Single & Crochet

CIANA SMOAK

Also by

Roses are Red

Shoot for the Stars

Single & Crochet

Book 1

Ciana Smoak

Dedication

Whether you craft for fun, or craft to escape. This one is for you.

Prologue

To:

itsanyleesmith@gmail.com

From:

s.keen@fashioninterational.or

Dear Anylee Smith,

11:30 AM

It is with great pride that I extend to you an invitation to be one of the featured designers for Fashion International in the Virgin Islands for our 2025 fashion show. Our team was so impressed with your designs and your work as a crochet artist. Your modern, sophisticated, and elegant designs have really blown us away. We would love to have your work showcased at our fashion show.

If you are still interested, please send us a bio of yourself, phone number, some model sizes that work for your designs and any accommodations you will need to have a successful trip. One of our team members will be giving you a call as soon as we hear back from you to answer any questions that you might have.

Congratulations again, Anylee! We cannot wait to see you during this year's Fashion International.

Sincerely,

Sapphire McNeal

Fashion International President

From:

itsanyleesmith@gmail.com

To:

s.keen@fashioninterational.org

11:35 AM

Oh my gosh! Thank you. I am so honored to be a part of this. My number is 561-349-2221. I will gladly send over any information you need. If it is possible, my designs are measured to fit certain people specifically. May I bring my own models or have measurements to craft pieces for each model?

I look forward to hearing from you.

Thank you,

Anylee Smith.

From:

s.keen@fashioninterational.org

To:

itsanyleesmith@gmail.com

12:30 PM

Hi Anylee,

Yes, you can bring your own models. Please send the attached document for specifics. We will give you a call shortly.

Sincerely,

Sapphire Keen

Fashion International President

Chapter 1

My champagne flute has not been empty since the party started. Why would it be? This event is to celebrate my accomplishment and I after all; Anylee Smith, the fashion icon or soon to be fashion icon (let's hope all goes well). I make another round through the floor once again in case more people I have yet to greet have shown up. I sip the sweet taste of the champagne and make casual smiles at the people gushing over my dress. The one I handcrafted myself using the perfect cotton blend not the stiff stuff from Walmart but the imported kind from overseas that takes about a month to get here.

It is floor length, tightly stitched with double crochets–took me forever to perfect my tension. The dress is a navy blue gown, deep v-cut at the bosom with pearls woven on the bodice. Not to toot my horn but the navy blue dress on my rich melanated skin is a magnificent combo. It's all about the look tonight.

"Sheesh…you sure you're not one of the models?" Samiyah says with a glamorous smile on her face. Her smile alone is one of the reasons I hand-picked her as a model for this special occasion. Her hair is a warm ginger color, with voluminous curls. She's wearing a bright yellow gown-length dress with a mid-thigh slit.

"You deserve to be on a runway!" My mouth drops, looking at her glowing skin against the yellow dress.

She poses as if she hit the end of the runway before laughing. "I'm so excited, Ny! You have no idea."

"That makes two of us." I sigh dreamily. For the past couple of years, I feel like I'm living in a dream. Sure, for the past year I have been hyper-fix-ated on making this goal of mine work and it has all paid off. I know my grandmother would be proud of me.

"I can't wait to see the designs you made." Samiyah's eyes wander behind me quickly before turning her gaze back to me.

My mind goes straight to the book where I draw all my designs. The designs I have for Samiyah hug her small frame perfectly. They show off her long toned legs and pair perfectly with her wild ginger curls.

"You know I think I have another design for you in mind." I think about another design in yellow, something that showcases intricate designs and flows down her body like water.

"You're always working, Ny. Do you ever take a break?" Her eyes glance behind me once more, her body radiating urgency.

"You can go if you need to." I say to her, her gaze snaps to me. She blushes a little as she reaches over and hugs me quickly.

"I'll have a drink with you later, okay?" She asks as she pulls away.

"Yeah yeah! Go to your man." I wave her off.

She laughs as she walks away in the direction of her eye candy. I take another sip of champagne and waltz through the party. The DJ plays upbeat R&B music making my hips swing softly to the beat as I stand alone off to the side. Multiple people dance to the music as they chat with friends.

While I know everyone here, there is something peaceful about sitting and reveling in your own success. My hips may sway to the music but my mind gravitates to every face that stares at me with admiration. I take in their gazes on me with a smile. My designs will feature on a main stage in just a few weeks. I won't only have 'influencer and crochet designer' on my resume. I'll be a certified fashion designer too soon yet this is only the beginning. My thoughts turn back to my designs. I itch for a pen and some paper hoping to sketch out the skirt design flowing through my head.

A shriek snaps my eyes open as I turn to see my best friend Kayla walk through the door. Her eyes are wide as she stares at me, tears tugging at her eyes.

"Bestie, you look stunning!" Kayla runs to me in a way that won't cause her to break her neck in her super high heels. Leave it to Kayla to put on the highest heels for such an event. She wraps one arm around me, careful not to get too much of her body glitter on me.

I grin at her when she eyes my dress. Her reactions are always flashy. Now that she sees the dress up close, she is nothing but speechless.

"Ny, now this is a dress." Her gaze cascades over every detail I put.

Her lips curve into a downward frown. I know exactly the reason for it.

"You know I told you I would make your dress for tonight." I cross my arms over my chest giving her a frown of my own. I have made so many pieces for Kayla over the past couple of years that I know her measurements to a T. It's one of the reasons I asked her to be my first model on the runway. I could have her in an equally stunning dress.

"Have you been working more than you should? Please, I would much rather have you work on your pieces for the upcoming runway in a few weeks. I know you'll have me looking the best out of all your models." She gently nudges my shoulder playfully. She's right but still it's the gesture that matters most. "Besides, I don't want to steal your shine tonight."

"My shine?" I laugh at the thought. I never shined before this. But what can I say? It is natural for me to shine.

"Yes, you could use all the eye candy." Her tone is stealthy as her eyebrows point to the reason just beyond my shoulder. I look only to find a man in a nice tailored suit the color of red wine. His hair is pulled back with a fresh fade surrounding his hairline and a smooth fade to his beard. He smiles politely when he notices my gaze. I smile back so as not to be too awkward. I turn back to Kayla with a huge pile of disapproval written on my face.

"No, absolutely not." I shake my head, careful not to shake the pins out of the updo.

"Why not? Isn't he your type?" Kayla smirks, gazing between the two of us. "Really, you two would be cute together."

"This is why I don't ask for your opinion." Everytime I ask for Kayla's opinion on my love life, she proves to be right, however, this moment I can just tell he's wrong for me. No matter how good this man seems to look. I realize this is the only man I'm pretty sure I don't know at the party. Must be a fan of my work then.

"Honestly you should have to, especially with the last one. Look at you pouring yourself into your work because of–"

"I just want to make a name for myself." I cut her off not wanting to rip open a wound I have carefully kept bandaged for the past year. I scan the room desperately looking for a way out of this conversation before Kayla starts lecturing me about my love life and how I should be happy with a guy who would give me a good D like that nurse from Romeo and Juliet. Only I don't wish to be Juliet and I definitely don't need a Romeo. Not after the last one.

Thankfully, my mom and dad walk through the doors of the party, their smiles beaming when they finally spot me. I am attracted to their beaming smiles like a moth to flame in the night.

"My parents are here." I'm relieved when they walk up behind Kayla.

"Hey family…" Kayla says as she hugs mom and dad. "Ny, we'll talk later."

"Of course." I smile even though I'm sure we won't be, not in the slightest.

My mother takes me in, eyeing my handcrafted dress with glassy eyes and a quivering smile as though she could break into a sob any minute now. Her hair is pinned up in an updo almost resembling a flower with an elegant black dress. My dad smiles looking proud, a slight shine in his eye, his salt and pepper beard trimmed along with the fresh haircut that he most likely did himself this morning. His suit matches my mother's dress perfectly. They almost look better than I do.

"You look beautiful, Anylee," mom places her hand over her heart delicately. My dad grabs my hand, lifting it up in the air as I twirl for my parents.

"Thank you, mom. Dad, thank you." I give them both big hugs. They squeeze me to themselves, releasing the stress from my body.

"How long did it take you to make this sweetheart?" My mom plays with one of the curls in my hair, fixing it as she admires the navy blue yarn on my skin.

"Only about a week," I feel a slight ache in my wrist as the words leave my lips. It actually took me three sleepless nights to get this dress made for this night.

"And how did you have time to fit any of this in? With the party, the final designs?" My mom asks a twinge of worry in her tone.

I smile in response not knowing what words to put together. With the party and final designs and my second job, this is the reason I had to stay up late after painfully remembering I hadn't made my dress. I had about two months to make it after completing the sketch.

"Either way, you look great sweetheart." My dad kisses the top of my forehead, his facial hair scratchy against my moisturized skin. I can't help but notice the twinkle of worry in my dad's eyes as he looks down at me with a proud expression. It took an insane amount of blending to hide the bags underneath my eyes.

She takes my hand, the softness reassuring as she squeezes gently. "As long as you're getting the rest you deserve."

"Of course mom, I am living the dream." I say with much convincing enthusiasm. Working for myself has always been a dream of mine. I have worked too hard to give it up just like that. I want to design more for the runway; design pieces for my favorite celebrities and have pieces so iconic that they put the pieces I make in museums. I can rest when I am accomplished, when the world knows my name. For now I'm Anylee Smith, the crochet influencer, yet I want to be Anylee Smith, the fashion designer. The icon.

"Okay sweetheart." My mother says worry reflecting in her voice. I squeeze her hand back before looking over her shoulder determined to find a way out. If there's one thing I didn't expect tonight, it's for everyone to box me in a bubble. What I wouldn't give to sit in a corner with some yarn and a hook until my mind stops running!

"Okay mom, dad, I will let you enjoy yourselves." I walk over to the bar where a couple people sit chatting. I feel relieved to see my friend, Tony who has graciously agreed to work the bar tonight as I wouldn't trust anyone else to make my drink. I rub my temples, closing my eyes to think of this design that has been stuck in my head. The delusional part of me thinks I can sketch and have it crocheted before the final deadline. It would mean missing out on more sleep though.

"What's wrong, you look like you need something strong?" Tony says, leaning against the bar. His strong scent of sandalwood was surprisingly pleasant to me. His forearms pop against the black t-shirt I told him to wear. It's as if the shirt is constricting his muscles.

"I do need something strong." I exhale as the DJ plays a more upbeat song instead of the groovy R&B he has been playing most of the night. I could definitely make something shake on the dance floor right now.

"Nervous about that speech you have to give in about," he pauses to look at his wrist watch, "five minutes?"

My eyes bulge as I grab his wrist looking at the clock that reads 8:25 PM.

"Oh my gosh! It's almost 8:30!" I facepalm myself. Forgetting how I wanted to thank everyone thirty minutes after the party and started thinking everyone would run on CP time but most of my important guests are here.

He chuckles as he stands up straight and nods so slow it's almost unnoticeable. He takes a small shot glass and fills it with a clear liquid. "I will make you something strong after you're off the stage. I don't want you stumbling and slurring in front of everyone." He slides the shot glass over to me just as the DJ comes onto the speaker.

I nod in appreciation taking the shot as the liquid burns the back of my throat. I instantly wish he gave me cranberry juice or whatever he has back there to follow after.

"Let's bring up the reason why we are all here, shall we? Anylee Marie Smith! Get on up here!"

Everyone turns in my direction clapping and smiling as I walk gingerly to the top of the stage next to the DJ who stares at me in awe as he takes in my dress. I could definitely get used to the way people stare at my designs.

"Hi everyone," I sing cheerfully into the mic. "Thank you all for coming out." I clap, signaling a wave of applause after me. "You all know we are here to celebrate the biggest achievement of my career as my designs will be featured on the runway this year during Fashion International 2025." My voice pitches into a squeal earning genuine smiles all around. "My handmade designs will be on the runway at the first stop at the Virgin Islands. First time they are being held there this year. So many celebrities will be there." The crowd erupts into applause at the news. I smile so hard my cheeks hurt but I can't stop myself from doing so.

"I just want to thank you all for being here and supporting me. I can't wait for you all to see my designs in Vogue and everything. A special thank you to my parents. Thanks to my grandmother for teaching me how to crochet. This one's for her."

A few whistles sound throughout the cheers. I see Kayla in the corner of my eye wiping fake tears. I giggle into the mic "Well, don't let me stop you from partying."

The DJ turns on a line dance, so many people run to the dance floor happy to have some actual music. I don't blame them after all. I walk back to the bar where Tony has a colorful drink set out for me.

"You did good up there." I take the drink from him and sip it slowly. It tastes like juice, something I know is dangerous when it comes to Tony's drinks.

"Thank you, Tony. This is really good, by the way." I motion to the drink as the straw still rests in my mouth.

"Don't have too much. I don't want you getting too torn up at your own party." He chuckles as he wipes a glass clean.

"Well, it's a good thing I didn't drive here tonight then." I shoot him a wink causing him to laugh fully.

Tony winks back at me before walking over to another customer who just had a seat at the bar. I admire Tony from a distance as I always have since we were kids. His deep melanated skin is perfect against his painfully white smile. His hair is cut low and swims in waves. His chiseled jawline that formed since working out over the years due to football practice. Tony is the most hardworking person I know. Just last year, we were celebrating him being the youngest D1 Head Coach in the history of college football. He would be the type I would go for if I didn't think of him as family.

I take a look at my drink, knowing that this drink is making me crazy for thinking of Tony like this. A strong hand touches my shoulder, a warm smile comes across the full cheeks I have grown to love.

"Great speech up there," Marcus smiles at me as he leans against the counter, his bright smile radiates onto me.

"Thank you, Marcus. Tell me you started packing?" I eye him as he laughs.

"Damn! Don't worry. I've had my suitcase picked since you asked me." He laughs again flashing those pearly whites of his.

Marcus is the most beautiful dark skin man I have met. He's also been one of the most talented models that I have ever met. I knew that this is the perfect opportunity to get him in front of the audience he deserves."

"Have a drink with me?" I ask, suddenly wishing I had someone to talk to since Tony is busy with clients.

"I will before the party ends. Just don't get too drunk." He leans his body off the counter and looks around the room. "Where are you about to go?" Curiosity gets the better of me. My grandmother always asked not to question people unless it concerns me. I know whatever he is looking for definitely doesn't concern me.

"Looking for my date. I'll see you later." He doesn't look at me before he leaves. I sigh watching him walk away suddenly exhausted from the multiple quick conversations I had with people. Nothing deeper than congratulations and my fashion show prep. And Kayla with her love talk. What I wouldn't give to have some type of release here for me.

Kayla finds me at the bar. She swoons a little when she sees Tony who has been her crush since forever. He smirks as she heads in my direction. "I'll have whatever she's having, Tony."

Kayla slides onto a stool next to me. "I think it's a little weird for us to be dressed up elegantly with this type of music. Don't you?" Kayla says, dancing in her seat to Red Nose.

"Look at the crowd. It's 90% African American here. We can be fancy and still be ourselves." I laugh as one lady seems to be giving everyone a show in the middle of the dance floor. The DJ calls her out causing the crowd to laugh.

"You're right. When I saw black tie event, I was thinking, 'Bouje,'" Kayla says.

I laugh as Tony puts down her drink in front of her. She takes a sip of her drink, eyes almost popping out of her sockets as she looks at Tony "Oh, you're dangerous!" She says

"I like that. Maybe that's what I'll call it." He leans forward, his muscles flexing as he looks hungrily at Kayla.

"I think you have something more dangerous than this drink that you're not telling me about." Kayla's eyes sink seductively as she takes a slow sip of her drink.

"Oh, just date already!" I roll my eyes, feeling like I'm intruding on some serious eye contact.

"Speaking of which," Kayla turns to me with a slight red hue on her face from the intense silence with Tony.

"Please, do not start." I say, tilting my head back already in agony.

"Look, I talked to Mr. Might-Be-Your-Type. He's a doctor, girl. They make lots of money." She gives me a playful shrug. As if I need another doctor. The man I used to date was a physical therapist. It's basically the same thing.

"I don't want a doctor." The words make my tongue bitter. I take a sip of the drink in my hand, wanting a sweet taste instead.

"Why? He can break your back and heal you when he's done." She wiggles her eyebrows.

"I'm going to pretend I didn't hear that." Tony stands up straight and walks to the side of the bar near the soda nozzles, far enough not to hear a lot but enough to hear some of it.

My cheeks burn from embarrassment, "I don't have time for distractions, Kayla."

"I'd want some eye candy for the cameras when I get back from the fashion show. The youngest fashion designer being single, I don't know if that's a good look. It's bad enough you came alone."

"You came alone." I roll my eyes. If I was still with *him*, I wouldn't be alone. I'd be with the person who believed in me from the beginning. I shake away the feeling. The sadness of him not being here almost hurts.

"I'm not the superstar here. You are. Someone would definitely want to know if you're taken in the interviews you'll be doing."

"It just means I'm young, exploring my options and working hard. Besides, I might get multiple suitors when they see my picture in the magazine."

"Yeah, walking STD rappers and sex traffic movie stars. But not a doctor." She scoffs.

"How many conspiracy theories did you watch this morning?" I ask, earning a hearty laugh from Tony.

"Listen, a baller is nice but a stable baller like a doctor?" She wiggles her eyebrows. "That's hard to come by."

I shrug.

"Well, you can talk to him and figure it out." She shrugs, taking another small sip of her drink as her gaze shifts slightly behind me.

"You didn't!" I feel my insides sink. Knowing I probably look pale.

"Oh, I did." Her eyes are set in stone as she sips more of her drink.

I reach my hand out "Tony, please give me another." I say, chugging the drink I had been sipping on for a while.

Kayla reaches for the cup before it gets too empty "No, girl! I'm not letting you screw up your chances with Mr. Doctor because you're drunk."

"Kayla why?" I whine.

"Girl, I am tired of you being sad and depressed about what happened to you and he-who-shall-not-be-named. I know you're not looking for anything serious but you're pouring so much of yourself into work. I can see the eye bags under your makeup…" She puts her hand gently on top of mine.

It's been a year and as much as I like to tell myself I'm coping. I only am because of crocheting. It gives me the endorphins to forget about him and a sweet release of happiness.

Tony hands me a drink and looks between the two of us. "This is the last drink for you." His voice is authoritative as he places it down in front of me.

I nod in acknowledgement of what he says and push away any thoughts about he-who-should-not-be-named as I sip on my new drink.

To me, it feels as though I have done a good job of not worrying about my ex over the recent months. I didn't have time to share the news of my biggest accomplishment with him yet I couldn't help but want to tell him about it as soon as I received it. I recall him staying up with me all night as I reread my pitch to him as he helped me pick out some sketches while he rubbed my feet, hands and wrist after creating a crochet video that he helped me with for my YouTube tutorial. He held my hand as I pressed send and kissed me gently when the word 'submitted' popped up onto the screen. What I wouldn't have given to kiss him when I received the word 'congratulations' in my inbox about a month ago.

Kayla nudges me gently out of my thoughts as she points to Mr. Doctor who's across the room. Our eyes meet for a second which invites him over even though to me my eyes signal *please stay where you are*.

"I'll be over there if you need me." Kayla picks up her drink and walks to the other side of the bar about three people in between us.

Making it four people now, as the doctor slips his way into the seat next to me. He looks stunning up close. His locs are pulled back into a clean ponytail, not a single strand out of place. His eyes are a dark brown deeper than the toffee colored complexion of his skin.

"Hi," I choke out.

"Congratulations on having your work displayed on the Fashion International runway. That's huge." His tone is excited, seeming super genuine. It slowly melts the guard that I put up.

I smile brightly, "Thank you, at first I couldn't believe I got in." I thought that the email was spam but there was no denying that I had got in after many confirmation google searches.

"I could. I mean, look at that dress. When you said hand made pieces on that stage, I could tell right away that the dress you're wearing was one of them. It makes you look so gorgeous though. There has to be a way better word than that."

I laugh nervously. His charm is smooth like the cream cheese spread I use for my bagels every morning. His voice is velvety and rumbles slightly, sending vibrations through my body. I can't help but smile at him truly at a loss for words.

"Well, enough about *me*,' my voice cracks on the last word, I cough before motioning at him, 'Tell me about yourself." I grab my drink hoping that it gives me some liquid confidence.

"I'm a doctor, well a surgeon. A very rewarding profession." He says humbly

"Really?" I ask, not knowing what to say. I shoot a glance at Tony hoping he could save me but he's too busy.

"Yeah, besides the money, helping people is great. I bet you feel the same way watching people put on your designs."

I nod. "My designs don't cure wounds though." I giggle

"I would say so. They definitely make people feel good on the inside."

I smirk, nodding slowly. "Okay you got me there." I take another sip of my drink, almost finishing the last drop in the cup.

He chuckles before motioning to Tony, "You want another drink?"

"Soda." I say, earning an approving nod from Tony.

"I'll take a beer, whatever you have."

He places his phone on the counter as he reaches for the QR code on the edge of the tabletop to send tips to Tony.

His phone lights up just as Tony places the drinks in front of us. I get a glimpse of his phone wallpaper, a photo of him with some girl sharing a kiss between the two of them, no doubt about that. He smoothly flips his phone over. His smile never falters as he takes a slow slip of his beer.

"Family man?"

His smile falters just a little bit but still shines brightly. "I visit my mother's house every Sunday for family dinners."

"Oh okay," I say awkwardly, pretending to make eye contact with some-one across the room and smile at the wall right behind him. "I will be back." I slide off the chair and walk toward the bathroom. I let out an exhausted sigh once I am away from him. I walk into the bathroom, find the biggest stall and place my back against the wall.

I fiddle with my thumbs. "I knew it." I whisper to myself, squeezing my eyes shut as I fight back tears. Even with the great feeling of what I have accomplished, it doesn't cure the hole inside of me.

I scroll my phone to the shared photo album between him and I. The one we used to share. I look at the last picture we shared before we broke up. Our smiles reached both our eyes, as he looked at me hungrily like he could never get enough of me. It always felt like that when he stared into my eyes. I wonder when that hunger ran out or what snapped inside for him to toss me to the side just like that. I just wonder how it got to this point where I'd be celebrating one of my biggest accomplishments without him.

I close my phone and lift my head up high. I walk toward the mirror and make sure I look flawless, not a curl out of place nor a crease in my makeup. I'll have to do many more accomplishments without him after all. And it didn't start tonight, it started when the word 'congratulations' was written in the header of that email.

Chapter 2

Small streamers hang from my office as the floor is littered with a rainbow of confetti. I smile at the slightly crooked 'congratulations' banner hanging in front of the window. My coworkers clap as I slowly make my way into the office.

"AwwW...thank you guys. You didn't have to do this." I say looking at the small cupcake with the plastic candle on top of it.

"You're the first person in our office to actually do something cool. Of course, we wanted to do something special for you." Ashley says with an expression that questions any need I have to protest the gesture.

I smirk at the comment, it's not like we are not working at a firm managing influencers with brand deals. Just last week I helped a client with a Nike deal. I thought that was pretty cool. Or when one of our clients had got to go on a free cruise by working with one of the major cruise lines. I was jealous just looking at her itinerary.

"Thank you guys, seriously." I place my hand over my heart as I take the cupcake off the table to see my favorite sweet thing. A chocolate cupcake with whipped icing. I have no doubt they bought it from the grocery store. I'm not complaining though. It seems that is the only place to get some decent whipped icing. The many recipes I followed online didn't taste the same.

"Of course, girl! I can't wait to see the designs you kept top secret for the past year." Jasmine wiggles her eyebrows as she looks at my bag that no doubt has my sketch book inside.

"I can't wait for you guys to see them all. I worked hard redoing them." I hold my bag closer to me, protecting my sketchbook from her unwanted gaze. Not like she could see anything through the bag.

I have been working on these designs since I told my coworkers about the fashion show, even way before that. I came up with all new designs. Those I never featured on my channel before or even showed to my followers. These designs were so hard to keep secret. I desperately wanted to show Kayla some of them, especially the pieces I made for her. The countless times I pricked myself with pins and almost stabbed my finger into sewing machines from a lack of caffeine; I just hope their mouths drop to the ground when they see all of it. My work.

"I just hope you crocheted something to make it fit the models. You know how they are stick-skinny." Ashley holds up her finger to demonstrate. She flips her braids over her shoulder and runs her fingers through the small curls that hang loose from her goddess braids

"I get to bring my own models. I didn't want anyone to recreate my designs or anything."

I was grateful that this is a policy for this year's show. The models I chose are people I have worked with in Fashion School alongside my close friend,

Kayla who thankfully was forced to do some pageants when she was a kid. The only thing is I had to make sure I had 6 models in total. They want some pieces for men as well as pieces for women from me. Luckily, I have always wanted to design some pieces for the men in my life. I already had sketches in my notebook for it.

"I feel like you are living a dream I didn't know I had." Jasmine says, running her long purple nail across her cheek to mimic a tear.

I shake my head, hiding my smile. "Don't you have some emails or something to get to?"

"You're right I have a meeting to prepare for." Ashley sighs.

"We'll let you get to work then, girl." Jasmine says as she walks out of my office along with Ashley.

I sit at my desk and the first thing I do is check my email for anything important only to find that all my meetings and schedule have been cleared for the day. Nothing short of what my boss' doing. I check my personal email to see if I have any important emails from Fashion Week International. Of course the first email that shows in my inbox screams to be read.

To: itsanyleesmith@gmail.com

From: j.wilkins@fashioninternational.org

Dear Anylee Smith,

We are so excited that you and your designs will be a part of our Fashion International Show at the Virgin Islands. Please make sure to double check your email for any attachments as tickets for you and your models have been sent. Please let me know as soon as possible if tickets have not been sent out to you. A reminder that any designer who is bringing their own models needs to have a diverse cast of models, original designs, and makeup/hair looks sent by the end of this week for our team to look over. You will receive itinerary for events leading up to the day of the show that all designers and models need to participate in for publicity and promotion, however you are free to enjoy yourself outside of those events however you choose. Attached is a list of things covered by Fashion Week international for our designers.

I or someone else from my team will be reaching out to you with more information in the upcoming days. We look forward to your arrival on the island and can't wait to see your designs on the runway.

Sincerely,

Jayana Wilkins

Fashion International Pub Team

My heart pounds in anticipation. Sometime tomorrow I will be landing on the island, checking out my beautiful hotel room and relaxing for the first time in a while since finding out about being accepted. The nonstop preparation, sketching, and growth of my social media, all worked out for me. Granny always said I had a drive that just won't stop no matter how many times I'm told to step on the brakes. If only she could see me now.

After changing tabs and refreshing my screen for the two hundredth time for something important, nothing pops up. Not even a message from the team group chat. I check my to-do list which is like my schedule that has nothing slotted except for my lunch break. The meetings I had for this week have all been pushed to the first available week after I return. I sit back in my chair regretting my last minute decision to come into work. Definitely nothing special going on for me to do here today.

Most people would call out of work before they go on vacation but I decided I could use the extra money coming in. I took this job to bring in extra money for yarn expenses which I probably don't need to do now. Nonetheless, it gets me out of the house. I could go home to pack but I triple packed all week making sure I have everything I needed for the trip and the runway. Makeup, extra yarn and hooks, fabric in case I need to sew in some lining, my sketch book for designs, etc. I didn't want to miss a single thing. Yesterday after the party, I distracted myself with another repack of my suitcase, putting everything back to where it was just to make sure I had everything. I might do it again tonight just to quadruple-check to make sure everything is in my suitcase.

"You know you are the only person I know who would throw a party, have a vacation planned and still come to work on Monday like it is a regular day." My boss, Chantelle, stands in the doorway of my office taking in the sight of my celebration decorations.

"Well, it is a *normal* day." I shrug. I still have one more day until the rest of my life changes.

"Yes, but you also should be home making last minute preparations. I'm excited to hear all about your trip." She stares at me with pride rich in her eyes. "I knew you could do it." She smiles. Chantelle hired me when I was a small influencer. She witnessed me grow in more ways than one after the passing of my grandmother. Besides my tight knit family, she was the first one to believe in me.

I come to work on occasion wearing skirts that I crocheted. One of the reasons was to declutter my room of the yarn taking up my yarn wall, plus I was experimenting on some designs. The majority of those designs would be nowhere near appropriate for work but would definitely be on the runway. I made sure to pack some of the most creative ones. Regardless, Chantelle has always loved when I came to work wearing them. She liked how I branded myself which as part of being an influencer is what I do. Brand myself. Branding myself is what got me into this very position today. It's why I'm so good at doing my job.

"Thank you, Chantelle. You know, I'll tell you all about it. I'll even bring you back something." I smile.

"Thank you, love. You know what I want? An autograph when you come back and one of those skirts you make."

My heart pangs with happiness at the thought. "Yes, of course!" I can see myself picking up some yarn at the market over in the islands. Crochet is especially popular over there. I'll crochet her skirt while at the beach. Her umber skin tone lets me know yellow would be the perfect color for her melanated skin.

She nods a bright smile on her face "I cleared your schedule for today. Make sure you go home early tonight."

I nod to give her the satisfaction. Maybe she is right. I should be going home to relax for the couple hours I have left before taking an early flight for the islands tomorrow. Just the thought of lounging on an island makes me happy. I have yet to tell my followers or make a YouTube video about it. Maybe I should do that instead of working. I will do just that. Tell my close knit supportive strangers and get back to the drawing board with some of my sketches.

I pick up my work bag, snatch off my water bottle from my desk and say farewell to my coworkers before heading out. The cool breeze of the spring pushes back my wild curls as I walk to my car. I settle in and place my phone on the tripod, immediately opening the instagram app. I click my story and fluff my hair to frame around my face before holding down the record button to greet my followers.

"Hey y'all! Be sure to check out my YouTube channel at six pm tonight. I have a surprise you all are going to love." I upload the video before putting my phone on silent.

Before heading home, I make a stop at my parents' house. It's *definitely* not because they have one of the best bakeries near their house and I crave something sweet but because deep down I can't stop the nervousness coursing through my body.

I park in front of Robinsons Bakery and walk into the building. The cute small bakery has cases filled with cupcakes, cakes and cookies. My eyes beeline to try out free samples of the new flavors they are always experimenting with their cookies. I take in a deep breath as the never ending smell of vanilla makes my stomach rumble with hunger.

"Good morning, Anylee." Mrs. Robinson lights up when she sees me. Her light blue apron matches her walls and is stained with flowers. Her short hair is pulled up in a mini bun on top of her head. She is the only person I know who is shorter than me by an inch or two.

"Coming by for your usual?" She asks as she wipes her hands on the apron. I'm surprised she doesn't have my picture hanging up in her bakery that says 'Number One Customer' on it.

"Good morning, Mrs. Robinson. I think I want to try something new today." I stop in front of the case, surveying the case of the freshly baked donuts and muffins that I should eat for breakfast.

"I'm sorry I wasn't able to make it to your party. I had to cater a wedding, you know it's that time of the year." Mrs. Robinson's last couple words come out in a sigh. Spring and Summer are her busiest times. I'm surprised to actually see her in the shop today. She leans her curvy frame against the glass. I can tell the wedding yesterday really drained her. The faint bags under her eyes let me know everything I need to know. The prep for this show has me feeling the same way.

"You know it's not a wedding without Mrs. Robinson's baked goods anyway." I say as I gaze at a strawberry shortcake cookie. It takes all self control for me not to lick my lips like a maniac while staring at them.

Mrs. Robinson comes out from behind the case with the tray of samples in her hand. "Mind tasting this lavender sugar cookie sweetness?"

"Lavender?" I put a hand on my chest in surprise. I take a cookie off the tray and admire its golden color before taking a bite into it. The crisp edges and soft insides mixed with the sweet flavor make my eyes roll back into my head. Mrs. Robinson chuckles as she watches my reaction.

"Give me a minute." I say, turning back to stuff the remaining cookie into my mouth.

"I'm glad you like them." She laughs "What can I get for you today?"

"Let me get a dozen of these cookies. Half a dozen strawberry shortcake cookies, chocolate cupcakes and a blueberry muffin." The words spill out of my mouth almost instantly. Mrs. Robinson smiles wide as she walks back behind the counter to pack up my order. She comes back with three big boxes and a small one for my cupcake and muffin.

"What's the third box for Mrs. Robinson?" I take the boxes with curiosity.

"Your gift to say congratulations on this big accomplishment of yours." Her eyes shimmer as she looks at me. I know the exact thought she is thinking. I can see the pride in her eyes. A look that everyone I ran into today has given me.

"Thank you, Mrs. Robinson." I pout to let her know I appreciate her and as a way of hugging her since my arms are full of precious cargo.

"Make sure your mom tries one of those cookies." She says as she comes around the back to hold the door open for me.

"If they make it to the house." I lick my lips tasting the lingering flavor of lavender there. She laughs as she walks me to the car, giving me a hand with the door. I place the baked goods down and buckle them up in the back before turning around to give Mrs. Robinson a hug.

"I will be back with a gift for you from my trip." I can probably find a special ingredient for her next batch of cookies. They would be perfect for her summer menu. My mouth waters just thinking about it.

"I have no doubt that you will. See you when you get back honey." She says waving me on. I watch Mrs. Robinson fade in the background until her short frame leaves my rear view mirror. I take the short drive around the corner to mom's house. My stomach rumbles feeling the effects of only a cookie and coffee for breakfast. I curse silently thinking of the cupcake I left on my desk that my coworkers got me. Now breakfast for my trash can or whoever walks into my office later. I pull up to my parents house and text dad that I'm outside with goodies. Not even five seconds later my dad comes waltzing out of the front door with a wide smile on his face.

"Well, if it isn't my baby girl. No work today?" He asks as he opens the back door to grab the boxes of goodies in the backseat.

"My boss forced me to have a day off." I sigh out in relief. I am honestly grateful for the break. It gives me time to eat these cookies and sketch in my book.

"Your mother is going to love hearing that." He says, carrying the boxes and leading me inside the home. The smell of a lemon candle fills the house. It is how I know my mom just got done cleaning the house for the day.

"Babe, our princess has arrived and she brought goodies." My dad calls out as he sets the boxes down on the dining room table.

My mom walks out from the kitchen with a spatula and a wide smile on her face. "Why isn't it Anylee?!" She walks over to give me a hug and kisses my cheek. "I'm just finishing up breakfast." Her face questions why I'm here as she stares at me for a few seconds longer before walking back to the kitchen.

"Her boss gave her the day off." My dad gives me a wink before opening up the boxes to see what is inside.

"Oh really?" She re-emerges from the kitchen, surprised. I know she's secretly happy that I get a break. I'll never forget her look of worry at the party before I ran away from them. I can still see a hint of that worry on her face but I know that it's just a mother's instinct to worry about her child. And not at all about the spiral of depression after my ex dumped me, or after the passing of grandma which sent me into a spiral of working too hard.

"Yeah. I'm all packed and ready to go so I'm going to spend the day relaxing." I take a seat at my favorite spot at the table and rest my head on my hands.

"What are your plans for the day?" Dad asks as he grabs a cupcake. Mom walks over to smack his hand, silently scolding him.

"I'm making breakfast." She mutters under her breath. Dad and I share a laugh.

"I'm saving myself one before Anylee eats them all." He looks at me with a wide grin before laughing at his joke.

I frown and turn away from his gaze to roll my eyes before watching mom flip pancakes. "I plan to sketch and do some crocheting to answer your question, mother."

She smiles slightly at my tone knowing that I'm annoyed at my father's joke. Leave it to him to make fun of me for my sweet tooth addiction. I swear being addicted to sugar is some type of disease.

"That's your plan? To do what you always do as a form of relaxation?" My mom says, that worry tone coming back to her voice.

I choose my next words carefully before she makes me sit home all day with her playing board games or something. I still have to get home to make my YouTube video.

"I just want to do some crocheting for myself, not for the fashion show." I say, which isn't a lie. I have some ideas brewing that I want to crochet for my wardrobe. My problem is that I never know where to wear the outfits but after the fashion show I know I'll be invited to many occasions where I can show off the outfits. At least I hope I'm able to.

My mom walks out of the kitchen setting plates of bacon and pancakes on the table with serving utensils.

"Okay sweetheart," she puts her hand on my shoulder and the tension that has been built up releases at her soft touch. "I think you should visit the garden before you head out today."

I nod knowing her intentions to destress me after serving myself some breakfast. During breakfast, dad goes on and on about safety for the trip. Listing the type of precautions I should take and how I should share my location with them at all times. Mom nods in agreement to his lecture as she eats and chimes in about making sure to call them whenever I feel overwhelmed. After breakfast and a 10:00 AM college lecture from my parents I head outside to enjoy the warm spring sun.

Mom has the best sunflower garden in the whole state of Pennsylvania. I walk to the edge of the garden to be greeted by the tall stalks of flowers. The orange hue of the yellow leaves comforts me as I sit close to the dirt, face to face with one of the smaller sunflowers. I take in a deep breath smelling the scent of the flower mixed with freshly wet dirt.

"Please, let this trip go as planned," I whisper to myself as I take in the scent of the sunflowers again. I reach over to touch the delicate petals instantly feeling the relief I needed. Whenever I was angry or sad while I was younger, mom would tell me to go smell the flowers. Whether they were in a vase or the garden, they were always sunflowers. Mom and grandmother's favorite flower. I smile at the thought and give the petals one last touch for good luck and comfort. I wish I could bottle them up and take them with me for my trip.

One thing that I miss about my ex is that he would help me set up the camera, and make it sit perfectly still whenever my tripod was not acting right. In this case, it's being stupid. I refuse to get a new one as this is the first tripod I ever owned, the one my grandmother bought me when I first told her I wanted to be a crochet fashion designer and influencer. I remember her face lighting up when I told her. The next day, I found a brand new tripod resting on my parents' porch. Now that I moved to my own house I was able to have my dream yarn wall which works as the background for my YouTube videos. Honestly, I have more views when I post with it rather than without it.

I sigh in frustration when the camera tilts creating a crooked frame.

"Please, God let this be steady for once." I cup the base, holding the camera straight for a couple seconds before slowly releasing it. Like magic, it finally rests straight. I sigh in relief and get my station set up before recording. I definitely don't need negative comments about my work space while recording big news for my channel.

I hit record and fluff my hair one more time before putting on a smile.

"Hey guys! It's your girl Anylee. Instead of a crochet video today, I have exciting news for you guys." I take a deep breath and smile at the camera. "Sorry guys, I'm just really nervous. For the past two years I am so grateful for the support you all have given me and for the half a million of you all that love my designs and patterns. It means so much to me. Which is why for the 2025 Fashion International Week, my designs will be featured on their runway and in Vogue magazine. I couldn't have done it without you all. So, my schedule will be a little different but I will definitely get some content out to you while on this journey for the next three weeks. I am forever grateful for all of you."

I hit the button ending my recording and decided to make a montage video of my journey over the last couple years until now with the video. I put the video into an editing software when the doorbell rings.

"Who in the world?" I get up just as the second ring happens. I fix my face and take in a deep breath to push away my annoyance. I open the door to see Kayla in front of me with two cups of coffee and a treat bag in her hand.

"Coffee at 1 pm?" I ask as I move to the side.

"No girl, this is hot chocolate! I know you need to relax in order to get some sleep tonight." She pushes her way inside of my home and places the cups down on the coasters on the coffee table.

"I don't need to relax." I say, closing the door behind her. My body is actually screaming for a break but I know it will be worth it in the end.

"I saw your announcement on Instagram. I know you're editing that video right now. You're also probably going to try and crochet something before bed or doodle in your sketchbook."

Shit. Am I that predictable?

I open my mouth to speak but Kayla is already shoving the warm cup of hot chocolate into my hands before pulling out a brown paper bag from her bag.

"Thank you, Kayla." I blow into the lid of the cup before taking a sip.

"Since you're here, you might as well keep me company while I edit this video." I put down the cup, about to grab my laptop when Kayla's next statement makes my legs fumble.

"Not so fast. I want to hear about what happened with the doctor." She takes a sip of her hot chocolate with a curious expression on her face.

I reel back as if I have been stung. Kayla frowns at my response "That bad, huh?"

"The dude had a girl." I roll my eyes at the thought of it. Something about a grown man cheating on his girl doesn't sit well with me. At the big age of twenty-two that doesn't sit right with me.

She inhales a shocked breath "No way! How did you know? How did you find out?"

"His phone snitched on him." I laugh at the memory. That phone lit up right on time. Just before I got too flirty with him.

She shakes her head disapprovingly. "I'm sorry girl. I should've scouted him out better."

I shrug. "It's not your fault. You just want me to be happy."

Her smile is small which almost makes me feel bad that I'm the friend who is the most heart broken. I've been fighting it but when you lose two people who mean the world to you back to back it takes a little while longer to bounce back. My heart couldn't take the double homicide. I push the thought down and force a smile before turning on my heels.

"Now to my office." I lead the way, walking up the stairs straight to my back room where the colors of blue yarn peek through the cracked door.

"I haven't been in this room forever." Kayla says, sitting on the fluffy chair in the corner where I do most of my crocheting.

"Yeah. Well, it's because I only ever ask you to come in when I make something that I don't feel like modeling."

"You're so modest." She laughs at me.

"What is that supposed to mean?" I scrunch my face at her comment.

"You crochet some really cute things but you don't wear them. You're a great designer but you're the most unfashionable girl outside of that." She laughs.

"I have my own style." I say "I like to wear baggy clothes then show off when I feel like it."

"That's what I love about you, because it sure is a damn show-stopper." She takes a long sip of her hot chocolate, wiggling her eyebrows.

We share a laugh before I turn back to my computer and begin editing the video. It takes only about an hour to finish all the editing before I schedule it for upload to YouTube. I create a cute thumbnail before clicking the upload button.I look at Kayla who seems to have passed out in the fluffy chair. I shake my head and snuggle my way onto the other chair and pick up my hooks for another crochet project. I want to make some type of dress with mermaid bra cups. I reach for a caramel colored yarn and crochet the cups that I think of in my head before making tweaks. I make the cups about three times before perfecting how I want them. I continue double crocheting until I finish the top part of the dress as Kayla snores in the background. I guess I'm not the only one who falls asleep after drinking hot chocolate.

I check Instagram and YouTube after a while of responding to different comments. Before I get bored, one particular comment sticks out to me. A comment from @jisbatman, "Proud of you, LeeLee. Go get that bag."

I stare at the comment thinking of the small number of people who actually call me LeeLee. I haven't heard that name since *he* called me that but the man I know, his name doesn't start with a J. I shake the thought from my head and sip the rest of my hot chocolate which is now a cold *chocolatey* mud as it swings down my throat.

There's no possible way he would check up on me after all this time. I have him blocked on everything under the sun. I even deleted my fake pages in the beginning of the relationship just so I wouldn't have to watch his stories anymore. Anything to cure myself of the heart break that is *him*. That is the man who-shall-not-be-named. The man that broke my heart yet is the reason that I am even in this situation in the first place.

"LeeLee..." I whisper to myself as I close my eyes thinking of the memories that have broken free. I always liked when he called me that.

"Why are you looking at your phone as if you've seen a ghost?" Kayla asks groggily.

I turn to her and notice her eyes still closed. They open slightly when she feels my gaze on her. I open my mouth to speak out the multiple thoughts that flood my mind on hearing the name *LeeLee*. I close my lips instead and shake my head. Knowing that Kayla would turn our hang out session into a therapy session if I tell her.

"Nothing just overthinking this whole thing." The lie comes out effortlessly. It's a feeling I used to have but have nothing close to the feeling now.

Kayla stands up from the chair and grabs my hands, dragging me into the living room. "Alexa! Turn on 'Savage' by Megan thee Stallion." Kayla shouts.

I groan. "Please, don't make me dance out my problems."

"You already know I am." She lets go of my hands and begins dancing that old trendy dance. It makes me laugh seeing it again.

"I don't think you're doing that right." I laugh seeing Kayla freestyle.

"Well, how about you show me then?" She frowns with her arms folded over her chest. Her expression pulls me to the center of the living room. Just as the chorus repeats I do the dance just as I've seen it a million times on social media. My little cousin had gone out of her way to teach me how to do it.

Just as I finish, Kayla pushes me playfully onto the couch. "Don't be a hater just because you can't dance."

We laugh before dancing to a few more songs. This definitely counts as my exercise of the day since I haven't gone to the gym this morning or in a few mornings at that. I walk to the kitchen and grab two water bottles from the fridge and bring one to Kayla who sits on the couch scrolling through her phone as Beyoncé plays in the background.

"I hope you danced all your worries away." Her words are still a little breathy as she graciously takes the water bottle and chugs half of it.

I take a sip of my own water moving my hips slowly to the beat filling my living room. I stare at Kayla's phone with an urge to grab my own to check out that comment one more time.

"I actually could dance to a few more songs."

Kayla throws her head back with a loud groan. "Fine! But you're buying me Ramen to reup on all these calories I'm burning."

"Yeah yeah." I laugh just as Rihanna comes on the radio.

Chapter 3

"You called off your job a week early and you're still not ready?" I sigh into the phone. Leave it to Kayla to be the last one to get ready. I packed an extra bag just in case, with extras of stuff I felt were necessary like yarn, socks, undies and some dresses that I thought would be good in photo ops. But my main bags have been packed for weeks. I itch to text my models and make sure that they get to the airport on time but I don't want to be annoying before the trip even starts.

"Listen, I was waiting for my vacation clothes to come. Okay? They just arrived yesterday." I can hear the rustling on the other end of the line. The struggle of a suitcase being pulled out of the closet.

"So, why weren't they packed yet?" I took in deep breaths trying to regain my composure as I know that Kayla is always like this but between the excitement and the stress to be perfect, I'm one small inconvenience away from a break down.

"I had to try them on and wash them. Some of the clothes smelled like packages." I hear the struggle in the background followed by a loud zip drag.

"Are you packed and ready because I'm pulling up in a second?" I turn the corner to see Kayla's house is already in view. Her hedges had been freshly cut and by the looks of it her sprinklers had just gone off. Great. I couldn't handle Kayla telling me she needed a change of clothes.

"Yeah yeah, just let me get my stuff downstairs." The multiple thud sounds in the background tell me something is falling down the steps and I know it's her suitcase. I let out a silent prayer hoping that her suitcase didn't pop open, making her have to repack everything all over again.

I hang up the phone and park right in front of her door and pop my trunk. Not even the warm spring air and fresh sunflowers blooming in front of me could ease my mind right now. I need to put my feet in some sand ASAP.

Kayla comes busting through the front door trying to carry all her bags at once. I laugh and get out of the car to help her. She is disheveled. It's clear she truly spent the last minute packing. I try to fight the smile that threatens the corner of my lips.

"We could've just taken multiple trips." I say grabbing two of her bags. She sighs dramatically as a *thank you* and walks toward my car. She and I have the same outfit for our flight. A two piece long sleeve shirt with matching pants and some comfortable sneakers. Kayla and I have been friends since we were five so I know one of these bags contains her shoes.

"And miss being two hours early for our flight?" Her voice drips with sarcasm as she stops at the car giving me a face that screams boredom. I would laugh but we still need to get our bags checked, go through security, find out where we are boarding from plus the lines are brutally long.

Definitely not a thirty minute ordeal. It might take us two hours to get through all of that.

"Sorry about that bestie but we need ample amount of time." I throw her bag into the trunk and rush to get the last bag she's holding. I close the trunk, spin on my heels and almost run straight into Kayla.

Her eyes shine with concern as she scans my face silently for an answer. "What's wrong with you?"

I ignore her question and step past her, entering the car. I wait for her to get in and quickly get us on the road. My fingers tap on the steering wheel as we drive down the street. I feel her eyes fixated on me and shift in my seat as her gaze burns into the side of my face.

"Why do you think something is wrong?" I ask, checking my mirrors while moving out of the spot in front of her house. My GPS says that the airport is just ten minutes away. *Perfect.* Definitely enough time for us to settle in. I let out a small sigh and internally tell myself everything will be okay. I actually repeat this saying over and over again until Kayla's voice interrupts my thoughts.

"I don't know. Maybe it's because my best friend who was hyped about this trip is now looking like a dumpster fire. What happened to the confidence, babe?" Her eyes soften as she turns her body as much as the seat belt allows her to face me. I don't bother looking in her eyes knowing that if I do my confidence may go to shit. I look at myself in the rearview mirror, straighten my slouchy shoulders and turn my gaze back to the road.

"I am confident. I am excited to have my best friend be a model for me. I'm stoked about the opportunity to even be featured and I have prepared for this moment for over a year and–"

"Then why does it feel like you're missing something?" She eyes me suspiciously. "You're not sad about what I think right? I'm sorry if I messed up your confidence with that stunt I pulled. You don't need a man." Kayla pokes her glossy bottom lip out into a pout and reaches out to squeeze my shoulder for a makeshift hug. I reach up for her hand and squeeze back quickly before placing my hand back on the wheel.

"Nothing is your fault, bestie. I just want everything to be perfect." I merge onto the highway, my thoughts vanishing as I drive on my least favorite road of all time. I would be lying to myself if I didn't say that I stayed up late watching YouTube videos of fashion designers, overthinking what could possibly go wrong and fighting the urge to call my mother in the wee hours of the morning for a pep talk. I wished my grandmother was here. She would know just what to say to make me not have to worry at all. I think about what she would say but nothing comes to mind. My made up thoughts are nothing close to the comforting words she would speak to me.

"Girl, have you not seen your designs? Everything is perfect when it comes to your creations. It's the sole reason why you are in this show. It's because of that perfection. I know it, so does everyone who jumped up and down in excitement when you asked them to stunt on that runway for you. Now don't be a Debby Downer before the trip has even started. Everything will be perfect."

I pout my lips looking briefly at Kayla. It may not be what grandma would say but this is definitely what I needed to hear. I never doubted myself at all during this journey. Look where it got me! Why should I doubt now? "What did I do to deserve a best friend like you?"

"Honestly? It's a miracle we even found each other."

I remember the day I met Kayla back in sixth grade. I spilled chocolate milk on my white shirt at lunch one day. I ran to the bathroom to scrub it off and Kayla came in and offered me a clean shirt from her gym bag. I still have the yellow shirt with the sunflower and sun glasses on it. Hoping that I could re-gift it to her at her wedding or baby shower but we're both in the same boat. Single and no one lining up to change that.

Once the airport is in sight my shoulders sink with relief. Planes fly overhead and cars line up to drop off loved ones and unload quickly for the next car to take their place. I drive as fast as I can to the parking garage and try to find the parking spot that Fashion International graciously paid for.

Nerves get the better of me as I walk into the airport, the sound of wheels rolling on the tile floors, the array of colorful suitcases and box braids fill in around us. We follow the signs ahead of us leading us to the security where we wait in the devastatingly long line. I know it'll be worth it feeling the warm sun once we land on the beach. Once Kayla and I are free from the tedious stuff we look for our flight.

"Are the other models joining our flight?" Kayla asks as we walk through the airport. The smell of coffee and fast food waft through the air as we find our boarding zone. My stomach grumbles for the Mickey D's breakfast sandwich even though it's currently occupied by nerves.

"They took an earlier flight. We will be meeting them there." I say as we reach our boarding zone.

"Why didn't we get an early flight?" She asks as she slips into one of the empty seats next to me. A curious look on her face.

"I did not want to risk missing our flight because you don't know how to get up early." As much as I would love to be on the island already drinking from a coconut or a pineapple with my feet up, Kayla does not like to get up early in the morning so I asked for an afternoon flight. Plus, I don't see myself unpacking my suitcase for the trip so I don't need the extra time to settle in.

Kayla throws her arms around my neck the scent of strawberries invading my nostrils.

"You know me too well." She wipes a fake tear from her eye.

"Just trying to save my own ass." I think back to the email needing the same amount of models and everything forwarded to them about hair and makeup. I would hope my models are all heading to the island. I take out my phone and send a quick text to the model group chat for some updates. Considering my text hasn't been delivered I know they're probably still on the airplane.

"You're internally freaking out again." Kayla says, looking intently at me. I quickly relax my face knowing that I should work on having a better poker face especially if I want to freak out internally without having to be comforted. I haven't stopped internally freaking out since the party but she doesn't need to know that.

"I'm okay. Just thinking." I put my phone away and look around the airport, anything to avoid Kayla's stare

I feel Kayla's presence as she scoots closer to me. She shoves her phone in my face showing me a picture of some lady swimming underwater with fish surrounding her.

"We have to do this." She scrolls slowly showing me more pictures of underwater activities.

"You want to swim with fishes?" I ask, noticing Kayla's eyes light up when she sees a picture of a couple snorkeling. I'm definitely not doing that.

"Yes! We are also on a vacation. I want to do everything. Tubing, kayaking, swimming with *sharks*..." Her voice squeaks at the mention of sharks.

"I don't know. I'll do some stuff but I also have interviews and things that I need to prepare for. I can't get my hair wet everyday and–"

Kayla stops me with a raised hand. "If you don't relax at all, you will be sleeping with the fishes." Kayla points to the TV screen showing that our plane is arriving sooner than expected. "I don't need you to work yourself to death. Also I believe that's what they do now. They throw your body in the ocean when you die." Kayla gives me a joking glare before turning back to her phone.

I roll my eyes and try to breathe evenly. My nerves mix with excitement which feels like I drank three cups of coffee in a thirty minute span. My body can't handle too much coffee. This feels so much stronger than a few caffeinated beans. I can't stop thinking about what this opportunity could do for my life but I also can't stop the amount of worry rushing through my mind. The thoughts of which yarn colors need to be ordered when I get back home, checking my P.O. Box and following up with brand deals that I pushed to the back burner because of the prep.

What if this show flops and my brand deals stop coming in too?

"You know what they say about thinking about those negative thoughts?" Kayla says, butting into my mind-meeting with myself.

"Don't worry nothing bad will happen on this trip." I reassure myself out loud. I take a deep breath and think about the Anylee I was back at my party a few days ago, the kick ass fashion designer who crocheted her breathtaking dress in three days, showing everyone that attended a reason to celebrate my accomplishment. Who else would be able to say their clothes, made completely out of yarn, are on the runway in front of the biggest audience in the world? I push my shoulders back taking the thought in with pride. I worked hard for this moment.

"I'm sensing my girl got her bad bitch energy back?" Kayla questions a small grin creeping on her face.

"You know it." I reach into my bag and pull out one of my comfort projects, a cropped crochet cardigan with a soft peach color.

I pull out my favorite five millimeter hook as the speaker above us crackles to life. "Boarding to the Virgin Islands will begin in twenty minutes. Please make your way to boarding area A23. Again boarding to the Virgin Islands begins in twenty minutes."

I ball up my project and decide to work on it during the plane ride over instead. I have never been a fan of the flying death traps.

"Excuse me…" A soft voice pulls my attention to the person behind it. A girl who could be around eighteen with long box braids the color honey blonde, wearing black rimmed glasses and smiles wide when she sees the peach colored yarn waiting to be zipped up in my suitcase.

"Please, don't think I'm weird. Are you *'It's Anylee'* from YouTube?" Her voice is small as she asks the question, a look of hope glimmers in her eyes.

Kayla's eyes almost pop out of her skull as a wild grin follows. She nods her head approvingly.

"Yes, that's me." I smile in shock to see one of my supporters in person.

"Oh my gosh!" She squeals, earning a few looks from people in the airport. They watch intently trying to see what kind of celebrity I might be. I don't know how to show that I am just an ordinary girl who just happens to make YouTube videos.

"You wouldn't mind if I got a picture with you. Would you? I know you're on your way to the Fashion Show, right? I saw your announcement the other day." She blushes as she rambles. Her whole adorable vibe warms my heart.

"Of course, we can take a picture." I stand up as she squeezes close to me and lifts her phone up for a selfie. We make cute faces into the camera taking a couple pictures and a boomerang before she puts her phone down smiling at the photos in front of her.

"I can't wait to see your designs. I'm following some of your tutorials." She beams with excitement.

"Girl, make sure you tag me when you are finished. I would love to see how it turned out." My phone buzzes as an Instagram notification pops up on my phone.

"Oh, I will! It was so nice to meet you." She grabs her suitcase and runs toward a group of people who hang back to wait for her.

Kayla jumps up and down excited. "Girl, I can get used to being the best friend of a celebrity."

I giggle and zip up my suitcase. "Definitely not a celebrity."

"You will be after they see those killer designs on the runway." She says matter of factly

I smile just as the speaker sounds again getting all the attention, "Now boarding for the Virgin Islands."

I always say I would never get on another plane after getting on one. It never sits right with me that the sky can get bumpy when there is nothing but pillowy clouds and air. I know clouds don't have rocks in them for those fluff balls to make the plane shake a little bit. Turbulence be damned!

I stand up waiting to get my bag from the overhead compartment, eager to get off this plane. I snack on one of the biscoff cookies that Kayla snagged for me while I took a nap to ease the jitters of excitement coursing through my body.

Kayla looks back at me, the eager feeling to get off and see the island vibrating off her. I know exactly how she feels.

As soon as it was our turn to get off the plane, we snatched our bags and walked down the steps to the island airport. We walked down the steps and into a building that somewhat resembles a strip mall. As we head inside the building, our ears are flooded with island music as one of the men offers us shots of white Hennessy.

"Girl, I can get used to this." Kayla says, taking a shot and tipping the man a ten dollar bill. She dances as she tosses the liquor back.

"Welcome to the Virgin Islands, ladies!" One man with long locs down to his waist smiles at me as he hands me a flyer for a nightclub on one of the islands we will be staying near.

"Thank you." I say looking at the address seeing that the place is only a ten minute ferry ride. I remember looking up the island and seeing that we can take a ferry to other islands like Puerto Rico which I would be happy to visit while I'm here.

"You're welcome, beautiful." He says his accent thick as he walks over to the couple behind us.

"You can get you an island bae." Kayla says as she follows me to baggage claim.

"I am here for work, not a man." I snap. I point my finger at her, a silent warning for her not to try and set me up this whole trip.

Kayla holds her hands up defensively and waits to pick up her last couple of bags. "I hear you," she nods slowly as if I have a weapon pointed at her. "But how are we getting to the resort?" She says swiftly to change the subject.

"We are supposed to be getting a car to pick us up." I say as we walk through the building seeing the many taxi services, liquor stores and valet for certain hotels. We continue walking until we reach the other side of the building toward the exit where the taxi's line up for tourists and eager people willing to explore the island. As we walk out of the building we instantly come face to face with a sign that says *Anylee Smith*. "Speaking of which."

Kayla looks at me impressed. "Please, promise that you will bring me to all your fashion shows." She drops to her knees and hugs my legs.

I laugh at her dramatic antics as always. "I promise. Can't do this without my bestie." I smile.

"Anylee?" The driver asks. He looks formal despite not wearing the typical driver outfit. He has on cargo shorts and an island shirt with pineapples and sunglasses tinted throughout. I smirk at his shirt and nod, "That's me."

"Your carriage awaits." He walks and takes our bags, putting them into the back.

The air smells of salty warm water. The sound of music and chatter fills the air as our driver comes back to open the door for us.

I take in the scenery as we drive throughout the island, the colorful buildings filling the hills surrounding us. Some homes are blue, orange, bright pinks. Many people fill the streets. Men with locs that hit the floor seem to be on every corner. I stare at them in awe knowing that I need their hair routine. The sky is bright and sunny, nothing but clear skies ahead of us.

"This place is beautiful." I say in awe as we pull up to a dock. Awaiting us is a white boat with two stories that make me feel uneasy. If there's two things that I'm not a fan of, it's boats and planes. I don't know how I can go anywhere if I'm scared of every type of travel.

"This boat will take you to the resort." Our driver says to us as he unbuckles his seat belt and heads out of the car to open our doors for us.

"We're taking a boat to the resort?" The sight of the boat alone makes me want to puke. I rub my temples. I didn't know I would have to add boat travel to my list of reasons to stress.

He chuckles hearing the nerves in my voice.

"Girl, we are on vacation! Live a little." Kayla beams as she sees the boat, excitement radiating off of her body.

"Don't worry. It will only be a five-minute ride." He assures me handing our bags to a man who loads them onto the boat.

"See? You can survive five minutes." Kayla assures me as she steps onto the boat.

"A lot can happen in five minutes." I mumble under my breath as I follow suit carefully, following Kayla onto the boat. Despite this anxiety fest about floating on water, the boat is cozy with blue furniture and multiple life vests hanging on the walls. It makes me happy seeing that they care about our safety. I eye the closest life jacket knowing that if something goes down I will push anyone out of my way for it.

"At least we are inside with life jackets." I whisper to myself as I grab a window seat.

"What's on the docket for the day?" Kayla asks as the boat begins to start up.

I open up my email and check the schedule they sent me earlier this week. After a few minutes of refreshing my email with no results, I resort to checking the screenshots I had taken on my phone in case this sort of thing happens. I make a mental note to change phone providers after this trip

"I just see some time allotted for us to settle in and stuff. Then we have to meet up tomorrow for them to go over the rules again."

As soon as we get to the island, I need to contact my models and make sure everyone arrives either today or tomorrow like the schedule made time for. I opted to come for the first day as did the rest of my models. I want to do some team bonding before the serious stuff takes over.

Kayla smacks my arm pointing out of the window as the resort comes into view. The island looks stunning from here. Many villas line the grassy hills of the island, a private beach and restaurant comes into view as the bright greens, whites, and blues make this place feel so surreal, making it feel like I am experiencing nature for the first time. Multiple golf carts drive through the pathways of the island. I can tell I will really get some cardio in walking around the hills and crevices of this place.

Multiple boats dock in the water near us as we pull up to the dock where a couple of people stand around waiting for us or to get on board. We head off of the boat to see one woman's face light up as she sees us.

"Anylee right?" She says to me as soon as we walk off the boat. The workers grab our bags and pile them onto a golf cart.

I nod and shake her outstretched hand.

"I'm Jayana, the one you've been in contact with via email about every-thing."

"Hi! It's so nice to meet you." I take in her short frame. She's about two inches shorter than me. Her hair is done in fresh box braids. Her smile is wide causing her full cheeks to frame her face in an almost baby-like manner. If I didn't know she was the lady I had been speaking with, I would've thought of her as a child.

"I hope your trip was okay." Her smile is radiant and very much contagious as she looks over me with eager eyes.

"It was fine, I'm just ready to rest." I return her smile and stretch my body.

She laughs innocently at my response. "Of course there will be time for you to do that. You're able to rest and see the resort as much as you like today. We just ask that you come to the meeting at 6 for fashion designers. It's on schedule." She smiles.

I nod. I had completely forgotten about the meeting. "Is the address on there?" I look at my phone to see if the schedule of the meeting includes the address information but it doesn't. There is just a designated time.

"We scheduled a car to pick you up about half an hour before every event from your resort rooms. We want to accommodate time for traffic and trust me you'd be surprised how much traffic there is."

"I can only imagine. This place is so beautiful everyone must be excited to explore it." I look around in awe at the amount of cute villas on the hills and warm pink flowers covering the front of the lawns. A breeze flows from the ocean causing goosebumps to pop onto my arm.

"Ready when you are ladies." One of the workers says cutting us off from our conversation.

"I will let you two get settled into your room. See you tonight?" Jayana asks as she rubs her hands on her hot pink skirt.

I nod reassuring her that she will see me tonight before Kayla as I hop into the golf cart. Our luggage is currently ahead of us being dropped off to our rooms.

"I know I say something similar every five minutes but I really can get used to this." Kayla says, closing her eyes as a warm breeze passes over us.

The spring sun is already feeling warmer than the sun back home. I know as soon as I get to the room I will change into some type of shorts or sundress.

The golf cart stops in front of Kayla's room first. I look at her room, impressed and hope that my room is just as nice as hers.

"Meet up in an hour or two?" She calls to me as she walks to the doors of her room. I nod just as the cart pulls off and signal for her to text me before she's out of sight. Just around the corner is my room which is simply breathtaking. It's like a mini house with nothing but screen doors to bring in the natural light. A small rock and palm tree with flowers rests in front of my room looking over the private beach and restaurant.

This is the perfect place to take pictures. I make a mental note before heading inside seeing the mini castle before me. This space has more than one bedroom, probably one for me to work, another to sleep how thoughtful.

I pull up my phone taking video of the whole resort, the kitchen, the living area and bed room. My mouth drops at the pool in the back of the room and the mini jacuzzi. Thank God, I won't have to fight to get into the public one because I have my own.

As soon as the Wi-Fi connects, I send a message to my parents and Kayla to let her know I've arrived.

I take in a deep breath. The sweet smell of fruits waft to me as I look around my room. Complimentary flowers and wine wait for me on top of the dresser along with a gift bag with Fashion Week International's logo.

"I could get used to this too." I reach out my phone and text my models to meet me in an hour for some bonding. I want to know how they are adjusting to island life. I want to know if they all have that similar feeling of getting used to this treatment too.

"To Ms. Smith! May her name be known everywhere so that we can keep doing extravagant shit like this." Sean says as he holds up his cup in the air. The others and I follow suit celebrating this accomplishment.

"For real, girl! We're going to have to go out every day just to celebrate. You know I've never been on an island vacation." Tazlyn says to me.

"Yeah Florida is the closest I got to an island." Reef chimes in.

I laugh at their foolishness. "We all can definitely go out, we just have to find a time to go out together. I know you all don't want to go out every night." I say taking a sip of the champagne Sean had bought for the occasion.

"As long as Fashion International pays for all of this I will gladly hang out with you." Reef says sitting on the couch.

"Such a gold digger!" Samiyah shakes her head at Reef as he pulls out his phone to record a video of his fresh hair cut.

"It's hard out here. I'm broke," he says, making the rest of us laugh. I know how hard it is to break into a paid modeling gig. I always come to my friends' shows to support and even have them model some of my designs on my Youtube/Instagram to give them some exposure. I definitely made sure to add them to my Youtube montage and post them on my Instagram hoping that this event will be even more life changing for them than it will be for me.

"Where is Marcus and Kayla? I want to make sure they can have at least a swig." Sean asks, pausing mid pour of the champagne bottle.

"Kayla told me she was taking a nap and then would head over. Should be over soon though. I haven't heard from Marcus." I pull out my phone to check if I have any missed calls or texts but haven't heard anything.

"Don't worry. I just texted him." Reef says confidently as if a simple text is good enough to get him to come over.

I nod before taking another sip from the glass flute. I look at my friends chatting with each other, excitement radiating from them. I can't wait till I make it bigger than I imagined. They will all be my permanent models. I can pay them their worth and have their name on the big stage for the rest of their lives. My phone dings in my hand snapping me out of the blissful dream that is now my life. I gaze at the screen seeing Marcus' name and a feeling of dread crushes into me as I read the words on the screen.

> Marcus: *Hey, I know I should've said something sooner but I can't make it. Something came up with my family. Please don't hate me.*

I read the text over and over again thinking maybe this is a sick joke. I check the group chat to confirm if what I see is right. I found that all my models liked my message and expressed their arrival, seeing their *'on the way'* text. Marcus had even liked the message. Three men and three women are needed. Not two men and three women. Where am I going to find a model that can come to the islands at the last minute?

Without Marcus I am out of compliance and can kiss this opportunity and my dreams goodbye.

Chapter 4

Me: SOS

Kayla: What happened?

Me: Marcus just told me he dropped out and I have
no backup.

Kayla: What the fuck???

Kayla: I'm going to be at your door soon.

I pace back and forth after Kayla's last message. Maybe she was right. Thinking about all those bad thoughts conjured something. Something that could break my career before it even starts. I think back to the night of the party when he told me he was ready. He seemed to me happy at the opportunity. Maybe it was just a front.

A knock comes swiftly on my door before my overthinking gets worse which probably would create more bad mojo for me on this island. Next thing you know they'd tell me it was a mistake that they chose me for the show. Such a beautiful place for someone's career to end.

I walk to the door seeing Kayla dressed in a floral sundress. She just missed everyone by two minutes. I lied and told them I wanted to take a nap but I honestly could not have my models watch me freak out. They didn't have an issue either. They walked away to take naps of their own or explore the island. Which is something I would do if I wasn't internally freaking out.

"What do you mean Marcus canceled?" She says, taking in the worry on my face. I can see the rage building up in her the longer she looks at me. The protectiveness steams off her like a protective sister.

I show her the messages between Marcus and I. I continue pacing as she reads the messages. I don't bother looking at her face yet. Scared of what kind of thoughts could be visible on her face as she reads.

"Okay." She says her voice radiating annoyance. I stop pacing to glance at Kayla but her face shows no emotion. She sits there quietly deep in thought, which makes me uneasy. I called her over here to freak out with me not to sit quietly. Maybe she's thinking of some way to torture him when we get back or better yet a way to fix it. I pray she's thinking about a way to fix it. My brain doesn't have the capacity for it at the moment.

"Okay what?" My hands roll forward as I urge her to continue on. I couldn't contain the eagerness in my voice. I'm screaming for her help internally

"If Marcus wants to bail, that's his loss." She hands my phone back to me with a small smirk on her face. I stare confused. Out of all the reactions I was expecting from her, this is definitely not one of them.

"How is this his loss when I am the one that's at risk of being kicked out of the fashion show because of this?" I couldn't help my voice from wavering. It already took an insane amount of willpower not to have tears spilling down my cheeks.

"First take a deep breath," Kayla says, starting the motion by taking in a deep breath and breathing out slowly. I follow after her, closing my eyes, taking in a couple of deep breaths. *Everything is going to be okay.* I think to myself as I take in another deep breath. I open my eyes to see Kayla holding out a complimentary bottle of water for me to drink which I sip slowly.

"I'm guessing you have a plan?" I say looking at the mischievous smile on Kayla's face. I can almost see the light bulb lighting up above her head. That look alone worries and calms me down at the same time.

"Listen, we are on an island full of people who are no doubt here for vacation or to see this show. After your meeting we can go outside and find us a model for you. When do you have to get everything submitted to the team?" Her eyes scan my face eagerly. Confidence radiates from her as she looks into my eyes with a bright smile on her face. If anyone can fix this, it could be Kayla.

"I have sent everything but if I need to send revisions, I have to do so by early next week." I hated how weak my voice sounded. What happened to the confident Anylee I was a while ago? The one who wasn't crying over her ex, the one who worked hard to grow her brand and make a living solely doing what she loved? I want that Anylee back here dealing with this situation. Not the weak deteriorated one that took residence after my grandmother passed. I don't know how to shut my brain down now. Imposter Syndrome might be biting me in my ass a little too hard these days.

"You have time to get another model and with your speedy self I know you can whip up another outfit for them. I know you brought your yarn and hooks. This is just a tiny setback." Kayla places her hand on my shoulder before pulling me into a hug. She rubs my back in tiny circles as I keep still. My arms keep limp by my side to help me fight back the damn tears threatening to break behind my eyes. I know that if I wrap my arms around her in a full fledged hug tears will run down Kayla's shoulders.

"Trust me, Anylee everything will be okay. If I can help it, I'll even burn Marcus alive for you."

I nod chuckling slightly and take into account everything Kayla says. If I get a new model, then I can sacrifice my first week of sleep and partying to get ready for them. The only problem is we need to find someone today. Kayla lets go of me and sits on the couch.

"How in the world are we going to find one today?" I rub my temples and try to take in some small breaths. What I wouldn't give for a cookie or some herbal tea right about now!

"You just leave that to me. You get some rest and enjoy yourself before tonight's meeting. You and I will do some hunting for a model afterwards." Kayla types away on her phone, probably looking up some tourist attractions with the most people to find models. I might lay down and do the same thing. Maybe I can run into an influencer who is here for a trip or better yet taking a long trip in hopes to see the show. They might want to join, I'll have to check it out later but then again I may have to skip my nap for this. Lack of sleep is one of the things I planned to give up after all.

"Should I go right now? I don't know if we will find anyone in the evening," I ask with a plague of worry in my tone. Waiting until the evening makes me feel like I should be popping some blood pressure medicine.

"Girl, that's when all the hot ones pop out." Kayla smiles wide which somewhat eases my nerves.

I laugh weakly at her joke wishing I could give her a full on 'Anylee' laugh.

"It'll be fine." She wraps me in a hug again and rubs my back for a few more seconds before pulling away.

I want to believe what Kayla says to me and tricking myself into peace seems much more fitting than wallowing in self pity for things I can't control. I make a mental note to find a bakery later or something to stuff my face with cake before my head blows up from the pressure.

"I'm going to take a nap or something." I mention, hoping that Kayla would leave me alone to worry in peace.

"Okay, make sure you eat and change into something cute after the meeting. We have a model to find."

She exits my room and leaves me alone in comfortable silence. I walk to the bedroom and sit on my bed taking out my phone to look over the positive comments from my followers that always make me feel better.

I read the amount of proud messages and even repost my fan that I met at the airport who was the sweetest soul ever. If anything, I should do this for the people who support me. My friends, parents and followers. I know I'll find a model. I mean strangers support strangers. My followers are living proof of that.

Before my mind overwhelms me, I stand up and unpack some of my yarn that I have and some clothes for a refreshing shower. I desperately need a fresh start to wash away all the events from the day. Hoping that the second half will run smoothly with a clean slate.

A car comes to get me at exactly 5:30 PM and not a second later. I am greeted by yet another handsome driver dressed in a nice polo t-shirt and pants. This one must actually work for the agency. His skin is a rich umber making the bright blue shirt he chose to wear today pop against his skin. His hair is in soft spirals on top of his head. The closer I get to him the more tropical and musky he smells. He is a nice distraction from the fact that I need to worry about a model. Maybe he would be interested in becoming a model for me.

"Ms. Smith, I will be your driver for the entirety of the trip. I believe they gave you my card with your care basket. If you need anything at all please don't hesitate to give me a call." His smile is blinding against the sun's setting rays.

"Thank you Mr...?" I pause, hoping he can fill in the blanks for me. I look up to meet his gaze. The sun's brightness behind his head forms a halo around him.

"No mister needed just Chance." He takes a small bow and opens the car door for me. The inside of the car looks as if it has been freshly cleaned with an all black interior. The smell of spearmint is strong from the air freshener hanging from the rearview mirror in the car. He probably took it straight out of the package.

"Pleasure to meet you, Chance." I smile at him before getting into the car.

"The pleasure is all mine." He winks at me as he jogs over to the driver seat. I take out my phone and immediately text Kayla.

Me: So many fine men on the island.

Kayla: Are any of these fine men coming home with us tonight?

I close out of her messages with an exaggerated sigh as we head toward the agency. If I thought that the island was beautiful, before it is gorgeous now. As we ride to our destination, Chance slows down when we pass one of the many beaches on the island and I am truly in awe. The light blue water against the pale white sand has never been more breathtaking. The sun is glowing warmly as it prepares to set. I could get used to sitting around the many trees on the mountainous areas looking over the beach.. So many people fill the beaches. It reminds me of home when my family used to force us to Wildwood. We drive past pathways that lead to island mansions hidden behind luscious foliage and fruit trees. We stop just outside of one of those hidden pathways. The trees wave in the breeze to greet us as we ride up the driveway.

I hold in my breath as we pull up into the biggest building I ever saw. The hot pink bricks scream out to me as we pull in front of the large mansion with the Fashion international logo in front of us plated in gold.

"Welcome to the Headquarters, Ms. Smith.'" His accent rolls over every syllable as he opens the door, letting the warm breeze of the water and the smell of the ocean invade my nose. Below us is a private beach, one with rocks covered in sea moss that appear as if someone sculpted them to perfection a perfect cave as water flows between the hollowed area. Completely perfect for a photo shoot if nobody thought about it before.

My phone dings with a message from Kayla

Kayla: You promise to tell me what happens after the meeting? Or if anything happens with you and any of these cute dudes, right?

Me: No dudes.

I respond back with a smug smile on my face. The only breathtaking view I need is the view of the ocean, not some handsome islander. Although both would be nice.

Chance leads me to the building where he opens the door for me showing the bright white interior of the building. The floor is marbled scented with lemon cleaner and lavender air freshener. Statues and pictures from magazine appearances line the wall surrounded by royal blue furniture.

"Anylee, so glad you can make it." Jayana says to me. She appears to be the same height as me now that she has heels on.

"This building is so..." I trail off looking at some of the icons who line the walls. I take it all in awe. Unable to finish my sentence as I look at the iconic designs and designers that have been featured in Fashion International's presence.

Jayana follows my gaze and nods. "You do have a taste for fashion," she says as we take a look at Lovely Davis. She made headlines in France a couple years ago with an iconic dress that looked to be torn. So many people have copied her style since then to make it their own, especially fast fashion. I have a couple of pieces I crocheted inspired by her designs. I didn't create a pattern for them of course. I didn't need them to sue me over it. I'm too broke to fight against them in a court of law.

I look at the wide grin on her face. Unsure of how to take her comment as an insult or a compliment. Obviously if I didn't I wouldn't be here.

"Please, follow me to the other room where the other guests are waiting. We will get started in ten minutes."

I check the time noting that we will be starting exactly at 6:00 PM like it says on the schedule. I remind myself not to be late for anything in the future. When it comes to the schedule, they really mean to start on time around here.

Jayana opens the door for me. It takes everything in me not to fall to my knees when I see some of my favorite designers here in this very room. Michele Lovet who has designed items for big named fashion brands like Gucci and Dior. I'm pretty sure many of these artists have done the same but she is my favorite. Then there is Jose Tenio, the man who has not designed outfits for those big name brands but has also been the stylist to some of my favorite celebrities.

I almost feel ashamed being in the same room as these people as I am just a crochet fashion artist who just so happens to have a big following. If Kayla was here right now, she would smack me for having such thoughts. I am 'The Anylee Smith' and should start acting like it. I definitely have made a name for myself to get here. My work has already been featured on the major blog sites.

"Looks like we have fresh talent." Jose sits up in his seat no longer looking bored when I come fully into the room. He stares at me with complete interest, a hint of a smile on his face.

"I'm Anylee." I say, taking a seat by the door. The smell of coffee beans permeates through the room. I suddenly regret not eating before coming here. My stomach is on the brink of an embarrassing rumble in this room.

"Ah, the crochet artist!" He smirks looking at my hands, nodding impressed.

"You're the artist?" Michele beams "I love your work. I looked up all the designers who are featured and was shocked when I saw your work. It must take you hours to crochet those beautiful pieces." Michele chirps. She pulls out her phone and shows the rest of the group some of my work who nod impressively along with the rest of them. I sit there with the goofiest smile on my face, unable to speak. *Starstruck much?*

"This is my first fashion show. I'm a little nervous." I manage to choke out. I'm pretty sure they can tell. My throat feels unreasonably dry all of a sudden. I try to swallow as much spit as I can.

"It's okay, kid. We all have some level of experience. We will show you the ropes." Jose smiles.

I smile at the gesture and sink into my seat waiting for the meeting to start as the rest of the group talk about their upcoming designs, their struggles with color schemes, which type of look they wanted for each other of their models. And that's when it hit me. I forgot about the need for a new one.

"Alrighty since everyone is here, let's get started. I promise not to take up too much of your time." Jayana says as soon as she walks in. She shuts the door behind her and stands at the front of the room instead of sitting in the chair in front of us. It's clear who runs things around here.

I sit up attentively when Jayana speaks. Her voice demands attention as she starts to go over the details of the event.

"I know that for some of us these details will be overkill. And for the others these are new, so please make sure you pay attention. For those of you who zone out, there will be a copy of what I say sent to your email with a lot more details than I am sparing you from."

I nod when Jayana scans the room looking to make sure she has all of our attention before she begins.

"So all details about the categories and pieces have been sent to you in advance. I trust that each of you has created pieces to fit each category for every single model."

We all nod in unison. "Great, all details have been sent to you but we also need all your details sent to us by the end of next week to prepare for the line up. We want show stopping looks last so if you could send your outfit details, your makeup and hair looks to your department by then we can have everything ready by dress rehearsal which will take up most of your time."

"The dress rehearsal is to also have new models practice in case they never had the experience." Jose chimes in looking in my direction as he mentions it.

I mouth a *thank you* as Jayana smiles nodding in my direction. "Of course, we have a schedule that is pretty light. We want to give you ample time to make sure all designs are finalized to be sent in time for dress rehearsal. We also want to make sure you enjoy your stay without overloading you. Next week the promotion will start."

I raise my hand while simultaneously asking my question, "What happens during promo?"

"A lot of pictures and stuff for the magazine. Not with your unique pieces but with models and stuff. We have already started promotion obviously but highlighting models, designers and stuff. We trust you're not camera shy when it comes to pictures and interviews."

My body feels like it should be bursting with nerves but mostly it's exciting for me. My whole brand has been preparing me for this moment. I, of course, brought some of my old work as I planned to wear some of them to flaunt during the interviews and photoshoots so this works perfectly for me. Honestly everything has been working in our favor so far. Except the Marcus incident.

"Which brings me to my last and final point. Models." Jayana says. I can't help the pit that forms in my stomach.

"Just like the rest of your submissions that will include models so we can set up interviews and things of that nature. So you should send that to us early next week before the photoshoots and things of that nature. We want to have diversity and gender equality plus all those other things that make us comply with certain rules and regulations. So we need each designer to have diversity, whether that's gender, race, or sexuality. Believe me when I say people care about that kind of stuff. We want this show to feel like everyone can be seen on our stage. Not just thin, pale models."

A few of the designers chuckle and the looks on their faces show that they had their fair share of this problem before. I wonder if they could spare a model or so for me. I remember them saying they would provide for me and maybe they still would.

"Since all of you have brought your own models, there is nothing to worry about. All of the spare models we have are enjoying a much needed vacation so we thank you for bringing your own team." Jayana's giggle guts me out like the fish that I feel like at the moment. *Damn, I shouldn't swim with sharks if I can't handle it.* I pray silently hoping that Kayla's plans to find me a new model happen soon and fast.

I whip out my phone typing furiously at Kayla.

> Me: Definitely need that model.

> Kayla: I'm on it.

I should be relieved when I see those three words on my screen but I can't help it. Kayla is good for finding flings, one night stands and last minute dates but models? I don't think any guy would be willing to put on makeup and pose for the camera.

"Before you head out make sure not to post anything behind the scenes unless approved by the team. Definitely no final looks. Enjoy your time with us." She chirps before walking swiftly out of the room to who knows where.

I get up from my seat walking toward the back where a single donut and a pot of coffee sits. I take a cup and pour some of the black liquid into it, chugging it down to give me a boost of energy, instantly feeling the jitters in my system. I need to stay up tonight. My stomach rumbles from the coffee that sits bitterly on my tongue.

"Need some energy, Smith?" One of the designers comes up behind me to take the pot of coffee for themselves.

" I sure do." I smile tightly.

I'll need all the energy I can get to find one more model by tonight. Fast.

Chapter 5

"Why do I feel like you're not helping me?" I ask as Kayla holds up short dresses against my body, my hair already in wild loose curls to apparently top off my aesthetic for the night. According to her, I need to look the part. I immediately guess the part is a seductively irresistible fashion designer. To me though, it will be more desperate than sexy.

"I am helping you. How are people going to believe that you're a designer if you don't look drop dead gorgeous tonight?" She hands me a stack of dresses in various colors, all deadly short. I wonder how many of these Kayla packed for this trip. I have no doubt she will wear every single one of these dresses too. Let it to Kayla to be the life of the party out of the two of us.

However, I can't help but consider her words. Maybe she is right. I can't have people thinking I am scamming them or anything. If I go to the club dressed in some work attire, they might think I'm crazy or still living in the early 2000s.

"Okay, and do you know how we are going to find those models?" I don't mind taking Kayla's advice on the fashion piece of things. She did go to the School for Fashion Design and Business to open up her own little boutique. We mentioned multiple times about having my work in her store but I don't think my wrist can move that fast.

Kayla nods. "Remember that flier that the man gave us when we got off the plane?" Her eyebrows dance with mischief.

My shoulders drop unimpressed. "You're not talking about that night club, are you?"

Kayla winks at me, "Bingo!"

I let out a groan that could scare a small dog or baby. One place that I don't want to find a model is the club. Sure, there are some attractive men in clubs but there are even more of them just wandering the street. I think I saw at least twenty of the sort when I was riding to and from headquarters earlier.

"Do you need a model or not?" Kayla's weight shifts onto one leg as she puts her hand on her cocked hip scolding me.

"I do." I mumble softly, officially shamed at how she's looking at me. What I'm more ashamed of is the fact that I'm looking for a model in the club. I'll try my absolute best to feel sexy and not desperate.

"Good. Now go put on that black dress. That looks the best on you."

She turns toward the vanity in my room and fluffs her hair in the mirror, her perfect ringlets shaping her face. I walk to the bathroom and slip on the dress feeling silly until I look in the mirror. I nod impressed, admiring how it hugs my body tightly. It matches the look Kayla is going for, 'looking so good no man can say no'. A free stay in exchange to be a model seems like a sweet enough deal for me.

Stepping out of the bathroom, Kayla beams as she sees her work nodding in approval. I switch my jewelry from silver to gold. I want to show that I mean business and that I may also be made of money. It matches perfectly with my dress and rich brown skin tone.

"Perfect! Now throw on these heels and we are good to go." Kayla texts away at her phone before throwing it in her clutch

"I'm not throwing on any neck breaking heels." I look at the ones laying in front of me. I can't do heels more than an inch and these black strappy high heels look like they are about five inches too high.

"Don't worry! It's a perfect height for a newbie like you." She says smiling. "Hurry up! I told the others in the group chat to join us. I think letting loose will be good for you right now."

I sigh, staring at the heels. Kayla moves to help me strap them on but I swat her away. "I've worn heels before." I stare blankly at her.

Kayla shrugs me off as I strap on my heels and grab my clutch before heading outside to catch the taxi already waiting for us. My phone buzzes with messages from the others. I glance briefly at my phone to see a string of party emojis from Reef in the group chat before closing my phone.

"You had this scheduled?" I ask as the driver holds the door open for us.

"Since you told me about Marcus." She says confidently. I think back to Kayla being on her phone earlier wondering what she could have possibly been doing during my time of need. It was a plan to save my ass this entire time.

Tension releases from my shoulders as I look at Kayla who looks ahead with a confident gleam in her eyes. As long as one of us is confident about tonight, I will have a new model for the show before dawn breaks.

Music booms through the speakers so loud you might think you are inside the club already. The moment I step out of the car so many eyes look toward me lustful and hungry. It makes me want to turn around and ask the driver to take me right back to the resort where I can switch these clothes for my comfortable sweatpants and oversized t-shirts. I brought plenty of those with me for this trip. Thinking I would have time to crochet some personal pieces and make content in my down time.

I grab Kayla's arm and pull her close to me, "I don't think this is a good idea." I speak into her ear as one man in an unbuttoned shirt looks in our direction. He intentionally bites his bottom lip at me as we make eye contact. I roll my eyes and turn away in disgust.

"Look at the eye candy," Kayla says, fanning herself. "This is the perfect place."

"I don't–"

Kayla puts her hand up stopping me mid sentence. "Come on, the others should be inside already." She grabs my hand leading me into the building where the club is packed with people. I feel like sardines packed in a can as we move through the crowd. So many people on the dance floor slow grind to the music playing around us. There is an upstairs and downstairs bar that seems like even with the double bar it would be impossible to get a drink. Colorful lights change colors slowly from blue to green to yellow to red. The fast pace music is loud enough to cover the chatter of what feels like thousands of people. At least you can't hear hustle conversations here. It'll be easy to hide the shame in case my sales pitch is a complete shit show.

In the corner of my eye, I spot my models standing by the wall. I tap Kayla on the shoulder and point to them. We walk over to the spot that seems spacious enough for me to breath and hug each one of them.

"You look good, girl." Tazlyn says to me, eying my outfit, "You came here to get yourself a boo or what?"

I roll my eyes. "As if. I just wanted to get out of the house. I need to relax." I instantly feel a tiny bit better now that I'm around my friends. They all look so good, I fight the urge to pull out my phone and ask for a group photo. It would be too cringey for me. They all look good. Tazlyn in her dark blue strapless dress that stops just before mid thigh and hugs her curvy figure. Samiyah wears high heels with tight black leather pants and a bedazzled bralette.

"Yeah, I won't lie to you, Lee. You *were* looking like a stress ball earlier." Sean says to me. His outfit much like the islanders a calm two piece set, his shirt unbuttoned to show off his physique

Samiyah smacks him on the top of the head. I can feel the glare coming from Kayla.

"You're not the one who is under pressure with all the designs, all you have to do is look pretty." Tazlyn crosses her arms as she scolds Sean.

Sean shrugs. "You're right but as much as this is a business trip you should also find some time to relax."

"I agree with Sean. I don't need my designer getting into the hospital." Reef chimes in. He sports a two piece set too in the color black to match Samiyah's outfit.

"Aren't you guys considerate in your own way?" Samiyah says sarcastically.

I watch as they all talk amongst themselves dancing here and there to the music. I can't enjoy myself as much as Sean and Reef are right about me needing to relax. I desperately need to find this last model. Once I find them, then I can relax however until then I'm working overtime.

I turn to Kayla and pull her over to the side once the worry gets too much for me.

"What now?" I ask, suddenly feeling self-conscious about my outfit instead of the bad bitch I was originally supposed to feel like.

"Mingle. That's the only way we are going to find the perfect fit. I don't think you standing around with us is going to get you a model." Kayla shrugs.

I nod looking at the room. Kayla grabs my wrist softly pulling me in the direction of the bar. "You seem like you need a shot to loosen you up girly."

"We'll be right back." I call out to the others not that they could hear me over the booming bass.

I need to get it together. Now isn't the time to be the shy girl that I grew up being. That was all meant to be behind me when I started that YouTube channel, dating, building up my followers to be living this dream right here. This is for me, my career and my grandmother.

We reach the bar and order drinks I don't need to have. The sweet burning poison of alcohol gives me liquid confidence. My adrenaline only adds to the fire.

I throw one more shot back and order one more this time with some sweet fruit juice to wash it down afterward.

Kayla's face scrunches as if she smelled a smelly diaper. "I don't know what they put in these drinks over here but they sure are stronger than my bra straps." She sticks out her tongue in disgust causing me to laugh for the first time in what feels like days.

"They must dilute the drinks back home." I say, almost chugging the whole cup of juice to get that burning feeling out of my throat.

Kayla nods in agreement before scanning the area around her. She looks like a lioness scouting her prey. I turn to look around the club seeing who would be willing enough to be my model. It would be great if I can find someone who is native to the area. That way they can't hop on a flight to head back home out of forgetfulness.

"Okay, so here's the plan,' Kayla says, snapping me out of my thoughts, 'You search the bottom, I'll search the top?" Kayla asks before ordering two drinks that sound fruity. Hopefully, they aren't two strong. I don't want to slur my words trying to explain my pitch to them.

"Sure." I say, taking one of the drinks she bought off the counter.

"This is for aesthetics. Meet me back here in like forty five minutes," she says, snatching up the straw in her mouth, heading in the direction of the steps. I stand by the bar for a little while, sipping on my drink before gingerly walking to the dance floor. I make sure to hold my drink close to my body so nobody knocks it onto me.

Twenty minutes go by and I feel like I haven't gotten close to finding a model yet. So many cute guys around here but some of them are strictly here to party and find someone to take home for the night. Well, all of the guys are. The amount of "What are you doing after this?" after two minutes of a conversation made it clear they aren't interested in a single word I have to say. None of them scream *model* for me at Fashion International although most of them definitely have the face and cockiness to do it.

"How about you model for me instead?" A dark skinned man with tattoos and earrings speaks softly into my ear. I can hear the slur from the many drinks he has had as his hand trails from my shoulder to my lower back. I push back as gently as I can without trying to offend this man.

"No, thank you. I don't think it would benefit you." I turn on my heels before my face shifts from polite to a *'have you lost your damn mind'* expression. I need to look friendly, vulnerable, sexy if I want to trick men into coming up to me to ask them to become my model. Unfortunately, the men here just disgust me. I don't know why I let Kayla convince me that the club was the best idea for finding a model.

I scan the crowd and from a distance I see a fine group of men. One of them wears a button up shirt that's of course unbuttoned with cargo shorts which seems to be the dress code around here. Still he looks stunning, you can tell he works out. His chiseled muscles popping through the fabric as if he did a workout before he came here. I fail to look away fast enough so we lock eyes, a small smile creeping onto his lips. We move toward each other moving through bodies in the crowd before finally meeting face to face. His smile is charming. It might be the alcohol talking but I have to remind myself, I'm not looking for a body, I'm looking for a model.

I look at him up close, his plump lips smooth and pretty pink. His eyes pierce through me as a small smirk spreads across his kissable mouth. This man was attractive, irresistible like the cupcakes I can't ignore from the bakery around the corner from my mom's house. I shake the thoughts out of my head. Clearly, it is the drinks getting to me.

"Hi there," I say awkwardly before taking a small sip of my drink. I need to find a place to sit this cup down.

He leans in close to me, the smell of his cologne invading my nostrils. "You're too beautiful to be here by yourself." His voice rumbles like the bass from the speakers.

As corny as his words sound, my face heats up from the compliment, not the crowding bodies on the dance floor. I take another sip of my drink. I need to throw it away before my brain gets foggier. I'm already questioning my reasoning for being here with him standing in front of me.

"You look gorgeous yourself. Runway Handsome." My words come out a little slurred from the liquid courage. The words are sweet on my tongue. What is this flavor again? Cranberry? Pomegranate?

"You saying I have the face of a model?" He places his hand underneath his chin pretending to pose for me. I couldn't help but giggle. This is the most progress I have made all night.

"Face and body of one" I say, eyeing the pecs popping out of his shirt.

"Oh yeah?" He smirks and takes a little step towards me. His body radiates warmth. The smell of sweat and musk permeating the thin space between us.

I nod. He grabs my hand leading me closer to the wall where he no doubt wants to kiss and feel me up as sensual music plays in the background but I am here for that. Maybe getting him to think I am can lead him to wanting to model for me. You know...sex appeal and what not.

"LeeLee," I hear a deep voice say, his voice rumbles through me like thunder.

I look up to see the man holding my hand, his face drops as he looks right past me.

"Your Anylee, huh?" He says dropping my hand as if I disgust him. If I didn't know any better, the expression on his face looks like he will throw up just by looking at me. What sticks out to me though is the fact that he knows my name.

"Is something wrong? We can talk, maybe do something more. I just have a favor to ask of you." I bite my tongue hearing the desperation drip through my voice. Honestly, I hate it but I need this guy to be my model. He is literally my only hope. I cringe at myself. I have never stooped so low as to give my body away in order to get something I want. Nevertheless, I can let him think that I will.

"You'd go home and touch up on my best friend, huh?" I turn around, my heart dropping when I meet face to face with he-who-should-not-be-named. My heart flutters making me feel warm on the inside. That warmth quickly turns to anger. Out of all the places he could show up, he shows up here.

"Santoro, what the fuck are you doing here?" I snap

He takes the drink from me and places it on a small shelf looking at things around the wall.

"You had too much of this," he stumbles forward, almost knocking me over as his hands grip my hips for support.

"Oh, *I* had too much?" I roll my eyes trying to fight the feeling of electricity that courses through my body when his hands touch me after so long. Of course, my body would have this reaction when I'm supposed to be mad.

I look up into his eyes not believing him, not for one second. The hazel eyes staring into mine can't be him but his caramel complexion and musky scent prove me wrong. Why is he here?

"What are you doing here?" We say in unison. I push his hands off my body instantly, missing the warmth of where his hands once were. I curse myself for the desire to touch him again.

"Vacation. My birthday was last week." He says, scanning my face feverishly, taking in every part of me as if I could disappear from his sight any minute from now.

"Yeah. I know." I hold myself suddenly feeling cold. I had a gift that I was making him that I finished about a week before he dumped me. I kept that gift balled up in my closet for the past year or so.

"What about you?' He says, "I didn't take you for the airplane type." His chuckle has a hint of nerves to it as if he doesn't know if this is a time where he should be cracking jokes. I definitely don't want him to see me smile. He doesn't deserve it.

"I'm here for work." I fold my arms over my chest and stare up into his hazel eyes trying not to let my expression soften.

"You got it, huh Cupcake?" Santoro grins wide as his eyes gleam with pride.

"I'm not a cupcake." I snap at him though my body weakens at the look of happiness in his eyes. He remembers? Of course he does. He helped me with some of my designs, helped me put together my application and heard me talk about it for a month. Yet, I thought maybe since we weren't together it would slip his mind. Obviously it didn't.

"Yeah, well, you know," I shrug, trying not to get all choked up. This is not the right time to have a breakdown. I was not expecting any of this to happen to me. Not the disappearance of Marcus, not needing to find a last minute model. None of that. I am on vacation, the opportunity of a lifetime. This is no time to continue this sad girl parade. I need to make all these hiccups work out for me in some way. *Especially since one of the reasons is standing right in front of you living his best life.* I need to show him that I too am living my life.

"So, what's this favor you wanted to ask my friend?" He leans against the wall staring questionably at me. If I didn't know any better, I can see a hint of anger on his face. I know Santoro isn't jealous. Is he?

"Nothing you wouldn't get it." I look anywhere but his face. His knees and hairy legs, the heels that are making my poor feet ache the longer I walk around in them. I don't want him to try and be my saving grace.

"That's what I'm trying to do though *understand*. If you need anything, you know you can ask me." He smiles a little bit trying to downplay the jealousy in his voice.

"Says the man who left me when I did need him," I snap. I take in a deep breath. This is not the time for this. I don't need this going on world star. This is not how I want to be famous. I lower my voice and take in a huge breath to calm down.

The smile on Santoro's face falls as quickly as it appears. He nods slowly taking in the hurt tone of my voice. His eyes travel across my face before they scan over my body.

"You look good, Cupcake." Santoro says to me trying anything he can to make me feel something. When the only thing I want to feel is nothing. He deserves a swift kick in the balls.

"I stopped eating those." I quickly reply, even though I scarfed down so many before vacation. Thank God for fast metabolisms.

"Since when LeeLee?" He chuckles deeply as if calling my bluff. I shake my head unable to stand around and let the deepness of his voice and newly found muscles break down the walls that I have built so carefully from our time apart. Him and cupcakes were always my weak spot.

I stand up on my tippy toes scanning the crowd for Kayla. I hope that the forty five minutes are up as I rush back to the spot Kayla and I agreed to meet back. Her red dress eases the tension on my shoulders as I sit next to her in an empty seat, my ankles and calves thank me for the rest. I grab Kayla's drink that she sips from and chug it down until there is no more left. I need something stronger. I no longer want to get a model. I want to get drunk.

"Easy girl. We will find a model for tonight don't you worry. I met a few guys that are interested." She wiggles her eyebrows, sliding me a few numbers written on napkins or tiny slips of paper. I hope she means they are interested in being my models and not getting in her pants. Kayla has that flirtatious personality. I don't understand why she didn't volunteer to do all the work for me. She is much better at this than I am.

"Thanks, great." I say quickly, unable to get Santoro's handsome face out of my mind. I lean forward trying to see if I can find a bartender and fast.

"Can I have a Long Island?" I practically shout at the bartender when I spot them. The bartender whose hair is pulled back in a long ponytail shoots daggers my way before reluctantly making my drink.

"Woah woah! Tell me. What happened?," Kayla asks, eyeing me with concern and some amusement. "Tell me before you get so drunk and can't tell me anything until tomorrow. I don't think I can wait that long."

I roll my eyes and give her the finger before taking a sip of the new drink placed in front of me. My face scrunches at the strong taste. "I saw he-who-should-not-be-named."

"What?!" Kayla practically screams earning a few looks from the people around us. "You mean–"

"Santoro? Yes, he's here." I take in deep breaths, his name alone enough to bring butterflies. Scratch that! Make it cockroaches. I take a gulp of my drink this time. Maybe these drinks are making me hallucinate but then again, that man, his best friend looked at me like I was dog-shit when he asked if my name was Anylee. He must know I'm off-limits.

"Wow! Okay," Kayla looks off into the distance looking nowhere near as angry as I thought she would be at the news. Her silence starts to scare me.

"What are you thinking about?" I ask her as she has gone silent for one second too many times. I stir my drink before taking a sip appreciating the tea tasting flavor hoping this wouldn't bite me in the ass later.

"You need a model, right?" Kayla says slowly. Her face screams *hear me out* but honestly I would rather go deaf. I shake my head already knowing her next words.

"Ask him." Kayla says shrugging. She doesn't make eye contact as my face turns up as if looking at the most disgusting dish made to man.

"Ask who what?" I spit looking at her hoping she can come up with another idea in two seconds.

"Santoro. If you're acting like this over him, then he might feel the same about you and help?" She shrugs and orders another fruity drink from the bar. Something about Kayla is she is always calm and collected in these situations yet between the two of us she is the natural dramatic. The flip of the switch is a little scary.

"Feel the same? I don't have feelings for that man anymore." I take another sip and flag the bartender down for another.

Kayla gives me a *'liar, liar pants on fire'* look before looking at the cup in my hand.

"I'm pretty sure if you didn't you wouldn't have to drink your feelings away or wouldn't be hyperventilating over the fact that your hot ex is here in the same room as you and you want him back." Kayla smirks as if she has all the answers "You sure do want to jump his bones."

"Did you just call my ex *hot*?" I ask, everything else she said not registering something about a drink I think.

"See? Jealous." She grabs my drink from me and pushes it far out of my reach.

"I can get another drink you know." I shrug.

"And I'll spill it all over this bar." She says, staring intently into my eyes.

"*Kayla,*" I whine, not doubting that she would in fact spill my drink if I got another one.

"Listen here, Anlyee Marie Smith. I know losing Santoro was hard on you. I hated seeing you cry but if we are being honest this is the only real chance you have. Think of this as an IOU for breaking your heart."

"An IOU?" I laugh but find this nowhere near amusing.

"He helps you stay in compliance. You do a killer show and then never have to see him again. I don't see what's the problem with that."

Never have to see him again, those words should sound like music to my ears but all they do is bring fear into my heart. Asking Santoro should bring some sort of relief to me for the fashion show's sake but I can't bring myself to do it. If there's one thing I want more than anything it is to have Santoro back in my life instead of being pushed further away. I'm tired of losing the people I love.

"No!" I shake my head. "I can't go through that again. One goodbye was enough."

Kayla looks empathetically at me before pushing my drink back into my reach. I take it slowly, staring into the dark liquid as if it has all the answers that I desperately needed to drown my thoughts away even if it's with a few cups of soda. Crashing from a sugar high would be better than a hangover in the morning.

"I get that. I do. How about we just contact some of these dudes tomorrow afternoon and see if they are still interested? I don't think any of them were too drunk to forget this." She dances in her seat as if to say they weren't too drunk to forget her. After all, it's the reason we are dressed this way, to look irresistible.

I nod. "Should we still look or have fun?" I breathe out in a sigh hoping she will drop this for the night. One thing that I need for the first time since arriving here, is some fun. I know if I connect with my friends they will definitely help relieve this heavy feeling in my heart.

"I don't know about you but there is a fine islander calling my name somewhere. You can look if you want but I'm going to party."

I smile. "I think I'll do the same." I stand up searching the area to see if I can spot Reef or Tazlyn.

"Good. Go grind up on a stranger and forget about he-who-should-not-be-named." Kayla smacks my butt before grabbing her new drink and heading to the dance floor. Some man in pink shorts and a wife beater comes up to Kayla instantly.

I toss back the last of my drink and follow Kayla's lead to the dance floor. As the music slows and my body sways feeling the effects of the drink coursing through my veins, I don't mind when a stranger comes up behind me and places his hands on my hips. Letting loose and having fun is the only thing I want taking up space in my mind at this moment.

Chapter 6

I didn't know these villa things had doorbells. That is until it rang consecutively for the fifth time in a row. I sit up slowly rubbing my temples in circles to ease my pounding brain. I silently curse those strong drinks that made me addicted to the bar last night. Now it's biting me right in the ass.

"Who is at my door this early in the morning?" I throw the blanket off my head, the intense sunlight and my pounding headache are not ready to greet each other yet. I open my eyes slowly coming face to face with the digital alarm clock on my nightstand. It in fact is not morning but 1:30 PM in the afternoon.

I dig my toes into the furry bedroom carpet and stretch my body cracking all my muscles awake. The sun is blinding me. I curse the hotel for not giving us black out curtains for this place. It's like they don't want you to sleep the day away which I so desperately want to do but the sun is shining like crazy and a madman is ringing my doorbell forcing me out of bed early.

My eyes stare off into the distance. My brain is trying to process what I'm going to do for the day before the doorbell rings again.

"Ugh! Go away." I cry out, walking to the kitchen and setting the coffee pot up. I rest my elbows on the counter and place my face in the palm of my hands. Hoping I can heal myself with a quick *woozah* moment. I desperately need this coffee to combat this terrible headache. If there's one thing Kayla would do for me in our college days, it was making sure to put on a fresh pot of coffee. If I had the strength to walk back to my room and grab some pain killers I would do so in a heartbeat. Yet my body feels like heavy cement as I lean against this countertop. Impossible to move.

The doorbell rings one more time, igniting a fire in me that burns through my body as I stomp towards the door ready to give whoever's behind it the curse out of the century. Pain be damned!

"What?!" I snap, the intensity of my voice hurting my throat and sending a shock of pain to my already aching temples.

I swing the door open to see a well rested and handsome Santoro standing in front of me.

"Good morning, Gorgeous." He chuckles leaning against the doorframe. I slam the door in his face, quickly turning my back and taking deep breaths.

"What the hell?" I mouth to myself looking at myself in the mirror in the living area only to see that I was in fact not gorgeous. I have a white streak of dried up drool on my face and the smell of my breath is enough to send any man running. My curls stick up on all sides of my head as if I had just got shocked by lightning. I fix my wild curls in the mirror and wipe the dried spit off my face with fresh saliva as the doorbell rings again. I swear I'm going to break that thing. I place my hand on the door knob and do a quick breath check. I gag at the smell, run to the bathroom and place a breath strip in my mouth. Well, two that I find in the cabinet and throw back some pain meds accompanied by sink water before racing back to open the door. I swing the door open to find a smiling Santoro standing before me.

"Good morning," I reply dryly, opposite of what I feel. My heart can't stop racing as I look at this man. He is dressed in a blue and white button down shirt with matching shorts. No doubt in my mind that he bought this from Fashion Nova or something under vacation wear. Still he looks great in it. Blue always looked good against his caramel brown skin. He has that one shiny stud in his ear. I look away quickly before I get any other thoughts crossing my mind.

"You okay?" His eyebrows lift as if to silently ask again if I'm good. His voice sounds a little annoyed. I would be too if my ex slammed the door in my face. Even though I will never put myself in a situation for that to happen. You will not see me showing up at his apartment ringing his doorbell a thousand times to beg him to talk to me.

"I'm fine. What are you doing here?" I ask, putting myself fully into the doorframe to block him from coming in. I suddenly become self-conscious of my unmade bed that's waiting for me to crawl back in and rot until I find the urge to get up for the day to continue my model-hunt.

"You told me to stop by in the afternoon to get my measurements. You didn't text me back so I just came over." He flashes his award winning smile at me waiting to see recognition of our conversation in my eyes. All he gets when I look at his face is a pile of confusion

Text me back? Measurements? His words sound like another language because I don't recall saying anything to Santoro about coming over at all. Maybe this is Kayla's doing. This can be some sort of sick joke she would pull on me.

"You look confused," he laughs a hint of nerves in his amusement.

"I'm sorry when did I say this?" I try to think back to our conversation. The last thing I remember is dancing with a sexy stranger. Was it a stranger or was it Santoro? Either way. Nobody woke up next to me so I take that as a win.

"Last night?" He pauses as if that would jog my memory of something that I supposedly did.

"I walked away from you last night." I clearly remember that. I remember the charm he tried to throw on me with that vile Cupcake nickname that I used to love so much. I thought for sure by that time I was tipsy dancing on the dance floor he would be gone but apparently not.

"Yeah but you came back." He shrugs. I can tell he's hiding a smug smile. It's probably boosting his ego that his drunk ex came crawling back to him in a nightclub. Jokes on him because it doesn't count if only one of us remembers. The fact that keeps bothering me is I came back. Okay, so maybe this isn't Kayla's doing. I try to think back to the events of last night. Kayla and I talked after shutting down the idea of having Santoro become my model as compensation for breaking my heart before we decided to let loose and have fun. In fact, we should be meeting up soon to go over the people she found who wanted to be models for the show. So why was Santoro actually here?

"I'm still confused about why you're here. Can you fill me in on what happened last night?"

Santoro laughs wildly, causing heat to flood my face. "You get black out drunk now, Cupcake?" He pulls out his phone to pull up our messages, I'm assuming to prove his point.

My nails dig into the skin of my palm, "Don't call me that." I fight the heat that wants to show on my cheeks. This is why I don't drink. If I do, I need Tony. He holds me to three drinks max. I don't even remember how many I had last night.

"My bad, LeeLee." He holds up his hands innocently, amusement still in his eyes. He hands me his phone and shows me the messages. I gasp when I read the exchange between us. Right there are my text messages in plain gibberish but the concept is still there. Why would a drunk me do that?

I shove the phone into his chest and cross my arms over mine, "It's Ah-Ny-Lee. Not LeeLee or Cupcake." I spit, angry at his charm and good looks. Nicknames won't have my knees buckling today for Santoro. Not today, not tomorrow, not ever.

"Okay Anylee," Santoro shrugs. "Well, last night after you stepped away for a little bit, you came back over and we danced. You told me about your fashion dilemma and after a few drinks I brought you back here. You and Kayla."

I look at him appalled. I told Santoro about my fashion dilemma? I guess putting up walls is useless when you are drunk. I didn't have the intention of telling him. I had planned on him watching my success and sulking about me back home. Obviously he's in the drama now. My face heats up at the thought of what else I could've done when I was drunk out of my mind last night.

I clear my throat, "We didn't..." I trail off, hoping that he wouldn't say what I thought he might.

"Cute that you would think that Cupcake. But nah, I just made sure you got here safely." He smirks which turns into a full blown devilish grin.

My face burns with embarrassment. I look down at my freshly painted toenails suddenly interested in the plain white color, "Well, thank you."

"You're welcome, Cu–I mean Anylee." His voice is low and intoxicating like my favorite R&B love song that I can never get tired of.

I look up at him, his tall frame towering over me. He winks as soon as our eyes connect with one another. He tilts his head to the side with a questioning look.

"So we are doing this or what? From what you told me last night you're in need of a model and bad." He places his hand near my arm as if that is the key to moving me aside and letting him into my room.

"You don't seem like the model type." I slap his hand away, not wanting him to touch me or come into my room for that matter.

"I'm not but you are in a tight squeeze and if that means extending my trip a few more days then that's okay with me. I didn't see everything I wanted." He shrugs.

Our eyes connect briefly again. If I wasn't mistaken, it was almost like a pull to them. As if he was begging me to let him into my space, to let him stay here on the island. Begging to let him help me out. I'm desperate but am I that desperate? I just don't want him to think that I still need him.

"Fine." I huff and move to the side. "Only because I need one more model since Marcus canceled on me" I have half a mind to cuss him out when I get back from my trip because of this.

"Marcus,' Santoro looks up at the ceiling pondering, 'The one you took that class with?"

I slowly look up at him as I shut the door behind him and nod, "Yes, you remember him?" There was no need in hiding the shock in my voice. After all, they did meet a few times at parties I dragged Santoro to when we were dating. Each time they met they acted like they never knew each other or would have a 'Oh, that guy' moment. I don't think Santoro ever liked him.

"Yea, I remember all your friends. I never liked Marcus though. He always seems to have those hater vibes." Suspicion confirmed. Though, I wouldn't think of Marcus as a hater.

"Anyway, if we do this you're only here to help me and that's it. You don't text me unless I text you about the show. I'll send you details and stuff about it later."

Santoro nods unmoved by words. I shift uncomfortably not knowing how to feel about my ex in my space as he looks around the room to see remnants of the Anylee I am back home.

I walk over to the coffee pot and make myself a nice cup of coffee with extra cream and sugar. The sweet smell relaxes the tension in my shoulders. I almost forget Santoro is here if it wasn't for the fact that I can feel his lingering presence behind me.

"Do you want coffee?" I yell out, not looking behind but instead at the light colored drink I had transformed in front of me. I take a sip and almost shiver from the sweetness but at least I can't taste the bitter coffee.

"Yeah, give me a cup." His voice makes me jump as I step back a little bit, elbows brushing against his blue shirt. I grab my chest and feel my racing heart inside. The adrenaline from the little sip I took and the scare from Santoro make it feel like my heart just ran a marathon.

"Okay, another rule." I spin around practically body to body with Santoro. If I look up at him, our lips will be inches apart. I don't think he will mind that I sure will. I step back against the counter creating enough breathing room between the two of us. I turn, grab my cup of coffee and take a sip.

"I need my space so you can't be all up on me like this." I motion to the space between us even though the gap is pretty spacious I don't need him within three feet of me. Just the fact that he's here right now makes me not able to focus on what I'm doing.

"My bad, Cupcake." He puts his hands up in defense. His lips turn up into a smirk. What I wouldn't give to wipe that smirk right off his face! My face twists into a scowl. "Another rule." I put my cup on the counter and point a finger at him, hoping that the gesture is threatening even though I can't threaten to kick him off my modeling team now. I desperately need him.

Santoro's eyes roll playfully, I fight my facial muscles for the smile that threatens to break against my lips. I turn to look at the floor for two seconds to regain my composure before turning to look at him.

"No nicknames, no touching me, no friendly type of things. This is business."

He nods slowly as I turn on my heels making his coffee the way I remember him liking it. Two creams and two teaspoons of sugar. I always called his order borderline black.

"So, you just combine like five rules into one?" I can hear the playfulness of his tone.

"Do you want to take your coffee to go?" My eyebrows shoot up daring him to challenge me.

He takes the coffee and sips it without ceasing eye contact with me. As he looks up, an approving nod at his drinks he continues his same intense staring. "Yes, Ms. Smith."

His voice rumbles through me causing those damn butterflies in my stomach. I nod approvingly at the 'Ms. Smith' remark before turning to face the counter.

I grab my coffee and lead him to the spare bedroom where my tools are waiting for me. I motion for Santoro to sit down while I dig through my suitcase, looking for my measuring tape. When I used to make Santoro items that I never saw him wear unless it was for video purposes, I wouldn't measure him. I knew his size perfectly but considering it looked like he put on a little bit more muscle mass, I need to measure him. I don't want to crochet him something too tight or too baggy for the runway. Making personalized outfits is sort of my specialty.

As I dig through my bag a comfortable silence falls between the two of us. Something I can get used to when we continue to work together.

"Celebrities and stuff are going to be there right?" Santoro says trying to make some type of small talk. *There goes the quietness I was starting to enjoy.*

"Yup, some of them will be models too." I couldn't help the excitement that poured into my voice.

I know Jose and Michele brought celebrities as their models. I overheard them talk about it at the meeting the other day. I have no doubt there will be some in the crowd as well. I can't wait for promotions and dress rehearsal. I'll get to meet these celebrities in person. I wonder if it will be too unprofessional of me if I ask for their autograph. It is a dream of mine to have a celebrity walk the runway in one of my designs. I hope one day I can create a custom piece for one of my favorites.

"That's dope. You know ever since you told me you wanted to make an outfit for one of your favorite artists I knew you would do it eventually." I can see a glimmer in his eyes when he looks at me. My heart continues to flutter.

Of course, he remembers that too. Nevertheless, bringing up old memories won't make me fall for him again. Memory lane is a dangerous place to visit. It almost made me dye my hair again one time yet I had just got it to grow back to its natural color.

"Stand up," I grab the measuring tape, holding a notepad under my arm as Santoro peels his shirt back.

"You need as few layers as possible, right?" He queries, his biceps flexing a little bit as I put the cool tape on his shoulder. I roll my eyes while trying to fight the heat that threatens to rush through my body.

"You could've kept it on," I say to him as I smooth the tape down just below his pelvic bone and write the number of his measurement.

"I just remember when you–" he begins to say.

"Shut up!" I cut him off quickly in horror, knowing exactly the memory he was going to bring up. One I keep pushing down as I measure his body.

He closes his lips fighting a laugh as I wrap the tape around his bicep.

I measure shoulder to shoulder, front to back and get a few measurements around his waist for bottoms and all. Thankfully, he doesn't say another word. In fact, he doesn't look at me as I measure around his body, probably feeling uncomfortable and awkward knowing that he'll be modeling on the big stage not just a random body in my YouTube videos this time.

"Okay, all done." I say in an airy breath. The relief of getting this done and over with being the most important thing that has ever happened to me.

"So, what colors do you think will look good on me?" He asks with a curious tone.

Immediately, the blue he's wearing and pumpkin orange color scream out to me. I can tell with those colors that people will not take their eyes off him even if they try. I know from personal experience.

"I don't want to ruin the surprise. You'll see during dress rehearsal. Can you give me your information again?" I say, opening up my laptop and sending Jayana a quick email about the newest model, explaining to her how I got one last minute to fly out and how I'll need everything to be switched over for him.

Santoro writes his email down on a notepad using the pen left for me to write notes to the cleaning service. He slides the note in my direction. I write his information down in the email and send it straight to her. The swoosh sound of the email being sent feels like a weight has been lifted off my shoulder.

"Okay, so everything should be set. Are you sure you want to do this for me?" I ask, probably a little bit too late.

"Considering you just sent over that email saying I was in. It might be a little late to back out now." He laughs, pulling up a seat and sitting down next to me. I notice the distance he puts between us. I internalize my gratitude and nod.

"You're right but that didn't stop Marcus." I let out a sigh. Just the thought sets my insides on fire.

"I'm not Marcus." Santoro says his eyes are holding intensity as he stares into mine.

I nod. He's right. He isn't Marcus who dropped out the day of and did not tell me. He's Santoro Reeves. The man sitting here who would do anything for me yet also the one who left me stranded with a broken heart without a single fuck to give.

Just the thought of it brings the anger back and the cockroaches flowing through the pit of my stomach. The disgust of him coming back. He may not be Marcus but he's something worse than that. He's Santoro.

"Well, that's all. Thanks again." I say, my voice clipped. I sit back in my chair hoping that it will create more space.

"No problem, LeeLee." He shrugs nonchalantly. It's hard to tell what he's thinking about. Not like I should care.

"It's Anylee." I groan. "If you're not going to listen to a word I say..."

"Relax. I'll follow all your little rules." He says, cutting me off. A hint of a smile forms across his lips. It takes everything in me not to slap it off his face.

I stand up and pack up my supplies and begin walking out of the room with Santoro right on my heels. Swiftly, I open the door and wave him toward the warm sun rays. "That will be all of your service."

"You don't want to get food and fill me in on everything?" He scratches the back of his neck looking insanely cute with how nervous he looks.

"I'm pretty sure Jayana has sent you all the information and stuff. She's good like that. Look over it after lunch."

He nods and steps out of the room before he can say another word. I shut the door and run to my phone which is thankfully charging on the nightstand in front of me. I had to be the doing of Santoro because drunk Anylee must have definitely forgotten to charge her phone.

An email notification from Jayana releases the tension in my shoulders. With the little issue fixed and everything back up to speed, I just need to figure out how I'm going to get through this pageant with Santoro as one of my models.

I pick up my phone and triple text Kayla.

I think I made a mistake

Please, help me!

Talk over lunch?

Kayla sits quietly chewing on her onion rings from a small diner we found on the island that specializes in greasy food, something we both needed after last night. The perfect cure for the hangover we both still have. I desperately need to get this out of my system. I need to stay up late tonight making clothes for Santoro's runway debut. I wait for her to respond as she takes in every last detail of what happened with Santoro this afternoon.

"And here I printed out headshots of all our other candidates." She frowns as she lifts up the white folder she brought with her.

"Kayla for real, be serious..." I plead, grabbing an onion ring from the basket between us.

"I am being serious. I thought we were picking someone else. You were so against the idea yesterday. Even though it was a great idea, I guess I should be happy. These other guys could be creeps." I look around the diner looking at the blue and white sailor decorations to mimic the feel of a boat. I look everywhere but her eyes.

"Be serious! I thought I said no too. Apparently, this happened when I was drunk yesterday." I rub my temple. The thought of getting drunk is giving me a double hangover.

"Ahh...so the real feelings came out." She sits back in her chair with a smug look, dipping an onion ring in ketchup.

"Real feelings?" I roll my eyes and grab another onion ring from the basket.

"You know they say the truth comes out when you're drunk." She slowly presses her manicured fingers to her temple and rubs her forehead. I can tell she's having a worse hangover than I am. Kayla usually bounces back before I do but we still are in the same state. Hoping pain meds, coffee and greasy foods cure us.

"No real feelings came out, we just made a mutual drunken agreement." I say even though I'm pretty sure I was the only one drinking.

"If he's the only one who remembers what happened last night, I'm pretty sure it wasn't a mutually drunk decision.."

I groan as the live band begins to play music. A few people stand up and dance to the music. I feel like my body is already swaying to the music even though I'm sitting perfectly still.

"Listen, you set your boundaries, you have a model for the biggest accomplishment of your life that people can only dream of. Don't let the fact that you're worried about falling in love again distract you from your goals. Even if you were to get together again I somewhat support it." Her lashes flutter as she gives me an innocent smile to distract me from her last comment.

I roll my eyes and give Kayla the finger. She laughs. I don't need him throwing me off my game now. I finally get everything I need to not have to stress about this.

"I'm not worried about that. Besides, he pretty much caught me flirting with his friend last night." The image floods my mind, making me cringe with embarrassment.

Kayla roars with laughter. "I'm pretty sure that doesn't matter. He probably knew you were off limits as soon as Santoro came around."

"Whatever." I shove down the fact about how painfully right she is by pretending the people around me that are dancing in the middle of the restaurant are more important than this conversation and greasy food, a conga line starts forming as the band changes to an even more upbeat song.

"Let's just get out of here. It feels like my brain is doing the conga." I lift my hand for the waitress, signaling at her to bring the cheque.

Chapter 7

Reef: Only my third day out here. What's the plan?

Shawn: I'm down with whatever.

Samiyah: I say we all meet at the beach in a little bit.

Reef: I like the sound of that. Meet in 30?

Shawn: I better see everyone there too.

Tazlyn: If I didn't know better, I would think that might have been a shot @Anylee.

Kayla: Lol…

Kaylya: What are you being messy for @Shawn?

Samiyah: Fr

I laugh at the messages pouring through my phone as I continue the repetitive motion of yarning over and pulling through the loops on my crochet hook. I ignore the messages briefly to count stitches, making sure that everything is in the right stitch count. I pull out the measuring tape and make sure that the length across is still perfect. One thing I can't afford is another mistake.

I put my feet up on the coffee table and turn my attention back to the TV after everything measures out correctly. I haven't moved from this spot in nearly twelve hours. I pull the comforter off my bed to snuggle me as I camp out on the couch. Take out containers sit on the other half of the coffee table barely touched and probably cold. I ordered room service about an hour ago or maybe two. Either way, the food needs to be heated up now. Water bottles and a half drunk bottle of Pepsi sit beside it and my coffee cup has a little swig still next to me. I have been up since 5:00 AM. I could use all the caffeine I can get. Yarn scraps clutter the spaces around me. My notes and sketch book lay across the couch in cluttered comfort next to me. I glance at them every so often to remind myself of the vision. Now is not the time to add new things to the designs.

The repetitive motion continues. Yarn over pull through two, yarn over pull through two. I continue that until row after row is finished. I measure the piece one more time, calculating how many rows I need in order to reach my desired length before the doorbell to my villa rings.

I groan out, throwing my head back onto the back of the couch.

"Just when I am nearly done." I say to myself as I throw the blanket off my warm thighs. The cold air from the AC makes goosebumps cover the exposed skin, as scraps of yarn fly to the shaggy carpet.

The doorbell rings again and then one more time after that. Yelling at me to come to the door.

"Hold on, damn!" I stumble, trying to pick up the yarn scraps off the floor, while hurrying to the door. I don't bother to check the peephole before swinging the door open to see Kayla on the other side. Kayla wears a purple bikini with a sheer cover up overtop of her swimsuit. She takes in my immediate appearance. My hair has been in its scarf since waking up, having not seen the light of day. My university hoodie has seen better days as it swallows me whole.

"Tell me you have eaten something today? Drank some type of water?"

I nod. "Yes, I have drank water." I stretch, hearing the frequent cracks that follow suit after that.

"And you have eaten too?" Her weight shifts to one leg as she crosses her arm around her chest.

"Yes, of course. I have." I nearly yawn but stop myself. I don't need her questioning how long I have been up next.

"Oh really? What did you eat?"

I think back to what I ordered off the menu but it all feels like a fever dream to me. This was when I was running off fumes and coffee had barely hit my system yet.

"You're taking too long to answer."

"I had something with Chicken...I don't remember." I say, holding my hands up pleading innocence

She rolls her eyes and grabs my hand, taking me straight to my room and away from my work.

"Where are we going?" I say as Kayla takes me to the bedroom and pulls out my suitcase.

"I know you saw the group chat. We are all going out tonight, I don't want to hear anything against it."

I throw my head back in another loud groan. "You know I need to get this work done."

"Yes, I know that. But you also need to relax before you stress yourself into a heart attack." She throws a blue bikini at me and pushes me to the bathroom. "Now put that on, fix your hair and freshen up a little bit. We need to meet the others at the beach. I think Reef booked us an excursion."

Before I can ask what kind, she shuts the door in my face. Leaving me with my reflection in the mirror. I yawn and instantly gag at my coffee and sugar-filled breath. I freshen up quickly and fix my hair into something cute. I opt for my loose curls fluffing them out and spraying them with a little bit of water for some TLC. After putting on my bikini, I gloss my lips and fluff my hair once more before exiting the bathroom.

Kayla nods in approval before tossing me a cover up dress and some flip flops.

"Hurry up, girly! We are already late."

I throw the shoes on quickly and follow behind Kayla who is already outside with the door held opened waiting for me. I grab my room key and exit outside, shielding my face from the bright summer sun.

"That's what you get for playing caveman all day." Kayla shakes her head and loops her arm around mine as we walk gingerly to the beach on the other side of the island.

A cool breeze whips around us as we walk to the beach. The sun begins its slow descent down to earth, making the golden hour especially beautiful. Kayla takes videos of her fluffing out her big curls. She puts the camera to me where I blow myself a kiss. Both of us are natural hair baddies.

As soon as we touch the sand, the others are there waiting for us. Tazlyn and Samiyah match Kayla and I with the bikinis. Tazlyn wears a pink bikini while Samiyah opts for her signature yellow. Sean and Reef stand off to the side talking to Santoro laughing up a storm. Samiyah rolls her eyes and turns her gaze away from the boys into our direction. Her face lights up when she sees us. She taps Tazlyn on the arm, pointing to us and the two of them hop through the sand straight to us.

"Thank God, the two of you are here! The boys had started becoming...well, boys." Samiyah rolls her eyes.

"Yeah they began to talk about sports and stuff. You know I don't do sports." Tazlyn says.

"Let them have their guy moment." I say, slowly moving my gaze to Santoro. His swim trunks are a black color with sharks on them. I stifle a laugh at the sharks.

Kayla fluffs her hair and points her phone up to capture us all in frame. "Pose like you mean it ladies." We put on our selfie faces taking as many photos as we can, until the loud cackle from Sean turns our attention to the guys on the far edge of the beach.

"Must be gossiping about us." Tazlyn crosses her arms over her chest and looks over the three of them. Their bodies are turned away from us. Their voices are slightly quiet so we can barely hear.

"Speaking of gossip." Samiyah turns to face me and Kayla. "What happened to Marcus and why is um...your *ex*...here to fill in?" She says the word ex questionably as if the fact that Santoro being here to fill in constitutes us getting back together.

I roll my eyes and Kayla lets out a loud groan.

"So the day we all got here, Marcus canceled on me. I had to find someone here at the last second. Um...surprise, surprise! Santoro was here to celebrate his birthday."

Tazlyn and Samiyah exchange a look "And you're okay with him around?" Tazlyn questions. I can feel Kayla's gaze on me. I know she is probably wondering the same thing.

"I just need someone to fill in for me. This is just a work thing. We already talked about it." I sigh in relief. They all exchange glances before coming to some kind of silent mutual agreement.

"Okay, girlie!" Samiyah puts her arm around me as we all head over to the guys to find out Reefs plans for us.

All three of them stop talking as we approach. A wide smile appears on Reef's face as he holds his arm out for Samiyah to fall into them. He kisses her on the cheek and holds her close to him. Tazlyn pouts at the cute romance blossoming between the two of them.

"Let's go to the bar before I have a feeling that we could use a drink before we start." Reef chuckles as he leads us over to the cute hut in the center of the beach.

"Whatever this dude has planned, I know I'm not going to like it." Shawn whispers to us as we head over to the bar "Dude wants us to calm down with a few drinks first."

Kayla and I share a laugh which makes a wide smile appear onto Shawn's face.

"What can I get you people today?" The bartender asks as we all sit at the bar. We take turns ordering our drinks. I order myself a rum punch. Kayla orders a mango mojito which I will be getting when we get back from the beach.

"Whatever Reef has planned, this drink sure is going to help me get through it." Kayla says before taking a dramatic sip of her drink.

"I asked the bartender to double mine," Shawn says with a sigh.

"Oh, stop whining!" Tazlyn says "I'm sure it's not going to be that bad. I'm excited."

"You have the tallest drink here," Shawn shakes his head

"My drink is watered down." Tazlyn motions to the amount of ice she has in her cup.

"Sure, watered down." Shawn chuckles, earning a playful smack on the arm..

Santoro laughs while sipping his soda.

"No drink for you, playboy?" Shawn calls out to him. Thankfully Shawn's head blocks my view of him.

"No, if we're going to be in the water, I'd rather have a clear head. You don't know what could happen out there."

Shawn turns his head looking at the liquor that fills half his glass before pushing it away.

"Scared huh?" Tazlyn teases.

"I rather not die from DWD." Shawn shakes his head calling out to the bartender for a change in beverages.

"What is DWD?" Kayla asks

"Drowning While Drunk." Shawn says before ordering a soda from the bar.

Everyone bursts into laughter but the thought of drowning makes us hesitate picking up our drinks for a while.

Once everyone finishes their drinks, we pay our tab before heading back over to the beach. Reef rubs his hands together, excitement burning through his expression.

"Y'all ready to go kayaking?" Reef asks with a grin wider than the beach. He moves to the side to show the little boats we will all be in shortly.

"I don't know about this." I say hesitantly. I hardly like catching the ferry boat. These boats are tinier and I have to control them myself.

"Don't worry you'll have a partner, unless you're skilled." Reef reassures me. Santoro gazes my way at the word partner, his body language halted between asking me and leaving us alone.

Kayla wraps her hand in mine, intertwining our fingers, "Bestie is my partner."

Reef holds Samiyah close to him. "I already got mine."

Santoro looks between Tazlyn and Shawn before pointing to one of the single boats. "I've been kayaking a few times. I can handle it by myself."

"You sure?" Tazlyn questions.

"Yeah, I spent half of my life in the water. I'm cool." Santoro walks to the single boat while the others follow suit in grabbing their boat and paddle.

Santoro was not lying when he mentioned spending most of his time on the water. He loves to swim, fish, kayak, all of the above. Santoro's grandmother's backyard is basically a creek. When we visited her, Santoro would swim in water while I crocheted on a blanket a few feet away. The boy lives for water and the swimming trophies and medals at his parents house attest to that.

I take off my swimsuit cover up and wrap my phone around it before throwing it on the ground. I can't afford to lose my phone to water damage out here. Kayla follows in my footsteps before handing me a life vest.

"Girl, have you ever been kayaking?" Kayla says to me as we put on our life vests. I shake my head nervously as I look at the water. Although the tide is calm, I still don't trust these skinny boats to carry me safely anywhere.

We grab our boat and safely try to fit inside with just the two of us. Kayla sits down first and holds the boat steady as I try to get in the boat myself. I try to step in the middle of the boat, careful not to tip Kayla into the water and sit down right across from her.

My heart pounds and the sounds around me are muffled as a new fear unlocks inside of me.

"Stop looking like that, you're making me scared." Kayla looks around us, her chest rising and falling at a rapid rate as we both hyperventilate.

I grab my paddle and lay it across the boat. I reach over with my palms up and Kayla leans forward to lay her hands in mine.

"Don't let us die." Kayla would be the one to tip us over. She releases her hands from mine and smacks my shoulder playfully. I laugh and grab my paddle.

"Are we all set?" Reef asks as he paddles his kayak in front of the group. We all pause and look around making sure everyone is set, not to leave anyone behind. "Alright let's paddle." Him and Samiyah begin paddling, followed by Santoro, Tazlyn and Shawn then Kayla and I. We slowly paddle behind the rest of the pack, afraid to go too far away from the shore. Small boats and yachts are docked along the beach making it a little too hard to hug the side of the shore line. The sun sets deeper into the horizon and the ferry rides to another island in the distance.

"I don't like this. The sun is about to go down." Kayla says as she barely paddles. Although we barely move our paddles, the tide pushes us along deeper into the ocean. I scold the tide at its betrayal.

"We're just paddling to the other side of the beach. You'll be fine." Shawn calls out over his shoulder.

I try to straighten my spine to see how far away the other side is from here. "We can let the tide take us there." I vouch as Kayla picks up her paddle.

"I don't think that's a good idea. We might end up drifting off to sea."

I pout and pick up my paddle feeling a heated gaze on my skin. I turn to my left to see Santoro paddling away from me, his face turned slightly making sure that I'm in his sight even if by a little.

Kayla and I continue paddling. All my energy has been focused on paddling to dry land for my survival. The sun has set deeper into the horizon, dark streaks of oranges and reds color the sky as we continue to paddle. The others have gone out a little farther than us, paddling slowly while they laugh at each other's jokes. Santoro stays a little bit behind them, a smile on his face.

"I think we're doing this wrong." I put the paddle down, trying not to let my frustration tip us over into the water.

"I think if we paddle the same way we can catch up." Kayla pauses in deep thought, making a paddle motion with her hands to figure out which way she should move her hands.

I sigh, "I thought we were doing that?"

"It feels like we were just moving in a circle literally." Kayla laughs and motions for me to pick up my paddle. We try our best to move forward, the tide helps push us along, as we move toward the others. As we paddle to the other side, my heart beats heavy in my chest as we near the side of the beach where all the boats float along the current.

"Don't get hit by a boat." I nod toward the boats behind Kayla. She looks nervous for a second but her face wipes clean of the emotion. We continue paddling, coming too close to some boats for my liking. A docked boat grazes our tiny kayak as we get closer to the rest of the group.

"Oh my gosh!" I stop paddling, afraid to hit more of the boats, hoping that the tide can carry us through the rest of the way.

"Don't stop paddling now, we might get hit with a–" Before Kayla can finish her sentence, we're under water, peering up at the bottom of a boat. My eyes widen as I struggle to get free from the boat. Kayla frees herself first and tries her hardest to free me next. I close my eyes as I hold my breath. I feel my body come free from the boat as it floats upward toward the surface. My body is wrapped around another as we break the surface. I gasp for air and turn to see Santoro looking down at me, his arm wrapped tight around my waist as he holds us close together.

"You saved me." I say in awe, like those girls who had just been saved by a glorious super hero. He looks down at me with a wide smile.

"I couldn't lose you again." He says softly, a small smirk on his face.

Before my body can process his words, Kayla snatches me away from him and wraps her arms around me squeezing tightly.

"Anylee, are you okay? Oh my gosh!" She scans my face briefly before breaking out into a hysterical laugh. I stare at her as if she grew three heads.

"Yes. Are y'all okay?" I turn when I hear the silky voice of Santoro, his hair is wet. His paddle and kayak float abandoned in the ocean.

I nod slowly, taking in the water dripping from his body, the slight smile on his face almost like pride.

"Santoro, I'm glad your ass is part fish." Kayla says as she lets me go.

His chuckle sends butterflies through my body. I turn towards Kayla and swim to meet the others as they sit on the opposite side of the beach where more kayaks and paddles rest. I sit on the sand, happy to touch earth as I crawl up next to Tazlyn. Kayla sits next to me a few seconds later.

"So, when is the next excursion we're going to do?" Kayla squeals as she rests next to me in the sand.

"I heard you can swim with exotic fish." Tazlyn says excited as she pulls her phone out of a protective case hanging around her neck.

I pop up from my spot on the beach and shake my head. "You too have fun with that, I'm going to go get my phone."

"Get mine too!" Kayla calls out.

I wave her off and continue walking, a cool breeze whips around me sending goosebumps down my arms. I stare off into the distance, trying to shake the feeling of butterflies that still flutter around in my insides.

Chapter 8

Sunscreen, hydration, crochet hooks, and yarn; the four most important things a crocheter can have on a vacation with me all laid out on my bed. When Kayla texted me early this morning begging to see some of the beaches, I immediately said yes. With the weight of the drama finally lifting off my shoulder, there was no way I could pass up an opportunity to relax on the beach. Especially, when the excursion yesterday almost resulted in my early demise. We have a couple more days to relax until the hectic Fashion International schedule and I intend to soak up as much of the rays as possible.

Kayla busts through my door with the spare key that the villa had given me and plops her items down on the floor of my bedroom.

"I'm getting ready with you today. I don't know what they put in these mattresses but I cannot stop falling asleep." She yawns, stretching her body to the point where I can hear the little cracks of her bones awakening. She drops to her knees and opens up the bags that she packed. She yanks out two tiny articles of clothing no doubt her bathing suit and walks to the bathroom to put them on. Before I can respond, the door shuts behind her meaning I have less than probably five minutes to change into my own bathing suit.

Of course, since I'm here celebrating my accomplishment, most of the clothes that I brought are handmade by yours truly. I have no shame wearing a scandalous piece that I made for vacation. My bra cups are a bright purple and baby blue triangle shape with chains that drape over both sides of my body making the curves of my body enhanced from the illusion. My swimsuit bottoms are also crocheted into a thong like piece with the same baby blue and purple color that I adore so much. I used bathing suit panty liners for the inside not wanting to feel the yarn on my lady parts. I don't know how other designers can stomach it. The piece is made of the softest acrylic yarn that I ever worked with. Thanks to a soaking method that I use when I work with cheap acrylic but you wouldn't know the yarn was only three dollars when you feel the texture.

I pick up my phone typing away at an open note to make a video of the process. I know so many girls who follow my channel would benefit from this hack. It's tried and true. My grandmother taught it to me before she passed. I just spruced it up a bit.

"Remind me to get you to crochet me some bathing suits." Kayla says basically drooling at the mouth. I twirl doing a little dance as I roll my shoulders and shake my hips.

"Get it girl! But seriously, I want a bathing suit like that so I can dance along with you." Kayla pouts as she folds her arms across her chest frowning in the mirror at her own bathing suit

"I gotcha girl just say when." I say checking myself out in the mirror. I fluff my hair, admiring the perfect shape of my voluminous curls.

"When." She pulls out her phone and motions for me to pose for the camera.

"I'm not the model that's you." I giggle walking over to her and push her camera down to view her pedicured toes instead. If there's one thing that I don't do that often, that is model my own creations. There's simply something about making other bodies look good that just does it for me.

"Come on, girl! You look too good to not have pictures taken in this creation. You know the girls would go crazy for this piece." She touches some of the dangling chain designs. Her eyes widen as she rubs the yarn between her thumb and pointer finger. I laugh as she awes over the softness. Definitely making a tutorial for this soaking

"And ask for a tutorial." I chime in. I already have a written pattern for this design that I plan on selling along with the multiple other patterns that I made. I've been keeping some of my intricate patterns hidden from my followers since I've been focused on making my designs for Fashion International. I've been uploading some easy quick designs that have my own spin to them that I see trending but my dresses and other patterns I haven't uploaded yet. Maybe taking pictures of my bathing suit on vacation will help with the promo when I do go to sell them. I believe the YouTube video I made of the announcement was the most viewed and most liked video that I have ever made. Kayla picks up her phone aiming it at me with a slow creeping smile.

"Fine but only get pictures of the front of my body," suddenly feeling self-conscious of the thong-like design. Maybe I should've brought a regular bathing suit.

"You're not going to give a little peekaboo action?" Kayla says standing off to the side popping her hip to one side to make her butt pop out a little more. "A little side butt?" She wiggles her eyebrows

"No, thank you." I shake my head, scrunching my face in disgust at the idea.

"You're no fun." She pouts and waves her hand off to the side of the room with the best sunlight directing me where I should stand. I head over there feeling a little awkward. I've done a little modeling in school but nothing like this.

I stand off to the side posing for the camera. The longer I stand there, the more comfortable I get taking the pictures. I bend over and blow a kiss to the camera. No doubt the peaks of my butt will show but I won't post *that* picture.

"Girl, you are a natural in front of the camera. You're sure you don't want to be a model instead of a designer?" Kayla asks, flipping through the pictures we took with a smile. She shows me a picture that has my butt looking good and raises her eyebrows with a *"you better post this"* look written on her face. I swipe it away looking at a picture of me with a cute smile on my face.

"I definitely don't want that." I laugh. I barely get comfortable posting myself on social media with the followers I have, let alone pose in front of big time photographers and be displayed on a platform with millions of followers like Fashion International. I'll stick to my cozy half a million and youtube subscribers.

Kayla walks over to me and hands me her phone to see the pictures. I send myself the ones I like and delete the ones that are never reaching the internet let alone my phone. I just hope she didn't save any of them and plan to post them on my birthday. I don't need random guys sliding into my messages with a happy birthday message in an attempt to get my number.

"Thank you, girl. Now let's finally enjoy our stay while we can." Kayla picks up her beach bag before we head out of the door together.

It's the first time since we've been here that I finally feel excited about the fashion show happening soon instead of stressing over not being able to participate because of stupid Marcus' drop out. Or the fact that I had to pull magic out of my ass to find a new model (even though I sucked at finding one in the first place). Not even the thought of having my ex fill in for Marcus can stop me from enjoying this vacation.

Kayla loops her arm around mine as we walk out in the blazing sun. The bright greenery of the island pleases me as we stroll towards the beach, smelling the salty water waiting for us in the distance.

"I hear that the private pool area is always lit around lunch time." Kayla says, flashing me the time. 11:30 AM. No doubt Kayla wants to join in on the fun. She's always been the party animal of the group. I still feel like I'm recovering from our night out at the club. I'll probably limit myself to one drink max. Or better yet get me a virgin drink instead.

"Just give me an hour at the beach." I sigh. Knowing my plans to crochet at the beach all day is going to go straight out of the window. I'll probably do most of it later in my room with some type of reality TV show playing in the background.

She squeals excitedly into my ear making me regret looping our arms together in the first place. As we step onto the private beach looking out at the boats and yachts docked in the water, the smell of charcoal from one of the huts on the far side of the beach wafts the scent of fresh grilled meats in the air.

Young children kick sand in the air as they run from the high tide while other people build sandcastles, bury themselves in sand or simply relax. I plan to be on the beach right with them. I want to smile at the kids on the beach occasionally as I work on my crochet pieces.

"I think I'd like to try his *meat*." Kayla points in the direction of the grill under the hut labeled Thomas Grill where a man with the longest locs I ever saw slaves over the hot charcoal. He flips burgers in a floral button down shirt and shorts. His muscles flex as he flips the food, his face poised in concentration.

"You're disgusting." My face contorts as she playfully hits my shoulder. I shake my head somewhat questioning why I opted to go the beach with Kayla instead of my friends, Tazlyn or Samiyah

"The actual items on the menu, dirty. I haven't eaten breakfast." Kayla fights a smile, the corner of her lips turn up slightly "I know where your head is at. Santoro got you–"

"Don't even think about finishing that sentence before I bury you in the sand." I point my finger at her mouth making her instantly be quiet. I move my finger when Kayla attempts to bite it. I turn on my heels walking toward the grill with Kayla right behind me. The smell of food makes my stomach sing to the island music. I guess I forgot to eat breakfast this morning too.

"Please, bury me in the sand. I loved that as a kid." Kayla's eyes seem distant as she thinks of past memories. Probably family vacations at the beach. I hate being buried in the sand but I can bury my dad in the sand joyfully.

The closer we get to the restaurant, the more heads seem to turn in our direction. The man on the grill looks up just as we are a mere five feet away. He stares at us with intensity but it might be the sun's brutal glare on our bodies that makes it hard to see us coming.

"Welcome ladies!" His dark eyes stare everywhere but my face as if he's carefully unraveling each stitch from my swimsuit. He looks at Kayla the same. The slight gleam of his eyebrow and the small sultry smirk on his lips already let me know before he can speak to me. This man is trouble for the ladies.

"Do you have a spot for us under your hut, *sir*? We're *starving*." Kayla's voice is sweeter than usual and the fact that she even pulled out the word sir tells me she doesn't mind a little trouble herself. I'm going to have to keep an eye on her.

"Right this way." He motions for us to enter the hut where a few tables are occupied with happy customers. I take peaks at their food looking at the savory food before them. My mouth waters at the sight of lamb chops. I turn back to Kayla who is still staring at the eye candy on the grill

"Don't even think about it with that one." I say once he is out of earshot. Something about that guy just screams trouble to me. I don't need Kayla getting caught up with this guy's player ways.

"So you felt it too?" Kayla says to me with an ear to ear grin on her face.

"Felt what?" I ask as we sit down at a table in the center of the hut. I make eye contact with a waiter. The subtle nod he gives me lets me know that he'll be with us in a second. Thank goodness because I am starving.

"Felt the bad boy vibes radiating from that man." Kayla practically drools as she stares in his direction at the thought of him. Her curls drift forward covering most of her face. I look over at the man to see he is also staring at Kayla back to undressing her with his eyes. I shiver, feeling disgusted when he did it to me just a few seconds ago.

"Girl no. No men while we are here." I sigh exhausted always having to have this talk with her. Kayla is a beautiful girl with rich brown skin and loose 4A curls that are big and long. She attracts the attention of every guy, and she lives for that attention sometimes. Her relationships don't seem to last more than three months. She dates flashy guys with money after the first dude she loved turned out to be good for nothing. I guess my bestie is a little bit of a gold digger but you would raise your standards too after such a heartbreak.

"We will be here for three weeks and you're telling me I have to hold on when there are so many fine melanated men walking around this island?" She scoffs as she surveys the hut again taking in the amount of men around the island. She's right, so many beautiful black men are here even I felt crazy for that statement. But I'm not looking and something about that thought feels equally crazy.

"We're not here for–" I begin to say before Kayla cuts me off.

"A summer fling is fun and for sure on my bucket list." Kayla winks. "I don't need you to shoot it down, just support me." She begs with her eyes.

I let out a deep sigh. "Since it's for *your* bucket list," I drag the words out like it exhausts me just to say those few, I know I'll be hearing all about it soon.

She jumps in her seat and smiles. "This is why I love you." She looks at me lovingly while I roll my eyes at the thought.

After a few minutes, the waiter comes over and takes our order. I order for the pineapple and shrimp rice bowl. Kayla orders the chicken and mango rice bowl. Of course, we have our cocktails to match. I ask for only a little bit of alcohol in my drink not wanting to relive the night from before.

"Hopefully, when they bring me the check the cook writes his number down," Kayla sighs as she draws small circles on the table.

"You're still talking about this." I can't help but roll my eyes.

"How about you get a fling? Look around this room and pick someone." She points her finger at me with a serious expression across her face.

"I'm not doing that." I take a bite of my food and pretend to be interested in random videos on my phone.

"Just pretend to be for my sake, for me. You make me feel like I'm being a whore." She folds her arms over her chest and leans back in her chair. I look up with a raised eyebrow which she returns with a pouty lip. I sigh and entertain the thought for a moment before scanning the room myself, seeing some attractive men yet nobody that catches my eye. Kayla taps my hand as my gaze lands on a man with red swimming trunks and a ton of tattoos up his arm. He has a clean cut on his head with a smile that could make my heart flutter.

" I think I found someone." I slightly begin drooling.

"Found someone for what? I thought I was your model?"

I freeze hearing the deep raspy voice that I used to love so much. I make quick eye contact with Kayla who slowly nods her head to confirm my suspicion. I silently pray it's just my imagination but with the slight jealousy I heard in his tone there is no doubt in my mind it is him.

She looks up at him and gives her biggest smile, "Hey Santoro!"

I look up behind me to see his hands resting on the back of my chair. He looks down at me, his hazel eyes fixate on my face. He looks as if he's trying to figure something out about me.

"We're just trying to find people who might want to be Kayla's summer fling." I shrug. Suddenly feeling guilty about the lie or the fact that I was looking at another man. I'm starting to wonder if I'm over Santoro like I said I am.

The food comes out to us swiftly looking too good to eat. A pineapple is carved out into a bowl that's filled with colorful peppers, onions and pineapples with glazed shrimp on a bed of fluffy white rice. My stomach growls a little too loudly but the sound of music in the distance covers up the viscous growl.

"That looks good," Santoro says, his eyes only briefly looking at the plate before his gaze turns back to me.

"Will you be joining them sir?" The waiter asks as he places Kayla's food in front of her. I sit there like a sitting duck waiting for his answer which I hope is a no. I don't think I can stomach this food and him sitting right here with me.

"Yeah, will you?"Kayla asks politely though by the slight tone of her voice we both know she doesn't want him around either. For my sake. Or she might be trying to mess with me.

"Yeah actually I'll stay and have a drink with y'all before heading over to whatever party they got today. Get me something brown." Santoro slides in the seat between me and Kayla. I reach for my phone instead of looking at Santoro whose gaze burns into the side of my face. I take a picture of my food and post it on my story with a cute little gif to accompany it.

"Still taking pictures of food before you eat it, huh?" Santoro smirks as he continues his watchful eye on me.

I follow the sound of his voice to see his softened eyes staring back at me. I look up right into his eyes which seem to melt into mine.

"You know the camera eats first." I reply, trying not to let my voice sound sweet to him.

He nods and eyes my food before turning his body to the waiter who places his drink in front of him. I turn to eat, feeling uncomfortable eating in front of him but I don't want to offer him any of my food. That will give him the wrong idea.

After a few minutes of awkward silence, I look up at Kayla and plead with her silently to say something to Santoro to make him go away. He can throw back his drink and leave any minute now.

"What party are you going to?" Kayla questions as she takes another bite of her food. I look down at her bowl to see it's almost gone.

"The one in the villa. They always get lit in the afternoon." A mischievous grin appears on his face before he takes a sip of his drink. Something tells me this isn't his first time going to the parties here.

"I wonder why they party during the day." I ask with a little shrug. I would love to just bask in the sun today and soak my feet in some warm water and then party at night but I do make a living crocheting so my grandma stage is well into effect.

"Well, it is vacation and everyone goes off looking for some type of adventure on the other islands at night. It's nice to have the jacuzzis to yourself. " He smiles at me which is enough to bring back those damn butterflies. A pit of warmth falls in my stomach when he winks at me. It's enough to have me melting in my seat like a popsicle being left out in the sun. I can't talk to him. Not until the official show prep happens like I planned it to. As childish as this may be, I need to give this man the silent treatment. I can't risk another one of those smiles.

"Anylee and I, we're going to head over there when we are done." Kayla beams excited. She dances in her seat. And I dread the next couple of words that come out of Santoro's mouth

"Word? Maybe we can go there together. I'm supposed to meet my boys over there. They leave tomorrow." He looks between the two of us. Kayla and I stare at each other speaking silently. This was not the plan. It was food, beach then party. Not food, party then beach

"What about the beach?" I say looking at Kayla with a slight pout in my tone.

"We can go afterwards. The beach doesn't close down but the party does." Kayla dances in her seat again before turning to her bowl to devour the rest.

After we finish our food, we head over to the party with Santoro who claims he is meeting some friends there. I hope that's true. I want to be as far away from him as possible. Kayla and him chat about island activities given he has been here a few days longer than we have before we extended his stay. I secretly eavesdrop thinking about how I will be swimming with dolphins on this trip one of these days.

As we enter the pool area of the villa, the DJ plays Megan Thee Stallion making some girls twerk on top of the jacuzzi. Santoro rubs his hands together looking in the direction of the dancing girls. I fight the suppressed jealousy down and turn to Kayla, "Drinks?"

Before Santoro can say anything to us about joining, I grab her hand and pull her along to the bar. The area is crowded with people. Everyone moves in sync with the music. The bartenders are busy pouring drinks into empty glasses and gladly get people drunk in the middle of the day. People soak in the jacuzzi talking as lovers give little pecks to the music. No doubt feeling sensual vibes.

"Two rum punches please." I say to the bartender. I watch as the bartender makes them quickly. My eyes nearly bolt out of my head when I see the amount of rum she pours in the drink. This is going to be my one and only drink for the day.

"Girl, this place is off the chain. Don't worry there's so many people here you will barely see Santoro here the whole time." She says knowingly as she looks at the tall glasses of rum punch in front of us.

I look out into the sea of people, the bodies huddled together everywhere. I take a deep breath realizing how right she is. There are so many people and attractive people that Santoro might not cross my mind

"I hope you're right." I say taking a deep breath. Something that I don't want is to be on the lookout for him when I should be enjoying myself.

"And if I'm not?" Kayla says with a raised brow.

"Then I won't give you the number the cook gave me for you." I turn my back to her and sip my drink to keep from laughing at her shocked expression

"Santoro! I swear." She says before silently cursing under her breath.

The music changes to more Hispanic club music that played when we first arrived. The music no doubt has me moving my hips to the rhythm as I sip the little drink left.

"Another one please." I say to the bartender whose attention is on us since most people are dancing on the pool decks. I'm going to need something to keep my liver healthy after this trip. One drink my ass!

"You might as well find a dancing partner before you get that stool pregnant." Kayla laughs.

I roll my eyes playfully and take the new drink placed in front of me.

"I could say the same thing about you Ms. I-want-a-summer-fling." I take a sip of my drink and raise my eyebrows questioning her silently as to why she wants one. She doesn't seem to take my hint and motions toward the dance floor.

"I'm serious, just go dance." She grabs my hand, pulling me out of the seat and pushes me towards the dance floor. Luckily, none of my drink gets on my bathing suit. I place the cup on an empty spot on a jacuzzi deck and move to find a comfortable spot on the dance floor. One where not a lot of bodies are squished together and the smell of chlorine and body odor doesn't leave a bad smell lingering in my nostrils for the next thirty or so minutes.

"Is the crowd making you hot too?" Santoro says into my ear. I turn my body coming face to face with him and his sly smirk. Leave it to Santoro to not be immersed in a party he was so eager to attend.

I open my mouth to speak but decide against it instead. I fake a yawn and sip my drink. My social battery is somewhat starting to drain. I will give myself about another thirty minutes or so before I take my bag and I to the beach to continue crocheting pieces for Santoro.

"Are you tired? The sun got you beat already, huh?" He smiles that signature smile, the one that I love so much before taking off his shirt revealing the tank top that lies underneath. His tattoos on his upper biceps glisten with sweat as he uses his shirt to wipe the perspiration from his forehead.

I look away not staring at him or his beautiful body that he created after our break up at the gym. Was that his way of getting over me? Of course not, he always talked about getting back into it after his football days. Santoro did everything he put his mind to. *Everything.*

"So you're excited for your big break or what?" Santoro says, staring down at me. His gaze shifts from my face to my swimsuit. It's then when his eyes bulge in their sockets as if this is his first time looking at me today. Like really looking at me. I fight the smirk of satisfaction seeing his reaction to my swimsuit. Instead of me having a flustered reaction.

"You made that didn't you, LeeLee?" He says breathless. His arm flexes as if he wants to reach out and touch me. I know he does. "You look good."

He stares into my eyes and an intensity that wasn't there before takes over. I watch as he seems to struggle with his words. He doesn't hide the slow scan of my body before returning to my face. I nod in acknowledgment. His head tilts and his eyebrows lift in curiosity.

"Are you ignoring me, Anylee?" An amused smirk plays on his lips.

I don't say a word as I take another sip of my drink. He laughs at my nonverbal words and licks his lips, sucking me in with his eyes.

"You are." He steps a little closer to me. I can smell the alcohol still lingering in his breath.

I shake my head *no* as I move my hips to the music.

"Then how come you're not saying it?" His smirk grows wider.

I turn my back to him, continuing to dance. Ignoring him and not talking is the best thing to do. This is what we need to do. I shouldn't be around him right now. This isn't what I agreed to with him. Being friends and hanging out outside of the show is something I shouldn't be doing.

"Stay silent if I can dance with you then." He grins.

Shit.

Santoro turns me around pressing his body to my backside as the music slows down bringing our bodies to slow down with it. Santoro's scent of cedarwood and now what smells like lime from his drink lingers in my nose as he puts his face inches away from mine. Our bodies slow grinding on the dance floor. All I have to do is speak right? Speak and he goes away?

"You look so good." Santoro speaks breathlessly into my ear. A deep rumble that I missed over the last few months. He holds me close, hands gripping my waist. His touch burns my skin. His thumbs graze the tiny bit of fabric that covers the delicate parts of my body.

I miss these moments, the ones where it felt like nothing could break us apart. Those late night conversations and early mornings when he first woke up, when his voice was filled with desire for me. That desire does not need to be needed now.

I quickly spin my heart pounding out of my chest when I see the desire staring back at me. He takes a step forward causing me to step back and bump into someone behind me.

"I have to check my email. I think an important message for the models and what not is coming to my email today." I stumble on my words as I quickly turn on my heels and run away from Santoro.

Chapter 9

To: itsanyleesmith@gmail.com

From: show2025@fashioninternational.org

Good afternoon, fellow models, designers, and the team for the 2025 Fashion International Show in the Virgin Islands.

We are looking forward to seeing your designs and working with you over the next couple of weeks. We would like to cordially invite you to our event tonight. You will have the chance to talk to other designers, models, makeup artists, photographers and others that will be working on this special event with you. This particular event is casual. Wear what you would like.

Please, let everyone in your team be reminded to show up. It is not required but encouraged.

Sincerely,

Fashion International Team

Please do not respond to this email.

I, in fact, did have an important message to send to the models. The moment the email landed in my inbox, I passed the message along to my team. Making sure that they can plan for it accordingly. I was excited to see the email in my inbox for a few reasons. 1. It makes me not a liar. 2. I am excited to see my favorite designers and ask them about their experience in the fashion industry without sounding like a total newbie.

Ever since I came back from the party, I've been crocheting. I even snuck to the beach for a little bit before the sun got too much for me and instead of burning in the sun I opted for my air conditioned room. The repetitive motions of my hook distract me from how close Santoro and I were. Hiding in my room just makes me sure I won't see him out in public. My phone has been going off since I sent the message in the group chat. Everyone chattering about their outfits, possible nerves and cracking jokes like usual. A high pitch ping of my phone announces back to back messages. I know those messages are from Kayla who is no doubt freaking out about what she should wear tonight.

Kayla: What are you wearing tonight?

Probably wearing something you crocheted.

I'm jealous.

I laugh at the text knowing that I will indeed be wearing something that I crocheted. It's a red dress with a corset top design and a short skirt in my favorite stitch. The shells stitch with red lining to accompany it. I didn't want people to see through my clothes twice in one day. Although the email said casual, I wanted to dress to impress today with my favorite designers being there and what not.

Whatever you wear is going to be gorgeous I know it.

Kayla: You're right. Let me channel my inner bad bitch.

I laugh and pull myself off the couch to get ready for tonight. I take a quick shower to freshen up and get dressed in my handmade dress and put on red lipstick to match. Instead of makeup, I opted for moisturized skin from my face wash routine that I neglected to do this morning and fixed a few of my stray curls.

I look good. I know it.

The red pops against my tanned skin from the hot rays of the sun, making this the perfect color to show off in. I take out my phone to snap a few pictures and make a mental note to film a get ready video for my next event for content. I cannot neglect the content.

Slipping on my shoes, I rush out of the door and head outside to wait for the car which should be here in about 5 minutes. The low sun hanging in the sky cooled down the island just a little bit as a warm breeze still swept through the villa. I take in the fresh scent of salty water and sit on a chair outside of the room. I sit back and close my eyes, sudden exhaustion from late night crochet sessions and the warm air washes over me. I wish I was taking a quick nap instead.

The sound of tires rolling up stray rocks on the pathway awakens me. An all black vehicle pulls up in front of me getting into park as Chance comes out of the car with a smile on his face.

"Good evening, Ms. Smith, you're looking beautiful." He winks at me with that warm smile still on his face.

He flashes his shiny teeth at me and honestly if I were to have a summer fling like Kayla it definitely would be with Chance, my driver. I'm pretty sure that would be an awesome love story. Too bad I'm too traumatized to find out if that would be true.

Chance opens the door for me as I scoot into the roomy backseat and cross my legs together. He jogs to the driver side and gets in the car, and looks back at me to check that I am buckled before shifting the car in gear. Lauren Hill plays low in the background.

"Ready?" He asks as he starts the car a small shimmer in his eye.

I nod my head as Chance turns around to put the car in drive. He glances at me in the rear view mirror a couple of times before heading toward our destination. I can tell by Chance's reaction, his stolen glances and compliments that I look good. Undeniably so and in something that I made at that. Mission accomplished.

Walking into the beautiful building with a marble interior will never get old. The setting sun in the background accompanied by the soft instrumental music playing for ambiance has me feeling like I am on a movie set. I can tell by the faint lemon scent this place has had a deep clean.

"When I get rich I will definitely get a house on an island." I say to myself as I walk around the party. There's not many people here, not enough bodies to cover the floor but to scarcely place them for private conversations. The intimacy of this event is deeply refreshing to me. The event night is casual but the atmosphere speaks grown to me and as a barely 22 year old, this event feels like something my mom would be invited to for work.

I walk over to the back of the room where a punch bowl and a few snacks wait. I fill up my cup with a punch that smells of sweetness from the fresh fruits swimming inside. I feel relieved sipping on the drinking knowing I won't get tipsy off of this. I scan the room for Jayana, hoping that I can talk to her but she's nowhere in sight. Maybe this shindig isn't her doing.

"Hi," a soft voice speaks to me as she comes closer to the snack area. "I love your dress." She ogles. "I couldn't stop looking at it when you came in." She says before filling up a cup and sipping from it. She looks to be the same age as me or younger. Her face is more babyish than mine. She's dressed in yellow wide leg pants with a lace white crop-top that looks great against her dark skin. She rocks bora braids with a hint of blond in them.

I fight the urge to say *thank you*. I made it because *duh* isn't that why some of us are here? Instead, I scan her looking at her flawless makeup. The natural look with the pops of color to match her pants are stunning. I guess I'm not the only one who wanted to dress to impress.

"Thank you. You look amazing yourself. Who did your makeup?" I question, admiring her work. Her eyes really do pop against the subtle shades of yellow she painted across her eyelids.

She smiles shyly and smooths her hand over her braids. Getting a glance at the sunflower design on her nails, my eyes almost pop out of their sockets. We definitely need to be friends.

"I did,' she beams, 'I'm one of the new makeup artists for this year's show."

I nearly scream with excitement. A million thoughts run through my mind. I definitely would like her to be the makeup artist for my models. I need to do a collaboration with her for a YouTube video. So many more ideas rush to my head that I notice I didn't speak after the scream. I glance to see a slight look of confusion and amusement on her face.

"I'm one of the designers," I smile, hoping to ease the awkwardness. "Hopefully we can work together during the show."

She nods and smiles brightly as if those were the best words she's heard all day. "That would be awesome!"

"You think Jayana would take a request?" My voice pitches up in eagerness, causing her to laugh.

"I think she gets so many requests. One more won't hurt." We smile in unison.

Just as I open my mouth to agree, Kayla's voice sings throughout the space between us.

"What's this look for? Santoro?" Kayla smirks at me when she sees my dress "Because you sure as hell will get his attention in that." Kayla strolls over, closer to me wearing a pretty sundress in a solid dark purple color that looks amazing on her skin tone. Her hair is pulled up into a simple bun, probably either annoyed from having it down all day or frustrated from not knowing what to do with her hair for the event. Knowing Kayla I'm pretty sure it's the second option.

I excuse myself from...*damn* I didn't get her name before walking over to Kayla willing her to be quiet before she embarrasses me anymore. I don't need everyone in my love life drama. I pull Kayla to the side and cross my arms over my chest with the word *really* written across my forehead.

"Don't look at me like that. I'm asking if this look is for Santoro." She fights a big grin.

I roll my eyes. "This look is for me. I wanted to make a statement. My favorites might be here." I say, scanning the room for them hoping they would be able to see one of my favorite designs. So far, no one is in sight.

"Well, you shouldn't have wasted that dress on this because your favorites aren't here." She sighs, looking around at the very few people at the event. I check the time to find it's almost seven and only a few more people have shown up. I turn back to Kayla and frown.

"What do you mean they're not here?" I didn't make my hair and skin look perfect just to show up and be disappointed. Story of my life.

"This event is basically for the newbies. The snacks and all the other things are mediocre at best. The people I've talked to mention that it's the first time here in one way or the other."

At the mention of her news, my chest deflates. I take a look around at the nervous people that are just like me, also slightly overdressed, scanning the room too every five seconds in hopes of finding someone. I suck my teeth. Such a waste of a perfect outfit!

"Don't be sad. I hear that when the real events happen like the after party and such, that is when the celebrities come out and everything." She basically squeals at the mention of it. I know she's hoping to see a singer or a celebrity. My only hope is that she doesn't expect to date any of those players

I nod. "Yes, but this dress was it. I wasted my dress on this. Nobody's even here." I couldn't help but let the disappointment seep out of my voice.

"Cheer up, girl! Just make the dress in another color. I know you got notes on how you made it somehow. Take pictures of this one on a mannequin and then pop out in the new one. Blue really is your color anyway."

"I think you look good in any color." Santoro says. I hear the desire in his voice.

I turn around to see him in his casual outfit, a simple white t-shirt and jeans. For some reason, he looks extra good. Maybe it's the spicy scent wafting to me from his body, a clear sign he showered before he came here or it's the fact that he and I danced together earlier and now my perception of him has been distorted. I can still feel his body pressed against me and the deepness of his voice admiring my looks.

With the way his hazel eyes swallow me up, I know he's thinking of that moment too. He runs his tongue over his bottom lip before releasing a long whistle. His eyes scan my body once more.

"I think you should be on the stage up there modeling." He has yet to look me in the eyes, too distracted by my dress to even pay any attention to me. He's not being subtle about checking me out *at all*.

"I can't. I'm the designer, not the model. I make the clothes for you guys." My words come out clipped. Hoping that those words are enough to get him to look me in the eyes instead of my nipples.

"Some pieces look better on the one who made it," he shrugs.

Santoro and I make eye contact and the sincerity in his stare lets me know he means every word.

I open my mouth to speak but Kayla grabs my hand and pulls me over to the floor to ceiling windows where the background overlooks the ocean with multiple fruit trees. The image it creates looks like a picture, an artist would paint and have an old grandmother hanging it up in her house.

"Is there something you need to show me?" I ask Kayla, turning to her confused.

"I had to get you up out of there before you made out with him or something." She says, looking back at Santoro.

I laugh loudly so hard that it makes my stomach hurt. Me? Kiss him? That thought hadn't crossed my mind since I saw him on this island. If anything, the thought of slapping him certainly crashes into my mind.

"Anylee girl, I'm serious! The chemistry is *cheming*," Kayla says as if she knows something I don't. So she thinks.

"Okay, now that's funnier than the last thing you said." I giggle with what's left of my laugh.

The Anylee of a few months ago would jump at the chance of getting back together with Santoro. At one point, I considered him the love of my life but now he's just a pain in my ass. One that will go away as soon as the last model walks down that run way.

"I try my best to avoid him. He just keeps popping up. It's not my fault." I'm starting to think maybe Santoro has a tracker on me or something. I could've sworn I stopped sharing our location when we broke up.

"Maybe this is a sign from God telling you to go get your man back." Kayla smirks with a wiggle of her brow. Very childish. I'm surprised she doesn't pretend to make out with the air after that comment.

I shake my head. "No, God wouldn't want me to get back with someone who broke my heart." I reply matter of factly

Kayla raises her eyebrows "How do you know leaving you didn't hurt him too?" She crosses her arms over her chest "He seems to miss you a lot. You still have a dangerous effect on him after a year still."

I laugh again. The bold words coming out Kayla's mouth don't sit right with me. Is Santoro being sad about leaving me? I doubt that. If he is, he has one hell of a way of showing that he loves me or has feelings for me especially since love is a strong word. He was the one who left. Sadness coming from him doesn't seem like a feeling he would have after dumping me. Maybe regret is the better word.

"I see the way he looks at you LeeLee. Like you're the most beautiful thing he has ever laid eyes on." She says with a look of yearning in her eyes. Like she knows that's exactly what he's thinking by watching our interaction. It's not my fault I've always been pretty.

"Not my fault crochet pieces have that effect on people. Just wait till you're walking down the runway, people will look at you like that too." I couldn't hide the defensive tone in my voice.

Kayla nods a small smile coming across her lips but her eyes droop with pity. I know what she's thinking. However, just because I look good doesn't mean I'm doing so for him. And just because he looks at me like *that* in those pieces doesn't mean he loves me. That *love* could be lust. I should know better after the grill cook looked at Kayla and I like he was undressing us. What Santoro was doing was basically the same thing. I can't control when I see him either so if I look good, I look good. Not to mention he did see me hungover and crazy a few days ago and it's not my doing that he pops up literally everyday. He might just be trying to find me. Because I damn sure am not trying to find him. This is a professional relationship now. Rules have been set.

"You can stop looking at me like that. I promise everything is fine." I furrow my brows seeing the same pity in her eyes as before.

Her hands shoot up as if she has been caught redhanded and nods repeatedly before giving me a salute.

"I understand." She nods.

A soft hand touches my shoulder and a floral scent fills my nose. "What's going on? It looks like we're in a secret huddle." Tazlyn's sweet voice sings to us. The somewhat thick tension that was left between Kayla and I dissipates at Tazlyn's presence. She wears a soft pink dress with a strapless top and a puffy skirt. Her hair is in perfect ringlets that elongate down her back. Tazlyn's style is super adorable. It matches the rest of her personality.

'We were just talking about men." Kayla says "You know regular girl stuff."

Tazlyn nods while surveying the area. "That is very understandable but we are here on business."

My shoulders drop in relief. "Exactly." I roll my neck at Kayla who rolls her eyes at me.

"Listen, you two can be too serious sometimes. Yes, we are here for work but also to make connections. Right LeeLee?" Kayla looks me dead in the eyes. Tazlyn looks between the two of us with confusion on her face.

"I don't know what we are talking about but it does not seem like we are talking about *networking*." Tazlyn pulls out a few business cards from her small clutch. "Speaking of which, I want you to take a picture of some of these business cards that I got so far. I think you could collaborate with some of these people here."

I take the business cards from Tazlyn's hands and smile, flipping through them as if they are rare collectibles.

"You two are boring me. Where are the rest?" Kayla says scanning the crowd for others.

"Last time I saw them, they were at the bar on the second floor. Reef was chatting with a photographer." Tazlyn says as I place the business cards back in her hand.

"Great, would you show me the way Tazzy?' Kayla smiles mysteriously at me before she loops her arm around Tazlyn. 'Just so you know he's coming back this way." She whispers to me before walking away with Tazlyn, giving me very little time to react before I feel his presence lingering nearby.

I look over my shoulder and see Santoro strolling over in my direction. He smiles as if he's shy and continues walking over, never taking his eyes off of me.

"This party is...fun" He shoves his hands in his jean pockets and rocks on the heels of his feet. His shoulders seem to be stuck in a half shrug. I can tell by the expression on his face that he's bored.

"Yes Santoro?" I ask, not wanting to engage in small talk. At first, he looks at me confused then a spark of recognition sprinkles over his features.

"Oh, I wanted to ask, have you been recording for your channel or anything lately? I think this vacation can be really fun to record, you know? You could do a vlog or something. Or a couple of them. That's if you still do those things." His words come out jumbled and rattled as if he doesn't know what to say to me. He smiles awkwardly. I don't know if it's me or the fact that the party has him saying anything.

"I've been taking some videos of things here and there. Not much to record yet with nothing happening until next week." I shrug.

I can whip out my phone and record something from this event but I doubt my followers will be interested in something like this. There's nothing really happening here.

"Right...I was just thinking. Of course, you thought of that idea." The confidence comes smoothing back over his voice. I can't help but feel a little happy that he remembers my channel. Of course he does, he used to help me especially when my camera wasn't acting right. There were some days I uploaded crooked videos until I learned how to edit the videos to fix that problem. That just adds more time to how long I spend editing my videos.

"Hey! Can I actually talk to you for a second?" He digs his hands further in his pockets as if that's possible considering the small pockets on his pants.

"You weren't talking to me before?" I question him. He chuckles nervously but I can tell he's enjoying the sass. I'm trying not to be soft for this boy anymore but rough like sandpaper.

We stand around awkwardly. Nobody says anything to break the ice. I hold myself, anything to put enough space between the two of us. He steps a little closer to that scent of spice, flooding back to me. Memories of him slowly grinding on me returns. I shiver at the thought.

"Yes Santoro?" I keep my voice even with a small smile. Though my heart is pounding so loud in my chest I'm pretty sure he can hear it.

"I know we haven't been on the best of terms lately." His words come out slow, filling my body with torture.

I shift in my stance hoping he isn't about to ask what I think he is.

"I don't want things to be awkward between us while working together so I was wondering," he pauses again, the slight pauses leaving me anxious for more. I suck in my breath anxiously awaiting for his words

He is about to ask me out. I know he is. I repeat in my mind during the dramatic pause.

"Would you like to hang out just one time to, you know, break the ice?" His eyes bore into me, scanning slowly as if he can see the answer written on my pupils.

Santoro wants to hang out with me? Willingly? As if these past couple of days we haven't been forced to be in the closest proximity to each other where it's almost like we already were hanging out. As far as I'm concerned, these things count and that should be enough for Santoro even if he doesn't want it to be. Kayla's words about Santoro's feelings come barreling back to me. I would hate for her to be right.

"I think the rules will help us." I say before I overthink it. As long as he doesn't cross that boundary, we will be okay. "We can keep a professional relationship and things won't be awkward between us kind of like they are now." I shift uncomfortably, avoiding Santoro's gaze.

He nods slowly. "Right." He scratches the back of his neck and shifts on his heels. "I didn't think that would've counted tho. I mean I am asking you to hang out after you know,' he pauses and clears his throat, 'some time."

"Oh!" That's all I manage to say. I turn and see Kayla chatting lively with another girl who looks to be a fellow model. She holds a salt rimmed glass in her hand which leads me to believe Tazlyn successfully showed her the bar. Kayla turns to grab another piece of food and the slight glance she throws at me before turning back is the sign I need to get away from this conversation.

"I have to go. Kayla needs me." I turn and practically run from Santoro. Again. Before he can see into my obvious lie, I practically float over to Kayla who in fact doesn't need me. Not even a little bit. She and the girl she's with are talking about their favorite perfumes when I finally reach her.

"Kayla," I call to her, almost out of breath. Speed walking with a racing heart feels like I made a full sprint to her. I feel the need to call my doctor after this.

She excuses herself and turns to me.

"What did he say?" Her eyes are hyper fixated on me. They scan my face waiting for the answer as if it's written on my face.

"He wanted to hang out with me." I say after a long pause to catch my breath. I turn to look back at Santoro who has found himself someone to talk to.

"And you said?" Kayla asks, her voice full of anticipation. I can see the threat of a smile approaching her lips.

I take a deep breath, "No." I say my voice sounding a little disappointed. Kayla lips pout for a quick second before she nods her head understanding. I'm thankful for her not mentioning *I told you so*. I nod, despite feeling confused about the sudden feeling of disappointment in my chest.

Maybe it is the conversation we had before that made something flutter in my chest at the thought of Santoro having feelings for me again. Maybe it's because I do want to hang out with Santoro just so we can ease some of the awkwardness. I can't though because deep down I know Kayla is right. I can't create more opportunities for us to be around each other. I need to keep myself focused. Getting back together is something old Anylee would want but I'm past that now. I need to focus on the present. At the moment, there's no room for Santoro.

Chapter 10

Avoiding. That's all I've been doing. Avoiding Santoro. Avoiding crocheting his pieces. Mainly because avoiding the latter means I don't have to invite Santoro over to try on the pieces to see if they fit. I have made pieces for him multiple times before but with his new found muscles the best option is to have him try them on rather than have a malfunction on the runway. I know I'll finish his pieces tonight but he doesn't have to try them on today. He can try them on in a few days when everyone has to meet up for the run throughs and such. I'm pretty sure I can get through a couple more days without seeing him.

I snug up against the living room couch crocheting a piece that I want to give a tutorial for. A simple cocktail dress that requires some fitting and measuring. Nothing my loyal followers can't handle. I love seeing their recreations on their social media. My patterns make anyone look good. As long as they follow the step by step directions. I usually know what they didn't do when they complain that it didn't turn out right.

My phone vibrates with notifications from instagram. It has been vibrating since I posted the pictures wearing some of the crochet wear that I bought on the island. A couple of heart eyes, fire emojis and of course people begging for the pattern. I'd promised to put the patterns up on my shop when I'm back home with decent WiFi but I can't let the girls wait.

I decided to record a pattern for the flower motif durag that I put on in the mirror yesterday. I didn't bother to weave in the end, just tucked them away while I took cute photos in the mirror. Something I usually do when I'm hype to show off my design. When my wrist needs a break from crocheting, I sit on the couch and weave in all the ends on the pieces I didn't feel like weaving in the ends for.

My phone rings. Mom's picture fills up the tiny rectangular screen. I pick up the phone immediately, eager to hear her sweet voice.

"Hi mom!" My voice sounds chipper and high pitched. You would think I am a child.

"Hey baby, how is it going over there?" I practically hear the smile in her voice. It makes me relax as I lay back on the couch, positioning the phone between my ear and my shoulder before resuming the crocheting project I'm on.

"I'm just enjoying my time on the island before things start up in a few days. I like the built-in vacation part of the whole thing." I really appreciated them for flying us out early to relax, unwind and even get some inspiration. I already thought of a color pallet for some newer designs based on the vibrant warm colors on the island. I know that if we were to fly out here and get into the dress fittings and rehearsals immediately it would have been a nightmare. I'd really be working myself into the ground then. Mom and dad would have had to fly out here to pick up my body.

"That's great honey. You deserve a vacation. You work yourself so hard." Her voice drips with happiness. I can almost see the pride in her eyes behind the phone.

I nod as if she can see me, "I know mom but look where it got me? I can finally slow down." Knowing me, slowing down won't happen until I have my own fashion line and clothing store.

"By slowing down, you mean quit that unnecessary job at that management company. Your crochet has taken off so much I don't know why you even have that job." She says, rambling and I can only dream of how long she's been wanting to say that to me.

She's right though. I make well over six figures from my crochet patterns, one-of-a-kind pieces and clothing that I sell online. I only got that job to distract myself from Santoro. Not that I need it anymore but the money and the hours are good. Again, not like I need it.

"Mom, I know but you know why I took it." I don't bother finishing the sentence. Out of everyone, mom knew how tough it was to lose two people all in the span of a couple weeks. The amount of depression that filled my body when the two people I could count on for comfort were no longer around. The only thing that would distract me then was literally getting out of the house and doing something.

"I know sweetheart but I don't think you have to worry about him anymore. You're doing so good without him." Her voice is cheerful as if she's waving her pom poms at me as I cross the finish line.

I laugh at that statement. If only she knew that he was here, asking for quality time and making me feel uncomfortable.

"Why are you laughing? Am I wrong about that?" She questions.

I lay silent, unmoving as if the words that threaten to come out have the power to break every bone in my body. My mom clears her throat as if to clear pressure in the conversation. I know I can't lie to her.

"No mom, it's just...' I pause trying to phrase the words properly but instead I blurt out, 'he's here."

I can picture her on the other end of the line, her lips turned down into a frown, her forehead wrinkled with confusion. "What do you mean *he's here?*" I can hear a shift over the phone as if she's settling down to process the information.

"Somehow, I ran into Santoro on the island. He was here celebrating his birthday." I think back to the night I met him in the club. The look on his face when he saw me with his friend. I'm getting secondhand embarrassment again. I make a mental note not to get drunk in front of Santoro ever again.

My mother makes a *hmm* sound as she thinks about what to say next. "Well, it was only for a couple minutes. I'm sure you can relax now." There's a pinch of worry in her tone as if this would send me spiraling backwards. Little does she know it's only making me spiral forward.

I take in a deep breath letting a weak laugh escape through my mouth.

"Is there something you're not telling me?" I can hear the slight challenge in her tone. I didn't tell my mom about the model situation obviously because she would be worrying about me being worried. I want to keep her blood pressure and heart rate at a normal level. She clears her throat again and I sigh before letting the words spill out of my mouth.

"One of my models had an issue and couldn't come so I had to ask him to fill in for me in order to still be able to do the show." The words come out of me in a rush. My mother is silent for a while as she takes them in.

"He's just helping you, right?" She asks, a twinge of worry in her tone.

"Yes, mother. That is all." I say the words so perfectly even I believe them.

"Okay," she sighs, 'I just don't want your heart broken again."

I frown, "Me too." I mumble. Believe me, that's the last thing I want to do. My heart is already aching with the thought of it. I now know how to keep my boundaries. I can't afford another heartbreak. I don't want to lose myself again.

"Well, I'm going to talk to you later. Tell daddy I'll call him after work."

"Okay, sweetheart. I love you." My mom sings into the phone.

"I love you too." I smile and make a kissy noise before the phone beeps signaling the end to our call. I frown, missing my mom and dad, hoping that I am right about this whole situation. Talks with my parents always make me question my sense of adulthood. My mom and Kayla worrying about me is making me self conscious about my behavior. One more thing I don't need to worry about right now.

The doorbell rings eliciting a loud groan from the pit of my stomach.

"Ugh! Who could it be now?" I roll my upper body back and forth on the couch in a fit, hoping that whoever is on the other side would just go away. Today is a day for me to work on crochet pieces. That is what I set aside to do. All the outside activities will be had later.

I hop to my feet as a pounding sound shutters throughout the living area. I open the door coming face to face with Santoro mid-knock. I sigh, shifting my weight to one side of my body.

"Why is it that you are always popping up unwanted?" I roll my eyes seeing that this is the new thing that he likes to do these days.

"I was just checking in on my outfit. Seeing if you needed me to try anything on while I'm in the area," he says, leaning against the door frame. Part of me wants to call his bluff.

"You always seem to be in the area." I say

"What can I say? Two halves can't stay apart for so long." He shrugs, content with his response. I open my mouth to speak but decide against it, not to give him anymore fuel to what's being said. It's quiet between us after that. We stare at each other silently for a couple of minutes letting the awkwardness shift our body weight while we fiddle with our hands and pick at our fingernails. A few more minutes pass before I finally speak.

"I'm not finished but I will be tomorrow. I'm in the middle of setting up to record a YouTube video." I lie, hoping that will make him go away instead his eyes light up.

"Oh yeah?" He smiles as he makes his way into my room. I stare at him confused. "What tutorial are you filming today?"

The excitement in his voice throws me off.

"You can subscribe to my channel and see when I upload it tonight."

He frowns. "How are we supposed to have a professional relationship if you keep treating me like that?"

"Like what?" I ask, removing the hostility from my voice for a second.

"I'm asking because I care."

I roll my eyes and turn back inside my room and grab white flowery durag off the couch before heading back to the door to show him.

"I'm filming a tutorial for this." I point to the orange one currently in the works on the couch. "I posted a picture on instagram and the girls were crazy over it."

He holds his hand out for the garment. I reluctantly hand it over to him as he eyes it with intrigue. His eyes light up with that same impressed look he always gives me when I show him my creation. The feeling sparks an ignition of pride in my heart. *Stand your ground, Anylee.* I exhale, making him look down into my eyes.

"I like this, Anylee," he says. He twirls the garment in his hands looking at the flowers that I made for the piece. He nods in appreciation, obviously impressed before handing it back to me.

"You should make one for the guys. But you know..." He trails off.

"Not girly?" I smirk while finishing the sentence for him.

"No. Not that. I mean not as long and without flowers. Surprised you're not out here selling those loc hats."

"Loc hats?" I laugh.

"Yeah. You know those things that the cinnamon stick guy from the Apple Jacks commercial used to wear?" He says shyly, making his face turn a darker shade of brown from embarrassment.

I can't stop the chorus of laughter that erupts from my mouth. It makes him smile wider than I've ever seen him smile before.

"I used to want one of those but I don't think locs fit me that well." He chuckles and scratches the back of his neck. I picture him with locs but it doesn't add up. There's just something about the flowing curls of Santoro's hair that just suits him. Don't let him put his hair in a man bun. I used to love it so much when he did that.

"Thank you. I needed that laugh." I say to him, the smile locked on my face slowly melts as I stare at the floor embarrassed. *Why am I smiling at him?*

I clear my throat. "But yeah the pieces should be finished tomorrow so if you don't mind." My eyes shoot for the door. Hoping he gets the message to leave.

"Do you think I can help you with your crochet video?" Santoro looks into my eyes pleading.

"I think I can do it." I say quickly without a thought. Afraid that if I think about it for only a second I will say *yes*. Matter of fact, I know I will.

"I doubt you have a tripod that can face down and be steady with you." He says with a shrug, the confidence in his tone lighting something up inside me.

"And why would you think that?" I cross my arms over my chest. Looking up at him intensely.

"I just...' he pauses, the muscles in his shoulders relax, 'I don't think filming YouTube tutorials was a part of your plan when you came here. You might not have the right tripod for that." He looks at me with sincerity.

He knows just what to say. I would hate for him to be right but he is. I wasn't planning on filming tutorials, cute vlogs and updating videos but I missed talking to myself–as crazy as that sounds–and giving little tips and tricks for crochet tutorials. I made a list of about five different videos that I wanted to record right away when I got back. I thought maybe using the tripod that I bought for my vlog would be enough but what if it isn't? I don't know if it can even record in the right angles.

"Listen, I'll be quiet and still, like I'm the camera. You won't even know I'm there." The plea in his voice is undeniable as he shifts uncomfortably waiting to hear what I might say. He doesn't have to look at me for me to know he's begging me with his eyes.

"Fine." I say without looking.

Santoro looks up with another one of those huge smiles. I swear his eyes grew as well.

"No talking. No distraction. No flirting." I say pointing a little finger at him like it's a deadly weapon.

"The last one might be hard." Santoro says, stepping a little closer to me.

"I'm serious, Santoro. This needs to be professional. Or you can gladly walk towards the exit." I point to the exit before placing my hand on my hip hoping it shows that I'm serious.

He stands with his back straight looking into my eyes as he salutes. "You got it boss. Show me the way."

I roll my eyes thinking multiple times that it's not too late to change my mind as I lead him to the second bedroom where I plan to shoot the video. I pull a chair over to the dresser and move it up a little bit for Santoro to be able to fit behind with the tripod and my phone. I hand him the phone and grab the materials for the video.

"Your phone is blowing up. Isn't it?" He says as it vibrates in his hand. No doubt the multiple social media notifications are the reason for all the buzzing.

I turn to see him staring at my phone. *Nosey much?* "Put it on silent. Will you? Or 'do not disturb'. I don't want calls coming in when I'm recording."

He nods doing exactly what I ask so far as I gather materials. I use some red yarn this time with some black flowers. I grab the crochet hook from the work in progress that is lying on the couch and head back to the room. The whole time I take to get everything set up he doesn't say a word or make a comment which puts me at ease. He's taking me seriously for once.

"Okay, I'm ready." I sit in the chair and fluff my hair out for the camera before signaling for Santoro to start recording.

"Hey hey! It's your girl, Anylee, back with another video for you guys and–"

"Wait!" Santoro says abruptly before stopping the video and resting the phone and tripod on the table. He looks at me with an expression that begs for me to hear him out.

"What's wrong?" I ask for a slight hint of annoyance in my tone.

"This setup isn't right." Santoro squeezes past the dresser and moves it towards the other side of the room. I watch him, confused as he starts rearranging the room.

"What are you doing?" I ask as he sets up my space closer to the windows. He nods in satisfaction before waving me over.

"Come here," he says, motioning me to sit in the chair facing the window.

I walk over and sit down at my newly positioned space. He picks up the tripod and takes a quick video of me before turning the phone over for me to see.

"You look much better over here." He shows me the difference between the two videos. The lighting is definitely much better, making my camera quality much clearer than the last.

I tilt my head and stare at the clear video in shock. "You're right."

"I know how to make you look good." He winks before picking up the camera and tripod to focus on me.

He leaves me in awe at his words as he gets the camera just right for me. Was this a gesture of professionalism? Before I overthink, I snap out of it and fix my hair one last time before moving to Santoro to record.

"Hey everyone! Welcome back to my YouTube channel. My name is Anylee, if this is your first time watching. I'm back to give you guys a tutorial of this flower motif durag."

I look up at Santoro who looks up behind the camera smiling at me as if I'm his favorite star on television.

"Yesterday, I posted this photo on instagram and the girls have been begging for a tutorial so this is my gift to you guys for supporting me during this journey. I may be away for Fashion International but I'd do anything for you guys." I make a heart with my fingers and make a cute kissy face for the camera. Santoro's deep laugh rumbles throughout the room. Making my heart flutter in surprise

"Without further ado, let's get started on the materials."

"You'll need yarn of your choice. I'm using a thin four weight yarn but any will work. A six millimeter hook. Stitch markers, scissors and darning needle." I hold up each item individually and twirl the skein of yarn to show them the brand I will be using.

"In this tutorial I'll be showing you how to color-change during the flower motif design. This is for the long version so that way you can wear it like a headwrap like I did or you can choose the short version. The number of chains for each length will be posted in the description box below. The steps will be the same no matter the length. So grab your materials and let's get started." I smile at the camera for ten seconds before putting a thumbs up to Santoro to stop recording.

"How was it?" I ask

He nods at the video with a big smile on his face as he positions the camera over top of the desk to get my hands crocheting.

"You're natural. This is what you were born to do." He says as if he is a five-year-old kid walking into a candy store.

I couldn't help but smile back at him. The tone and the way his face lights up as he watches the video back pull on my heart strings. Anybody supporting me, it really doesn't matter if it's my parents, Kayla, Santoro or my followers that support does push me forward.

He looks up at me with those hazel eyes and a smile in them as he waits for my directions. This professional thing between us could work. He helps me work and then we part ways which seems so simple. Working together and nothing more.

After a two hour shoot, my stomach rumbles for some lunch on the island and a nice cold drink. Maybe a mock tail this time. Or just plain old juice since my body likes betraying me.

"After you record this durag on my head and move the furniture back, we're done for the day."

Santoro nods, aiming the camera over my durag. We finish recording how I tie it and sign off before I take it off my head. I thought it would be best if we just get some extra footage for my social media.

"Ready whenever you are." He waits for me to give him the signal.

I put my manicured nails over top of the fresh piece, making sure the rings that are a little too big for my fingers are positioned upright so that the sun shines on the gems. Of course, I put them on for this occasion.

"Okay, I'm ready." I say trying my best not to look up at him and ruin my position.

Santoro puts his thumbs up letting me know the camera is rolling as I slowly drag my hand over the durag as he slowly gets a 360 of the finished product. I hope the video turns out as cinematic as it did in my head.

"Alright,' he says as he hands me the phone, 'didn't know you could make a durag look so sexy." He smirks. I wonder how long he's been holding that comment in.

I roll my eyes. "Don't they have shirtless guys modeling on durag packs all the time?" I raise my eyebrow questionably.

Santoro's features twist as he looks at me. "I can tell you've never bought a durag."

I howl with laughter as I clean up my materials and any stray pieces of yarn from the ends that I wove in.

"I'm just saying everything is sexualized these days. You never know." I shrug and clean up yarn scraps, putting all the items back where they belong.

He shrugs watching me clean and placing everything back into the bag before he moves the furniture back to where it was. I don't need him stepping on any needles or crochet hooks that may be lying on the ground.

"If you find me a sexualized durag video, I'll give you 20 dollars." Santoro offers after the comfortable silence between us.

"Hmm…" I shift my weight onto one leg pretending to think about the deal. Twenty dollars is not how you speak to a lady. "I don't want 20 dollars."

He smirks. "How about a Cookie Monster cupcake from Goodiva bakery?"

My eyes widen at the proposal of the cakey cookie dessert. I usually have that cupcake in my hands on special occasions. I have every plan of buying that expensive cake when I finish with Fashion International. It's been a while since I last had one and sometimes it feels as if I'm going through withdrawal symptoms without it.

"Deal, but I want the jumbo size." I raise my eyebrows, seeing if he will get me the dessert I've been craving for months.

He chuckles and tilts his head with that same smirk on his face. "I thought you didn't eat cupcakes anymore." His eyebrows wiggle and suddenly I'm reminded of the lie I told him just so he wouldn't call me one of the many nicknames I loved hearing coming from his mouth.

"I can never say no to a Cookie Monster cupcake." I shrug.

He chuckles. "Okay then, but if you can't find one of those videos you can't eat cupcakes for a week." he shrugs.

I gasp dramatically, "Cupcakes are another food group for me." I place my hand on my chest mocking a fake offense.

He chuckles, "I know," placing his hands in his pockets as he leans against the wall.

I squint my eyes searching for his bluff before holding out my hand for him to shake. "You're on."

"Bet! The video has to be from a durag company, nothing else. Not any of those weird videos that you used to send me on Insta."

"But you used to laugh at those videos." I say poking out my bottom lip in a pout.

"I did not." He shakes his head.

"Anything else?" I smirk.

"You know, nothing from a hair company video or a reel posted from some random Instagram model," his voice has a twinge of irritation to it.

I fight back a laugh, "I know, I know but what if the hair care company sells durags?"

He shakes his head, "Strictly durags." He points menacingly.

I struggle to keep my laugh inside causing his somewhat serious scowl to become a small smile.

"Okay, fine. How long do I have?" I ask curiously.

"Two days before the fashion show." He shrugs and makes his way out of the door. I look at him curiously as he heads for the main entrance.

"Where are you going?" I ask, he stops suddenly. The moment I say those words is the moment I realize my mistake. I shouldn't care where this man is going. I should be happy that he's leaving my room so I can crochet or go out to the private pool in peace. I shouldn't want to enjoy his company but...maybe I do.

"I'm heading out to lunch. I'd ask you to come with me but I know you'd say no." His eyes shoot up questionably, waiting for my response. I stand there frozen already feeling convicted from my previous question.

"I'm okay. Not hungry," Though my stomach feels as if it's going to cave in on itself, I give Santoro a weak but hopefully convincing enough smile.

"Right." He nods slowly, "Don't forget our bet, Anylee."

He closes the door leaving me in an empty resort room by myself. I shouldn't feel lonely but for some reason I do. I pick up my phone and text Kayla determined to win me that cupcake. He didn't say I couldn't get help.

Me: You know any sexy durag commercials?

Kayla: Sexy Durag?

Is that what turns you on these days, sexy durag commercials?

Kayla then sends me a screenshot to the address of a mental institution which I respond back with laughing emojis. I can't tell her about the bet with Santoro, not yet anyway. I don't want to feed her any more information that will have her claiming I'm falling back in love with him. Instead, I reply again with something more interesting than boys and durags.

Me: Are we going out tonight?

Kayla: I was hoping you'd ask. Texting the others now.

Kayla: Bring bikinis, swim trunks and full stomachs people. Meet at the docks in 15.

Kayla: The queen wants to party @Anylee.

Shawn: We lit!

Reef: I'll bring some bottles.

Tazlyn: I'll bring some as well.

Kayla's message brings a fury of reactions in the group chat. I know by the instructions alone, I am getting into some trouble. As long as I stay sober enough to finish the pieces tonight, that will be a win for me.

I wear a light blue bikini with mint green swirls in the design almost like fades of ombre. I put on a crochet cover up before heading out the door to the dock where Kayla wants us to meet. The setting sun leaves a comfortable warmth over the island as I walk down the slight incline toward the dock. As I pass the island restaurant the smell of shrimp searing, makes my stomach rumble. The leftovers I had in my room's fridge have to suffice tonight.

As I get to the dock everyone is in sight besides Kayla. Santoro is the first to notice me, but I keep my eyes trained on Reef's broad shoulders and the sunset behind him.

"There goes the queen," Samiyah says as I reach the group.

She gives me a hug and tries to hand me an unopened bottle of tequila. "We're letting loose tonight. Right Ms. Workaholic?"

I push the bottle down with a nervous giggle "What did I get myself into?"

"Some fun, Sweetness." I hear Tazlyn say from behind me as she drapes a flower necklace over my neck.

I turn to see Tazlyn wearing one and the guys in similar fashion. She drapes one over Samiyah's neck and slides the extra one for Kayla down her arm.

"It's giving *luau* vibes." Samiyah says twisting her hips in pretense of wearing a grass skirt.

"Hawaii should definitely be our next trip,' Tazlyn's eyes light up at the idea 'Or better yet model there."

Samiyah gasps at the idea, "You just read my mind Tazzy."

"Guys, over here!" I hear Kayla's voice out in the distance. I turn my body to see her standing on a big white yacht.

"Is that Kayla on a Yacht?' Reef asks in shock, 'How did she get that?"

Shawn shrugs. "I didn't know the boutique was popping like that."

I smack Shawn's arm as I head over to the Yacht. I hear him wince from behind and mumble under his breath as the group follows behind me.

"Kayla, how did you get a yacht?" I ask when she's in earshot. Behind her are rows and rows of similar yachts. Some with banners that hang from the side to showcase a special occasion.

"Don't worry about it." She waves me off and turns on some Beyonce before holding up two bottles. She moves her hips to the music and turns around farther into the boat. "Come party with me!" She calls out as loud as she can over the music.

"Kayla knows how to party." Shawn says as he rubs his hands together before getting onto the boat. I follow along with the others, careful as I walk up the small ramp to get on. Kayla's pouring shots in the back by a tiny bar waving us over to grab our cups. I stay back a bit not wanting to have my first sip of alcohol yet. I watch as Kayla saunters over to me with two shot glasses in her hand. She hands me a glass and sits us down on the built-in seats along the edge of the boat.

"You are unbelievable, you know that?" I shake my head at Kayla, putting the shot glass down next to me.

"Just trying to make sure my girl has the most fun possible." She gives my shoulders a squeeze, the smell of her vanilla perfume wafting into my nose.

"Let me text the guy to sail this thing." She grabs her phone immediately typing away before hitting send.

A few moments later the boat jostles gently forward as we sail a little out into the clear blue water. We don't sail too fast, careful to ease our way out from the other boats. The wind is slightly pushing my hair as we sail. I watch the tiny ripples of water around us as we push smoothly forward.

"You know, I was thinking we were going to have fun on the island somewhere." I tell Kayla, watching us drift further and further away.

"*This* is somewhere fun on the island, plus it's just us as a team. Way more fun than anything else. Did you want Reef to plan another death trap?"

"I would much rather be here than on that kayak." I shiver just thinking of the moment where my body forgot how to swim, when Santoro pulled me up above water. I look up glancing at him, he's talking to Shawn and Tazlyn off in the distance, probably asking them about their modeling goals or personal life back home. Samiyah and Reef dance and take selfies with each other off in front of the golden sun.

"And I much rather you be here. I don't want you pouring yourself into working on those pieces for him. You know you don't need more reasons to think about him. Not with your career taking off."

"Weren't you the one who told me, it was a great idea to ask him to fill in?"

Kayla looks at me appalled, "Of course, it's a great idea still is but I know you, Anylee. You get so heartbroken yet the moment that person comes back around that pain goes out the window."

It's one of the things my friends in high school noticed about me, and straight out told me they didn't like. Sure I cry and sulk and hate the person though that hate can't last forever. However, with Santoro, he crushed my heart. It's not going to take a few slick charms to get back with me.

"Okay, enough about relationships. We're here for vacation at this moment." Kayla stands up and winds her hips to the music. "Get up, put your bad bitch face on and let's party."

Kayla dances her way back to the bar, "Who wants more shots?!" She yells, making the rest roar in agreement right after. I look at the still full shot glass and throw the liquid down my throat. I walk over to the others with the shot glass raised over my head. "Don't forget to fill mine up!"

About five shots in and two dances later, my body is calling for me to go back to the villa and rest. The late night crochet sessions are catching up with me and the only thing that can fix that is sleeping in until dusk the next day. I walk over and lay my head on Tazlyn's shoulder. She places her hand on my curls, "Awww...is my girl tired?" She questions in a motherly tone.

"Yes, Tazzy. I have, like, one more item to finish up for Santoro then I am all done." I rotate my wrists to stretch them, thinking about the last of it.

"You know, he was just talking about you too. He's really excited to see what you created. We all are!"

I smile. "Thank you, I had to modify the original designs a little. Because you know Marcus wants to bail and all." I lift my head off her shoulder just in time to find Tazlyn's severe eyeroll.

"After telling us about what he did, I reached out to him to see what was going on and he left me on *read*. How rude!"

I shake my head, "I wouldn't be surprised if he blocked us." After that message Marcus sent me canceling on me at the last minute, I haven't spoken to him again. I'm not surprised the others reached out to him expressing their frustrations. He almost sent them home packing if it hadn't been for Santoro stepping in at the last possible minute.

I haven't checked his social media either to find out what he's up to. He burned a bridge with me and as much as I put effort into making sure he looked good on the runway, he made an attempt to make sure none of my designs were to be seen.

"He wouldn't do that. You know he likes to flex on his haters." Tazlyn says.

"And who said we were haters?" My eyebrow lifts in confusion. If anything the way Marcus is behaving gives off clear hater vibes.

"You know men and their delusional minds. Always thinking someone is against them."

I try not to think about how true that statement is even though I've seen it first hand a few times. Hell, Reef always thinks someone is a hater!

A laugh escapes my mouth at the thought.

"What's so funny over here?" Shawn questions as he and Santoro walk back to us.

"Where were you two? Dancing?" Tazlyn teases.

"Exploring the boat." Shawn sneers.

Santoro and I share a laugh which I end abruptly when his eyes look into mine. I cough, earning a look of concern from him.

"Are you okay?" Santoro questions.

"Yeah, my throat is dry. I need something other than alcohol." I squeeze the empty shot glass in my hand.

"Only liquid on this boat is clear and brown, maybe even bubbly." Sean says with a shrug.

"Whelp, I won't be drinking anything else for the night. I need to make sure my mind is still intact to finish my work, which Santoro if you stop by anytime tomorrow I should be done. You can try them on."

A smile slowly stretches out over his lips. "Bet." I trail my eyes down the length of his body, the exposed skin of his arms, the open sides of his shirt.

I turn to Tazlyn not wanting to get roped up in his features for long. "Dance with me?" I ask almost breathlessly. I look down slightly hoping she doesn't catch the heat rushing to my face.

She catches on quickly before taking my hand and walking to the center of the boat. We dance to a new Megan, the Stallion song that blasts through the speakers.

"Let me see what you got." Tazlyn says as she dances like one of those trending social media dancers.

"Oh my gosh! The internet corrupted your moves." I shake my head as she rocks her hips and pretends to lasso me.

"What's wrong with them? They go with every song." She giggles.

"Not every song." Kayla calls out before she joins us. She shakes her hips and butt to the beat.

"This is how you dance to the stallion." She calls out.

"I know that's right." Samiyah unwraps herself from Reef and runs over to dance with us. Tazlyn and I join Kayla as Samiyah adds her own flair.

I look up to see the boys standing there, awkward. Reef and Shawn stand off to the side chatting with Santoro but his eyes are on me, heat burns in his stare as his tongue basically falls out of his mouth. Seems like I'm not the only one who could use something other than liquid courage.

"Aye!" Kayla yells, causing all of us to laugh in unison. We all stop breathless just as another song comes onto the radio. "I need to sit down." Samiyah says as we fall onto the bench next to each other a small smile forming across my lips. Kayla pulls out her phone, snapping a quick picture of all of us together.

"I think I need to get in shape." Samiyah says breathlessly, causing Tazlyn to laugh.

"Don't worry once we practice walking that runway. It will be all the cardio you need."

Chapter 11

One more night until the real fun begins. That's what the words on the email stated this morning. Then it's full of prep, interviews and photo shoots. I'd be lying if I say I was not up most of the night thinking up the worst case scenarios and how I could prevent any more issues that may arise, like a wardrobe malfunction, one of the pieces not turning out quite like how I imagined. You can say I'm stricken with nerves but I know a relaxing evening in the jacuzzi, nights at the club and nighttime sandcastles will be the trick to helping me deal with the stress. An evening in the jacuzzi is exactly how I plan to kick it off.

I sink into the warm water, an unopened bottle of Rose that I bought from room service rests next to me. I grab the glass, pouring me some before taking small sips of the drink. Lauryn Hill sings through my Bluetooth speaker. I close my eyes, resting my back against the edge of the pool.

"Nothing even matters," I sing slightly off key. The bubbles from the water are like the warmest hug I didn't know I needed. The song does this moment justice. Nothing even matters right now, pieces are done, models are in check and I can finally relax. Nothing matters besides this feeling of relaxation.

My phone buzzes causing a slight pause in my music. I silently curse why I forgot to put my phone on 'Do Not Disturb'. There goes the relaxation that I need.

I pick up my phone and see a couple of messages from the model group chat. Most of them are super excited to finally get into the modeling stuff. I plan on asking as many designers about their process as possible. Knowing how they have been planning for months for this event and everything should be running smoothly for them. I just need to figure out how I fit into this smooth show they laid out for me..

> *Santoro: You think they might make me look emo if they put makeup on my face?*

> *Attachment*

I click the text thread opening up a picture of a past fashion show where the model's face was painted a deathly white with thick black makeup underlining their eye.

I shake my head laughing out loud as I text my response. Leave it to Santoro to be cracking jokes.

> *Me: I won't have you wearing makeup.*

When I picked my models for this thing, I chose the guys I know were the most attractive that I went to school with. Their clear skin with a fresh haircut is all the makeup they need. The light just needs to shine on them at the perfect spot and everything will go as planned.

His response comes immediately.

Santoro: Thank God!

I wipe the smile that I catch myself giving the phone. I place it next to the bottle of Rose. I take in a deep breath, willing down the flutters at the base of my stomach. I can't keep entertaining this man. My phone buzzes one more time. I know it's him.

Santoro: Wyd?

I look up at the rapid currents surrounding me, Alicia Keys' 'No One' playing in the background under the clear starry night. My thumbs have a mind of their own as I text Santoro back quickly.

Me: Relaxing in the jacuzzi.

Santoro: I'm outside.

Reading that message makes my heart drop. *What does he mean he's outside?* I sit up in the jacuzzi looking through the glass doors as though I can see him from here. My doorbell rings, instead of getting up to answer it, I turn up the music, Alicia singing her heart out through the speaker. I stare at the door, heart pounding as another text comes through my phone.

Santoro: I can hear the music.

What am I doing? I basically walked into that one.

I rise from the water setting down my glass and wrap a towel around my body. I stand on the cool tiles surrounding the jacuzzi. My heart continues racing as I stare at the inside of the hotel room from here. *Do I let him in?* My feet answer for me as I walk through the glass doors. My feet squish against the floor as I walk across the living area, the cold air making me shiver instantly.

I grab the handle feeling the cool metal on my hand. I take a deep breath before swinging the door open. I see Santoro leaning against the door like this is some type of music video. He looks down at me with a sensual look in his eyes. It's enough for me to turn into a puddle.

"What the hell are you doing?" I say, my chest heaving up and down taking in as much air as I can. This man still leaves me breathless.

Santoro moves me to the side gently to let himself in before walking to the back of the room. I follow behind him curiously as he walks out the back where the music and jacuzzi reside.

"You're living the life back here." He says, pausing before turning around to walk to the kitchen, grabbing a glass.

"What the hell are you doing here?" I ask again. Unable to say anything else.

"You told me to come by yesterday when we were on the yacht to try on my pieces,' he turns to face me with a slight smirk on his face, 'Or did you forget about that?"

I facepalm myself and take in a deep sigh. "I honestly forgot. I spent the morning finishing them though, time just got away from me."

"I can always come back." Santoro shrugs.

"No, it's fine. You're here now." I walk back to the second room where all my yarn and tools are held, hoping that Santoro follows me without guidance. Luckily he does. He glances around at all the pieces of scrap yarn laying across the floor, fabric scraps and thread all over the place.

"Sorry about the mess." I shrink, a little embarrassed.

He chuckles. "Don't apologize for being in your element, Cupcake."

I roll my eyes at the nickname and turn to grab a long strip of black fabric.

"What's that for?" his head tilts curiously as a slow smirk moves across his lips. "I don't think we are in the right bedroom to live out your kinks."

I push his shoulder and throw the fabric at him as he laughs. "This is so you don't see the pieces yet. I want it to be a surprise."

He picks the long strip off the floor, his expression turned amused. "And you had everyone go through this?"

"Yes, I want it to be a surprise. Don't worry, I'll help you." I take the blindfold from him and tie it around his eyes tight but not too much. Once secure I take a look to make sure the blindfold covers his eyes.

"Can you see anything?"

Santoro follows the sound of my voice and looks in my direction. "Not really. I trust you to take advantage of me in this blindfold."

I roll my eyes and give him the finger. "How many fingers am I holding up?"

He smirks, "Three."

"Okay, you can't see anything." I hold back a laugh as I grab the pieces for Santoro. I grab the protective plastic casings that I put them in and admire my work briefly before taking them out of the protective layer.

I take a glance at Santoro noticing he's wearing swim trunks and a tank.

"Did you go swimming before?"

"No, I plan to head to the beach after this. You were just on the way."

I sigh in relief before walking over with the top part of my outfit. I place the shirt over his head and grab onto one of Santoro's chiseled arms to guide him to the right spot. His warm muscles against my fingertips send an electric shock against my body. I clear my throat and make small talk with him. I don't think I can do this quietly.

"How's school?"

Santoro smiles. "Great actually. I graduate this upcoming school year. Finally become Dr. Reeves."

I smile wide as if this news is for me. "Congratulations!" I guide his other arm, allowing the top to fit just how I imagined.

"Thanks, it was rough. A full time student while working at a PT office is not for the weak." He chuckles.

"But you got a lot of good experience with it. Do you know what path you want to take after graduation?"

I grab the bottoms and hold them against his pelvic bone just to make sure they are at the right length. With effort, I ignore the slight flinch of his lower abs at my touch.

"Actually yeah, I heard the Physical Therapist at U.P is retiring, Tony put in a good word for me and they are considering me as a part of the team."

"Oh my gosh, Santoro! You're going to be a physical therapist for a D1 college." I couldn't help the squeal from my voice.

He chuckles. "I might be." He shrugs before lifting his leg into one of the pant legs.

"Don't think like that. You will. I know the athletes will love you over there. Plus, you're like their age anyway."

"I basically *am* their age. I just got a little bit of a head start."

"Yeah, because of how smart you are." I say, adjusting his pants to fall right where I want them on his waist. I stand back to admire the piece on him before fixing a few crinkles in his outfit.

"You are pretty smart. That's just going to make the athletes love you more. Who knows? You might become a personal Physical Therapist for a major athlete because of this."

"That's part of the plan. I had some success on social media with my tips and what not." Santoro's cheeks darken at the mention of his social media.

I begin to help him out of the outfit so we can try on the next one. "Santoro, you do content creation now?"

I look shocked as I gather the pieces and carefully put the piece back into its protective casing.

"A little something here and there. One of my friends kept sending me videos like it on instagram so I decided to do a little something to have more exposure."

I pick up the next plastic covering, eyeing him suspiciously. "What's a little something?"

He chuckles knowing that I'm catching on to his humility.

"Look up Torofitness on your IG. I can't because my eyes are held captive."

I roll my eyes, not like he can see. I grab my phone and look up his fitness page. His page is nothing but aesthetics. All of which are him at the gym, giving workout advice, tips on how to relieve pain, and more. His videos have thousands of views, especially the ones where he's shirtless. Heat rises to my chest and up my neck.

"You have twenty thousand followers. I don't think it's a little something. This is awesome!"

He shrugs. "I guess dating a content creator for a little while, I sort of knew what to do, still not on your level though."

"People love your content,' I say, looking through the comments on his video before putting my phone down, 'I would say that is on my level."

A wide smile spreads across his face, "Thank you, Cupcake."

The rest of the session is quiet for the most part, everything fits perfectly and looks great just in time for everything else. I let out a sigh of relief and pack up the last outfit, putting it all on the rack with the rest. I take the blindfold off Santoro and watch as he blinks to adjust his eyes to the light.

"How did I look?" He questions.

"Runway ready," I say, waving my hands towards the exit. I could use the warmth of my jacuzzi right now, for more than five minutes.

"Eager to get back to that jacuzzi, huh?" He chuckles and catches a glimpse of the outside of my hotel room. His eyes widen a little. "They really hooked you up."

Santoro walks out the sliding glass doors and onto the tiles by the jacuzzi. Before I can stop him, he walks around the pool surveying it as if he's trying to figure out if anything is wrong with it. He dips his toes in the water instantly removing them as if he'd put his hand in hot grease.

"That shit is hot." He yelps a little followed by a chuckle.

"It's a hot tub." I laugh.

"You said it was a jacuzzi. I was expecting just the bubbles." Santoro says, shaking his head.

Before I know it his shirt peels off his body, revealing all his progress in the gym, the tattoos on his forearms flex as he throws his shirt down on the floor.

He steps carefully into the water, his muscles flexing and twitching as he sinks fully into the water. He sits there stiff for a moment warming up to the water before moving swiftly to the bottle of Rose pouring himself a glass.

I stand there in shock as I watch him get comfortable.

"Are you going to stand there or are you going to get in with me?" He smirks, taking a slow sip of Rose, "That's good stuff." He licks his lips to taste the Rose one more time.

"You must be paying for my new bottle." I drop my towel as he takes another sip. His eyes bulge as the towel hits the ground he removes the cup from his lips and puts his arms up in the air trying to save his life from his coughing fit.

"You okay?"I ask as he puts the cup down, the cough worsening a little bit before he takes in slow deep breaths

"Yeah. Went down. The. Wrong. Pipe." He says in between fits of coughing.

"It's just one pipe." I laugh as he takes another breath. A small breeze blows bringing more air for him to inhale. I look up into the starry night, the trees waving around us. I look back to Santoro who clears his throat and continues taking deep breaths

I scoot my body closer to him and lift his arms higher up in the air.

"You need to keep your arms up and take deep breaths." I say my fingers lightly touching the base of his biceps as if that gentle gesture is enough to keep his arms up in the air.

I watch as he struggles to breathe a little bit more before his cough disappears into a wheezy breath.

"They weren't lying when they said beauty kills." His voice is raspy as he slowly puts his arms back to his sides. I can feel his eyes burning a hole into the side of my face. I stare at his shoulders scared that if I look at him I won't be able to control myself.

"How come you always pop up on me? I could've sworn you're supposed to leave me alone until tomorrow." My hope for this was to only use him for the modeling so that I would never have to see him after that but the more he pops up I don't know how true that will be when I get back home. My fear is that I'll actually miss him.

Again.

"You keep dodging me. So, I thought I'd come to you. I'm telling you I want to see you, Cupcake." His voice sounds utterly sweet. I make the mistake of looking into his eyes, an intense look of desire as he looks my way.

I look away and push away from him, going back to my corner. I pick up my glass chugging the remaining contents before pouring myself another glass.

"You're stress drinking?" Santoro says matter of factly. "Are you nervous about tomorrow?"

I shake my head. If only he knew what he's doing to me right now. Or maybe he does and that's why he's here to torture me.

"I'm not stress drinking. I'm fine." I put the bottle down and sip on my glass looking at everything but Santoro and his beautiful body. I look up at the sky and say a quick prayer before taking a long slow sip of my glass.

"I don't make you nervous, do I?" He asks, raising a brow as he rests his elbows on the edge of the pool.

The question makes me start to choke on my drink. Santoro sways his body over to me, taking my drink and lifting my arms into the air. His touch sets my skin on fire. Please, get this man away from me.

"Why. Would. You. Ask. That?" I question between coughs.

He shrugs. "Maybe because you always run away from me or the fact that every time I ask you to hang out with me you say no." I can feel his eyes burning into me. "Or maybe I'm projecting."

"And why would I want to hang out with the man that broke my heart?" I snap, looking up into his eyes. His eyes are gentle and caring, the complete opposite of how he looked when he broke my heart. Cold with no compassion

His expression looks pained as if the words offend him.

"I didn't mean to break your heart." He says softly, his words so low that I almost miss what he says over the music playing in the background.

"Oh, so you did it by accident?" I put my arms down moving away from him to create space between us, making some water slosh over the edge of the tub in the process.

"Listen to me, LeeLee." Santoro says his voice is calm and relaxing. It almost makes me actually relax. He looks as if he wants to say something important. Is this what he came over for? To talk about our breakup as if I haven't begged him for a month to explain why. Do I really want to know why now?

"I want you to understand. I was going through a lot of things when I broke up with you. I had to make myself better." His voice is still raspy from the coughing fit.

"Better?" I scoff.

"Yes." He says his words gentle.

I swallow multiple times as the lump I am avoiding forms in my throat. I push my shoulders back, willing myself not to cry in front of this man. He doesn't deserve to see me in tears. Especially, when I gave all of them to him a year ago.

"I accepted every part of you, Santoro. I was always by your side." My voice doesn't come out as angry as I want it to be, instead, it comes out cracked and a tad bit small. Making me feel like the weak girl I felt when he dumped me.

"You don't understand, LeeLee. I love you for that but you became my source of happiness. I couldn't depend on you like that or I'd drag both of us down." He sighs.

His words pang deep into my heart. I remember the Santoro I knew when we both met, the one who was nonchalant and closed off until we started dating more. I never questioned if he liked me despite his closed off nature at first. He showed up with flowers and always made me smile like it was a competition how many smiles he could get out of me on one date. I also remember the times where he didn't want to talk, when he felt off to me with sadness and just wanted to be around me or hold me while I went to sleep. I always wanted to ask what was on his mind but that seemed like a delicate topic. I knew about his past and he knew about mine but none of that changed anything.

"Santoro..." I whisper. I don't think he hears me over the music, *Soul Child* playing on the speaker but he stares into my eyes, our breathing synced.

"I couldn't do that to you, LeeLee. I had to find myself again. I just didn't know when I lost myself. I didn't want to lose you. I wanted to get better."

I take a deep breath as hot tears flow down my cheeks, "Do you know how bad it hurt me to lose you and my grandmother at the same time?" I whisper toward the water. I feel Santoro pull close to me in the current. Right after my grandmother's funeral the next day is when Santoro dumped me. My heart was broken back to back. I used that pain to get me to where I am now so I guess it counted for something.

"I called you so many times and you didn't answer the phone." I couldn't help but feel bitter and I tried my best to fight that bitterness for so long. Dealing with two heartbreaks at the same time was torture. Mourning the loss of two people who made you happy was like losing a part of yourself. I dug myself deep into my crocheting at that time. Making pieces that I knew were difficult, different. Instead of staying in the comfort zone that my grandmother was always pushing me to get out of. I did that for her and to show Santoro that I could do this without him.

Yet, now I wade in water across from him, doing this with him instead of shoving this accomplishment in his face.

"I had started therapy at that time. I didn't want to contact you until I knew I would be ready for you." He wipes his hand over his face

"Then why now? Why do you keep popping up now?"

There has to be something more to the reason he keeps coming to see me. There has to be if this is an intervention from God himself.

"I've been wanting to contact you for a month now but I thought you hated me." He chuckles nervously.

"I did." I say, crossing my arms over my chest. Do I hate him now? The more he's around, the more I'm opening myself up to him. To gently let him in nonetheless, he's still so close to my heart that it seems pathetic. I know I'll want more from him. Hating him is safer.

"Okay, ouch." He gives me a charmed smile "When I saw you here I had to stop being a bitch, and finally try to have you back." His voice is more gentle this time. His arms flinch as if he wants to reach out to touch me.

"Is that what you called those multiple times you came to bother me?" I ask to lighten the mood. It gets a smile out of him and chuckle.

"I wouldn't call that bothering you." He puts his thumb and pointer finger under and over his chin.

"Oh really?" I cross my arms over my chest."What would you call that?"

"Satisfying my brain when I can't get you off my mind,' he says moving a little close, 'I crave you all the time, Anylee."

I look up to find Santoro's lips inches away from me, our heated breaths making the air hotter around us. The pull he has on me is too strong. I can't seem to pull away from him.

"I don't know how satisfying that's been," his look of longing sucks me in deeper as the words come out of my mouth

"I can never get you off my mind. You're everywhere." The smell of Rose is subtle on his breath. His spice scent fills the space between us. The sound of Keisha Cole blasts through the speakers as he presses closer to me making my back press against the edge of the tub.

He closes the space between our lips slowly. His lips getting closer to mine, the steady stream of his breath felt on mine. My heart pounds as we stay close seeing who will budge and connect our lips first.

I look up into his eyes, placing my hands on the side of his face feeling the stubble along his sideburns. He smiles before pressing our lips together.

I knew once we started kissin' I'd found love. The words blast from the speaker as his kiss deepens, our lips slightly parting as our tongues connect. This feels like that kiss I wish for when I watch romance movies. The sparks and fireworks exploding around the couple though now it feels as if those fireworks are exploding inside of me.

I pull back slightly, taking in a deep breath, "Toro..."

The nickname felt familiar on my lips having spent such a long time without feeling it on my lips.

He smiles, "It's been a while since I heard that name come out of your mouth, Cupcake." His hands caress the curves of my body leaving every inch of skin on fire from his touch.

He nods, seeming to understand before lifting me up. I giggle as my legs wrap around his waist. My thighs resting in his hands.

"What are you doing?" I ask, not caring what he does to me at this moment.

"Dancing." He says as he holds me swaying softly to the music.

I rest my head on his shoulder. This closeness, the feeling, it's one that I've been avoiding since seeing him again that night at the club. I can't give into it now. Not with everything happening so fast with the fashion show. I can't afford distractions like this one.

"Santoro..." I lift my head looking into his eyes.

"Yes?" He asks his voice sweet as honey

"We can't do whatever this is." I say, a pang of sadness in my voice

He stares questionably at me.

"Not with the fashion show coming up, I–"

"Don't want distractions, right?" Santoro says, cutting me off. His voice hints sadness but quickly turns back to the confident tone he always has.

I nod my head. He lowers me down and treads through the water to grab his drink. I instantly miss his touch and the warmth of his body.

"What are you doing?" I ask as he leans back with his closed eyes enjoying the warmth of the water.

"Not being a distraction." He says with a quick clear of his throat.

I couldn't help but feel a pang of sadness in my chest at those words. My emotions should be labeled bipolar. I should take it in stride that he actually listened to me but I can't ignore the other part of me that was hoping he wouldn't. The one that hoped that I'd be wrapped in his arms, swaying to the slow music and sharing more kisses under the stars. It was wishful thinking. Reality is, this is what needs to be done for my sake. I move over to my cup to take a sip hoping that the drink eases those thoughts. I sip slowly, not wanting Santoro to think he's the reason I'm stress drinking.

"You should invite the other models over and have a party." He says with his eyes closed I'm guessing so he doesn't have to look at me.

"A party?" I grab my drink and take a slow sip.

"Yeah. You know to get the spirits high for tomorrow." He shrugs.

"You're right." I pick up my phone and send a text to the group chat and head over to my room. I text them the number and tell them to bring their own drinks. This could be the distraction that I really need. The one that will help me forget the feeling of Santoro's lips on mine. Though I desperately want to enjoy this time with just the two of us.

Kayla hooks up her phone to my speaker when she shows up, claiming my R&B music had her wanting to call her ex and beg him to take her back. Both of us know that can't happen. Kayla hasn't spoken to that man in three years.

"Shots anybody?" Samiyah asks as she holds multiple glasses of brown liquid.

She walks around steadily, handing everyone a shot before lifting it up in the air. "To our fashion designer for this amazing opportunity! We're proud of you girl and happy you chose us to model your perfect pieces. To Anylee! May this be the start of many."

I pout, faking a sad face as they all click their shot glasses. Even though, in reality, I do want to cry at Samiyah's words. I couldn't have done it without them.

"Girl, thank you for being the first one to respond with a *yes*." I say before taking the shot.

"You know I wouldn't miss my big break." Samiyah says, causing every-one to erupt in laughter and nod their heads in agreement.

"You guys were my buddies in school. I wouldn't want anyone else to be my model." They were my friend group in college of course I would ask them. To me there is no one more talented than this group.

"Anyone but Marcus." Shawn says, shaking his head at the lack of his presence.

"Can you believe that asshole? Canceling her the last possible second." Tazlyn chimes in.

"Almost ruined everyone's bag."

"Yes but at least I was able to find a replacement." I say with a smile

Everyone claps and looks in Santoro's presence who seems to shrink under everyone's applause.

"It was nothing. I'd do anything for Anylee." Santoro says his gaze never leaving mine as he says those words.

I smile staring back at Santoro. Knowing how true those words are.

"That makes all of us." Reef says, walking around with an open bottle of Don Julio pouring more into everyone's shot glasses. We take a few more shots before Kayla turns the speaker music all the way up as the sound of Glorilla fills up the small backyard area.

Tazlyn and Samiyah stand on top of the chairs singing word for word of *Yeah Glo* as it plays through the speakers. I get out of the jacuzzi, my fingers wrinkled like raisins as I step onto the slippery surface.

"I'm proud of you." Kayla says handing me a bottle of moisturizer.

I take the bottle and squeeze the product in my hands before working it into my skin. "I know. You're the person I wouldn't be able to do this without." I smile.

She smiles and gives me a big hug. "I love this for you. We're going to kill it on the runway in your pieces. I know we are."

We laugh together as Santoro walks over to us, his presence towering over us. Kayla lets go of me and shields me with her body.

"Sorry sir but I want to hang out with my friend for the night." She says, holding her shot glass like a weapon.

He chuckles and holds up his hands backing off from me. "I'm actually here to tell you ladies goodnight."

"What?" Kayla says "But we all just got here." She pouts but we both know that won't work on Santoro.

I look at Kayla and nod. "You are a part of the modeling crew." Hoping that would be enough to get him to stay. I don't want him to leave just yet.

His gaze shifts from Kayla to me. "Yeah but I've been partying since I got here. I need to rest this beautiful body for tomorrow."

He winks and walks away before I can say anything, wishing the rest of the other models a good night before walking out of the villa room. I wish he would stay, as crazy as that sounds.

"How long has he been here? Like five minutes." Kayla says as she pours herself some Rose from my bottle that she took from the edge of the pool.

I open my mouth to protest that he's been here longer but decide against it. I don't need Kayla rubbing my love life in my face. I don't need her coming up with cute nicknames for shipping us together.

"At least he showed his face." I shrug.

Kayla shrugs. "True, you wouldn't be worried if he showed his face or not."

"I wouldn't care if he showed up. I was going to see him tomorrow anyway." I lie to her.

Kayla eyes me suspiciously before shrugging it off. "Yeah yeah, whatever. At least you got to see each other, right?"

I roll my eyes hoping that soon the party will end and I can go to sleep. My dreams are only one eight hour sleep away from becoming a reality. I can rest peacefully tonight, my clothes will soon be modeled on the big stage for the whole world to see.

Chapter 12

A few more hours until the prep begins. I've added a few more stitches on Santoro's outfits just in case. It took multiple nights and crochet beach sessions to get it done. I would like to think that I have outdone myself. I swipe through my phone looking at the pieces I made. I took pictures of them last night on my portable mannequin and fought the urge to post them on my private instagram account. My heart pounds in excitement. I can't wait for people to see these pieces. I scoop them up in my hands and hold them close to my chest. I tried some new stitches on some of these pieces from a book that my grandmother had in her attic. After dusting it off, I decided to put it to good use. I just hope people think they look great on my models like I do.

"Alright girl! It's time for some real fun." Kayla says walking into the living area, surveying the amount of yarn and stray pieces scattering the floor. I may have gone through and weaved in all the ends of Santoro's pieces at 3 AM, not on purpose either. I woke up to use the bathroom and remembered that was what I had to do. Thank God, for my overworking brain. I probably would have been weaving in the ends right now if I hadn't remembered to do so last night. Missing out on sleep for that was necessary. Just don't tell my mom.

"Don't say anything about the mess please." I shift uncomfortably, looking at the mess. I walk over and close the door to the room hiding the resulting shame of my late night crafting session. I'll come back to that room later and pick up all the yarn on my hands and knees. I should ask the villa staff to borrow a vacuum instead of resulting in hard labor.

"I wasn't going to say anything workaholic. Go put that stuff down and let's party." Kayla shimmies her shoulders before pulling out her phone for a selfie. I notice the cutesy outfit she has on. Her dress is a short orange color that hugs her body. Her hair looks to be freshly curled and coiled to perfection.

"How many parties are we going to go on throughout this whole trip?" I groan not wanting to party too much. Swimming at the beach or soaking up the sun rays seems more interesting to me. I'm not much of a party girl.

"So, you don't want to go to the yacht party?" She asks confused as if this is a shocking revelation. I look at her confused.

"Yacht party? How did you even manage to get another yacht?" I have seen many yacht parties sailing the ocean while sitting on the beach and they all look like they have more money than I could make in my entire life. It makes our Yacht party look like a kid's birthday party.

Kayla smirks, "Remember Mr. Grill Master?"

I nod slowly, holding in my horrified expression. I don't want Kayla to talk to this guy, he screams 'womanizer' and no offense but judging by the doctor she tried setting me up with at my party. She seems to know how to spot those *types* of men. I wonder what kind of men I spot.

"Well, he owns one and he is inviting us to his party." Kayla breaks out into a little dance, twerking a little bit in her dress. I pull at the hem, fixing the bottom so that her butt doesn't pop out from the shortness. The motherly urge to make her change is a demon I'm currently fighting.

"Why do I feel like you're holding some valuable information from me about him?" I scan her face as she avoids eye contact. She picks up one of my skeins of yarn and tosses it at me.

"Please, this is the last outing we are having before we're worked up on fashion show stuff. I even invited the other models." She says with a smile.

"But Kayla," I whine. I don't want to go.

"Don't *but* me girl. What will the other models think if their designer isn't there with us to party with them, like to celebrate the first day of this historic occasion? Cause it is historic, you know..." She pouts trying to use her signature face to get me to go with her.

I let out a small chuckle. "Trust me. They'll understand that their designer is busy." I walk to the back room and put the pieces of clothing that I made onto the spare bed. I remove the clothes from the clothing bags labeled 'Marcus' and replace them with the outfits I made for Santoro. I look at the pieces that I made for Marcus, the sketches I did to change each piece to make it feel like they were for Santoro, and not feel like he was just filling in. My brain smiles at the work and the creativity and hard work it took to finish it all on time. I'm going to list the pieces that I made for Marcus in my shop so that people can buy them. No need in letting them rot in the closet.

"You know, I am dying to see those pieces." Kayla walks over looking at the tan bag in front of her. Her name is written on the tag using a blue sharpie. She grazes her fingers along the plastic as if connecting with a long lost lover.

"They're coming to get these in a few minutes. Right on time, right?" I say putting the last of the pieces on the clothing rack and dragging them out into the living area.

I couldn't wait for today. Apparently, I'm being interviewed first and a photo shoot will happen afterwards with my models and I. The other designers I heard will be talking about logistics for their shoots apparently they want something bigger. But for the rest of us we have photoshoots and interviews scheduled all week for different magazines.

Just the thought of my clothing line being featured in one of the biggest fashion magazines in the world is enough to make me drop to my knees.

"Once they come to get the clothes, shall we go partying then? We have like five more hours before we have to head over. This can be our relaxing time. *Please...*" Kayla begs.

I shift my weight to one leg as I cross my arms over my chest. "Girl, you forget that I know you. Parties are not relaxing. I would rather sit on a beach somewhere," which I feel like I have yet to do without a crochet hook in my hand. I definitely have some books that I have yet to read.

"You're no fun. You know that? Besides, we can dance to some island music, drink a cocktail out of a pineapple," her eyes widen as she waits for my response. Drinking a cocktail out of a pineapple does seem appetizing but I'd rather go to a beach bar and bring it back to my house.

"I don't want to drink today. Not till after the photoshoot anyway." I can't risk getting drunk before the interview. How embarrassing would it be to stutter from nerves and slur my words at the same time! They would tear me to shreds in the Instagram comments.

I imagine those comments. 'She needs to go to an AA meeting.' Or 'Wow! They let alcoholics become designers now?' I don't want that type of publicity especially since the world can be so cruel. It's easy to switch over an account and troll in the comments. So many people do it, they live for that. I don't need my confidence destroyed before my career even starts.

"We don't have to drink." She assures me, like it's the easiest promise in the world for her to make but when Kayla has fun everyone around her must have fun. She'll shove drinks in my hand like my liver is made for it. I'll be dumping shots overboard for hours. The sea creatures will get drunk on my behalf.

"You can go. I want to make sure that I get my outfit ready for the day." I say to Kayla.

"You're going to take five hours to get ready?" She huffs.

I nod, "Sure I'm."

It won't take me more than an hour to get ready. The longest part might be my hair as I won't be wearing makeup. They might put some on me for the interview portion when I get there. I don't want to overdo it, especially since I might do it wrong.

Kayla pouts one more time, her final attempt at getting me to go with her. It won't work this time. I'm in a new state of mind. No distractions...officially starting today.

"Sorry Kayla. We can party afterwards." I poke my bottom lip out, mimicking her pout.

"Fine...' she lets out a long sigh, 'but you better look drop-dead gorgeous if it's going to take you that long to get ready." She stares daggers at me. I know she is deadly serious about it.

I laugh and drag the cart with the outfits over by the front door. As if on cue, the truck with Fashion International's logo pulls up to the front. A couple of workers hop out of the car and greet me with a huge smile. They take in the sight of my small rack and the tension in their shoulders instantly releases.

"Is this all you have?" His voice was rich with the island accent. Something that I have grown to love the longer that I stay here. It makes me want to raise kids on this island specifically for the accent. I'd never get tired of hearing them talk with an accent like that.

"Yes, this is it. All bagged up and ready to go." I smile as the one worker with a fresh low-cut fade pretends to faint at the news.

"Thank the heavens!" One of the workers with small studded earrings cries out.

"One of the designers had so many things. You would've thought it was her own private show." He shakes his head and helps his coworker lift the clothing rack in the back of the truck. I laugh picturing which designer that could be. I know some designers have accessories they make and new designs they have yet to reveal with big name brands that they will show on the runway as well. I can't wait to see them all.

"Thank you." I smile, both of them nod in my direction.

"Pleasure is all ours! We look forward to seeing your work." They give me a pleasant smile before hopping in the truck and driving away. I watch my work drive away from me in the distance as they get ready to wait in their new home. I sigh at the sight as Kayla comes up to stand next to me, her bag in hand obviously ready for the party.

"If you change your mind, I'll be at the party for a few hours. I'll text you." She looks at me with a hopeful look, hoping that I'll decide to put on my best swimsuit and join her.

"Okay, be safe and back to your room on time for the driver." I call out to her as she walks down the steep hill of the island.

She looks back at me and lifts her phone up. "In case you change your mind I just sent it to you."

I laugh and check my phone. "Okay, Kayla. Got it." I say, blowing her a kiss.

I, in fact, will not be joining her. Instead, I go into my room and grab the almost finished bottle of Rose from last night and head outback to the private jacuzzi. I kick off my shoes and peel back my clothes stepping into the warm water awaiting for me. As I relax, I mentally go through my checklist.

- ~~Models accounted for~~

- ~~Pieces completed~~

- ~~Content created~~

- ~~Relaxing on the island~~

- Killing it at my first fashion show (soon to be checked)

Nerves fill my body as Chance pulls up to the Fashion International building. I've been watching and reading the comments on my Instagram story about the short 'get ready with me' video that I recorded before heading out. My curls are popping and smell like pineapples from a new curl cream I bought. My outfit is handmade and a beautiful pink color. The admiration and praise I get from my followers about it is just what I need to boost my ego.

While I walk into the building, the empty area that I have walked into twice before has been transformed with multiple backdrops of different scenery. Tripods and different lighting are set up in front of each station. I think of the multiple types of magazines here to take pictures. I don't think we will get through most of them today. Some of the photographers are here to capture pictures for magazines native to the island. I have to get myself copies of them before I leave.

Photographers and videographers stand around chatting with each other showing different shots on their high quality cameras to each other. The lighting is almost blinding as I walk past one of the photo areas to get to my group of models.

I scan their faces hoping to find all my models in one spot. I'm missing only two of them, Santoro and Kayla. Leave it to the two of them to be *fashionably* late. Santoro probably has a curl out of place or tried to find a last minute barber on the island. I know Kayla timed the whole party wrong. I take a deep breath to calm down.

"Where are Toro and Kay?" I ask as I get close enough to the crew who turn in my direction when they hear my voice. I try to look calm as I get closer to them hoping they have some type of information for me.

"Santoro went to the bathroom. I haven't seen Kayla yet." Samiyah shrugs, looking at the rest in case they might have more information about the two missing models. They just softly shake their heads *no*.

I pinch the bridge of my nose and take a deep breath. Tazlyn and Samiyah look at each other before Tazlyn turns to me. "If you want to get your makeup done before the shoot, they have a makeup artist ready. Samiyah and I went up there earlier," she says.

The natural look with a touch of color on her eyelids is stunning especially with the green sundress she wears. Samiyah has a natural look and a hint of blush on her cheeks that is subtle yet stunning.

Just as I am about to open my mouth to compliment them a soft hand touches my shoulder. I turn and find Kayla. Her hair is voluminous without a curl out of place. Her makeup is equally flawless. I underestimated her.

"Sorry I'm late, bestie." She gives me a quick hug, filling my nostrils with a lavender scent.

"If you didn't look stunning, I'd be so mad at you right about now." My voice is mushy against her herbal scented skin. She even changed into a long dark blue dress.

She smiles brightly, "I'm actually living for your outfit this minute. Can you make me a skirt like this when you have the time?" My skirt is a shell stitch that stops just before my knees. The dark pink color isn't my go-to but it looks great against my skin. I even made a long sleeve top to match.

"If you promise to be on time for the dress rehearsal, then yes I'll make you a skirt." I hold up my pinky.

Kayla loops her pinky around mine. "Promise!" She kisses her hand. I kiss mine too, a promise now set in stone.

Jayana claps her hands then stands front and center of the room demanding everyone's attention. She smiles warmly at us, noticing what feels like hundreds of people standing in this space. Much more people than the shindig they threw a few days ago.

"Hello everyone! Welcome to what I call 'promo' week. This week is important. As you know, we have been advertising you guys for the past couple of months. It's now time to get a little serious. This week is all about pictures, interviews and trust me there is a lot. Different magazines will be coming to interview you. Some small, some local and a few big name magazines from the United States."

We all clap at the news as Jayana beams with pride.

"Everyone will have the chance to be interviewed separately as well with their models plus our president Sapphire who handpicked each of you." She smiles.

My heart suddenly feels like it's about to stop. The president of Fashion International picked me herself? I hope this is some type of joke. Something they tell everyone who wants to be a designer but the way all the veterans nod collectively as they survey the room tells me that they are not, in fact, joking.

"We will have veterans go first with the interviews while the newcomers start with photography. It will open you up more for the interview portion. By the time you get to be interviewed, you won't be camera shy." There's a collection of laughter. I don't think anyone here is camera shy. At least not anymore. "We may not get everyone done with the interviews today. Some may have interview heavy days. Others may have photography heavy days. But everyone will speak and take pictures with everyone."

We nod in agreement before Jayana dismisses us. I turn on my heels swiftly, eager to get started with the events. As soon as I turn, I smack my face into Santoro's chest. It feels as though I've smacked my face into a brick wall. He smirks.

"You heard that, Cupcake? You were handpicked." Pride shines in his eyes as he stares down at me.

I take in the tan button up and dark colored shorts he's wearing. The gold chain he wears is perfect against his caramel skin and by the two buttons unbuttoned at the top of his shirt I can see that he's not wearing an undershirt beneath.

I take a deep breath, fanning myself between the Santoro's looks and the overwhelming amount of information I just received. Just that one sentence is shocking enough. I'm surprised that I'm still standing upright on both of my legs.

"Yeah, that both shocks and terrifies me." I say, fanning myself some more. I hope I don't pass out onto this marble floor and embarrass myself. That's definitely something I can do. Santoro's fingers graze the bottom of my chin as he gently tilts my head to look me in the eyes.

"Hey, calm down, love. You know your work is beautiful, that's why you're here with all the big shots." Santoro looks around the room at the other designers while I fan myself faster, nerves getting the best of me. I haven't done one thing yet.

Santoro grabs my fanning hands and takes them into his. His thumbs rub over the back of my hands. His voice is as smooth as cupcake frosting.

"Toro, what if my new designs underwhelm her and I stick out like a sore thumb on the runway?" My intrusive thoughts blurt out before I can stop myself from speaking them. The comfort that his hands give me puts a crack in the wall I'd put up, not to mention that I just called him *Toro*. I can't help it though.

I've been working on my designs since I submitted my application. I crocheted day and night to get the perfect design, after the multiple sketches I trashed, dreaming of being able to blow them away with my pieces. I never once lost confidence in myself as I worked on them. Making sure to mimic each piece with the perfect color to match their skin tone for each of my models. I worked super hard to make sure that they would absolutely shine because of me. What if they look the exact opposite?

"I think you're overthinking. You usually sabotage yourself when you do that." Santoro looks into my eyes, the hazel looking slightly greenish in the light.

"I do not." I turn my face up at him, the accusation too outrageous for me to believe.

"You do. Remember when you made that one top and wanted to delete the picture five minutes after posting it?" He raises an eyebrow, a pull of a smile on his lips

"Yeah. The color didn't look right on me. I hated the pictures. It was just–" I shake my head hoping the gesture finishes the sentences for me.

"Woah! You hated those pictures that I took?" He *fake* frowns.

I laugh, "Yeah, I did. One because I looked ugly." I think back to that horrible coral color. The design was perfect. The color was not. I should've made it in black but I wanted to see my stitches.

He stares deep into my eyes before shaking his head. "I don't know about ugly but I'm going to act like you didn't just hate on my photography skills."

I laugh while rubbing his broad shoulder in hopes of making him feel better. Secretly, I just wanted to touch him. I stop before he gets the wrong idea because I am getting the wrong idea.

"Anyway that picture went viral and you got a brand deal because of it. Don't get in your own head. I don't want you to have any more regrets." I think back to that top. It did get me my biggest brand deal and the pattern went number one in my shop for a good six months after I posted it.

I look up at the calm, serious expression in his eyes. "You're right. Thank you, Santoro."

He smiles, "Anytime." He grabs my hands again, rubbing slow circles into them. "Did you ever get that *video*? I believe your time is up."

As I open my lips I speak, another voice enters the space between us. I drop my hands and turn to the photographer in front of me.

"Alright! This group right here, if you would follow me." He motions for us to follow him. He's wearing all black like most of the photographers here.

"Don't they get hot wearing all black all the time?" Kayla asks as she walks close to me. She loops her arms in mine and pulls me close, no doubt being nosey about Santoro and I's conversation.

"They need to blend in with the shadows. So you don't know they're there." Santoro says, following us from behind. "I guess it's a camera shy hack."

"You act like you've done photography before." Kayla says with a shocked look on her face as Santoro explains what I think might not be a true explanation but sure as heck sounds true to me.

He shrugs. "I have but apparently. I make people look ugly." He says, the fake hurt in his voice evident.

I laugh as we follow the man outside. Right by the greenery are cameras and lights ready to capture their subject.

I pull out my phone capturing this moment for my vlog. "Hey guys, we're doing some behind the scenes photography. I'm here with my models." I twirl, making sure I capture all of them in the footage. I'll edit name tags on them in the post later.

Kayla comes next to me posing in the camera. "My girl is vlogging. Make sure to capture my good side." She says, poking out her lips in a kiss at the camera.

"Okay, so we'll be starting you guys off with pictures over here." He says, pointing to his station while brushing his hand against his blond hair.

The greenery in the background makes me happy. The pops of pink and blue flowers give the feeling of the island. Definitely the perfect promo backdrop, especially since the show this year is in the islands.

"This is cute." I take a slow-mo video of the scenery that they will be posing in front of. I also take videos of the other backgrounds surrounding us. "You guys are going to have your work cut out for you."

"I would rather pose than all that yapping." Reef says, causing Santoro to laugh.

I shoot daggers at Reef before laughing at myself. I hope they have hot tea around here. I'm going to need my voice.

"Does anybody want to go first?" He says, picking up the camera from around his neck and holding it in his hands. He smiles perfectly as I look around to see who's eager. It looks like everyone is nervous. We are a bunch of rookies, especially my seasoned models. They don't jump at the chance. Shawn pushes Reef gently to get him to go first. Samiyah and Tazlyn look everywhere but the photographer. It's pure comedy coming from them.

"Well, since nobody is jumping for the opportunity, I'll go." Kayla says walking over to the center of the lights. The lights don't seem harsh on her, rather they highlight her natural melanin. I move a little closer, recording her for my vlog. I hope my views don't mind the shaky camera work. I'll have to figure out how to stabilize the video later.

I smile while watching her pose for the cameras. The way she plays with her hair and moves her hands to capture the attention, the subtle look she plays, I definitely can tell she's been practicing in the mirror for this moment. I know it was a joke to us forever but honestly it really paid off.

I clap my hands, "You go girl!" I blow kisses at her as she strikes a pose with her knees slightly bent. She laughs and blows kisses to me.

"That's the one." The photographer says as he rapidly takes pictures. The sound of his shutter clicking a mile a minute as he snaps her pictures.

She takes a few pictures with a soft look, no smiles, just a natural straight face.

Kayla bows when she's done, earning a big applause from everyone in the area. I look at the other models who seem to warm up to the idea of getting in front of the camera.

"Thank you, thank you!" She says walking carefully over to us. Her smile is as bright as the sun, pure joy radiating from her.

"You looked like a real model." Santoro says with a chuckle earning a mean mug from Kayla who no doubt feels like one now.

"How about you go next? Show me how it is supposed to be done, huh?" She cracks her neck and waits for him to budge.

He shrugs and walks over to where Kayla had been a few minutes ago. "I probably don't have to do much. My face should speak for me."

I can tell even with the joke that he's nervous, his hands shake a little and tiny beads of sweat form at the top of his hair line.

"Wait a second!" I say walking over to stand in front of Santoro. He looks at me confused as I reach up to wipe the tiny beads of sweat from his hair line. He looks down at me and smiles.

"There. You're perfect." I beam at him. He reaches down and squeezes my hand, before turning to walk over where Kayla was.

"I don't know what to do." He whispers quietly so the others won't hear him.

I grin goofy, letting the words slip out, "Think sexy durag."

I walk away as Santoro throws his head back in laughter. The photographer gives me a thumbs up as he takes pictures of Santoro who despite the nerves, is a natural in front of the camera.

"I don't know what you said to him but I hope his pictures don't look better than mine. They better not." Kayla jokes as we watch Santoro pose for the camera.

"Don't worry. I don't think anyone will outshine the other." I watch as Santoro makes sensual faces for the camera. His features in this light pop, proving him to be the eye candy that he naturally is. He was right, his looks *are* speaking for him.

"Is something going on between you two?" Kayla questions as she looks at me. She stares between us, back and forth multiple times before turning her attention to me.

"Why do you think that?" I ask, finally tearing my eyes away from Santoro only to be greeted by an amused smirk plastered on her face.

"Nothing is going on between us." I shrug. The sound of Santoro's laughter brings my attention right back to him.

"Really? Because you're drooling." Her smile widens as she watches me wipe my face.

"I'm not drooling." I cross my arms, annoyed even though she's quite right. I might as well have been drooling.

"Mhmm...whatever   you   say,   Ms. I'm-not-falling-back-in-love-with-my-ex." She sings as she giggles at her own words.

"Because I'm not." My tone is a little more defensive than it should be.

"You don't have to prove anything to me. I heard you for the first time when you said that it wasn't happening." I couldn't help but hear the amusement in her tone. It shouldn't irk me but it does.

"I can't have him distracting me." I say more to myself than to her.

"Oh sweetie!" Kayla puts her hand on my shoulder and pokes out her bottom lip. "Then you shouldn't have asked him to be your model."

I push her hand off my shoulder as Santoro walks over to me, a sense of pride in his eyes. *He's not distracting me.*

"How did I do, boss?" His grin is from ear to ear. Waiting to hear approval from me.

"You did great." I say. My voice is a little too chipper than what I intend. I silently hit myself in the forehead. *Keep calm.*

"I had a little too much fun." He says, chuckling. I look behind him to see Samiyah already in front of the camera. I take my phone back out and record videos of Samiyah, immediately remembering that I forgot to take some of Santoro. A video airdrops to my phone from Kayla. I silently thank her. I know I may catch myself watching this tonight. Over and over again.

"I could tell." I chuckle nervously.

"Your inspiration helped you're still not winning that bet though. You have until tonight." He pats my shoulder and walks off to the back to talk to Reef and Shawn.

"And you're *positive* nothing is going on?" Kayla teases. Anyone with eyes could see that the whole interaction was purely friendly.

"Of course, I'm positive! I'd tell you if there was." I shrug, hoping I don't have to tell Kayla anything. I can fight my feelings, the ones I'm telling myself that I don't have.

She nods in contentment with my answer before turning back to watch Samiyah pose for the camera. After a few more videos of Samiyah, I turn the brightness down on my phone and open the internet. I pull up google and search for sexy durag videos while I wait for my turn.

Chapter 13

After I took photographs with about three different photographers (there were a lot more and I don't think we made a dent). My crew and I went to the refreshment table to sip on some of the sparkling water and sandwiches that they have for us. My appetite was nonexistent as I was too excited from seeing my friends work their magic in front of the camera. I was a little nervous at the idea of being interviewed and thought that if I ate anything I would risk looking bloated in front of the camera. I wanted my body to have that flat stomach look that it always has. I recorded a little more content for my vlog.

Reef takes a bite of one of the sandwiches and immediately turns his face up at the piece of bread in front of him. He scratches his head confused at the sandwich before looking around at the rest of us.

"What's wrong?" I ask, amused, fighting back the laughter in my voice. I reach over to him and grab one sparkling water. I take a look at the can in front of me hoping that the water doesn't have me burping in front of the camera. That would be truly embarrassing.

"There's no meat on this sandwich." He says just as Samiyah takes it smoothly from his hands and takes a bite. I smile between the two of them.

"You're right. It's just a bunch of vegetables." She hands the sandwich back as Reef shoves her playfully. A smile forms on his lips as he stares down at her.

"You get on my nerves." Reef laughs and doesn't dare take his eyes off of her. Reef's not the most friendly guy around but he is super funny and caring when you get to know him. I remember when I first met him in class we had to do a class project together for the semester. It took me a while to get him to open up to me. I eye the two of them, internally fangirling over their relationship.

"Well, you know what they say...you have to be model thin." Santoro chimes, taking a bite of the sandwich, instantly hiding the disgust from his face. I hold back a laugh because I know that Santoro loves him a good turkey sandwich.

"Excuse me! But what part about me looks thin to you?" Tazlyn says, fanning her hands over her pear shape. She folds her arms over her chest, waiting for someone to say something about it. Nobody says a word. They simply stare at the sandwiches contemplating on taking their first or second bites.

"No, for real! I need a slice of bologna on my sandwich or something." Shawn says, opting for the bottle of sparkling water. He shakes his head before opening the beverage and taking a sip.

"You know they have actual models here, right? The ones that actually need to watch their figure." Kayla chimes as the rest of us exchange eye contact. I guess we all forgot we were rookies for the time being. Though the sandwiches could've been exchanged for some real snacks.

I forget that everyone here has different aspirations. While I chose models that were close friends of mine, I also made sure to pick people with different skin tones and body shapes to encourage future models who may look just like them. I can't deny that most of the models here are fit and skinny looking but since diversity matters to Fashion International that's exactly what I gave them with my model choices even though diversity doesn't seem like a big deal to some designers.

"As far as I'm concerned, all of you in here are models and you're going to go far after this shoot." I say, looking at each and every one of them. I make sure to give them a look that tells them they belong here. They wouldn't be here if they didn't believe in themselves.

"Awww...Boss Girl is getting sentimental on us." Samiyah holds the can of sparkling water to her heart. She pokes out her bottom lip and I could've sworn she's trying to make her eyes glisten. If she wants, she can easily become an actor.

"I can't thank you enough, girl. You know how hard it is for someone like me to be a model." Tazlyn's voice is quiet next to me as everyone chatters and cheers over my words but I can hear her loud and clear.

Tazlyn out of all the other models I invited is the one I've known the longest. She has been desperately wanting to get her big break. I always ask her to model some of my pieces to be size inclusive and always get positive feedback about her on my YouTube channel and Instagram page. I also know she has always wanted to do bigger things. She never misses telling me about a new photoshoot or modeling gig she is striving for. It mostly ends in bad news and us eating from a tub of Wendy's chicken nuggets with Top Model playing in the background hoping that one day Tazlyn will make it.

When I found out that I got accepted into the show, she was the first person I thought of besides Kayla. This was going to be her big break as well as it is mine. Sure, I had Kayla and Samiyah but I was always holding out a spot for Tazlyn.

She holds out her fist and bumps it against mine. I look up, feeling Santoro's gaze on my face. I look at him moving my head slightly and notice his eyes looking for me in the slightest. He seems out of it as he finally snaps out of his long stare. The corner of his lips tug upward slightly when he notices that I am finally staring back at him. I can't help but stare back. I fight the urge to smile at him in fear that he will come over and flirt with me about sandwiches. I already hope he didn't think I was flirting with him at the shoot when I brought up sexy durags. Speaking of which, I admit I lost this bet. I couldn't find one to save my life. *Good bye, cookie monster cupcakes.*

"He was *definitely* fantasizing about you." Kayla whispers, noticing the interaction between the two of us. Here she goes with this again.

I shake my head. "You're just seeing things." I turn so that Santoro is no longer in my line of sight and reach for one of the sandwiches. I look at the fluffy bread with the crust cut off thinking how aesthetically pleasing the sandwich looks. I instantly regret taking a bite. It's like they put diet mayo and tofu on here. There are two things that I hate. 1. Anything diet-related. 2. Fake meat.

I spit it out and chug my drink. Santoro laughs at me, his eyes drinking me up with his gaze. Heat rises to my cheeks as his eyes trail over the crochet two piece that I made. I take in a deep breath. So much for him not being a distraction. I can't help if just him being around throws me off my game.

"I take it that the sandwiches are, in fact, nasty,' Kayla stops her hand from even grabbing one and takes sparkling water instead, 'this water doesn't even have a flavor." She mumbles.

"Don't worry when we get out of here we will get something to eat." I hang my tongue out, trying to get the horrible taste off of my tastebuds.

"From the beach restaurant." Kayla wiggles her eyebrow as I roll my eyes a little too hard.

"I'm pretty sure what you want isn't on the menu." I cross my arms over my chest, looking at Kayla as she visibly tries to come up with an excuse.

She reels back pretending to be hurt. "You must not know about me then. I have a private menu for the rest of the trip." She says with an arrogant look on her face. I know she feels like she is getting the most special treatment in the world.

"Is what you want on the menu even edible?" I ask in horror. I gag thinking about what she could be talking about.

"I'm pretty sure it'll have a taste." She wiggles her eyebrows, giggling at her own remark.

I pretend to gag and take another sip. "I'm pretty sure these sandwiches are going to taste better than what you're talking about, *nasty*." I pretend to gag again knowing if I keep going like this I might actually throw up. It might actually be better than continuing this conversation.

"Oh grow up! Who said I was the one being nasty? You need to watch your mind. All that Toro fantasizing has you thinking muddy, my friend." She puts her arm on my shoulder. I scowl at her as she tries to hold back her laughter.

"Nobody is fantasizing." I haven't thought about Santoro in any type of way. I feel like I scrubbed my mind raw with soap and water after that kiss, doing any and everything to stop myself from thinking about him. Thinking is a dangerous game when it comes to the past.

"You might not be but he is. Whatever you told him sure has him wanting to get you alone when this is over." She laughs, taking a slight look at Santoro.

"Things aren't going anywhere with him. I keep telling you that. You saw me super heartbroken over him. I'm past that." I sigh, thinking back to the days where I wallowed in bed, crocheting and sketching new pieces for my YouTube channel even though my heart truly wasn't in that.

Kayla rolls her eyes. "You may be past the heartbreak but the love is still there, obviously."

I open my mouth to protest but she raises her hand to stop me. "We'll just see who's right and who's wrong by the time this trip is over. I suggest if you don't want to fall back in love with him, then you keep a little distance between the two of you. I want you to actually be careful of your heart, girl. I'd hate to see you like *that* again." Kayla's eyes soften as the last words spill out. She jokes all the time about us getting back together but I know she truly just wants me to be happy.

I look toward the floor. She's right about that. You don't date someone for three years and expect it all to just go away overnight. He is rustling a little bit of my feathers. If I want to get out of this trip with my heart intact, I need to do better at keeping some distance from him. How do I do that though when he just gravitates toward me like a magnetic pull?

Jayna walks in surveying us as we chatter amongst ourselves. She practically brightens when she sees me and walks with a pep in her step over to me.

"Hi Anylee!' she sings, 'mind if I pull you away for a quick minute?" There's a cheerful grin on her face. My heart pounds with excitement as I think about what she could possibly ask me. It may be my turn for an interview.

I shake my head. "No, I don't mind," I grab an unopened can of sparkling water before turning to my crew. "Guys, I'm going to chat with Jayana for a second. Make sure not to stick around here too long. You have more cameras to pose for." I say, clicking an invisible camera at them or making a mockup of it with this can in my hand.

"Yeah yeah." Shawn says behind me, the last of his words are muffled as I follow Jayana out of the room.

"One of the interviewers wants to meet with you today if you don't mind." She smiles brightly as if she is more excited for this opportunity than I am.

My heart begins to beat a mile a minute. "I thought I wasn't going to get interviewed until tomorrow?" I dig my nails into my skin to keep from panicking. Well, she didn't technically say that but when I was modeling with my crew by the cameras for a couple hours it was feeling like a possibility.

Jayana reaches out and touches my shoulder with a small charm bracelet peaking from her sleeve. She wears a cute white skirt with a black long sleeved shirt, almost like a tennis player but a little classy. Her hair is pulled up into a bun and there's a big smile on her face.

"It's okay." Her laugh erases some of my panic. "The interviewer just really wanted a chance to meet you today. They are really impressed by your work." Her eyes trail the crochet outfit that I made. I can tell she's not the only one. My insides melt with happiness.

My eyes widen, "My work?" Disbelief rising in my voice. I smooth my hands over my crochet skirt.

She laughs again with a quick nod of her head as she points up to the white marbled staircase. "Up there and to the left is where you can go to the dressing room to get ready for the interview." Her facial features soften as she looks toward me. It's as if she can read my mind when the last words come out of her mouth, "Don't worry. You'll do great."

I turn around to see my friends walking out of the room heading out to another setup. Part of me wants to call out to them, talk to them before I get out there and do the interview or make a fool of myself, instead I take a deep breath and give Jayana my biggest smile.

"I'll be up there shortly."

Jayana practically squeals as she jumps in excitement, "Awesome! This makeup artist will have you looking flawless along with your stunning outfit." She looks at my outfit again. I have no doubt that she might ask me to make her something before the end of the trip.

I smile looking down at my crochet outfit. The two-piece is flattering on my body. The color pops against the rich brown of my skin. Before I can thank her for the compliment, Jayna nudges me in the back toward the steps, "Don't keep them waiting."

With a click of her heels, she walks away to chat with the photographers about the day.

I take a deep breath before heading up the steps, my mind wandering about who could possibly be waiting to talk to me about my work. They did post about us on their website a couple months before so that way people who may not be familiar with our work would have a chance to take a look at it. I am sure if you were to google me, only my YouTube channel would pop up which makes me feel like the complete novice I am. My website also pops up along with some professional photos that I took here and there. However, most people know me as "It's Anylee", the girl who makes crochet tutorials. I still don't believe I have made it this far with those as my credentials.

As I turn the corner and walk into the room with the makeup artist, a few of the big name designers stand around with their MUAs who are touching them up a little bit before an interview or picture. The sight of this scares me a little bit. Some of the designers look far too pale for my liking as if they've been dipped in a bucket of paint to hide the tan or sunburn they got while on vacation.

I rounded the corner to find an empty booth for me to sit at which most were taken. Out of the corner of my eye, I see a station with lilac purple makeup brushes sprawled out on the table. Behind the table is a makeup artist that I had met at the little party they threw us a few days back. I am thrilled to see her and a glimpse of a familiar face. Her makeup is even more stunning this time, full of bright colors. The orange sticks out to me the most. Something that I can never pull off. The way it looks on her definitely makes me feel jealous.

"Oh my gosh! It's you!" I announce once we get closer to each other.

The mug on her face dissolves into a playful smile. "Oh my gosh! It's so nice to see you."

She waves me over to sit in her chair. "I didn't catch your name before I had to run away the other day." My face warms up in embarrassment. I'm not the type of person to leave before asking for someone's name. My dad told me that is rude.

"Destiny," she says warmly.

"That's a perfect name for you because you were destined to do make-up." I say, taking in the look of her art one more time.

She giggles. "It's a good thing that I am your artist for today then." She trails off the words, coming to a halt as she waits for something important like my name.

"Anylee." I fill in. If this was an interview, I am 100% sure that I would bomb it.

Her smile widens, "You'll look stunning for the cameras today, Anylee. I will make sure of it." She nods as if my wish is her command.

I smile as I slide into a chair in front of her. She picks up her brushes and gets to work. She squints at me through the mirror like an artist studying a blank canvas before turning me around to face her. She picks the best foundation for my skin and gets to work.

After a few minutes of work, she turns me around to face the mirror again. My natural face looks more *natural*.I don't know how that's possible. My cheekbones seem to be lifted more and the natural blush of my cheeks even subtler to give me a natural glow. My eyes highlight their natural gentleness. I can't stop staring at my eyes. If I was somebody else, I'd clearly be seduced.

"I look good." I turn my face, admiring the work in the mirror from all angles as I whip out my phone to take a picture. I take a few selfies of myself.These are definitely going on my social media later.

"Do you mind if I get pictures for my Instagram as well?" Destiny holds up her phone shyly.

"Of course, as long as you don't mind taking a picture with me?" I ask, positioning the camera where both of us can be seen. We smile at the camera together feeling like long lost friends. I put my phone down and let Destiny take pictures and videos for her social media pages.

"I definitely need to tell all my models to see you for their makeup. You think Jayana would let me reserve you specifically for me?"

"I don't see why not. Just email her and ask. Take my number down too just in case you want to tell me exactly where you and the models will be.I'll do my best to be in the area."

We exchange numbers just as the familiar sound of clicking heels rounds the corner. "Sorry to intrude,' Jayana says apologetically, 'I need to borrow Anylee." It must be my time to shine for the cameras.

I stand up from the chair and give Destiny a small wave before heading over to Jayana. Her smile is three times brighter when she sees my makeup.

"You look fantastic! Totally camera-ready." She grabs my hand and leads me out of the room.

"Are you ready for me?" I question my heart, seeming to beat a mile a minute.

"Yes." She stops abruptly, turning to me. She fixes my hair while giving me a reassuring smile. "You're a natural in front of the camera.I watched a few of your videos. Just think of this person as a guest on your channel." She smiles. Easier said than done. They seem ready for me. Am I ready for them? That is the real question.

She opens the door to the mostly black film room. It's much bigger than I imagined. The building itself looks like it can be someone's residence. It sure does fool you with its office like spacing and production studios.

"She's here!" Jayana shouts happily as she walks into the room, getting the attention of anyone in the surrounding darkness who could be setting up cameras and whatnot.

We turn the corner around the black curtains, careful not to step over any stray wires or break our necks from how dark it is here. In front of us, are a few chairs where a director or studio audience might sit, surrounded by a couple of chairs and a fake setup of an office. It is like we're filming some sort of documentary.

"Sorry, if the space isn't comfortable. We had to find something last minute opposed to our regular setup." Jayana says a little irritated with her eyes looking off elsewhere. I know she's going to send an angry email later today.

"It's fine as long as this isn't some horror shoot." I say looking around the dark spaces scared of what might come out.

"Don't worry, love, even if you mess up super bad our editors will make you look great." I look to my left to see a tall man wearing glasses on my left. He has a lighter brown complexion than mine with short brown locs pulled up into a tiki style ponytail. He smiles down at me as he holds his hand out for me to shake, "The name is William."

"Well, William, I'll try not to give them so much to edit out." I take his hand, noting the firm handshake he gives me. He must have been doing this for decades. He doesn't look older than 60.

"Something tells me this interview will be flawless." He beams at me as he takes in my appearance. I fight the heat that comes to my cheeks and let go of his hand.

He waves me forward to have a seat in one of the white chairs on set and sits in one of the chairs next to me. I run my hands down my skirt and ball them into a fist to rest at the base of my knees to keep them from shaking. I try not to sneak glances at the camera in front of me.

"Nervous?" William asks, looking at my shaking knee. A production assistant hands both of us two tiny water bottles to sip on. I open mine immediately, taking tiny sips on the water since I left my bottle of sparkling water in the dressing room. I pray I don't burp.

"Just a little bit." I take another tiny sip of water, my voice suddenly drier than before.

"You know, before I became an interviewer I had to practice being an interviewee so I could see how nerve wracking this is for you." He chuckles before taking a sip.

I try to give him a smile but it's like the nerves in my face have gone numb and won't work. I try putting on the confidence I usually wear when making YouTube videos or the one I wore way back while I practiced in front of a vanity mirror so that I didn't get too tonguetied in front of the camera. None of them calms me from the thoughts I have of the millions of people who will watch this video opposed to the quarter million viewers that watch mine. My viewers are nice. Though not everyone's viewers are nice.

I take in one shaky breath before looking into William's eyes "How did you get over the nerves?" I ask, quietly hoping it would mask my desperation. I don't want to mess this up for myself.

"I would think about the times when my fiance helped me. I'd pretend that it was her sitting next to me and asking those questions. It's the equivalent of the saying 'picture your audience in their underwear'."

I laugh before nodding going into my head to a time when I was myself in front of the camera whenI was more authentic. My mind easily runs to the times when Santoro helped me shoot videos. The times where he sat right behind the camera and locked eyes with me as if those hazel stars in his head could capture and record every moment of my video. It felt natural as if I was talking to him instead of a camera. There were so many times we paused and reshot because of laughter or because his handsome face was just too much for me and had left me tonguetied.

"I see you have someone in mind." William notices the big smile on my face which brings a little grin on his.

I nod. "I do." I let out a wistful sigh. *What has this man done to me? So much for distractions!*

William sits up in his chair and claps his hands. "Great! Let's begin before that memory goes away."

Chapter 14

The fashion angels have smiled upon us today because this has been smoother than I originally planned. Photos and interviews are checked off today's list. There's just one problem to fix. We're all starving. After the shoot, we decided to meet up to have dinner at the beach before going our separate ways for the night. I went back to change into a crimson colored bathing suit with a black swimsuit cover up. I planned on lounging at the beach after dinner, scrolling through my Instagram feed, DMs and comments while I dig my toes deep into the sand. Whereas I've been enjoying guilty pleasure, the jacuzzi, I miss digging my toes in the sand. Kayla and I meet up first before walking to the beach. Judging by her short pink dress and face still beat, she'll be out partying tonight.

"Going out tonight?" I ask as we walk slowly down the hill. Kayla grabs and holds onto my arm so she doesn't break her neck in those heels she has on. I look down at the skinny heel that looks five inches long. I could never pull that off.

"Girl, he's taking me out on his yacht in private. Then we're going to go to his brother's club." She squeals.

"That's great." I sigh. Kayla has been telling me to protect my heart. WhatI need from her now is to do the same for herself.. Summer fling or not, the Kayla I know has attachment issues.

"What's wrong, babe?" She stops and searches my face for any signs of stress.

"Nothing, it's just when we got back home I was hoping you and Tony would actually be a thing." I sigh with a playful grin, even though I am hoping that will be the case between the two of them. Their chemistry is undeniable. She rolls her eyes before grabbing my arm again, walking gingerly down the hill, "Maybe in a few months. Let me live off this high for now." I am sure that all Kayla will be talking about at the boutique for a little with her customers is her rich island boyfriend. She's done it before and always made up how she broke up with them so that she wouldn't get pity for dating a cheating, manipulative narcissist.

I shake my head. "You're just going to break my poor brother's heart?" I frown at the idea of it. Tony will make my drinks too strong if he suffers a broken heart. Trust me, it has happened before.

"He's not your brother. Trust me, he'll be fine. I just want to have fun for now." She shrugs, silencing the conversation. I silence myself from pushing further even though the questions I have about this man she's seeing are bursting through my brain. We walk toward the beach where the rest of the crew is waiting for us, some dressed in bathing suits like me or party clothes and casual for just this evening. Kayla takes her heels off before following me to the group.

"This restaurant better be good. I already ate some bullshit today." Reef says as a low breeze blows sand across the beach. "I hope no sand gets in my food either." He mumbles.

Shawn punches Reef in the arm playfully "You don't like extra seasoning in your food?"

"Not salt." Reef replies dryly before punching Shawn back.

"Believe me. This place is good. Ny and I went here earlier and had some of their rice bowls." Kayla says, rubbing her stomach as her tongue travels against her bottom lip. For my sake, I hope she's thinking about the food.

"Rice? I need something like steak with mashed potatoes." Reef frowns at the mention of what we ate causing Santoro to chuckle behind him.

"You sure need something to eat, huh?" Tazlyn says, a little annoyed.

"We all do. You all sound hangry." Shawn says, walking up to the restaurant he motions for us to follow him to the front. The smell of the grill burning through my nostrils makes me weak in the knees. I want to laugh at Reef and his hunger but he is right. Today, we haven't eaten anything nearly as edible as we would have liked today. I could use some steak and mashed potatoes. The closer we get to walking inside the restaurant, the more the smell of grilled meat makes my stomach rumble out loud. Thankfully, the loud crash of the ocean behind us covers up the loud roar.

"Welcome! Is it just the seven of you today?" The waiter asks, flashing a warm smile at us. His locs are neatly pulled back. He's dressed in a white polo shirt with colorful shorts. They must want to give the *island vibe* everywhere.

"Yes." I say as he rushes to grab seven menus.

"Follow me," he says and sets us up along the back of the restaurant with a makeshift table to accommodate all of us. "I'll give you a minute to look over the menu and be back with some water," he says.

Each one of us takes a seat at the table. I sit between Santoro and Tazlyn with Kayla, Shawn and Samiyah across from me and Reef at the head of the table, next to Samiyah.

"What's everyone's plans for the night?" Santoro asks the table as he scans the menu.

"Samiyah and I are going to go night kayaking." Reef says a smirk tugging at his lips.

"He begged me to get out on that damn water again." Samiyah says with a hint of annoyance in her tone.

"Good luck with that shit," Shawn says while chuckling, 'I'm going in town to one of the smoothie shops. Apparently, they're staying open for some late night performance." He picks up the menu, scanning quickly before putting it down, already deciding on what he wants to eat.

"Oh, who's performing?" Tazlyn asks excitedly.

"You know, some artists, poetry and things like that. I thought it would be cool." He shrugs, " the arts while we're here."

"If you don't mind, I will be tagging along." Tazlyn declares more than asks. Considering she is the only one who's casually dressed amongst us, she doesn't have plans for the night. Shawn is definitely going to go to the club after the event. I can tell by how his shirt is more or less unbuttoned.

If there's one thing about Tazlyn that I've learned over the years, it's that she loves her art. It's one of her first loves. She's always creating paintings and sculptures or doing some DIY crafts. She and I went to a few poetry slams before while in school and performed too. She is most likely staying till the brink of dawn.

"I'll be doing some partying,' Kayla winks at me,'You're more than welcome to join me at the club."

"Maybe after kayaking. I might need a drink after my near death experience." Samiyah rubs her temples, the mere thought of kayaking stressing her out.

"You'll be fine I got you." Reef reaches out across the table and places his hand on her shoulder. I smile at the two of them, fighting the urge to scream *relationship goals* at them.

"What about you?" Santoro leans down and whispers quietly in my ear. The smell of his body wash wafts through my nose. The clean scent of soap and eucalyptus is intoxicating. I don't turn to look at him fully aware that the loose tank top hanging from his body will distract me. I can see his tattoos from the corner of my eye as I try to focus on the menu in front of me.

"What about me?" I ask in confusion. Sitting next to him might not have been the smartest idea.

The waiter comes back just in time as Santoro opens his mouth to speak. The warmth of his breath sends chills up my spine. I will myself to look at the waiter instead of whatever expression Santoro's wearing on his face.

"What can I get everyone?" he turns and looks around waiting to see who might be ready to order.

"Psst!"

Shawn leans over the table to get my attention. The sight amuses me. "Yes?"

"Is the show paying for these meals?" He asks with a hint of a smirk on his lips.

"They pay for the restaurants and stuff on this island, yes." I laugh, remembering the long list of shops and restaurants they listed. I forwarded the message to them just in case. I didn't want them spending the Fashion International card at a designer store thinking they were getting some free Gucci too.

Shawn immediately sits up in his chair and holds up the drink menu to the waiter. "Get us a round of margaritas. Give us whatever flavor is the most popular and a bottle of tequila," he then surveys the rest of us for any objections before proceeding, 'Also give a couple glasses of coke or pepsi."

The waiter writes it all down before reaching out to each one of us for their individual orders. I order the pineapple glazed salmon with mango salsa and overhear Santoro's order. Island jerk chicken pasta. I scan the menu searching for where I might have skipped over it. I definitely would've got that had I seen it on here before.

When the waiter removes himself from between us, I immediately feel exposed. "So are you going to answer my question now?" His voice is playful yet I refuse to look at him. I sip on water and stare at the foggy glass instead.

"I'm just going to chill at the beach. Go night swimming or something." I shrug. I'm not afraid to get my hair wet. I was planning on washing it tonight anyway. I need fresh hair for the photo shoots.

Santoro puts his wrist on the table. His hand twitches as if he wants to reach for me but decides against it. I'm surprised this man still has the instincts to touch me.

"How about you hang out with me tonight? There's a place on the island I want to show you.."

I turn. His eyebrows are raised in anticipation. "Is it a club?"

He shakes his head, a slight chuckle escaping his lips. "Nah, little miss homebody. It's something you'd like, trust me. It's perfect for night swimming."

I scan his face for any signs of this being some sort of trick. *You don't need the distraction girl.* That is what my brain says. What about my heart? What is it saying? *Spend time with the supposed love of your life.* Logically, I should let my brain answer for me but before I overthink it, I let the words slip out of my mouth.

"Sure, I'll go with you." I reply, betraying my brain.

His smile returns, his eyes follow suit, smiling too. I look down at the empty place mat in front of me and silently curse my heart.

After a good meal, we split ways with each one of us going to our respective events tonight. I am certain that I'll hear all about them tomorrow or through a few texts in the group chat. They will be expanded tomorrow. Santoro gets a to-go box for his food so that he can save the little portion he strategically had left for the shoot tomorrow. I should've done the same. Who knows what kind of lunch they will serve tomorrow?

I stand half inside of his villa. I stare at the stars just in case he flashes me by spontaneously changing instead of putting his food back like he mentioned.

"You know, if you want to try some, you can. I am so sure you wanted to while we were at the restaurant." Santoro calls out from the kitchen area of his villa.

"What makes you so sure about that?" I say from the doorway.

He turns around and his face is clear of the obviousness. "Come on, girl! You always want to try new food." He smirks like he knows something I don't. Maybe the fact that I'm lying.

"I don't think jerk chicken pasta is new to me." I say, watching as he turns off the lights in the villa except for a small desk lamp near the front of the door. His muscles flex as he flips the switch. My heart skips a beat just watching the movement.

"Yeah but you never had it on the Virgin Islands so it is new to you." He grabs onto my hip as he slowly leads me out of the way so he can close the door behind us. I move forward out into the starlit sky. I trip while escaping his hand. The burning sensation of his touch lingers as I stand awkwardly a few steps away from him.

He smirks, obviously amused, as he checks his pockets for the keys. A slight sigh escapes his lips as he feels the smooth key card in his pocket.

We stand silently for a minute. He looks at me like he wants to laugh. Before I open my mouth to question him, he waves me forward and walks down the hill.

"Where are we going?" I ask while I follow behind him.

"You wanted to go night swimming. I know the perfect place." He says as we stroll toward the beach. Out in the ocean we can see a crew of the kayakers, I laugh silently knowing that those will be Reef and Samiyah shortly.

We walk around the outskirts of the island farther away from the normal beach area where people usually play in the sand or stargaze. We head in the opposite direction, toward the very edge where a huge rock lingers in the water only a few feet away. Santoro gazes at the moon reflecting off the water. He grins at me with a huge smirk before peeling off his shirt and kicking off his shoes.

"What are you doing?" I ask as he walks over to me. My heart pounds staring up at him with a smile.

"You want to go night swimming, right?" His eyes pore deeply into mine with a mixture of desire and nerves. There's something else I can't quite put my finger on that reflects in his eyes.

"Yes, I do but this is like in the middle of nowhere." I turn my head, looking toward the beach where a few people recline on beach chairs. From here, they look like ants. "Where I'm going to show you isn't anywhere. It isn't 'nowhere'. We just have to get there first."

"Get there?" I ask curiously. I thought we were already there.

"Do you trust me?" He grabs my hand rubbing small circles at the back of it with his thumb. His body is close to me. There is no way to move without touching some part of him. He did that on purpose. This has to be some form of manipulation.

"I do trust you, Santoro. Just a little too dark out here." Standing on this part of the island, there's barely any lamps from the street lights from the resort shining on this area. Not even a villa in sight where the light can reflect on us. I take off my swimsuit cover and throw my other belongings next to it in the sand. I shiver a little, feeling the cool ocean breeze on my more exposed skin.

He smirks yet again. "Trust me, love." He holds out his hand for me to take. I take hold of his rough calloused hands instantly feeling safe. He squeezes my hand for reassurance and leads me to the water. Despite the breeze in the water, it's a little warm though I know it won't be like that for long.

We walk out into water, deeper into it until we can't walk any more. Soon, my torso is covered in water and I'm floating in front of Santoro. His eyes scan my face before asking, "Are you okay? You're not scared, are you?" His hand gently touches mine as we float against the currents of the water

"I'm fine." My heart knocks against my chest, the fear of swimming at night and the closeness of Santoro being all so much for my little heart to take. When I said night swim, I expected to stop here and swim in the water but...we still have to get to this special area. I pray there are no sharks.

"Are you scared?" The whites of Santoro's teeth shine at me under the moonlight. There's a hint of challenge in his voice, one that I'm willing to take.

"You wish I was." I laugh, smacking my hand against the calm current before him soaking a part of his body that had yet to reach the water.

"You're funny. If there's a shark in this water, I damn sure won't save you now." He teases before walking deeper into the water where his body can finally float.

"*Toro.*" The nerves ripple through my voice making him stop in his tracks.

"What's up, Cupcake?" He turns to me with a look of concern etched in his face.

"Where are we going?" I hug my arms, freezing from the cooled water. He steps a few feet closer to me and points to the giant rock a few feet away.

"Right over there, to that rock,' he points ahead, 'Just follow me." His voice shudders through me, quiet and deep like the ocean around us.

I nod without saying a word. He takes my hand gently and pulls me deeper into the water until both of us are floating.

"I don't recall if you're that good of a swimmer," Santoro jokes as he floats, "considering what happened with our group activity I need you closer."

"I out swam your ass plenty of times at the pool." I roll my eyes. Thinking back to the times where we would race in the pool at my aunt's house.

"Funny, I'm pretty sure you weren't the one on the swim team in school."

"I was an athlete." I scoff thinking back to my glory days as a track runner in middle school.

"I was a four sport athlete." He smirks.

I roll my eyes, doubtful that he can see me doing so in the dark yet still he chuckles anyway. It's like he knows my reactions even when they aren't visible to him.

"Enough stalling." I respond irritated even though with the glowing moon and bright stars in the distant sky it's the perfect setting to what I wanted to do tonight. *Swim in the nice cold water.*

Without warning, Santoro swims toward the rock. I follow behind him, seeing the flutter kicks of his feet just a few inches in front of me. The water is cool along my body sending tiny shivers up my spine. I focus on swimming, glancing up occasionally to make sure he's still in front of me so he doesn't have to save me after all.

I follow Santoro's lead until we reach the giant rock. He touches the green moss on the huge boulder and takes my hand as I get closer, pulling me to his body to keep me close.

"What I want to show you is on the other side." His body rises and falls against mine. His warm breath wisps across my face as he pulls our bodies along the rock to get us to the other side where a giant cave is carved out. Plants hang from the rock to give it a movie-like aesthetic. Its interior has a few grooves where we can sit and put our feet in the water. Fire flies glow, pulsing light through the darkness every few seconds. I look up to see a small hole where the moon and a few stars shine above us.

"Toro, how did you find this?" I ask in awe as he leads me, pulling my hand through the water so that we're underneath. The water underneath this structure feels warmer than the water exposed to the moonlight. I stare at the moon through the foliage hanging from the rock. The image in my line of vision is so perfect I wish I could frame it. I turn my body to face him, the awe still shining on my face as he laughs.

"I found it on my second day here. The guys wanted to go day-drinking after a night out. I told them to go without me and after breakfast I just happened to stumble upon it." He shrugs, floating along the current.

"How do you just happen to stumble upon this?" I laugh.Would you believe me if I told you that a 100-year-old looking man with a gray beard and hunchback told me to swim out to it?" He says, chuckling.

"I sure wouldn't," I giggle.

"Too bad, cause he did." He shrugs, fighting the smile tugging at the corner of his lips.

I roll my eyes and splash him with the cool water. He turns immediately shielding his face from the big splash.

He moves closer to me and grabs my hands quickly before they can hit the water again. "You keep splashing me and we're going to have a problem." He says with playfulness in his eyes.

"Oh really?" I laugh. "What are you going to do about it?" I challenge him.

"Do it again and see what happens." He lets go of my hands and waits for me to make a move. I stare into his eyes, seeing the challenge and the playful threat inside them.

"Yeah okay, that's what I thought." He smirks.

My hands immediately slap the water, sending a splash his way and a chorus of giggles through the air. He lunges forward and picks me up. He lifts me into the air. My bare cheeks touch his forearm making me well aware of how on fire his touch is making me. His face is buried into my stomach as he holds me up. His laughter sends a rumble through my body making my insides warmer.

"I'll dunk you into this water right now." He says his voice is a little muffled by my stomach.

"Please, don't! I'm sorry." I cry out, laughing hysterically, keeping the thought of how close Santoro is to the delicate parts of my body at bay. "I think it's too late for *sorry*." He says lowering me down, holding me close.

I open my mouth to speak but he pinches my nostrils closed and dunks me without warning.

"Oh my gosh!" I scream as he lifts me up, my hair soaking wet against my neck and back. I wipe my hands over my face to remove the wetness. It doesn't work immediately. I wish I was back on the shore so I can wipe my face on a towel or cover up. I feel around the water with my eyes squeezed shut. Santoro's laughter echoes through the caves. It just makes the anger inside me boil more.

"Santoro, shut the fuck up! It's not funny!" I snap.

He pulls me close to him, warmth radiates from his body as I pull myself closer to wipe my eyes on his shoulder blades. He smells like the ocean mixed with a cool minty scent. My eyes flutter open. They feel heavy from the weight of the water. I have no doubt that they are red with irritation. I look up to find him staring at me. He grabs my chin and gently blows across my face. The cool breeze from his mouth is enough to do some good to my wet face. My anger fades as I stare into his eyes. My heart slows as his gaze drops to my lips and trails slowly back to my eyes.

"Did that make you feel better?" He questions.

My eyebrows knit together in confusion. "Did *what* help me feel better?"

He pulls me closer, his breath warming my face, "Using me as a towel." He chuckles a little. It slowly fades out, the amusement never present in the gesture.

"My face is still a little wet." My tone comes out a bit whinier than intended.

His eyes soften just a little, continuing to hold me in that trance that I'm too weak to pull myself out of.

"Let me dry you off." His voice is deep as he whispers into the space between us. His lips connect softly to mine, the salty water mixing in with the small taste of margarita from dinner. His body presses against mine, as his hands trail the curves of my body underwater. I lift my hands from under the water and touch the roughness of his body.

This feels surreal. It's as if I can see us out of body, the moonlight shining on us while the fire flies glow around us. Someone could look at us and see two people in love but I don't have time for that. My brain tells me not to be distracted. Should I listen to my heart instead?

I pull away just as Santoro cups my ass and lifts me up. We stare at each other breathlessly.

"Santoro... We–' I pause, still catching my breath the only word I manage to say next spills out, "Distraction." He stares at me, his own chest rising and falling at a moderate pace. "No matter how many times I tell myself I need to stay away from you I just can't"

His words do something to my insides. I scan his face with a sudden fear in my eyes. It's like no matter how hard I try I can't fight the fact that I relate to these very words.

"*Toro.*" I place my forehead against his, our breathing becoming in sync with another.

"I know what you're going to say,'" he closes his eyes as if the words he's thinking physically hurt him, 'Just let me hold you for a little while longer."

I let out a small sigh knowing that again I can't listen to my brain on this one. I rub my nose gently against his. The shock of the gesture makes his body tense for just a second. "I was hoping you wouldn't let me go, just yet." I whisper into the space between us.

Chapter 15

The walk back from the beach is quiet. I crossed a line when I let Santoro hold and kiss me like that. He has done it before while we were in the jacuzzi that one time but this time it feels different. Everything feels different. Is it bad that I want him to do it again? To feel his lips against mine, just for the night? I force myself to look ahead and keep my gaze from his body that's next to me. After swimming, he insisted on walking me back to my room. Why the hell does he have to be such a gentleman? My tongue itches to say something yet it feels like I'd be intruding on the conversation he's probably having within himself.

"I had a good time with you. I didn't know you could swim *like* that." Santoro chuckles, breaking the silence. I fight the urge to sigh in relief. Despite itching to say something, I know saying something before he did would have made things between us a little more awkward.

"Okay, Mr. Swim Team." I roll my eyes, a tug of a smile pulling at my lips.

"I was also a lifeguard too, you know that right?" He smiles.

I give him a playful shrug. "Leave me alone. I can swim. Deal with it," I mutter even though I am sure that I probably put a lot of doubt in his mind after the kayaking *incident*.

Santoro's laughter echoes through the night, making me feel warm on the inside. The easy-going vibe between us fades as we reach the door. I instantly feel cold as if this is our final goodbye. We both pause in front of the door. *Do I let him in for a nightcap? Do I tell him to kick rocks? Or should I give into the desire deep in the pit of my stomach?* I have listened to my heart too many times tonight. The best thing for me to do is to let him go. So, why does it feel so painful if this is what I really want?

"So..." Santoro says as we reach the door, the warm breeze blows between us as we stare at each other under the illuminated front door. The key I must use to open it feels like hot coal in my hand. I want to drop it on the freshly cut grass and let it rest there until it cools. Anything to keep Santoro and I from parting ways so quickly.

"Good night, LeeLee." Santoro's hand flinches when I take a step forward toward the door. I pause waiting for his feet to budge hoping he will reach his hands out to touch me but they never move. They stay by his side. Still.

I turn around and find myself eye to eye with the lust in his eyes. He moves towards me, slowly, closer and closer until the warmth of his breath lightly blows across my lips.

My heart thuds as his lips draw closer to mine. I suck in a breath as his soft lips brush against mine. "Is there anything I can help you with?" I whisper in the space between us. Each word I speak makes my lip brush against his, ever so slightly, making electricity shoot through my body.

He nods his head slowly. "Let me in," he grabs the key from my hand, unlocking the door. With one swift motion, Santoro lifts me off my feet. I drop everything in my hand at the front door. His hands grip the middle of my thighs as we walk through the door, the tension too thick between us as he walks us into the living area. I place my hands on both sides of his face and connect our lips together.

As our kiss deepens, Santoro lays me down on the couch, his hands trailing over the curves of my body. It sends shivers up my spine as my body adjusts to the once familiar touch of his. He presses firmer against me while I run my fingers through his curls. Our tongues intertwine and the taste of salty water encapsulates my taste buds. His hand touches the exposed part of my abdomen, setting it ablaze. My craving for him increases as he kisses my jaw, down my neck then trails back to my lips. Every inch of skin he kisses tingles like he's leaving a permanent mark that I can graze my finger on and feel.

I pull away, chest heaving as he pores into my eyes with a hint of a smirk on his lips. I scan his face. At once I see everything that I ever wanted. I used to stay up late at night mentally planning my wedding to this man. Picturing the rest of my life with him and so much more. I would think about the life we would have together if only we never broke up. That's what I see now. I am certain that once we go back home, this whole paradise love affair will be over. The thought of it alone makes my heart break into pieces. I look between Santoro's lips and his eyes debating whether I should carry this on and let us live in the delusion of 'us' just this one night.

"What's wrong?" Santoro asks, his forehead wrinkles in concern. He scans my face searching for the answer.

"What are we doing?" I speak softly in the space between us. I lower my eyes from his face and stare at his broad shoulder blades.

"What do you want to do?" He asks, lifting himself off me, creating more space between us. The warmth wastes no time making its exit. I sit up rubbing the goosebumps on my arm, instantly wishing Santoro is closer. I take in a deep breath, finally listening to my brain for once.

"I don't want to do this. This isn't the professional relationship we agreed on." The words taste sour coming out of my mouth but this is what I want. It is what will help me become successful.

Santoro nods, staring at the carpet intently. "I know that's what *you* want but...that's not what *I* want." He says it so nonchalantly that I am caught offguard. With the number of times I have found myself entangled in him, you'd think I'd easily change my mind this time but I don't even budge. Not one bit. Even though every part of my body wants to. I face him as his gaze slowly reaches my face. "We both agreed on it so that we could focus. We both know it's not working. There's no denying *us*." He says with a hint of pleading in his voice.

I stare into his eyes seeing the desire deep within them. I wonder if he sees the desire in mine. "But you know we can't be anything more than coworkers right now." I stand up, carrying myself off the couch. I rub my temples. This is the exact thing I was protecting myself from. Yet I can't deny the history between us no matter how many times I set up these boundaries. Too bad I have to stick to them. For the sake of my heart and this show.

"I miss you, Anylee." Santoro stands up from the couch taking delicate steps toward me. He reaches for my hands and they fall limp in his hands as his thumbs rub circles on my knuckles. Tears burn the back of my eyes as I tilt my head upwards to fight the sob his touch elicits. I look down, unable to look at him.

"Santoro *please*." I stare at his thumbs hoping the circles mesmerize me. "I just don't think we should be doing this. We need to go back to the way things were." I sigh.

His hands let go of mine, "So, not talking?" Hurt drips from his voice. My heart pangs with sadness on hearing his tone

"No. Just being professional from here on out until the fashion show is over." I respond with a voice so low that I don't think I hear myself either.

"And then what?" Santoro says after a brief pause.

"And then we see where things go." The silence between us is deafening as I stand there waiting for his response.

Santoro chuckles but there's no humor behind the gesture. "Right. Well, I'll see you tomorrow then."

I nod. "You will."

Santoro turns and heads toward the door. He lingers there for a while before leaving. I think about saying one last word but then decide against it. I instantly wrap my arms around myself and sit on the couch. I wait for a while before sending a text to Kayla, Tazlyn, and Samiyah immediately.

Please, come over. Bring alcohol!

"You're going to need AA when this trip is over. I have never seen you drink this much." Kayla comments as she sees me pour another glass of whatever brown liquor she brought. I didn't have the energy to turn the bottle over to see what it was when she arrived. By the taste of it, it's most likely whisky, something she must have taken from the grill cook. I have never known Kayla as a whisky drinker. It feels like a grown man's drink to me.

"I know...you can admit me to AA as soon as we get back." I can't fight the disappointment lingering in my voice. The events of the last couple hours are on replay inside my head. I need to know if I did the right thing. I would call my mom if it wasn't too late but it's nothing my girls and a nice drink won't fix. Even though Samiyah isn't here yet. She's probably still out with Reef, something I don't blame her for. She doesn't need to leave Reef out cold like I did with Santoro. I take another long swig from my cup before Kayla takes the glass and bottle from me, placing them on the floor next to her.

"You're not an alcoholic." Tazlyn says as she sits across from Kayla and I. She brought me cupcakes, my real addiction. I may need to replace Kayla as my best friend after this. She scoots next to me and rubs my back. I feel like crying on her shoulder which would be silly of me because this is what I wanted.

"I might as well be." I sigh, staring at the cupcakes in front of me opting for one of them instead. I open the wrapper and see the chocolate goodness. She knows me too well.

"What happened between the two of you that has you risking a hangover before we report back tomorrow?" Kayla asks with a raised brow.

"See, I sort of had a feeling that there was something between the two of you." Tazlyn says as if a mystery has been solved. Yet there is nothing that has been solved between us.

I let out a sigh. "Santoro and I went for a night swim." His shirtless chest flashes in my mind which leaves me breathless for a moment.

Kayla wiggles her eye brows, "Skinny dipping in the ocean, huh?"

"I didn't know you were into that." Tazlyn says with evident shock in her voice.

I glare at Tazlyn who laughs. I throw a cushion at Kayla, "No, not skinny dipping."

She lets out a huff. "If it was just an innocent swim, then I don't see the problem."

I look between Kayla and Tazlyn. She looks just as confused as Kayla. This is not what I was hoping for when I invited them over. I thought they would understand the situation.

"The problem was it was so romantic, like a 'romance movie-type' of romance." I sigh, thinking about the cave with shining fire flies who were no doubt paid actors.

"Awww...that's so sweet!" Tazlyn says, not helping my situation because those are the things that easily get me.

"Did he plan that? Did you kiss?" Kayla asks with a knowing smirk.

"I don't think he did." I doubt if he caught the fireflies and told the moon to be full and beautiful. The atmosphere of the cave was just so perfect. So beautiful.

"Okay, but did you kiss him?" She raises her eyebrows waiting for my response.

Tazlyn leans forward smiling as if my answer is a life or death situation. It's honestly amusing.

"Yes." I say, "but that's not all. We almost–"

"You guys almost did the *deed*?" Kayla cuts me off, her voice a little raised. Tazlyn puts her hand on her chest, shocked at the revelation. If this was a different situation, I bet they would be squealing right now. I know they want to.

"Yes, but I couldn't do it. He wants to be with me yet I said no and sent him home." I sigh.

Tazlyn looks offended. "That man has the most admiration for you and you turned him down? I have never seen anyone look at anyone with so much love before." She says dreamily.

"Right, I wish I could have that too, you know." Kayla says in a low voice. I snap my head in her direction when I hear those words.

"So, you do want a relationship..." I smile, grabbing a pillow and holding it close to me.

"Of course, I do. I'm just, you know, being careful." Kayla shrugs, a hint of disappointment in her tone.

"Don't worry. You're not the only one." Tazyn sighs, grabbing a cup of her own and pouring a drink. I look between the two of them wanting this to be a whole therapy session for all of us. I want to double down on Tazlyn and Kayla but that's not why they're here.

"I just…I don't want a cheater." Kayla shrugs.

"And I don't want a man who is broke." Tazlyn says bitterly. Kayla and I both look towards Tazlyn with curiosity. Judging by the expression on her face, if I push for more information, she'll explode so I stop myself from nudging the subject any farther.

"You guys will find your love, don't worry." I say, picking up a fresh cupcake to lick icing off of.

"I know, I know." Tazlyn sighs. There's a brief silence between us while we reflect. If I could, I'd become a match-maker for my girls. I'm afraid though that I think I don't have the best taste in men.

"So…" Tazlyn breaks the silence, "You and Santoro." She brings the conversation back to me. It's like Kayla comes back to us, remembering just that second the last bit of detail I shared before we all got taken up by our thoughts.

She snaps out of her trance with the look of shock on her face. "You know what? I'm the one who needs a drink." She reaches down, picks up my cup and drinks the alcohol left.

"Kayla, be serious please. I need your help. All of us can't get drunk tonight." Tazlyn laughs while Kayla sighs taking in all the information for a brief second.

"I think you did the right thing. For now. You definitely don't want any distractions." She says out loud more to herself than us before shrugging.

"Why for now?" I ask her curiously.

"Because, what will you do after this is over? Clearly, you need to be with this man again." Kayla's lips flatten in a knowing way as if that's the obvious answer.

"Agreed. It feels like you want us here to make you feel better for making that choice." Tazlyn's voice drips with pity. Something I definitely don't want.

"I don't." I cross my arms over my chest like a pouty child even though part of me wishes that I could feel the lingering magic of his kisses on my skin. I touch the place on my jaw where he planted his pixie dust hoping to restore the faded feeling.

"You do. Otherwise, you wouldn't be stealing kisses with this man under a starry night." She laughs a little.

"It was the atmosphere. I promise. I wouldn't be doing that if it wasn't for the vibe." My defensive tone pitches my tone higher than intended. I know for a fact I'm lying to myself. I definitely would. The atmosphere was too beautiful not to share a kiss. I'd probably kiss anyone under that cave. Even the grinch. Maybe Santoro did plan it. Maybe, it's destiny working its magic to make me change my mind.

"Sure, you say that now but we both know that's a lie." Kayla rolls her eyes. "The chemistry between you two is too obvious. Too strong for the both of you to keep fighting it."

"I think he's mad about how things played out. He basically confessed his love to me and I sent him on his way." The look on Santoro's face before he left flashes through my mind. The hurt in his eyes. The fact that he couldn't look at me before walking out of the door. I wonder if that's how he felt after our breakup all those years ago.

"Yeah, I'd be mad too if you sent me home with blue balls and a broken heart." Kayla says, pouring herself another drink.

Tazlyn laughs. "You know men don't play about their balls."

Kayla and Tazlyn share a laugh as if they are the bestest friends on this whole island.

I roll my eyes. "I didn't break his heart. And I certainly hurt nobody's balls!" At least I hope I didn't. I wouldn't live with myself if I did. Like the 'break his heart' part not the ball thing.

"Sure, but if he feels like he has no chance of getting you back then you technically did." Tazlyn says

"I never said he couldn't." I sigh hoping that that's not the impression I gave when I pushed him away. I said we will see where things go. Doesn't that give someone hope?

"You never said he could either." Kayla sips her drink and leans back on the couch, a cocky smirk rests on her face before she sits up. "I just want you to do the right thing with this. Even if that means you get back with the love of your life after this and live a happy ending or you just tell him to kick rocks. Either way, I support you."

"I support you too even though it would be fun if I attended one of my friends' weddings in the near future." Tazlyn says.

Kayla's eyes light up. "Oh my gosh! Yes, I want to be a bridesmaid."

"You guys are not helping." I shake my head, sitting back on the couch holding the pillow closer to me. It's comforting me better than these two right now.

"Just think about what I said." Kayla shrugs as if it's that simple. Even so, *simple* these days is like learning how to fly an airplane. Not simple at all.

"Both routes can cause heartbreak." I say more to myself.

"Only if you let it happen." Kayla looks at me with an unreadable expression on her face. Tazlyn rubs my back again in that comforting way a mother does.

"If you were me, what would you do?" I say, switching my gaze between the two of them.

"I'd finish the fashion show then follow my heart." She takes another sip before placing the cup down. When I face Tazlyn, she nods in agreement. I nod my head in understanding and let out a sigh of relief.

"If I'm being completely honest, we would've gotten back together if I was in your shoes."

I throw another cushion at her, earning a scowl from Kayla.

"I can give you advice without receiving the abuse you know."

Laughter erupts from Tazlyn and I, "Sorry but I needed that."

Kayla throws the cushion back hitting me square in the face.

"How was both of your nights? I want to hear all about it." I say, hoping that it will change the subject. Kayla shoots a knowing look at me before downing the rest of her drink.

"Well…" Kayla pauses, "What kind of details do you want?" She smirks.

Tazlyn leans forward intrigued. My shoulders slump in relief. Thankful that she took the bait.

"Give me everything. Don't hold back."

Chapter 16

"Can you take me to the flea market?" I smile at the driver of the doorless shuttle, an older man with a partially gray beard, gives me a semi toothless grin, a hint of his delicate teeth showing.

"Sure, sweetness. Only ten dollars." I hand him a crumpled twenty dollar bill that he takes eagerly and motions for me to sit in the back with the rest of the passengers. As I walk through the tight isle, I notice everyone clinging onto some part of the shuttle for dear life. I sit next to a young girl and secure my phone in the bag and look for a seatbelt but don't see any, not even a piece of rope to secure your body with. This explains why everyone is holding on to some part of the shuttle. I join in with everyone else, holding onto a red metal bar before looking up at the driver hoping he has some type of skills in his driving.

"Have you rode one of these shuttles before?" I ask the girl next to me who seems to be about sixteen years old.

"This is how my family and I get around the island,' she looks at my phone and purse, 'Word of advice, put your phone in the bag and put it on your shoulder." She says almost in amusement.

I nod slowly, a little confused and follow her directions. I explore some other parts of the island quietly before heading over to Fashion International. The past few days have been pretty much the same routine; Fashion International photo shoots, interviews, checking in on makeup artists and so many meetings. I haven't spoken to any designers, not since the first meeting. Everyone seems to be in their own little world now that the show is coming up soon. I hope to see at least one of my models on a magazine cover while out on the island. I saw a few designers posting pictures of the last edition of the islands magazine on their social media. One of my missions is to find a few copies to look at.

Two more people get on the shuttle before the driver sits in his seat and looks back at us with a sly grin across his face. "First stop? The flea market." I hold onto the bar in front of me like everyone else seems to be doing just as the man backs up abruptly, jolting everybody forward before flying through the street barely stopping at the stop sign and turning the corner onto the street where a flurry of shuttles also drive with no regard for human life.

While we pass tourist stops like beautiful trails and beaches, he slows down long enough for the tourists to take a picture. I would be a fool to take my phone out for a picture. I need it for content purposes. While the scenery is beautiful, the way this man drives the shuttle is like he is trying to fling us off. It almost feels like I'm riding a rollercoaster rather than a shuttle to go down the road.

Once we get to a congested area where driving recklessly would result in a lawsuit, I know we're close to the marketplace. I take out my phone now that it's safe to do so and check the schedule Jayana sent for this upcoming week. After the countless interviews and photo ops, there is still more to do before the dress rehearsals which is only two days away. Just thinking about it makes my palms sweaty. In a few days, my designs will be unveiled for the whole world to see. It makes me want to take all my designs away and start over.

"We're at the marketplace." The driver states while looking up into the rearview mirror making eye contact with me. I get up and smile at the man before heading off the bus into the busy streets. I walk across the street greeted by a smiling man holding a cardboard sign.

"Best smoothies in town. Come try it out." He says, staring into my direction. I avoid direct eye contact and smile at the establishment like a tourist would. I walk through the streets where people yell at strangers to come try out their diners and shops. Some people set up shops around the sidewalks making it a struggle to walk on without bumping into one of the tourists or the tables filled with products. Instead many of us walk through the streets, giving the buses and cars passing by a little bit of a run for their money. I continue walking on the street, with the sweet smell of pineapples filling the air plus the savory aroma of roasting meat at the dining options along the road.

I take out my phone and the portable tripod I packed for vlogs like these and take a slowmo video of the street view capturing the busy street and colorful buildings along the palm trees. One woman smiles at me as I pan my phone to her table. Her inviting gaze draws me into her table filled with beautiful turquoise blue jewelry. I pan over the table admiring the pieces before me. A turquoise stone ring catches my attention as it dazzles in frame.

"These are so beautiful." I say to her as I stand up straight and talk to the lady. She's dressed in a long blue dress with white swirled patterns that popped against the richness of her brown skin.

"Thank you, my dear. See anything you like." Her accent is thick as her jeweled hand scans over the table. Her smile frames her face into the perfect circle.

I smile and point to the ring that caught my eye earlier. "This one caught my eye."

She nods impressed. "You have a gift for picking out fine pieces." Her smile turns into a soft smirk as she stares at the ring that has caught my attention.

"Do you make all these pieces?" I ask as a warm breeze blows through the marketplace, causing one of the men across the street who's holding a sign to scream about cool beverages.

"I do. Most of my pieces are made of glass." She runs her hands up her head wrap where a massive curly pineapple rests on top of her head. I wonder if she makes the headwraps too.

"Why glass?" I ask as I pick up a bracelet with the same beautiful colored stone.

"Some places on the island have a little too much trash. I make art out of it." She says, her efficacious smile spreading on her lips

"That's beautiful." I say, placing the jewelry gently back on the table.

"How about you? Are you a creator?" She says, eying my mini vlog setup closely before looking back at me.

"Oh yes! I am a crochet artist. I am just filming a little vlog for my trip down here." I say, wanting to boast about my accomplishment yet fighting the urge to say it. Even though it's on the tip of my tongue, I swallow it. I doubt some of these people even know about Fashion International...

"Not just any crochet artist. She's one of the designers for Fashion International." I hear Santoro's soothing voice behind me. His body heat radiates to me as he stands behind my back, creating some instant shade for me.

The woman's face lights up as he says that. "Oh! I am in the presence of fame." She says to me, causing Santoro to chuckle.

"I wouldn't say that at all." I say as my face warms up. Santoro places his arm around my shoulder. I look up at him horrified as the woman steps away briefly to grab something for us.

"Don't be so modest, Cupcake." He looks down at me, his curly hair falling gently over his forehead.

"I'm not your *cupcake*." I say, untangling myself from him. My breath catches as he stands there in a tank top revealing his muscular arms. His shorts scream 'THIRST TRAP' as they stop mid-thigh. Suddenly, I wouldn't mind having him wrapped around me again.

"What are you doing here?" I cross my arms, stuffing them under my armpits feeling betrayed by my thoughts to touch him.

"I always come here when I'm done working out." He says.

"Of course, only *you* can find a gym here." I say, placing all my weight on the right side of my body.

"It's my therapy away from therapy." He smirks, making my heart flutter. It takes me back to that night in the jacuzzi, when our bodies were wrapped around each other, the plea in his voice when he spoke.

"You don't understand, LeeLee. I love you for that but you became my source of happiness. I couldn't depend on you like that or I'd drag both of us down." His words from before sing back to me.

The gym is his way of coping with his depression, something that I want to know more about. Since that night, I have always wanted to ask him more questions to get a deeper understanding of him. I feel it's selfish to know all his thoughts only when he looks happier and by the look of his body I can see that it definitely is paying off.

"You know if you ever want to go to the gym with me I do offer personal training as a side hustle."

"Physical therapy isn't paying enough?" I ask, tearing my gaze away from his tantalizing muscles.

"It's great but when you need a little extra money why not do what it takes to get it? You wouldn't work out with Doctor Reeves?" he asks stepping a little closer to me.

"I don't think I'd be needing your services in the future, Dr. Reeves." I look up at him, his cinnamon scent wafts into my nose.

"I like the way that sounds when you say it." Santoro stares down at my lips with a small smirk.

"Like the way I say what?" My heart knocks against my chest when I notice his hands reaching out for me.

"My name, 'Dr. Reeves'." He says, reaching out past me to touch a necklace on the table. He sounds amused like he knows my skin is on fire from missing his touch. I should feel stupid for thinking this way but I know he wants to touch me too.

He tilts his head gazing back and forth between the necklace and I. I see the thought and the question he wants to ask me as it forms in his mind yet what comes out isn't what I was expecting.

"Have you tried the smoothies here yet?" Santoro questions, snapping me out of my thoughts of him, something I need to stop with the show coming up in a few days.

"I haven't. Are they good?" I ask, smiling as Santoro gives me a knowing smile of his own.

"I'll take you to the spot where I get mine. You can be the judge." He says in excitement. I open my mouth to object but the jewelry stall owner returns with an article that has my face.

"I'm so glad you are still here,' she says, a little out of breath before holding out the article to me with a pen, 'do you mind, pretty girl?"

I look at Santoro who beams at me proudly. I face the woman and take the magazine article out of her hands and experience the surreal moment when I hold it in my hands. I scan over the article for a quick second, a megawatt smile forming on my lips. I need to find these magazines ASAP. I take the pen and sign my name at the bottom righthand corner of my picture. The woman beams as she grabs the magazine.

"Please, please, try on the ring." She says as she picks up the piece of jewelry and holds it out to me as if it is as delicate as an egg and places it in my hands.

"That's beautiful." Santoro says, followed by a slow low whistle.

"Thank you." The woman says with her head held up in pride.

"She makes them." I say to her as a slow but beautiful thought comes to my mind. "Do you mind if I buy some pieces for my models to wear? These will definitely complete the outfits." Excitement radiates off me. The vision burns into my brain as I envision myself coloring the beautiful pieces into the final designs in my sketch book. The pieces I made will definitely become complete with this jewelry.

"Yes! Stay here while I get the rest of them." She says, practically running to her car.

"They made the right girl famous." Santoro says with a wide smile on his face.

I blush and look at the ring still in my hand. "Shut up! I'm not famous." I place the ring on my finger and smile as the turquoise blue stone glistens against my skin.

When the lady returns, she brings with her a ton of handmade pieces of all different colors, different from the ocean blue stones I've been seeing. Some with pinks, yellow, green. All colors of the rainbow. A purple ring sticks out to me that will be perfect for Kayla. I pick up a small linked chain, the color of a green Heineken bottle and place it against Santoro's skin. He smirks looking at the piece against his bicep.

"It's fun watching you work, you know..."

I ignore him and pick up a few more chains in different colors.

I buy a few pieces for each of the designs I made that I think will pair nicely. I am excited to see the girls put them on during the dress rehearsal. I know they will be happier than the guys.

After shopping, Santoro takes over my attention. He holds the heavy bag of jewelry while I follow him through the crowd as he leads me to his favorite smoothie spot. Every fiber in my body is telling me to just walk away, slip into a crowded bar with my head down until he realizes I'm gone but I don't. I can't. I'm too mesmerized by his walk to leave. The way his skin is golden under the high sun. The curls of his head falling in the right places. I just want to reach out and touch the soft springy texture of his curls.

He slows his walk as we head toward a much more crowded area. I can tell by the way his back tenses that he's concerned by the crowd. He reaches his hand out behind him, opening up the palm of his hand toward me, a tiny wiggle of his fingers reeling me in. I place my hand into his rough calloused one, his fingers woven with mine as he squeezes my hand gently. Warmth rushes through my body as the sound of music blasts throughout the space making the crowd cheer.

"They're doing some type of performance." He looks at me over his shoulder and a slow smirk starts to spread over his face. "I know a shortcut."

He squeezes my hand again and leads us through a small portion of the crowd till we reach a clear opening on the sidewalk. We excuse ourselves from a few more people as we head toward an alley in between a few tiny restaurants. We clear the alley and find ourselves in a new area of the marketplace where more vendors are selling handmade items. Wooden carvings, handsewn hats and bags. Merch with the island's name and much more line up the streets.

Santoro turns with a huge grin on his face. "We can go shopping later if you want." He leads me to a small shack near the corner of the street. The smell of pineapple and mixed fruit fills my nostrils as a man high up behind the counter smiles down at us.

"Hi! Welcome to Mama Smoothie. What can I get you?" His accent rolls smoothly off his tongue as he pulls a pen out from behind his ear.

"I'll have the number 4." Santoro says, staring up at the menu above us.

"All fruit, okay? Pineapple, mango, raspberry, that works?" He asks, not taking his eyes off us.

"Yeah, that works." Santoro says.

The man looks up at me and smiles. "How about you, pretty girl?" He says with a huge smile on his face.

"I'll have the number 2." I say.

"All fruit, okay?" He asks with an intense gaze.

"Yes."

"Give me five minutes." He says. Santoro hands him a 10 dollar bill and waves him off when offered change back.

I look down at our intertwined hands, fingers lacing into each other. I want to pull away but I can't. Despite being against my better judgement, I don't want to.

"Number 2 is my favorite." Santoro's voice lulls me out of my head. I meet his gaze. His expression softens when he looks at me.

"Oh really? Have you tried every smoothie here?"

"Just about every single one that they have to offer. I've been avoiding the ones with coconut though. You know I hate that."

I smile, "Of course, I do." I think back to the time Santoro and I went out to a new restaurant earlier on in our relationship. I could tell he was trying to impress me when he took me to a place with a dresscode. I remember it vividly, the surf and turf he ordered plus the chicken dinner I ordered. The face he made when he took a bite of the shrimp and tasted the coconut. I have never seen someone spit out something faster like he did that night. I laughed so hard everyone around stared at us like we didn't belong. We didn't, of course, so we ended up getting McDonald's and sitting at the waterfront nearby, looking at the water and the bridge that lit up the night sky. My heart flutters at the memory. I tilt my head and gaze at his smile which instantly makes me weak in the knees. The desire I feel goes against every part of me that was screaming 'FUCK HIM' at the very beginning.

"Here you are, sir." The man hands us the smoothies. Santoro grabs them, removing his hand from mine. He hands me one and stares intensely.

"Yes?" I ask, putting the straw in my cup and watching the smug stare he gives me.

"I'm waiting for you to tell me how good it is." He chuckles.

He puts the straw in his cup and takes a long sip. His eyes practically roll to the back of his head. I laugh at the dramatic reaction and take a sip of my smoothie.

"How is it?" He asks for my honest opinion impatiently. He smirks as I take another sip, unable to deny the amazing taste.

"You might be right about this place." I say, not wanting to hype his ego too much.

"Might? Yeah whatever." He chuckles as we make our way toward the exit, a breeze flows around us making the air smell salty. The sun feels amazing on my skin and the vibes are all perfect especially with him next to me.

"*Toro...*" I begin, stopping in my tracks.

"Before you try to leave, let me show you one more spot." He says, moving his smoothie to the other hand holding the jewelry bag before taking my hand, not waiting for my refusal but for my permission."Take me then."

He grins and pulls me gently close to him so that we're walking side by side. He looks down at me with a smile as bright as the sun. He halts in front of me blocking my view of the area behind him. "I think of you every time I pass this place." He moves out of the way before showing me a table full of yarn. My mouth drops at the yarn shop.

"Why didn't you show me this sooner?!" I scream, smacking his chest playfully.

"You were always blowing me off." He shrugs and takes a sip of his smoothie.

I flatten my lips at his response and roll my eyes. "If you told me it was to show me yarn, I would've hung out with you sooner."

"Only for the yarn?" He asks.

"Only for the yarn." I avoid his gaze and walk to the shop touching the yarn on the table, feeling its softness and admiring the rainbow of colors on display. "Do you crochet or knit?" The woman at the table asks me with a smile.

"I crochet." I say, longingly look at a beautiful soft pink yarn. An idea for a dress comes to mind as soon as I spot it.

"How much for the pink yarn?" I ask. Santoro chuckles behind me. I look at him with a raised eyebrow. He shakes his head and puts his hands up in defense.

"What?" I cross my arms over my chest. "I just knew you had an idea for that yarn as soon as your eyes lit up when you saw it." He tells me.

I scoff, "My eyes did not light up." I think to myself about what he might have seen on my face when the pink yarn came into my vision.

"Are you two a couple?" The woman asks as she picks up the pink yarn and puts two skeins in a bag for me. I face her and fight the heat that rushes to my cheeks.

I hand her the money and take the bag from her. "No, we're just working together on a project right now."

She nods and turns her gaze to Santoro, something in her expression says she doesn't believe me. I follow her gaze and find him staring at the ground sipping his smoothie.

"We're having a crochet class shortly if you would like to join." She says with a smile. "You are welcome to join too sir."

He looks up and shakes his head profusely. "I don't know how to do all that."

"That's why they teach you." I say. His eyes shift to me and stare with a little bit of confusion in them. I hope he takes the bait and comes with me. I don't want our time together to end just yet as much as calling it off here is the best thing to do. I need to relax and think about the rest of the show preparations, the dress I'm going to crochet for the 'before and after' party of the event instead of having thoughts about him and the way he's making me feel when he's around. This is a high that I'm not ready to give up yet. Am I not?

He shrugs, "I'll give it a try." I watch as he walks toward me fighting the smile that threatens to break.

"Just go straight to the backroom. We will get started in five minutes. There are some people already inside." She says with a smile.

I look back at Santoro briefly before ambling inside the building where a rainbow of yarn fills the walls. Crochet hooks and knitting needles with special designs fill showcases at the back walls. I stare in awe as I see women in the back corner making yarn from wool.

"No way! She's making yarn!" Santoro says in awe.

"I definitely want to do more shopping when this lesson is over." I say, eyeing some yarn in the blue section of the rainbow.

We enter the back room where chunky yarn and hooks rest on the table. I saunter to the back table where no one is seated. I grab a hook and a skein of chunky orange yarn. Santoro slides in the chair next to me then picks up a hook and green yarn off the table.

The lady who I guess is our teacher comes in with a beautiful crochet granny square cardigan in blue, purple and white with a matching white turban wrapped on her head. She smiles as she takes command of the room with her presence.

"Are we ready to crochet?" She looks around at each table with a wide grin then picks up her yarn and hook at the center podium in the room. "Begin with a slip knot," she says, making a loop and pulling it closely around the neck of the hook. She pauses before continuing, 'everyone has a specific way of holding their yarn and hook so try to find a way that is comfortable." She moves herself from the podium and reaches out to anyone who needs help with making a slip knot. I make my knot and place the hook with the yarn attached on the table curious of what we might be making.

I watch Santoro unravel some yarn and pick up his yarn and hook. "Show me how to do that knot thing."

I giggle and grab the yarn from Santoro and slowly show him how to make the knot and attach it to his hook. "Does that make sense?" I say as I unravel it, handing him the yarn and hook.

He hands it back to me, with a small shake of his head. "Show me again." He rests his head in his left hand as he watches me cross the yarn and pull together a knot on his hook this time slower.

He nods and grabs it from me before making the knot, he jumps in his seat in excitement when he masters the motion and attempts to hold the yarn in his hands. "This isn't so bad,' he says, 'they might as well add me to the fashion show lineup because I'm about to make something dope."

I roll my eyes, "Sure you will." I hold back a laugh as the woman shows us the next motion. A chain three and connect to form a ring.

I make my chains slowly knowing that Santoro is watching and making mock-attempts of the motion. When I look at his hook and yarn he has three loose chains formed into a strangled ring. I snicker at the piece before following the next direction which is another chain three. At this point, I am certain that we're attempting to make a granny square so I will go ahead to finish it.

"Slow down, Cupcake. You can't move that fast." He shakes his head trying to mimic what I'm doing.

I laugh and point to the teacher. "You're supposed to be watching her, not me."

He laughs. "If only you knew how hard it was to take my eyes off you…"

Heat rises to my cheeks as I make eye contact with him and focus on the yarn. I allow it to melt away all the thoughts of him that threaten to take over my mind.

"Pay attention to the woman!" I say while on the third row of the granny square.

"I'm paying attention to *a* woman." He says, leaning closer to look at my work.

I turn and make direct eye contact with him. A slow smile forms on his lips. "I'm only here for you." He looks down at my lips and back to my eyes before sitting back in his chair and fooling with the yarn on his hook.

I continue making double crochets while ignoring the pounding of my heart as I work with the yarn. If only I had the guts to tell him that I'd rather have him here with me than anywhere else.

Chapter 17

"Do you think these lights can dry my skin out?" Kayla questions as she puts moisturizing cream on her face before applying eyelashes, the most subtle fluffy lashes that she asked me to choose from are the most dramatic lashes I have ever seen. I had to remind her what we are here for on the island.

"They might. I know we're going through the whole show." I say, thinking back to the schedule that Jayana had shown me. The show rundown is an extensive document with directions for just about everyone; stage crew, make-up artists, designers, host, the whole crew. I think this document is about fifty pages long with time stamps and clear cut directions. The one thing that I've learned about Jayana over the past couple of days is that she is meticulous. I need someone like her in my life.

Kayla turns to me and smiles, her face glistening from the cream that's not fully rubbed into her face. "Are you nervous about today?" She asks as rub the streaks of cream onto her face.

"I think *nervous* is the understatement of the century." I sit in the chair facing the vanity. Kayla makes eye contact with me through the glass and squeezes my shoulders. "Don't worry, sweetness. This is the moment we have been dreaming of,' Kayla says, 'You, the designer and I on the big stage.'"

I turn my head to look at her, "You've dreamt of being on the big stage?"

"Yeah. Just because I don't talk about it openly doesn't mean I didn't want to walk on the runway at least once in my life. Mom had me in a pageant once."

I laugh remembering her story. "I remember you telling me that you didn't like it."

"Oh, I hated it," we share a brief laugh before she continues, 'But I liked the walking part of it. I just don't like to answer questions. Feels too much like a test."

I nod, while I never did any pageants, I always did them with the dolls at my house, plus fashion shows. I think my spark for fashion started when my mom got me a mini fashion kit so I can make dresses for my dolls. I didn't know how to sew or use a sewing machine but I liked to create.

"Well, I'm happy I can make your dreams come true, just like you are able to do for me."

Kayla squeezes my shoulders one more time. "Of course, sweetness. Your crochet in my boutique has been selling like hot cakes."

I smile. "I bet it has."

A reminder from my calendar goes off. Hair and makeup will happen in about 15 minutes.

I grab some of Kayla's moisturizer and rub it on my face just as the hair and makeup artist file into the room.

"Make sure that you start with models first before the designers. Models need to be out sooner than later." I hear Jayana's voice from outside in the hallway, authority coating her voice.

I smile when I see Destiny walking toward her station. She gives me a huge grin when we make eye contact. Destiny and I chatted about the makeup looks that I wanted for my models a few times over the phone. I had a chat with hairstylists as well. Jayana sent me an email confirming my hairstyles before sending them off to the other stylist. As for my makeup looks, I specifically wanted Destiny to do it. All my looks are more natural. It's all I want for my team. The makeup part should be quick but a black girl and her hair? That's another story.

"I'm glad I am your main makeup artist. Some of the looks that these designers want are ridiculous." Destiny says as she puts her bag and folder down on her station.

"I can't wait for this practice then." Kayla giggles as we switch places in the chair.

"I think the host is in the main room practicing their lines. That's what I heard walking past." Destiny says as she looks through her folder for Kayla's makeup preferences.

"You would think that with all the interviews, meetings and rundowns we've been having I'd get used to it by now." I say more to myself than those around.

"Well, it's your first time in a show like this and definitely won't be the last." Kayla reaches up and grabs my hand comforting me. The gesture is small but it definitely calms the trembling of my hands.

"Yeah, plus I don't think I finished all my interviews yet. I'm sick of them."

A smile tugs on the corners of Kayla's lips, "But you know what? I will be grabbing every single copy of all your interviews. Make sure you sign it for me too."

I feel a pair of soft arms around my shoulders, the fruity scent of pomegranates filling my nose, "You definitely have to sign all my copies too." Tazlyn says.

"I will, but first you have to tell me what kind of perfume you are wearing."

She laughs, pulling the bottle out of her bag. "I'll let you borrow it."

I smile, taking the bottle and spritzing some on my body. I can't remember if I went with a more floral scent this morning. I hope it pairs well.

Samiya and the boys come in through the door exactly at 7:15 AM, the time we agreed upon so that we can have our makeup done a little after 8:00 AM. That's when everyone else is supposed to come anyway. We made a schedule within the schedule.

"We would've been here sooner but someone didn't want to get out of bed." Samiyah elbows Reef in the stomach who smirks knowingly.

"My bad, Ny! You know how mornings go." He shrugs the sly grin still on his face.

"I think I can guess." I laugh, Samiyah's face loses color slightly. She throws me a slightly grumpy face. When she sees the smile on my face, hers melts instantly.

I hang by my girls ignoring the fact that the bane of my existence and what might be the love of my life is standing right in front of me, chatting it up with the other men in the group.

"Guys, this is Destiny. She is our makeup artist. I met her and have been obsessed ever since. I want her to do everyone's face."

"She's not going to do anything crazy, right?" Reef looks skeptical as he eyes the makeup pallet.

"Don't worry pretty boy, your masculinity will still be intact." Samiyah spews.

"Pretty boy? If anyone is a pretty boy, it is Mr. Dark and Lovely over here." Reef says, pointing at Shawn.

Shawn smiles showing his pearly white teeth and runs his hands against his chiseled jaw. "What can I say? The blacker the berry..." He shrugs. The girls' eyes roll at him while I laugh.

"Anyway, before this becomes a beauty contest,' I cut in, ignoring the set gaze from everyone's eyes, 'Who will be going first?"

Kayla scoffs. "I'm already sitting in the chair. I think I'll go. I didn't do my skincare for nothing." She rests her hands under her chin and smiles with a slight head tilt.

Destiny's face lights up as she reaches in her bag and pulls out mini bottles. She hands two of them to each person. "Go down the hall and wash your face with that then apply the moisturizer."

Reef nudges Santoro and Shawn. "Looks like the girls got us to do skincare after all." He nudges his head toward the door and they walk off together. Santoro looks back at me. Is it wrong that I feel weird for our interaction? The fact that he hasn't tried having a conversation with me yet shouldn't bother me nonetheless it does.

"When they come back, I have green juice for them to drink." Destiny smiles as she shows us the mini fridge under her work station. It's then that I realize for sure that I picked the right person.

Destiny works fast. The boys were really easy to get done after all. Since I opted for a no makeup look, she finishes doing their skincare to get the clearest canvas possible. As for the girls, they look amazing in their natural looks with a little more effort. Destiny applies my makeup last. She was unsure if I would have any photoshoots or anything for later but she did it anyway which I'm thankful for. I don't want to walk around with caked up makeup from any other artist.

With makeup and hair done, the last thing to do is try on the outfits. I'm nervous for everyone to see what I made for them. I have seen it on them with a blind fold on their eyes. It's different this time because I get to see their reactions to the designs this time. Crocheting multiple outfits for them was a challenge, especially last minute for Santoro.

"Alright, I just want to let you guys know that if you hate any of it,' all eyes are on me as I stand in front of the plastic covered outfits, 'I'm sorry."

Shawn laughs and moves me out the way gently, "I don't think there is anything for you to be sorry for, really,' Shawn says, 'We've all seen your work."

I nod even though deep down, I still feel nervous when someone sees my work. I nearly throw my phone every time I post on my social media account. Sure, I get some hateful comments, the *'anyone can make that'* and *'it looks ugly'* stuff but my style is one of a kind. It took me years to get the style that I have now. Years of perfecting my tension and creating all types of tips and tricks to get my crochet neat and done efficiently. With all the years I have put into the craft, I still get nervous.

"The way these big designers talk about your work, I don't think you have anything to be scared of." Santoro stands behind me. His voice is soft enough for just him and I to hear.

My body tenses. Every part of my body tingles anticipating his touch. I hope he cools that feeling.

I push my shoulders back feeling the dim lights of the dressing room on me. "Okay, everyone grab bag one and find some place you feel comfortable enough to strip down."

"You want us to get dressed in front of each other?" Tazlyn says a red hue forming on her cheeks.

"Yes. You won't really have time to do it during the show. You've done this before."

"Not in front of dudes though." Tazlyn whispers shyly. When my school did fashion shows and had us work them, I had a chance to see that once you leave the stage you have to peel off every item and get into the next outfit really fast.

"It's okay, just be out in the open but out of sight." I say, hoping my words give her some type of confidence.

She nods. I hear the plastic bags unzipping in front of me. At that moment, all I wish is for the floor to cave out and swallow me. As much as a smile coats every inch of my face, seeing their reactions to the pieces I crocheted for them, I am still nervous for not only them but the people of this island seeing the last piece whose colors were inspired by them. I must specially thank them.

"Anylee! You did your thing with this piece." Reef says putting on the motif lace shirt I made for him along with the pants. My first design inspiration for the first pieces. It was a pain in the ass working with that thin yarn but it was worth it.

I watch as everyone puts on their items, the colors matching their skin tones perfectly. I sigh in relief.

"Anylee, can you come here for a second?" Santoro's voice calls out to me from a corner of the room. I walk over to his side, a mirror sits lazily in the crack. My heart melts, seeing the rich orange color on his skin. I nearly faint seeing his abs poke out between the fabric.

"You want me to wear this outfit like this." He flexes a little, no doubt enjoying the look of the outfit on his body.

"Yes," is all I'm able to choke out without stumbling over a response.

"Is there a reason for this particular one for me?" Santoro smirks looking at me through the glass of the mirror in front of him.

"No reason, honestly." I am mortified to tell him I thought about his body when making this. The breakup certainly did his body well, plus studying to be a physical therapist.

"You're sure about that?" Santoro fights back a laugh no doubt enjoying the slight blush on my cheeks.

"Yes, I am sure about that." I roll my eyes and turn away but Santoro catches my hand. He turns me around. I look back making sure nobody is watching as his hands lead to my waist and pull me close. I place my hands on his biceps staring deep into his chest.

"My eyes are up here." He says softly.

I look up and meet his beautiful hazel orbs.

"Unless you're trying to see if your name is written on my heart, then in that case I can tell you right now it is."

My lips twitch wanting to smile but I force it back. I can't get distracted. Not right now when everything is coming together.

"Is there something you want?" My heart thuds in my ear, adrenaline rushing to my brain, as I fear getting caught in his arms by the rest of the crew. I, for some reason, can't let them see me swooning over Santoro who in my eyes is the real pretty boy of the group.

"I just want to say I'm proud of you, Cupcake. And I know you're nervous." His voice soothes me. It's as if he can look into my eyes and know exactly how I feel at any given moment.

"I told you to stop calling me cupcake." I release a shaky breath and squeeze Santoro's bicep gently. The feeling automatically gives me comfort.

"Out of all the things I said, you're worried about the word 'cupcake'." He chuckles in a low tone, probably not wanting to get caught like this with me either. "If you want, I can get you a cupcake or a cookie later."

"You found a bakery in this place?" My voice is a little too loud. But you can't blame me, I love my sweets. There's nothing I wouldn't give for one right now.

"I can find one, if biting into some buttercream will ease how tense you are." His hands snake their way to my arms as he rubs my biceps. I drop my hands from his arms letting him rub the tension out of my body.

I can't hide the fact that this man knows me.

"Anylee!" Kayla calls, making me jump instantly away from Santoro's hands. I walk out from the corner of the room and find an excited Kayla.

"Jayana is calling for us. Grab the rack, it's showtime baby!"

I squeal in excitement as I grab the rack and drag it to the runway. I enter backstage where a batch of models is getting dressed in their outfits. I wave at Destiny as she applies finishing touches and corrections to one model's face. She waves back before her eyes bulge at my designs.

I park the rack in a space free of bodies and chaotic models. "Okay," I say while opening my phone to check the email that Jayana sent. "You guys will be back here. Someone designated to us will help you guys get changed into your next outfits quickly. I believe they plan on doing this all day so be prepared."

Shawn groans a little, "As long as they feed us actual food, I'm good."

"I could actually do without. I don't want to look bloated on the runway." Kayla says, looking at herself in her motif dress.

"Girls and their figures." Shawn shakes his head, making the rest of us laugh.

"Where will you be during all this?" Santoro asks

"I'll be here to help. Don't worry, I won't go anywhere. Except, right now I am." I say, stepping away from the others.

"And where do you think you're going?" Samiyah asks me. Her hair is in an slick elaborate high bun, something she is known for doing, which is why her looks are classiest amongst all the girls.

"I'm going to check out the runway, of course." I say quickly before rushing towards the doors that will lead me to the front. I plop down the steps, behind the back row of chairs until I'm parallel to the end of the stage. My mouth drops seeing the glow, feeling the aura given off by the runway. It calls to me, letting me know I truly belong. That alone wipes the feeling of nerves from my body.

The runway is long, which for me is huge. I stand at the bottom of the stage smiling at the long white stage that my work will be showcased on. The bright lights shine on the stage, as the bright star they are. I can't wait to see my friends, strut my designs on this glorious path, a path forward. I can only imagine the opportunities I'll have after this show. It's only the beginning. Jayana puts a hand on my shoulder waking me up from this trance of mine.

"Thank you for having your models already dressed in outfit one. They look so so good." She beams, her energy feeling like two shots of espresso. "I can't believe you made all of those by hand."

I look down a little shy. "It's just something that I threw together."

Jayana scoffs on my behalf, "Just something? Girl, those are works of art. Look at the details in that design right there." She points to the motif dress hugging Tazlyn's body. "That's more than something thrown together."

I smile. "Thank you."

"Of course, I can't wait for you to talk to Sapphire later. She is going to be so excited to meet you. I know, personally, she loves your work."

I freeze on hearing Sapphire's name. "I'm speaking to her later?"

Jayana looks at me confused, she picks up her ipad from an adjacent chair and taps through a few apps. "Oh, I forgot to send you the email this morning. I have been so busy. But right after this dress rehearsal actually you are speaking to her."

I can feel my face flush as the words come out of her mouth. I want to say something but nerves have overcome my body.

"You won't be here all day, once this rehearsal is over I'll send you up." She says clicking away at her ipad once more.

Before I can build the confidence to ask her something, she steps away from me and shouts as loud as she can toward the back stage.

"We start in twenty minutes people." She paces away quickly to the sound and lighting crew to make sure things are perfect. A photographer snaps an off guard picture of me while I stand in shock. With a few deep breaths, I walk as fast as I can toward the back and find my group of people. Kayla sees me first, her smile completely dropping when she sees my face.

"Honey, what's wrong?" She asks.

Her words are almost inaudible under the sound of my heartbeat. I try to take a few deep breaths before answering, "I meet with Sapphire today."

Everyone looks at me in shock before wide grins take over, "I am so happy for you!" Tazlyn wraps her arms around me. She must know I'm nervous. I am shaking with nerves.

"You'll do fine, sweetness." Shawn says to me as he looks in the mirror, further examining his curly top.

Samiyah pushes him away. "She's talking to the biggest fashion mogul ever. This is a big deal!"

Shawn catches himself before he falls. "Why would you do that? Can't get the masterpiece dirty." He shakes his head heading back to the mirror.

Samiyah rolls her eyes and turns her attention to me, "Anylee, I am happy for you girl. Let's get you some water or something."

"I know where some is, I'll take her." Santoro says before anyone chimes in. Without hesitation, I follow him. His hand grazes my lower back as we trudge toward a water filter with paper cups. I haven't been around these things since I went to the dermatologist in high school.

Santoro grabs a cup and fills it up for me. I can only see him standing before me. He shields me from the chaos on the other side as people scramble to get ready.

"Pretty nervous?" He hands me a cup of water. The liquid splashes a little in my hands.

"Just a little." I reply as I lean against the gray walls.

"Take a deep breath and sip some water." Santoro says as he rubs my back.

I do as he says. His touch alone is enough to calm me down.

"I would feel much better if you were there with me." I laugh nervously, thinking about how he might take what I just said. Yet, he just smiles and pulls something out of his crochet pocket. A small piece of paper that he unfolds. It's a picture of us together during a picnic date he had taken me on early in our relationship. It was unexpected. We walked through this rose hedge maze searching for an open garden space but we got lost instead. We picked a corner and set up there until one of the workers helped us. I smile when I see how happy we looked.

"When I want you near me, I just have something like this in my pocket. I won't lie. Today made me pretty nervous. I can lend this to you if it will help." Santoro hands me the photo.

"I know you don't have pockets."

I smile and put the photo in my bra without a second thought. He smirks and looks at where the photo lies on my chest. He probably can't wait to get it back now.

"That's one way to carry it."

I laugh, "I want to have it closer to my heart."

He smirks, "I respect that."

I'm not visibly shaking by the time I sit down in the interview room. The lights beat down on me to get the view right for the camera frame as I sit in a new space, comfortable blue chairs and an open window backdrop. Every time I take a deep breath, I feel the picture laying on the curvature of my breast, reminding me that Santoro is here with me. I take another deep breath, thinking about how proud my grandmother would be of me. I can almost see her watching this interview with my mom, a gummy grin on her face as she holds a frail hand to her heart.

The journey has been a way of making her proud too.

"I'm here." A sweet voice sings, a tall almond brown woman with deep silky blue hair steps into the light. She wears a gray women's suit that hugs the curves of her body and black heels. She lights up when she sees me. I stand to greet her, nowhere near as tall as she is, that's for sure.

"Anylee? My crochet designer." She smiles wide and greets me with a hug.

"You know me?" I ask stupidly.

"Know you?" She laughs "I handpicked you specifically."

Just hearing those words makes my heart pound. She takes a seat in her chair and waves me down to do the same. "What made you pick me?" I blurt out as soon as my butt hits the chair.

She laughs, her voice melodic. I don't notice the people in the background. I can see the glimpse of a red light flickering in the background meaning we're recording yet it does nothing to phase me. This fashion icon sitting across however does phase me.

"When I first saw your designs, I knew you were different. I looked you up after approving your application. I had to know more about you like you were my favorite singer."

I laugh at her comment, the gesture eases me.

"When I saw your social media, your YouTube, your shop, your other designs, I fell in love. I am a huge fan."

I smile, "I am a huge fan of your work too. I have your doll." I fight the urge of cringing at myself. *Get it together, Anylee!*

"I'm so honored." She giggles. "I would be honored if you could make a piece for me, after the show?"

She nods, "I always ask this of my favorite designer after the show. I would love to wear your design on the red carpet."

I struggle to keep my mouth closed. I nod my head vigorously, "Yes! Yes, of course!" I think back to the fashion designs that I have seen Sapphire McNeal wear on the red carpet. Daring. Bold. One of a kind looks from big name designers. Designers that my designs will share a stage with soon. I can't wait to see the pictures of her wearing my design. I can't wait to sketch up some ideas later tonight.

She claps her hands together, "Great! This really has made my day. We will talk right after this interview." Her smile beams as she grabs the note cards on the table next to her. "Should we get on with it then? I can't wait to talk about ideas."

"Yes, of course," I lean back in the chair confidently.

Sapphire looks at the camera and gives the cameraman a thumbs up before she code switches to professional.

"Tell me. What motivated you to get into crocheting?"

Chapter 18

I am so glad this is not my job. I can barely handle crocheting all the pieces, making sure they are perfect, let alone perfect my walk to model them. I commend my models. This is their fifth walk through of the day since 4:30 AM this morning.

Once Tazlyn finishes her last outfit she meets me at the front for our lunch break.

"Thank God, there's a break." Tazlyn says as she sits down next to me, wearing the clothes she arrived in. Comfortable yoga pants and a cropped t-shirt.

"I think we have to do it two more times after lunch." I yawn, definitely in need of a shot or two of espresso.

"At least it's only two and not five like it was yesterday." Tazlyn yawns and stretches her body until I hear the little cracks from her bones.

"Well, the party for the show is happening tonight," I take a deep breath, 'this is all in preparation for tomorrow."

Tazlyn's eyes bulge as she remembers, "Oh my gosh! You're right. It's a good thing we practice like this. I think I can get in and out of those outfits in like a second. I go back to the room and dream about them."

I laugh. "Thank you for doing this. You look really good out there."

Tazlyn hugs me, "Of course! Thank you for this opportunity."

I smile, hugging her back, "You deserve it more than anyone."

A throat clears above us, followed by the concealment of the glare from the light fixtures.

"Am I interrupting something?" Santoro hovers over us, his eyes only glued to me.

"No, not at all. I'm going to use the bathroom, Lee." Tazlyn gets up in a hurry, practically running to the bathroom. I roll my eyes.

"How are you feeling about the show?" Santoro takes a seat next to me. His arm grazes mine. Tension runs up my body a little bit.

"I'm feeling…" I pause. The word 'fine' wants to come out even when that would be a horrible lie. "Terrified. But at least I'm not up there burning under the lights."

Santoro chuckles. "Technically you are up there with us. It's your designs that we are modeling."

"Pfft! I'm there in spirit. Not physically." I lean back and rub my temples. The fashion show music is annoying me this time. I wonder who made this playlist anyway.

"How do you think I look up there?"

"I don't know. In fact, I won't know until tomorrow. I've been backstage with you guys perfecting looks until the last minute. I only got to see Tazlyn." Once I saw her walk, I closed my eyes for a good thirty minutes or so. Just to catch up on the sleep I'm desperately missing.

"Well, I guess you can let me know tomorrow?" Santoro asks. The brief second of silence is replaced by the rumble of his stomach. I giggle.

"Sure, if I will not be in the corner freaking out somewhere." I can 1000% see myself doing something like that tomorrow before the show. I always have some type of freakout before I do something big.

"Listen mama," Santoro says as he directs his body toward me and cups my face in his hands. I look into his eyes, the warmth in them making me feel safe instantly. "We're going to get you some food and then after two more rehearsals, some rest. I'm going to try to find a cupcake too to put your mind at ease."

I place my forehead against his. "Maybe I can edit this YouTube video to help me feel better."

Santoro chuckles. "You're always working. I said rest, Cupcake. Not more work. You have a big night tonight and tomorrow."

I lean back and sigh. "You're right. Sapphire will be at the party."

"How was she?" Santoro asks. I didn't get a chance to tell him about the interview, not with all the rehearsal and extra sleep due to the early morning practice. I sure did tell my girls though.

"She is a dream. A sweetheart really!"

Santoro chuckles, "So someone like you, huh?"

I roll my eyes. "This isn't the time to flirt with me."

"I've been doing so the whole time that I've been sitting here with you."

I shrug. "Maybe I didn't notice because you're simply a nice guy to me."

"I'm trying to be more than a nice guy you know."

I stand up from my chair just as the rest of the team walks off stage. They look as tired and drained as I do.

"Got enough practice in?"

Reef makes a swish noise. "Did? We have to come back here and do it two more times."

I laugh at his reaction, honestly feeling bad for them.

"I'm sorry Jayana is putting you through all this."

"I don't mind the extra practice." Tazlyn says joining us again after her bathroom break.

"You mean excessive?" Reef says

Santoro chuckles which sends a shiver down my spine. He feels so close. "Listen, if you want to bust your ass on the runway in front of multiple people, be my guest. I have no problem with it. At least we get to wear Anylee's amazing crochet designs." Samiyah smiles curtly at Reef. There must be a tiny bit of trouble in paradise. Reef gives her a look that Samiyah ignores, turning her attention to me.

"We have to come back here and do it again. Been like this all week." Shawn runs a hand over his hair and yawns big. Everyone's eyes droop as Shawn closes his mouth.

"Let's get food and the last two run throughs over with. Then it's 'go time'." I say. Santoro claps, making almost everyone jump out of their skin.

"You heard the lady! Let's get some pep in our step."

Amongst all of us, Santoro looks the most awake. As if he slept twelve hours before showing up this morning.

"How are you so energetic?" I ask him as we walk toward the doors.

"I usually get up at this time everyday to work out." He shrugs. "Then I have to go to work right afterwards so I'll be up all day."

I look at him in shock. "You're telling me that you get up at 4:30 AM everyday?"

"How else would I be able to look this good? My patients would clown me if their physical therapist was fat." He laughs and walks on.

"It makes sense." I laugh along with him. On our way out, we are finally greeted by the warm sun and island breeze. We head toward the nearest bar to get food.

"My stomach is touching my back." Shawn calls out at the head of the pact. I turn to Santoro but he's not next to me instead he's marching in the opposite direction. I pause watching the group ahead of me slowly backing away towards Santoro. I jog in his direction, inching closer before touching his shoulder turning him around. "What's wrong?" He looks at me with concern. For a second, I feel embarrassed. Had he told me he wasn't joining us? Did I miss that part?

"Um...how come you're not joining us for lunch?"

He chuckles. "I wanted to take a walk first to work up an appetite."

"Haven't you worked up an appetite yet?"

A smile forms slowly across his lips. "I do this everyday, remember?"

I nod a tiny bit embarrassed. "I guess you're right about that."

He smirks as his eyes travel up and down my body, lighting it ablaze.

"If you want you can walk with me,' he shrugs, 'I don't want you to miss out on part of your lunch."

My phone buzzes on receiving a text from Kayla asking for my where-abouts. I sent her the emoji that I used to send her back in school that'd let her know I'm with Santoro. I ignore the buzz that immediately follows and dart my eyes between the path and Santoro.

"I would love to, but I think I should go back with the rest of them. I am pretty hungry."

He nods, "I don't need you getting *hangry* anyway." He winks before walking away from me leaving me in the presence of trees.

"Anylee, come look!" Tazlyn calls out to me as a video plays on her phone.

She turns the video toward me just as I stand behind her. To my surprise it's Marcus, walking down the runway.

"Where is that?" I ask, vying to get a look at the banners in the back-ground.

"Looks like Nista-Fest in New York." Tazlyn says, clicking off his story.

"So, he double booked? He could've just said that in the beginning."

"At this point, forget Marcus. Nobody cares about that festival anyway." Samiyah rolls her eyes with an obvious huge twinge of annoyance over Marcus.

"I never thought Marcus was like that." I shrugged

"People code switch LeeLee." Kayla calls out.

"Yeah, probably why Santoro never liked him." I mention thinking back to the amount of times he faced off with Marcus in front of each other.

"Because Santoro has never played when it comes to you." Kayla says.

"It's because we were dating then."

"Might as well get back, the chemistry is still there."

"It's not."

"It is."

"I might tell you a joke but I'll never tell you a lie." I say to Kayla who frowns at me through the vanity mirror.

"You just lied." She says, not buying it, "So you're telling me you just went after Santoro to have a regular conversation with him?" Her brow raises.

Tazlyn and Samiyah sit on my bed in suspense waiting for the answer that will underwhelm them.

"Yes, one of my models was walking away. I wanted to know what's wrong." I shrug. Considering the amount of time Santoro has checked on me during this process, it's only right that I do so. Sure, Santoro has the body of a perfect sculpture and the face of a hunk but I can tell he's out of his comfort zone.

"What is up with you two, anyway?" Samiyah says as she stretches her body. We may or may not have had a mini sleep over before we decided to get ready together.

"That's what I would like to know." Kayla gives me a look that dares me to spill the tea. I lean back in the chair letting the cushion touch my back.

"Nothing is going on with us." I scan the crevices in my brain, the only body part that would make me feel otherwise before feeling confident in my answer.

"Are you sure about that? You two sneak around a lot." Samiyah wiggles her eyebrows.

"I hope you're not insinuating what I think you are." My face distorts in disgust.

"That's probably why you and Reef were having an issue this morning." Kayla laughs cutting in.

Samiyah rolls her eyes. "Definitely not, but whatever."

We stare at Samiyah waiting for her to spill the tea.

"Well...' Tazlyn pauses, "What is it then?"

Samiyah looks at each one of our faces before laughing. "Okay, it was that but I'll solve *that* problem later."

Kayla and Tazlyn laugh. I smile at them and continue to get ready for the party.

"The guys will be here any second now. We need to finish getting ready."

Samiyah stands up and grabs her bag. "They will be waiting in the other room because I need at least another hour to finish up."

"Make it fifteen minutes, princess." I call out to her. She turns around sticking her tongue out at me before entering the bathroom and closing the door.

Tazlyn walks to the mirror on the other side of the room to finish her final touches while Kayla and I share the vanity mirror. About thirty minutes pass before the three of us are ready except for Samiyah, of course. A soft tap comes from the front door, which means the boys are here.

"Samiyah, get your ass out of the bathroom!" Kayla shouts as I run barefoot, feeling the fuzzy carpet on my feet as I get to the door.

All three boys are standing on the other side of the door wearing different colored suits. Shawn in gray, Reef in burgundy and Santoro in a blue one. He knows exactly the type of shade that looks amazing on him.

"Come in! We're almost ready." I say as we stand there waiting. Kayla wears a beautiful purple gown with a slit up the side to show off her long smooth legs. Her hair is in a big curly afro. Tazlyn is dressed in a silky pink dress with two slits on both sides with her hair pulled up into a slick bun. When Samiyah comes out, she's wearing a red dress, with some lace details at the bottom. My dress of course is crocheted. I put together a long gown with a corset top in a baby blue color and allowed my curls to fall down my back.

"Oh, we look like a million bucks!" Samiyah says as she pulls out her phone for a selfie. We huddle together as we snap pictures before going outside and having a mini photoshoot of our own.

A thing I love about this island is how calm the night is. The sky is clear with stars littering the sky. A slight breeze moves the trees and a hair curl out of place as we walk to the dock taking the ferry to another island.

The calm water makes the travel easy so does the taxi driver that squeezes us all in. It feels like prom, or some big moment in my career that honestly feels like it should be recorded, something that should never and I mean never leave my memory.

Once we pull up to the Fashion International building it is decked out with signs celebrating the show, a couple of island vendors line up the entry way as people stop and look at the intricate crafts, before walking inside. I remember getting lost at the market a few days ago. Such a sight to behold.

"I'm going to go in and get drinks." Kayla says to me. Shawn and Tazlyn follow suit as Samiyah and Reef take pictures of each other.

I slowly walk through the line of tables, most things I have seen before, going into the building. The interior of the building shines as occasional flashes from photographers light up the place even more. Servers walk through, offering drinks and appetizers, somewhat resembling the farewell party that was organized for me a while back. What a journey it's been from then till now!

"Anylee," I hear Sapphire's sweet voice calling out to me. I turn and smile at her, embracing her into a big hug. "I am in love with your dress!" Sapphire is stunning as always. Her hair is still in the silky blue, and her dress is a long black gown that hugs her curves with diamond like shapes on her hips also encased along the bra cups. I bet that dress costs thousands of dollars.

Her eyes don't leave the light blue cotton woven together intricately to form my dress. It took me a while to make it.

"I'm so excited to talk to you after the show about making a design for you."

"You have my contact information, right? I will not let you leave this island without taking my measurements."

I laugh and pull out my phone. We swap numbers. If she wasn't standing in front of me right now, I'd be somewhere screaming, crying and throwing up. I just got Sapphire McNeal's number.

"Don't give my number away. I've had this one forever. My late stepfather and I had the same ending digits."

"Of course not, I will text you as soon as my last model struts on the runway," I say.

She squeals then hugs me again. "Perfect, I cannot wait!"

"That makes two of us."

Sapphire smiles before excusing herself and moving to someone else. The moment felt surreal as if we were best friends. *Don't tell Kayla.* It feels as though Sapphire is my biggest fan. The nerves definitely still get to me but hopefully working with Sapphire on her next outfit for the runway will melt all of those, even if she is one of my favorite fashion moguls.

I survey the crowd, before heading to one of the open tables along the big windows in the room. The lights dim as a performer starts introducing herself on the tall winding staircase in the middle of the room.

A server hands me a glass of champagne as the singer's smooth voice serenades my ears. I lean over the table, the thought of this journey coming to an end soon is somewhat bitter-sweet to me. No more staying up perfecting designs (for this anyway). No more finger cramping. The island vibes will be over a few days after Fashion International's show is over. I got exactly what I've been wanting. The only thing I can think about now is not royally screwing this up again like I almost did in the beginning or making a fool of myself by overly freaking out. I let out a deep sigh and take a sip of champagne, downing the glass before it's replaced by another server who swaps them swiftly.

"Thank you." I say quietly.

My mind drifts to Marcus how he bailed on me and his absence made way for Santoro to fill in. I like to think about what would happen if he didn't. I wouldn't have run into Santoro. I probably wouldn't be thinking about him right now if it wasn't for all this.

"What are you doing by yourself?" Santoro says standing on the other side of the table.

"I'm just here in thought." I say, swirling the liquid in my flute.

"Must be a deep one." Santoro puts his hand on top of my free hand making me sigh.

"Sort of,' I begin, 'Just thinking about life."

"My therapist says overthinking kills your joy." Santoro shrugs, putting his arm against the table.

"Yeah, that's pretty much common sense."

"Common sense isn't common." He chuckles, staring down at the table in front of him.

"The therapist told you that?"

"More like an old friend." He chuckles harder this time. Memory taking over his mind.

"Santoro, about therapy..." I begin but he cuts me off

"I went to therapy because I was depressed, if that's what you want to know."

I pause "No. But I–" I take a deep breath, 'The thought did come up once or twice."

He nods, "Guess you can say college, life and my own thoughts got the best of me. I don't like talking about myself much."

"You had to, though, for therapy."

He laughs, "That I did. I was comparing myself, destroying my own happiness, literally sabotaging myself. You know how I tell you not to do that."

I nod as he lets out a sigh "However, I'm not like that anymore. I'm happier, more observant of myself and others. The same way I know you're still in deep thought about something so spill it."

I sigh, "I'm just thinking about what's next for me. Sure, I accomplished my goal. Nonetheless, that doesn't mean anything if I don't have something lined up next."

"I saw you talking and hugging some lady, might have something there. It looked like something." Santoro shrugs.

I nod, remembering that I do have some things going for me. I laugh, the comment making me feel a little bit better. "Are you always watching me?" I laugh already knowing the answer to this question. I just want to hear him say it.

A server puts a flute of champagne next to Santoro before walking away. He never takes his eyes off me.

"I can't take my eyes off you. It gives me comfort to know where you are whenever we share the same room."

He rubs my hand while I take a sip of champagne. "You know," I laugh at the wild joke playing in my head, "Worrying about falling for you again has definitely made me stress less over all this." I say, gesturing to the place around us. Sure, I have been stressed about the show but seeing my ex again on an island out of all places and having him become my hero takes the cake. What girl wouldn't fall for the love of her life, with a cape draped around his shoulders? Santoro frowns slightly, the hold of his hand almost limp. "I can't help it."

I nod, not wanting him to continue further with his sentence. "I know, you can't help but fall for me."

I take another sip, feeling a slight buzz from the sparkling beverage. Has this drink made me a light weight?

"I'm holding on for a few more days, Cupcake." Santoro says.

"A few more days until what?" My tone challenges as I stare into Santoro's eyes. I remove my hand from his and empty the rest of my champagne. "I'm going to go dance or something." I say, moving my way through the party.

I fight the urge to look back at him. Is he going to take me seriously and let me go? The full moon greets me as I stand outside on the pool deck. People dance with each other, sip drinks as they talk. Much more of my vibe.

I walk over to the bar in the back of the area and order me a Malibu Bay Breeze and sip on that, dancing to the beat of the music playing through the speaker.

Jayana walks over to me with a huge grin on her face. Seeing her short authoritative frame always makes me feel as if I have my life together. "Hey, Anylee! I hope you are enjoying the party. I sent out a reminder for the show. 8 AM sharp." She says as she walks over to another person behind me and relays the same message.

I laugh and sip on my drink. Same Jayana always working, If I was slightly more buzzed, I'd have her take a shot with me. I spot Destiny over by the chairs. Once we make eye contact, she comes over. *Thank God.* I don't think I can get through this party alone. Especially while I'm drinking.

"Slow down on the drinks. I can tell you're nervous." She says, grabbing the drink from my hand.

I let out a sigh. "I know. I'm going to have to go to an AA meeting after this experience. This is the most I've ever drunk."

She laughs, "It's a fun island."

"You're right about that." People laugh and dance around us proving the point more. "I'd come back here for a regular vacation."

Destiny nods and lets out an exhausted sigh in agreement. We both laugh as I grab my drink from Destiny and place it on the bar calling out to the bartender to replace it with soda.

"Don't worry, girl. We will cross the finish line tomorrow. I can't wait to see what lies ahead for us in the future." She looks up at the sky dreamily as if she can picture the days ahead of her.

I could use another drink thinking about the future has me stressed. I have prayed for times like this. My grandmother supported me on this journey more than anyone. What if I cross the finish line and still fail? I look up at the sky and say a silent prayer, hoping that more good comes from this.

"I will be right back. There is someone I got to see. I will bring them over to meet you later." She beams before giving me a quick hug and walking into the crowd of people.

I pull out my phone for content and take a picture of my glass of soda to post on my insta story. I take a few selfies and videos for my vlog, that I will edit as soon as I land home, before texting the girls to save me out of boredom. I should've got drinks with Kayla or photobombed Samiyah a few times before taking a picture together with her. The wind off the water creates a cool breeze leaving the exposed parts of my body cold, making up the perfect excuse to walk toward the entrance only to stop right in front of Santoro.

"Come with me." He says before grabbing my hand and whisking me off to another place. He leads me gently through the crowd. We smile at other designers and models that we meet. We turn the corner where the bathroom and coat closets are. Santoro opens the door and leads me into a dark room. It's nothing but pitch black darkness. I can only make out fuzzy dots as my eyes try to adjust to the low lit room. I bump into hangers and clothes racks in the tight space between us. I can feel the heat from Santoro's body radiating between us.

I feel around for a switch and flick it on coming face to face with Santoro whose lips come crashing into mine. Without hesitation, I wrap my arms around his neck as I melt into his body. He presses me gently against the wall as I run my fingers through his curly hair. Santoro breaks our kiss and peppers my slightly exposed upper body with kisses.

"I know what you're doing, Anylee" His eyes reach up to mine as I stare down at his lips hovering over my skin. My heart pounds as I wait for his next move.

"What are you talking about?" My words are breathless as he stands up straight cupping my face in the palms of his hands. "Stop trying to push me away." He says, scanning my face for an answer.

"What do you mean?" I say, the coat closet clearly with a view of something that would be great in a heated movie scene.

"What you said back there all made sense for how things have been going. I can't let you push me away." He kisses my lips softly, pressing his body gently into mine. "I can't let you." He whispers between kisses.

"We can't do this right now." I whisper back feeling the slowness of his breathing against my lips.

"I know, but can we just live in the moment? I've been living for these." He places another supple kiss on my lips before trailing his lips down my jaw and neckline. I breathe out ecstasy as I live in the moment. God knows, I live for these moments too.

Chapter 19

"How nervous is my baby?" My mom coos over the phone. I sit up in bed, resting against the headboard with a snoozing Santoro next to me. I look at the alarm clock, the sun peaking out over the horizon, ready to shine over the island.

"I could poop myself. That's how nervous I am." I let out a shaking breath and stare down at Santoro's peaceful face. I reach down and play with one of his loose curls.

"If it makes you feel better, we'll be watching the live stream." I can tell she's smiling over the phone. She's proud of me.

"I hope you like my pieces." I smile back as I look down at the blanket wrapped around my body.The soft white blankets make me feel angelic on the inside. "I can't wait to see them. You've been hiding them from me for so long." She laughs. I giggle softly so that I don't wake Santoro up.

"I'm so proud of you, sweetheart. I know granny is too." Hearing those words make me feel warm on the inside like the first sip from a warm cup of tea.

"So am I sweetheart!" My dad yells in the background. There's a ruffling on the other end before his soothing voice takes over my ears.

"Hey babycakes! I hear you might be nervous." He chuckles. I smile when I hear his voice.

"Yes, I wish there were some sweets to help me cope." I sigh.

"No worries, babycakes. I'll get you all the treats your heart desires when you return." I smile and stare at the numbers on the alarm clock.

"Thank you, dad. I look forward to it. You better keep your promise or I'll tell mom."

He laughs. "Go get 'em today! I'm going into the garden with your mom."

"This early?"

"Got to get it out of the way early before your big day." His voice is full of cheer.

I smile "Thanks, Dad. I love you. Love you too, mom."

"We love you too." My dad says.

The nerves somewhat relax after talking to my dad. I lay down next to Santoro. His breathing is steady, the curls drape over his face like a perfect picture.

I play with the stray curls once more, run my finger along his jawline fighting the urge to kiss him in his sleep even though it's something I used to do when we were still together. That would make me long to be with him even more. Even now, I shouldn't have this man in my bed but we're still living in the moment. Right? Slightly longer but there's no time stamp on moments, right?

I trail my finger across his jaw one more time. Santoro reaches up to grab my hand. His voice is raspy as he groans tired. His eyes flutter open, and droop slightly, still heavy with sleep. He kisses my hand and gives me a small smile before closing his eyes.

"Why are you messing with me?" His voice is raspy and louder than intended. My insides melt when I hear the vibration of his voice.

The sun peaks out through a sliver in the curtains as he smiles, his eyes drifting closed.

I lay down next to him. His eyes open yet again before he shuts them quickly fighting off a foolish grin. He snakes his hand across my body and pulls me close to him. His body is warm as I lay into him staring at his thick, long eyelashes. The one and only thing I'm jealous of.

"You know I can feel you staring at me. They say taking a picture will last longer." He chuckles pulling me closer as his hand rubs up and down the curves of my body. He makes a gruff noise and shifts next to me.

I get closer to his face, our noses almost touching, if only I can stay in this moment with him.

"Today is *the* big day." He croaks before giving me a supple kiss on the lips.

"Please, don't remind me." I roll over onto my back, instantly missing his touch and warmth. Santoro sits up, sliding closer and pulls me back into his arms.

"I know you are nervous, baby girl. That's okay. Don't let the nerves ruin your day."

"But I'm so nervous." I let out a shaky breath.

"Tell me, what makes you so nervous about all this?" Santoro yawns and positions himself where he focuses on nothing but me.

"I know I'm not the one modeling the clothes but it's just...the fact that people will see my designs and not just the ones who watch my YouTube, not only even those who shop at Kayla's boutique or just my parents who love everything I sketch but people who are important to the fashion world. People other than Sapphire, probably bigger than her, are going to see my work and judge it for whether it's good or bad." I sigh, thinking about the possibility of people hating my work. I already suffer from imposter syndrome sometimes. Something like this could make or break my spirit.

"You don't know though. Those people could have been watching your YouTube page or following you on social media."

"I would see the blue check if that were the case." I sigh

"I feel like famous people also have backups." He chuckles.

It makes sense with what Sapphire told me. She looked up my other work and myself. No doubt she would give me a follow on her backup account if she had one. It would have to be something really out of the ordinary. I don't see many celebrities doing something like that.

"It's not only that but you have people from fashion agencies that also look at your work." Santoro smiles. "You're going to get an agent. No way can people look at those designs and not want someone as talented."

"What if multiple people want me, how am I going to choose?"

Santoro looks at me confused and pulls me closer so that I straddle his lap. He rubs my thighs, looking at me as if I'm a confused piece to a puzzle.

"Why are you stressing yourself out?" He questions, "You're thinking of only bad things under the sun for your career. It has barely started."

"I can't help but think of the bad." I stare at the gray headboard getting discolored by the shining sun. Santoro's skin looks golden under the honey rays. He sits up wrapping his arms around my waist and peppering soft kisses on my body. The fabric of my t-shirt shields me from the warmth of his lips. "Think of good things then." He whispers into my body. Though, even good things come to an end. Just like this moment will do shortly.

I lift his lips up to mine and place soft kisses against them. He leans back slightly and happily as if he is floating on a cloud.

"How nervous are you?" I ask, wanting to get the attention off of me.

"I'd be more nervous if we didn't practice fifty times a week." We share a harmonized laugh, smiles stretching across our faces. He pushes my curly hair back which is probably a mess from the sleep and the night before.

"I don't think I ever thanked you, like, truly thanked you for saving my chances."

"I remember you prepping for this moment. I always rooted for you. I'd hate for your dreams not to come true."

"Thank you." I kiss his lips over and over until no space can tear our lips apart.

It takes me more time to get ready since my curls are messier. I wash it in the shower before re-styling. I stretch my hair and fluff it out before making final touches. The front door slams shut. I know it can only be one person.

"Girl, today is the day!" Kayla shouts. She always has her eyelashes and her face looking dewy from the moisturizer. She scolds me when she notices that I am in the bathroom. I yank the towel from around my shoulders and fix my corset top back over my chest. I can't get my shirt wet.

"Now, how am I ready before you?" Her arms cross over her shoulders. When I check the time, it's only 7:25 AM. We'll be there by 8.

"I was a little distracted this morning." I lean forward, applying mascara to my eyelashes.

Kayla's scream almost makes me poke an eye out.

"What?!"

She looks at me then the bed and back to me. "You didn't!" She says breathlessly.

I roll my eyes, unable to hide the discoloration in my cheeks. I try not to smile as I apply mascara to the other eye.

"You are spilling the tea after this show, girl." She grabs the mascara from me and helps apply it to my eyes. She does the same for my eyeliner, just how I like it. I apply lip gloss and my favorite perfume then we head out. I hold my heels in my hand as I walk to the dock to catch the ferry to the building where the show will happen. I text the group chat and confirm that everyone is awake.

> *Is everyone heading to the ferry? Remember, we have to be there by 8.*

> *Tazlyn: I'm headed over now.*

> *Shawn: ^^*

> *Samiyah: Waiting for Reef to finish up in the bathroom. I think he's nervous.*

I laugh at the last reply and wait for Santoro's response which never comes when the ferry pulls up. Tazlyn and Shawn join us making it in time unlike Samiyah and Reef. I know exactly how he feels. I might have to hog the bathroom soon.

Everytime my phone lights up, I think it's Santoro. It was not that long ago when we split up to let each other get ready for the show today. I just hope he didn't fall asleep or get caught up somewhere. I let out a deep breath, "Think of the positive." I tell myself as I watch the island in the distance.

It seems to be in celebratory spirits as we arrive, everyone and everything is excited for the show. I like how Fashion International gets everyone involved. I know the people wherever they host their shows see an increase in tourism. I, for one, have loved my stay here. The sights are so beautiful. When I complete the show, tomorrow, I will be doing all the touristy things

I've wanted to do since I got here. Maybe it will give me inspiration for color pallets of the designs for my next few sketches.

"You seem in a better mood than you did earlier." Kayla whispers to me as we ride the car to the Fashion International building.

"What do you mean?"

Kayla rolls her eyes, "I'm your best friend, girl. I know when you're feeling anxious or something is wrong." She says to me as she reaches into her purse and pulls out a card.

"This is for you. I waited until this very moment to give it to you. I thought you could use a pick me up in something like this."

I place my hand over my heart. "Kayla!" I rest my head on her shoulder, "You know how sentimental I am."

She laughs "I know, so open the card."

I open the card and see a collage or pictures of Kayla and I over the years, the words *I'm so proud* scribbled in cursive on the front.

"I'm so proud of you, bestie. I want you to know that. So, stop getting in your head and let's kill it!"

I let out a sigh. "You're right. Are you ready though? No distractions? Is that guy you met coming to cheer you on?"

Kayla rolls her eyes. "I don't want to even speak about him."

"Yesss…" I whisper which makes her laugh. "You have to spill the tea about him later too."

She rolls her eyes but ultimately agrees when we pull up to the building where the magic will be happening.

The front path is lined with a red carpet. A banner that says *Fashion International'* rests in front of foliage and colorful flowers, no doubt the perfect place to pose on the red carpet. The driver uses a different route this time. We reach the back of the building where we are greeted with an intricate stone design and a smaller red carpet.

"Thank God!" I say as we get out of the car. I don't think I could handle getting out on the red carpet and walking down the long path to the building. The show isn't for another good couple of hours so that we can finish up any touches or have changes before everything hits the runway. I try not to think about my designs too much. They went through a rigorous process anyway. I can't sabotage myself mentally and physically.

When we enter the building, Jayana greets us. "Thank you for arriving on time." She sings to us as we walk in. The place glows more than usual, probably having experienced another deep clean since the party last night. "Makeup artists should be ready for you by 9. Breakfast is being served down the hall."

My stomach rumbles at the mention of food even though nerves just can't let me eat right now. Shawn and Tazlyn go straight down the hall towards the food. After a couple seconds of lingering, Kayla follows suit.

I walk around, looking at the mannequins displayed with the most iconic designs from Fashion International over the years. I stand in front of one huge display that shows the most intricate fashion pieces from sewing together socks.

"Anylee!" Jayana calls out. Her attention is glued to an ipad in her hands as she taps away at the screen. "I wanted to let you know that you have your own dressing room. While the models get ready in the main one, if you'd like a space to breathe it's there. All designers have one. Just look for your name on the door in that hallway."

She doesn't look up when she speaks to me. She walks on past me focused ahead as she greets the next couple of people that come through the door. I check my phone again to see if Santoro's name pops up. Still nothing. I panic just a little. No way he would go through with ruining my day, after this whole time? After what he said this morning. I feel a sort of anger come over me. I close my eyes and mentally count to five. There's still time left. Maybe he's on the way with Samiyah and Reef. He did stay with me so maybe his phone is dead. Those are the only things that somewhat give me peace as I join my friends before my mind starts to wonder even more.

They laugh and drink out of white porcelain mugs. I try my best to look normal and not at all worried as I stand next to Kayla.

"Here you go." Kayla says, giving me a small bottle filled with yellow liquid. "It's a ginger shot. Take that before you drink or eat anything. I don't need my girl looking bloated in her red carpet photos."

I smile somewhat weakly as I take the ginger shot feeling the burn of ginger and cayenne down my throat. Kayla takes the empty bottle and hands me a hot cup of coffee just how I like it.

"I'm surprised the carpet is red instead of blue." I say as I take a sip.

"Honestly, I was wondering the same thing." Tazlyn agrees as she takes a bite of a muffin.

"I looked up this Sapphire girl after y'all mentioned her the other day." Shawn says, "She rolls out a blue carpet for her biggest events of the year."

"You're telling me there is one bigger than this?"

Shawn nods. "I don't think the big event is a fashion show either but who knows? You might be able to tell us soon. You might be invited."

Tazlyn's eyes light up in agreement. "Yes! I can see that happening. I can already picture you on the blue carpet."

Kayla nods. "I agree, bestie. I also think they might roll out the blue carpet. The red one is just a placeholder."

I point to Kayla in agreement. "Definitely! Can't mess up the carpet before the show starts."

"See?" Kayla says before taking a bite into some eggs. "But don't forget about me when you are invited to Sapphire's event."

The thought of being invited to something that huge makes me excited and sick to my stomach.

"I could use something stronger than coffee." I mutter into my cup. "Hey, girl. I'm not letting you turn into an alcoholic on my watch." Kayla says, giving me a dangerous glare.

"I'm sorry. I just wish I had my hook and yarn I guess." I sigh, thinking of how the repetitive motion would calm me. I usually make blankets when I'm stressed instead of designs because usually the designs are the things that stress me. I'd be happy to sit back and crochet the king-sized fluffy blanket I've been working on back home.

"Did they get real food in here today or more cucumbers?" Reef asks as he walks through the door with Samiyah by his side. My shoulders droop in relief only to tense yet again when I don't see Santoro behind them.

"Did Santoro come with you guys?" I ask, checking the time. It's a little after 8.

Reef shakes his head before taking a ginger shot.

"I bet he's already here, probably sitting by the water." Kayla places a hand on my shoulder, placing the idea in my head as I stare at the brown liquid in my cup.

"That would be a Santoro thing to do." Shawn chimes.

I give them a small smile before turning to the food display. There's eggs and pastries, fruit and a variety of beverages yet nothing seems appetizing to me. I grab an apple and take a bite. The taste is almost bitter but I know it's not the apple tasting this way it's me.

"Alright, all models with hair and makeup." Jayana claps. "I want to get a bit more of a head start. It dawned on me that an earlier start will be better for all of us." She looks distant as if she's thinking of another horror story.

Everyone files out of the dining area and down the hall to the makeup room. Names are posted on every door along the corridor which reminds me of the little room created for me to breathe.

"I'll see you guys there. I want to see the dressing room they gave me."

"Share some of that complimentary gift basket with us." Reef says, giving me an amused smile before walking away with the others.

At the end of the hall by the window my name is written in a star. I smile and open the door entering darkness. I turn on the light and see a blue couch against white walls and a star rug in the center, and a few cute plants to make the place cozy. What intrigues me the most is the vase of sunflowers and medium sized pink box on the vanity. It's no gift basket but it's a gift none of the less.

I walk over and grab the little card sticking out from the top of the flowers.

I want you to go to your happy place.

~Santoro

My eyes close as I sniff the flowers, the floral scent already bringing me back home. I can almost feel the sun rays hitting my skin as I sit by the sunflower beds at my parents' house. The flowers tower over me, a cool breeze kissing my skin. My eyes flutter open as I stare into the brown center of the flowers. My hand rests against my chest as I bring the note closer to my heart.

I move my hand toward the box which has a white ribbon tied into a bow. From the door, the box appeared smaller but up close it's larger. The presentation is so cute that I don't wish to open the box. Nonetheless curiosity gets the best of me. I open it and my mouth waters. Sugar cookies. At least a dozen of them and two cupcakes inside with rich buttercream frosting. They are also chocolate cupcakes, my favorite.

I grab a cookie, the cleaner option and take a bite. It's still slightly warm like it just came out of the oven. As I breathe in the scent of the flowers, it takes over making me feel truly in my happy place. Sitting in the sunrays and eating sweets. The one thing I always do at my parents house.

I devour the rest of the cookie and immediately close the box. I have to find Santoro. If this is why he wasn't answering my calls, and was ignoring me, I need to find him, litter his face with kisses and shower him with love. No matter how much I try to fight it, I can't help but love him. I need to tell him that I love him.

I take one more cookie out of the box and place the card from Kayla in between the crack of the mirror and the wood. I place the note from my flowers underneath, feeling joy warm up my skin.

I leave the room, floating on cloud nine. I walk into the makeup room and look for Destiny's station. The entire room is filled with people applying makeup and styling hair. Models stand around stations wearing black robes and sipping from white mugs. I weave through people pardoning myself as I try to find a curl from Shawn's head, or the obnoxious laughter from Samiyah to draw me toward them. As I turn the corner, I see them by Destiny. I smile when Santoro stands with everyone else sipping Destiny's green juice.

"You're glowing." Destiny smiles when she sees me. I give her a hug and grab a bottle of green juice to drink with the rest of them.

"I'm feeling a lot better than I did." I think of the cookies and flowers in my dressing room. I look up at Santoro whose eyes are already piercing into mine. I need to talk to this man quickly.

The smell of burning hot tools fill the air as the stylist next to Destiny gets ready to do hair.

"We're all going to smell of burning hair and makeup." I say, scrunching my face up at the thought. I would hate to talk to one of my favorite designers only for them to smell burning heat protectant.

"They have perfume and cologne in the other room. You just need to air our first." Destiny says as Kayla takes a seat in the chair.

"Good because I want to smell like a million bucks, not like I work at a hair salon." Shawn shakes his head in deep thought about the comment, "I don't think that would be a good look for your designs either."

I laugh, "You're right about that." I try not to let the comment stress me out. I just came back from my happy place.

"Oh, I missed you yesterday. There was someone I wanted you to meet." Destiny reminds me. It was moments before Santoro swept me off my feet. I almost blush thinking of the stolen kisses in the coat closet.

"Right, I'm sorry. I got distracted." I smack myself with the juice bottle which causes Destiny to laugh.

Kayla smirks at me through the mirror and it takes everything in me not to kick the back of her chair.

"It's okay. I'll introduce you after the show." She jumps almost jittery.

"I can't wait." I say, moving behind Kayla's chair. We all squeeze to look at each other in the mirror. Kayla sits in the chair first with Destiny, Shawn, Reef, Samiyah, Tazlyn, Santoro, and I standing behind her, exchanging looks at one another that exude confidence. I fight back the tears of joy. My beautiful melanated models and team that I have no doubt will make my dreams come true. This is the moment that I have been waiting for.

"Are you guys ready to create magic today?" I scan each and everyone one of their smiling faces. "I know I am.'

Chapter 20

"Before I forget, I want to make sure you are all wearing your jewelry." I say, handing each person a set of jewelry I bought at the market for them to wear with the designs. "Jayana will have to kill me but I had to add these to the final touches."

They open their jewelry and look just as visibly impressed as I was when I saw the pieces.

"You do have a taste for fashion." Samiyah says as she examines the shiny ring on her finger.

"I would hope so since she did design all our outfits." Shawn says with a *duh* tone in his voice.

"Really? I thought my grandmother did." Samiah says sarcastically, making the rest of the group laugh. I walk away from them when I can't take the vibrations from my phone stinging my body anymore.

The show starts in an hour. My phone buzzes with congratulatory texts and tags from family members and social media. It's that buzz that snaps me back to reality whenever I drift into my own thoughts.

I stare at each one of my models in their outfits. They help each other with finishing touches as the crew helps them perfect hair and makeup before going on to the next. I laugh on seeing Shawn wince at the clear tube of gloss they try to put on his lips. He looks almost offended as if he knows his lips aren't ashy.

Santoro walks over to me with a smile in his eye. "How do I look?" He asks. He wears the motif opened shirt in the way I imagined. His muscles flex as I reach up to fix the placement of the shirt against his honey skin.

"You look handsome." I brush my fingers against his bare chest and fix a curl out of place with my free hand.

"I'm proud of you." He gets close to me and as much as I want to create another moment, I have to remember where I am.

"I can't get distracted, Santoro. Not now." I hope my tone is gentle. When I look into his eyes, I can tell he has taken my words for what I actually meant, the right way. *Thank God.*

"Anylee, please," Jayana rushes over to me and takes my hand. "You have to go out there and mingle with the big dogs. I have your seat in the crowd next to Sapphire.

Santoro and I exchange looks before he kisses me gently on the forehead. "Go get 'em." He joins the rest. I watch as he walks away, as if on cue he turns back around and winks at me.

"They'll be fine. We practiced a million times." Jayana drags me away from backstage and sprays a fruity smelling perfume on me. She's lucky it smells good.I check myself in one of the hallway mirrors before following her to the show room. So many people stand around mingling, talking as upbeat music fills our ears while we wait for the show to start. I weave through the crowd to find my seat which isn't hard. I spot Sapphire's blue hair and find my name written on the seat next to hers.

She smiles when she sees me. She talks to a gentleman wearing a nice brown suit, and nicely trimmed hair. I hesitate to walk over. I'm not one to interrupt conversations but I push my shoulders back and strut confidently to the two of them.

"John, there's someone I'd like you to meet." Sapphire says, guiding him to turn around and greet me, "John, this is Anylee. She is a crochet fashion designer."

His face exudes that he's impressed as he reaches out to shake my hand. "Crochet you say?" He looks to his right and sees my name on one of the white chairs. "I'm standing in front of your seat. Forgive me." He says as he moves out of the way so I can stand in front of my chair. Not like I'll be sitting down anytime soon anyway.

"Anylee, John owns a fashion agency in New York. I think you two should talk." Sapphire gives me a wink before turning to John. "Anylee will be designing my dress for my big event." Sapphire squeals which makes my heart drop. Clearly, she is only saying this to get me in good graces with John here. I silently thank her and make a mental note to actually put my whole foot in the design that I will create for her.

"Well, Anylee, if Sapphire has great hope in your abilities so do I." He gazes at the runway. "Will your designs be on display today?"

I nod. "Yes, sir. They will be."

He smirks slyly before handing me a business card from his suit jacket. "Send me an email. This is my direct contact information. We have to meet when we touch back to the mainland."

I stare at the card in shock as John nods to Sapphire. "Enjoy the show, ladies."

As soon as John is out of earshot, Sapphire hits my arm knocking me out of my trance. "This is your big big break, girl."

"You think so?" I ask, different colorful lights shine on the stage which tells me–from the rehearsal we made–that they're almost ready to walk the runway for a good thirty minutes tops.

Sapphire pulls out her phone and with a few quick taps, she shows me everything I need to know about John. He gave Sapphire her big break before she started her own thing. She's too big for an agent now. If I was her, I wouldn't need one either. Jayana holds things down for her like the boss she is. But John has some of the biggest names at his agency right now. Designers, models. My eyes bulge as I think about bringing my friends with me; Tazlyn, Samiyah, Reef, Shawn. I definitely need to find that man during the after party and talk to him about my friends too.

"With this guy and your team, I promise you, we'll be running into each other more often. But if that's not what you want I understand, I can train you to be like me."

"You would do that?" I ask in shock. She stares at me as if that would be the stupidest question to ask.

"Why, of course, I would! I love what you have going on with your image. I can help you grow it. You'd just need a personal assistant."

I think about the possibilities of being taught how to make my name 'Anylee Smith' into a brand like Sapphire.

She sits down and gestures for me to do the same. "I didn't get a chance to ask you this during your interview. All the questions were individualized, of course, but I'm curious with all you have going on. What do you want, Anylee? What's your dream?"

I could cry. Thee Sapphire wants to know my dream? "Well, my dream is to become a crochet fashion designer."

"Check that off the list." Sapphire smiles as she motions her hand around the room we're in. I smile and nod before continuing.

"I would also like to create one of a kind pieces for my favorite celebrities and models, have my own store with my limited edition creations in another country like Paris or London." My voice is dreamlike as I think about the possibilities of these things. I've been dreaming of them since I could draw my own designs. "I would like to achieve things no one has ever done before."

Sapphire sighs like she's just seen her crush walk past us. "I admire you, Anylee. All of those things are truly possible for you."

I place my hand on my chest taken aback "You admire me? You're the one who built this brand, I'd love to travel to other places and display other artist creations."

Sapphire nods. "I admire your journey. The things you are able to become besides just an artist. The part that you nailed on the head is becoming an influencer. I wouldn't be where I am if I didn't have that gift."

Thinking back, most of the styles I tried were because of Sapphire, some of her iconic looks and knowledge about fashion helped me discover my own style.

"You influenced me a lot." I nod "But it helped me to develop my own path."

Sapphire nods. "Of course, because a lot of people these days copy style, because they think they can pull it off better but I'm telling you, Anylee, you keep this up and nobody can rock your style better than you."

"I wish I could hug you." I say, unable to speak the life she has spoken into me, into her.

She holds her arms wide open, "And, why can't you?"

I give her a big embrace, her arms squeezing me as tight as they can. A photographer snaps a picture of us. After a few clicks of the brief flash, I turn to the photographer. He stands there smiling at his camera. His locs are pulled back into a ponytail. He's wearing a clean tuxedo too.

"Excuse me, but can you please send me those pictures?" I ask.

He chuckles and gives me a little salute. "Of course."

A woman comes up and steals Sapphire away for a moment. While I would like to get up and talk to the other people, designers that came to watch or are in the show, none of it will beat the conversation I just had with Sapphire.

"Good evening, everyone. The show will start in about five minutes."

I turn to find a cameraman setting up his lens right in front of the long runway. I pull out my phone and text my parents that the show is about to begin.

"Welcome, everyone! Welcome to the Annual Fashion International Show. I'm your host for this evening, Daniel Beckers."

The crowd goes crazy seeing the rising actor host this show. He's made his way from small side roles to major roles in movies over the past couple of months.

"I want to thank Ms. McNeal for allowing me to host tonight and witness this amazing fashion with the rest of you." Daniel places the microphone under his armpit and claps. Sapphire stands up and waves to the crowd blowing kisses at them before sitting down again. Her eyes are watering, She is a woman who loves her job.

"We have some of your favorite designers, displaying collection sneak peeks and new designers who I can tell you right now will become one of your favorites tonight." He surveys the crowd while smiling at individuals before looking at the cue card. "I promise I won't talk long. I'll let fashion do that for me." He walks to the back of the stage, slightly off center to where the models will walk. The light dims and a spotlight big enough to illuminate Daniel lights up the stage.

"Our first designer is Victoria Racker. Her collection wants to glorify the human body."

A tall male walks to the center of the stage posing slightly as he comes out draped in an array of nude colors. The piece he's wearing has holes in the pant legs and in the arms' area where certain parts of the body are usually covered. I stop myself from visually cringing and clap along with the other people in the crowd. More models of Victoria's group walk out onto the stage strutting their stuff and while this piece may not be my cup of tea, I still admire the way her models exude confidence as they walk down the runway.

"Victoria's color choices of nude shades are an epitome of the different shades of people who feel comfortable in their own skin."

"These people are basically naked," says a woman behind me who must have bought tickets to the show.

"That's how most people dress these days anyway." A man who I take is sitting next to her chimes in. I fold my lips in to keep me from laughing at their comments. Once they're done, Daniel invites the next line of a designer who goes by Naviard. He showcases beautiful tailored suits with specific designs. The art showcased inside the suit jacket is of stitched together silk fabric pieces to mimic a painting. A pumpkin orange suit had the design of fall leaves and a setting sun that was stunning. I can only think of the amount of times he pricked himself with a needle while stitching those together or the hours he spent slaving over a sewing machine.

"Those suits are incredible!" I gasp in awe as one by one, each man comes out displaying intricate suit jackets. The one that catches my eye is a teal suit jacket almost the color of the water on the island. The inside of it is perfectly painted scenery of what the beach looks like here. I can tell this man was an artist before he got into fashion. The creativity he uses to turn scrap pieces into art work is something that I would have never thought to do.

"Wait until you see the women's suits." Sapphire whispers as she claps at each design.

As if on cue, the models for the women's line come out one by one. They are absolutely stunning. A magenta suit with a beautiful sunset inspired by the island catches my eye. What intrigues me about this line the most is a rich yellow suit with the sunflower design inside.

I gasp so loud it almost feels like the whole room hears me. "I need that." I watch breathlessly as the model walks back down the runway.

"Consider it done." Sapphire nods and leans over to whisper in Jayana's ear.

I would love to get one of those suits for Santoro, a late birthday gift since I missed it. That's the reason why he came down here anyway. To party with his friends on an island.

"Could you get me his contact information too?" I lean into Sapphire, whispering the request. "I'd like to get one for a friend of mine as well."

She nods and says something else to Jayana. It's this moment that makes me want a personal assistant like her for myself.

We sit through more designs, some just as creative, which makes me question the ability of my own hands. One designer by the name of Joann designs beautiful dresses with the most sheer fabric. Another designer who is new to the stage, designs dresses and suits based on flowers and leaves that he hand makes himself. Some flowers are 3D and some flat. Looking at the amount of creativity and effort on these pieces, they all feel like limited editions, pieces that I can see some of my favorite artists and celebrities wearing. I wonder if they had them in mind. I would love to get my hands on some of these pieces for myself.

"Next, we have a crochet fashion artist, Anylee Smith. Her first collection showcases a variety of suits and elegant dresses, hand crocheted in motifs made of thin lace." I scan the crowd and note the amount of faces that look intrigued at the mention of my design.

Kayla walks down the aisle first, someone whistles from the crowd as soon as she hits the stage. I note the amount of awe in people's eyes as they see the elegant dress I created. The motifs I chose specifically for everyone were flowers. This was my longest creation yet. I wanted to have something that represented my family on that stage and what better way to show that than to have flowers.

Their garden is full of them so fragile just like the lacey motifs I put together. Kayla's dress is strapless with a mermaid-like bottom. Her body is hugged by lily motifs. I love when my mother plants them in the front yard. The light purple yarn compliments Kayla's skin nicely.

Tazlyn follows suit in a flowy rose motif dress that fans out puffy to match her adorable personality, then Samiyah rocking yellow and sunflowers in a long elegant design follows suit, each of them rocking their dresses. The men follow. Hooting and hollering comes from someone in the back.

Reef comes out first. I can see the appeal. The color red makes his melanin pop, something that I wanted for each and everyone of my models. His motif is roses. The thorns and beautiful flowers fit his personality. Shawn struts in after him wearing a green leaf motif. Then Santoro steps onto the stage in an orange hydrangea motif. If it could, my heart would leap out onto that stage just to be right next to him.

The crowd gets rowdier as Santoro walks the stage, strutting his stuff in a shy yet confident way. The orange does wonders for his skin. The piece was originally made for Marcus but after a few adjustments and extra lace, I was able to make something work.

I lean back and fix my face hoping none of the cameras caught me drooling or better yet, my parents. I won't live this down from my mother if she saw that.

Santoro stops at the end and winks at me before turning and walking back.

"Might this be the friend you'd like to get a suit for?" Sapphire asks, a sly smile on her face.

I can't hide the discoloration on my face. It almost feels like talking to my mother. "Yes." I say, suddenly thinking about how good he will look in a suit that color.

"Consider that done as well."

I stare at the side of her face and she nods in thought, "You have good taste in fashion and men." She says, winking before turning her attention to the next designer.

Not sure she will still say the same thing if she hears about our falling out yet something in me says she will think positively. I think it's her optimistic personality that has gotten her far in life.

The show goes on. A number of designs shock and inspire me. For instance this one woman who makes all her clothing out of silk ribbon. I am tempted to crochet with it too and see what would become of it, what it would do. Some of the designs make me question how they're considered fashion, but, you know what they say about art...it's subjective. Every time my name and new pieces are announced, I can't help but scan the room for people's reactions and listen to what they think. Some are hard to decipher but the ones who appreciate visually warm my heart. If my mother was here, she would urge me to stop looking around and calm down. Though, how can I avoid it when I'm in a room full of people who paid to see my art and silently judge it? The people pleaser in me wants to make sure that everyone likes my pieces. Judging by the room, I can most confidently say they do.

My last set of designs comes from an inspiration I got from the crochet community. It's one of the most jaw dropping collections that I crocheted. I cried real tears while figuring out these pieces. I had to try it though with limited hours of sleep plus imagination I created items strictly out of the crochet base. Chain stitches.

Tazlyn comes out first, wearing a piece that I'm most proud of. Her figure is curvier than the rest so when she comes out in an asymmetrical half chain stitch, half tightly knitted solid crochet design, the crowd cheers. Body positivity and the design both work in her favor. I admire her as she struts down the runway. What I wouldn't give to ruin the show by hugging her!

She blows a gentleman a kiss before walking back down the runway. I look around hoping the cameramen do their job and take pictures of my favorite piece.

"I need you to make me something just like that." Sapphire says with her eyes glued to the screen as her jaw drops. "I need a whole collection."

Jayana leans over past Sapphire to get my attention. "I also need a dress like that."

"This collection from the talented baby designer, Anylee Smith, certainly has the crowd turning heads. These designs are made from the starting base of every crochet piece and foundation chain."

Samiyah comes out in a dress that I mixed a little bit of motifs on the side while chains wrap around her body in a pretty coral like color. I made sure that the girls wore nude undergarments so the pieces don't reveal too much.

The crowd claps as the men too come onto the stage one by one strutting their stuff. Reef and Shawn make some women's jaws drop when they see the chains expose their abs and muscles in the shirt and shorts combination they're wearing. My focus is on Santoro. When he nods at me, the royal blue chains pop against his skin, begging to be free. I can't wait to get my hands on him when this show is over. I need to tell him what I've wanted to tell him ever since we ran into each other at the club. I fight the urge to ruin my moment by telling him now though. The pieces they wear shine in the spotlight. The glimpse of it all makes me smile proudly knowing I got the chance of making someone else's dream come true. Their dream.

Once the final collection is revealed, Daniel walks to the center of the stage.

"Give it up for our models and designers! Spectacular pieces have been displayed this year."

The crowd cheers as Daniel waves up Sapphire to the stage. He holds his hand out to her and helps her up onto the runway, she smooths out her dress and takes the microphone from Daniel.

"I want to thank all of the designers who trusted me to help them get their works out on the biggest runway of the year. It is because of all of you, the people of this island, those who submit, and the ones who love fashion. It is because of you that this is possible." The crowd erupts. Sapphire blows 'thank you' kisses to the crowd. "Thank you all so much for coming to the show. I definitely hope that I will see you all next year for another successful and amazing Fashion International Week. I hope to see you all soon. Who knows? I may be wearing a piece from one of these incredible designers you have witnessed today." She smiles down at me briefly before waving to the crowd.

"Thank you all. I'm your host Daniel Beckers, coming to you live from Saint Thomas." He winks and drops the mic. He gives a thumbs up to someone on the other side of the room before speaking back into the mic.

"The After Party will now commence. Go get some alcohol, people!"

The crowd cheers once more which makes me laugh. I walk backstage where models hug and congratulate each other. Some people add touches to their hair and makeup before the after party. I hear a pop from a champagne bottle and a chorus of laughter from a far corner. It isn't long before I spot Tazlyn, still wearing the dress made of chain stitches. I'm glad it looks amazing on her.

"Tazlyn, you did amazing!" I say, giving her the biggest hug, "Everyone loved you."

"No. Everyone loves you and your designs, Ms. Fashion Designer. I just wore it." She steps back and rubs her hands over the dress. "I feel so beautiful in this. I'm wearing it to the after party." She touches the necklace

I gave her and a sudden reminder sparks in her expression. "Do you want this jewelry back?"

I shake my head. "No, it's a gift. I want you all to keep it and the pieces too."

Tazlyn's eyes visibly water, her lips pout making me want to cry with her "Tazlyn stop! You're going to make me cry."

"How do you think I feel?" She fans her face, "I don't need mascara running down my face."

Kayla's scream silences the backstage for a second. Kayla and Samiyah run and embrace me into a big hug.

"You don't know how proud I am of you." Kayla says

"I'm proud of you guys! I came to tell you, you all looked great up there."

"All thanks to you! I'm definitely getting some Red Carpet pictures in this." Samiyah says, posing in the first design.

"Girl, I'm doing the same thing." Tazlyn says.

I laugh, looking around the room for the guys. This wouldn't be complete without them, especially without Santoro.

"So, who are you going to talk to first at the after party? Are you going to go out there and get an agent? Talk design choices with a celebrity or better yet..." Kayla holds onto my arm and looks at me as if I'm the last piece of candy in a jar, "Are you going to get us some free pieces from designers?"

The other girls nod in agreement. "I definitely saw some pieces I liked." Samiyah chimes in.

I laugh, "I'll see if I can do that."

I loop my arms through Tazlyn and Kayla's as Samiyah loops hers around Kayla from the other side. We walk out together ready to go out there and mingle with the rest of the people. I scan each group of people on the way out of the door hoping to find the guys. I plan on mingling with each designer and celebrity later. There's all night for that. The one thing on my mind is finding Santoro and no longer suppressing what I feel for him anymore. I know I said I want to be single and crochet but plans have changed. I want to crochet and be in love.

Chapter 21

As I walk into the party, I feverishly scan the crowd for Santoro. I don't see him anywhere yet. He must be with the boys changing into their party outfits or having a celebratory drink.

"Come, we need to take pictures." Samiyah leads us through the crowd as we walk toward the flashing lights along the front of the building. I glimpse people smiling under the starry night. And before us is the legendary Blue Carpet.

"I wish Reef was here. I'd love to get a picture with him on the runway." Samiyah says, walking gingerly toward the flashing lights as we wait for people to motion us forward for pictures.

"Where is Reef?" My voice pitches higher than usual. I can't help but show my curiosity, part of me hopes Santoro is with him.

"I don't know, he and the rest of the guys went for a walk somewhere." She shrugs before pulling us forward, a photographer waves us over for pictures. We take group photos posing as if we are runway models and celebrities. We hold back from throwing in a goofy photo here and there. I know not sticking out her tongue is literally killing Kayla. It's her signature look.

Once our time on the carpet is over, we make our way around the house to the private looking beach in the back where most of the party is happening. People who didn't attend the fashion show are pulling up in long sleek limos for the after party.

Trees sway softly against the breeze of the beach as we walk through the path. We ditch our shoes in a nearby bush lining the entrance of the beach to keep them safe and so we don't break our necks walking in heels. Thank God, I am not wearing a gown. I stroll through the beach, the gritty sand between my pedicured toes. I wave to a few models and designers who share the same barefoot idea.

"I'm going to find something to eat." Tazlyn says as she heads toward a bar on the opposite side.

"I'm coming too, Tazzy." Samiyah says, following her. They loop hands and tread through the beach together.

I turn to Kayla who has a glare in her eye. Her body is tense, so much so that I feel like if I pull her to the direction of the beach bar she'll strain a muscle. Following her gaze, I spot the man that'd caught her attention before at the beach restaurant we were at last time. He is flaunting a woman at his side. His hands rest on her jutting hips, as he speaks to the surrounding guests, sipping on a bottle of champagne.

"What is he doing here?" I say outloud, which judging by the annoyed groan that escapes Kayla's mouth I should have kept to myself.

"He's here because he's rich." She smooths sand out with her foot, her mood turning sour.

"Well, I know that he owns that cute beach restaurant." My eyes glaze over to him one more time, this time noticing the expensive suit he's wearing and the gold accessories and the diamonds that sparkle like stars around his neck.

"He's more than just rich. He's an asshole." Kayal mutters under her breath. The wind carries her words toward me. I don't like seeing Kayla hurt, or even used by men. I've had my share of heartbreak but Kayla is the one that could use true love right now. She lives it through me sometimes, or the flings she has. Kayla does deserve someone, more than just a fling.

"Are you going to let some asshole really ruin our moment Kay Kay?" I place my hand on my hip and dip my neck low to see her face looking down at the sand.

She looks up at me, having not heard that nickname from me in a while, a smile slowly forms on her lips.

"It would be stupid of me to let him do that, huh?" A wide grin covers her face.

"Kind of." I smile back, looping our arms together. "Let's grab a drink with the rest of the girls and get us something to eat if we can find it. I'm too hungry."

At that moment, Kayla is back to her rowdy self again. "I could definitely use something to drink." She lets out a dramatic sigh, "That show drained me."

I roll my eyes, pulling her toward the direction Tazlyn and Samiyah took. "Don't roll your eyes at me. You were there when they had us practice for that show. I swear Jayana is a drill sergeant."

Laughter escapes me a little too loudly, causing a few people to look in our direction as we head to the bar.

"Anylee!" I am greeted by Destiny and a tall man with rich, smooth brown skin walking beside her. His hair is in locs that fall past his shoulders pulled back. A camera falls against his chest. Kayla grips my arm tight seeing this man walk toward me but nobody can compare to my Santoro. Not in the slightest.

"Hi Destiny!" I sing as she gets closer. I hug her tightly knowing that this might be the last time I see her for a while. She hugs Kayla too. I can tell by the look in Kayla's eye she'll miss Destiny too.

"I wanted to introduce you to my cousin, Zacardi." He reaches his hand out to me, a charming smile falling along his lips.

"It's nice to meet you." His voice is deep, Kayla and I share a look before I turn my attention back to him.

"He has a photography studio. I think it's pretty close to you. I remember you telling me your from..." she pauses, "somewhere along the East Coast, right?" Her skin preens.

"Yes, Pennsylvania." I laugh.

"Yes, that's right! Anyway.,Cardi stays in New York and if you're in need of a photographer he travels."

I smile and nod towards Zacardi. "Thank you, Destiny." Depending on how things go, I most definitely will need someone.

"I took pictures of your models on the runway." He speaks as he loads up the pictures showing me the photos from various angles. My mouth is agape as I stand there drooling over every picture he took. He even got an off-guard shot of me staring up in love at my designs. Unless, it was Santoro I was watching. I definitely need that picture for my instagram.

"These are amazing. Could you please send them to me?"

His smile is bright as he turns the camera back to where only he can see the tiny screen. "Of course, I can send them to your email once I do some slight editing."

The way those pictures appear, editing may not be needed. This man is a magician behind the camera.

"Perfect! Destiny can send it to you. I don't have a business card or anything." Although it will probably be best to carry those around from now on.

"That works for me." He smiles before saying his goodbyes and walking away toward another photographer.

"Your cousin is a dream." Kayla says breathlessly.

Destiny laughs. "Well, he is single."

For the next thirty minutes, I sip on a Shirley Temple and chat with the girls about their future hopes and dreams. Samiyah and Tazlyn want to get into more modeling gigs and hopefully they'll land big with their favorite magazines and clothing brands. Kayla hopes to get some big names into her boutique back home. I smile while they chat livelily about their aspirations.

I haven't seen Santoro since his runway debut. I hope he's not somewhere ashamed of what he did. I hope not. Before, I wouldn't care where he was, because then the more he was away from me, the clearer my mind became. But now, my mind isn't clear without him next to me easing my rampant thoughts. I think about him way more than I would like to admit these past few days and the stolen more moments that I should have had with him but I can't help it. This is the man I was with for years and the only person I ever thought about doing life with. About sharing my dreams with.

I recall when we would lay in my small dormitory bed, sharing a bag of salt and vinegar chips talking about the duo we'd become. Santoro would be a traveling physical therapist for sports players and I, a fashion designer. My job could be anywhere. My perks would be sitting in the stands of any sports game I wanted to. His perks would be getting free clothes to fix his overly athletic wardrobe. He does clean up really nice but his clothes when he is casual could be a little more suitable, especially if he is going to date a fashion icon. Well, a future one.

I scan the crowd once more hoping to see my Toro's curly hair. I take a slow sip of my drink when my eyes find nothing.

"You seem down, Cupcake." A low voice whispers into my ear.

I turn to find Santoro in the blue crochet suit I made for him. His smile is wide, as relief sets into his body when he finds me.

"Santoro!" My voice is a little louder than it should be, which earns us a few curious looks from the girls.

I clear my throat and hop off the bar stool. "Can we talk?" I grab his hand. The electricity of his touch sends warmth through my body.

He nods and a huge grin spreads across his cheeks. "Yeah, I was hoping we could."

Relief finds me this time as I grab his hand leading him toward the big headquarters.

"I like the sight of this." Santoro says to me. I turn over my shoulder to see heat in his eyes as he stares at my body. "I just wish it was under different circumstances." He winks.

My heart thuds. Unable to form words right now, I ignore him and continue walking toward the building. I walk into the party, suddenly remembering I'm barefoot and make my way toward the hallway where my little dressing room awaits us. I let go of Santoro's hand, not wanting to make the scene look like how Santoro thought of as I dragged him along the beach.

Once we reach my dressing room, I open the door for him and flick on the lights. The delectable desserts and flowers still rest on the table.

I walk over to flowers taking in their sweet smell once more.

"Tell me...what are your thoughts about the show?" I ask, breaking the tangible tension in the room. I grab a cookie and lean against the vanity. I watch for his response as he leans against the wall while watching me.

"It surprisingly wasn't as bad. I think the best part about this whole thing was that it was on an island." Santoro shrugs.

"So, would you do it again?"

He shakes his head no immediately, "I only did this out of the kindness of my heart. You'll have to find someone else who's sexy to fill my spot."

"Oh, so you're sexy now?" I fight back a laugh.

"You don't think so?" Santoro puts his hand on his chest feigning hurt.

I put my fingers under my chin and pretend to ponder. "I have to think about that."Santoro shakes his head. "Wow! If I knew you'd felt that way, I'd let you choose someone else then. They wouldn't be me but it would fill your diversity criteria. People need to see some ugly models."

I open my mouth in shock. I pick up a makeup brush and throw it at his shoulder. He catches it, laughing hysterically.

"You know, you are so wrong for that." I shake my head.

"What? Nobody is better looking than me." He shrugs, a cockiness forming in his poise.

"Just because people cheered when you walked on the stage, it doesn't mean you're all that."

Santoro snaps his fingers and points in my direction. "So, you noticed that too..." His lips form into a cheesy grin. I keep my mouth shut, not wanting to feed his ego.

"Anyway," I drag out, clearly letting him know this conversation is going to take a turn for something more. "I...thank you so much for filling in. I know I said it already but you helped more than you know and this..." I motion to the flowers and cookies, "This is exactly what I needed."

He nods, "I knew you needed it. I could tell you needed a release. I didn't want you freaking out before the show began."

Santoro has been watching me like a hawk these last few days, even though he hasn't said much, and kept some more slight distance to avoid distracting me besides the other night. I can admit the stress, the worry has been getting to me. I needed it. I needed him.

The way Santoro knows just what to do to make me feel calm. The way he knows just when to sweep me off my feet or give me a laugh to make me feel lighter. He makes me feel lighter and while I've been trying my best to ignore the man, to push him away so I can focus, I need him. The plan was always to be single, crochet, and make a name for myself but I know now I need the old plan back. Every designer needs a muse.

"I don't know how you found sunflowers and a bakery but this just makes me love you more."

Santoro's eyebrows lift in surprise at my confession. He smirks and sits on the arm of the chair by the door stretching his legs out.

"I told you I like to explore the island." He says with a smile on his face.

"That you do."

The silence between us is comfortable, mostly because I eat another sugar cookie from the box as Santoro stares down at his shoes in thought. I grab a cookie from the box and walk over to him positioning myself right next to him on the couch. He smiles at me, wrapping his arm around my waist as he pulls me to himself so that we touch shoulder to shoulder.

"Here?" I say nervously, "Take this."

I hold up the cookie for him to eat. He stares at me not moving, not even glancing at the cookie in my hand. I lift it a little higher, my hand aligning with his chest. His face is expressionless as he moves his head down, taking a bite of the cookie in my hand. The eye contact is deliberate as the piece breaks off into his mouth. He chews the cookie slowly and nods.

"I'm glad it's not nasty." He chuckles, but I just hold the cookie limp in my hand until it drops. I grab Santoro's face, feeling his facial hair between my fingers and plant my lips firmly against his. He wastes no time lifting me up and sitting me on his lap, He falls back onto the chair, our kiss never breaking its hold. I pull back searching for air. Santoro's hands find my thighs as he rubs them softly.

"I was not expecting that." He smirks, tracing smooth circles into my skin.

"You weren't?" I tease as I play with one of the curls that falls along his forehead.

He shakes his head, unable to make out words.

"I can't pretend anymore, Santoro." I whisper into the space between us. He looks up at me intrigued by my words. He waits in silence silently begging me to continue, hope gleams in his eyes. "I thought moving on from you would be what's best for me. I wanted to focus on myself and rub all my success in your face." This earns a smile from him, "But, I don't want to do that without you. I want to fulfill my dreams but you were also one of them."

Santoro sighs up in relief and sits up in his chair. "Thank God, you realized that. I thought I would have to serenade you outside your room tonight if you didn't accept my gift."

"Gift?"

Santoro lifts me off of him and moves to the drawer on the side of the vanity. He pulls out a stuffed animal, not just any but amigurumi that was hand crocheted. I can tell by how the creature looks and the uneven stitches that he attempted this himself. My heart swells when I look at the deformed bunny given to me. I laugh a little as tears swell in my eyes.

"You made this for me?"

Santoro nods, rubbing the back of his neck, "I went back to that class we took together and tried to learn so I could make you a little something."

Tears silently fall down my face as I look up at him. He stares at the bunny probably avoiding my gaze thinking I'm judging him for his crochet work.

"But why do this specifically?" Out of all the things Santoro could do to win me back, he chooses to do something like this. Why?

"Because..." He lets out a sigh running his hands over his face. He walks closer, cupping my face in his hands to drive his next words into my heart, "I'd do anything for you, to make you happy, to be in your world. I need you, LeeLee. Being a Doctor may be one of my dreams but you are too."

I smile, "I dream you can make a better bunny."

He howls with laughter. "I can be better only if you teach me."

I smile, "I can teach you how to make a bunny."

"Can you teach me as my girlfriend?" He holds the back of my hands as we cradle the bunny together.

"I can definitely teach you as your girlfriend."

Epilogue

"Are you ready?" I ask Santoro as he adjusts the tripod just a little until it remains steady and stable. He lets go and watches the camera stay put.

"Ready!" He says, standing back from the camera and turning to me. He eyes the handmade dress on me with fire in his eyes. Swiftly, he wraps his arm around my waistline pulling me closer. "So, what is this video for again?" He asks as he presses kisses along my collarbone. His spicy scent fills my nose as he makes his way up my neck to my jawline.

"Santoro stop..." I push him away gently and fix the dress on my body.

"I can't help it. You just look so good." His tongue traces his bottom lip as he stares at me. Suddenly, I wish I didn't ask him to shoot this video with me in the first place.

"The faster we get this done, the sooner we can spend time together."

He laughs "This is us spending time together. I don't mind this at all."

I feel the heat begin to rush to my cheeks, "Right. Anyway, we have to unbox these packages from Naviard. There's something special right here for you."

He nods, staring at me with a hint of unease, "Really?"

"Yes, really." I sit down at my spot in front of the camera, making sure that the yarn wall behind me is just the way I like it.

Santoro sits next to me, a small amount of tension in his shoulders. "I'm only doing this for you."

I place my hand on his shoulder, rubbing it gently, "Don't worry, just be yourself."

The tension releases in his shoulders at those words. I stand up and hit record on the camera before framing my hair around my face the way I like it.

I turn to see Santoro watching me with a twinkle in his eye.

"I will never get tired of seeing you prepare for this." He laughs.

The smile that forms on my face is perfectly genuine as I start the intro to my video.

"Hey, what's up?! It's your girl, Anylee, back to you with another video. Today Santoro and I will be unboxing special suits from Naviard."

Santoro leans forward a little bit into the camera "I have no idea who this designer is but she saw them at Fashion International."

I giggle. "Sure did. And if you haven't already, my vlog for Fashion International is posted on my YouTube. If you check out my Instagram in the caption, my designs and models are featured on my page."

"So, without further ado, hit that subscribe button on my baby's channel and let's get to the unboxing." Santoro says as he wraps his arms around my body, pulling me closer until I'm sitting on his lap.

"Santoro, what if I'm blocking you?" I whisper to him

"You're the star of the show, everyone should be focused on you."

I lean forward softly pecking his lips, a wide smile slowly creeps across my lips. "We'll edit that part out."

He chuckles as he wraps his arms around my waist tightly. I smile, grabbing first the small white gift bag that I received as a complimentary gift from Sapphire.

"Oh, before we unbox the pieces from Naviard, I want to show you guys this cute bracelet that Sapphire McNeal gifted me for completing my first fashion show."

I pull out the bag a white box when opened lays a charm bracelet with two charms, the island's flag and a sapphire pendant.

"Whenever I travel for more shows, I need to get something that represents that country or that city. Isn't it cute?" I pout and move forward letting the camera focus on the simplicity of the bracelet for a few seconds before pulling it back and placing it in the box.

"You'll definitely be going to more places, Cupcake." He mentions as he rubs his hands up and down my thighs.

I clear my throat, heated by Santoro's touch.

"I think it might be soon too. I'm still confirming details but I will let you all know as soon as I hear details."

"You'll tell me first, right?" Santoro questions, his eyebrow arches in anticipation. I cup his face in my hands and give him a big kiss. "Of course, I will. I might bring you along."

He chuckles. "I'll book myself a flight there if you don't."

"Don't be a stalker."

"I think we all become stalkers when it comes to loved ones."

I shake my head in disagreement.

"If you agree with me, comment below in the chat." Santoro calls out the camera.

I cover his mouth briefly with my hand "Now, the moment we've all been waiting for."

I bring the gift boxes into frame and hand Santoro the box that is meant for him. "You didn't have to do that."

I giggle ignoring his comment. "So, when I was at fashion international, this designer truly caught my attention. Unfortunately, I didn't get to meet them later. However, Sapphire got me in contact with them after the show because I need these pieces in my life."

"What is so special about the pieces again?" Santoro asks before opening his pieces.

"The insides of the jackets are basically paintings that look like they should be hung in a museum, like water coloresque and all." I fully face the camera, "I'll try to find a video of the pieces from the fashion show and put it here."

Santoro nods. "That sounds cool."

"You don't seem impressed," I frown. "I thought of you when I saw the pieces."

"Did you?" He smirks. "And why might that be?" His voice raises a little in curiosity. His smirk turns into a full blown smile as his ego grows.

I roll my eyes and motion towards his box. "I'm going to allow Santoro to open his first."

"Oh, so I have to go first?"

"You're the guest on my channel." I laugh. "And the guests always go first. That way your reaction is more genuine. Mine is similar to yours in a sense."

"More genuine, huh?" He pauses, "Whatever you say, princess."

I watch as Santoro opens the box slowly, pulling out a suit jacket in that blue color that I so much love on him.

"Hold the jacket up so the people can see." I move back to my seat so the jacket can be seen in front of the camera.

He holds it up, visibly impressed at the quality and color of the jacket, "It's blue too." He says knowingly. If there's one thing Santoro knows, it is my love for the color blue on his skin.

"Open up the jacket!" I say with more excitement than is required.

"Hold on, mama! Let me build up anticipation." He puts his hand in front of me so I pause before he slowly points the jacket in the perfect position for the camera.

I sigh at his dramatics and watch as he slowly opens it to reveal a stunning portrait of the ocean inside. Not just any ocean but the one with the rock where Santoro and I slowly danced among the waves in the distant horizon of the piece.

He stares in awe letting out a low whistle. "Well, I'll be damned!" He utters in shock, making me laugh.

"See? I knew you would love it." He nods his head before showing the inside of the jacket to the camera.

"In the box are the pants that match the jacket. Though, we don't need to get into that right now. It's just pants." He says. I laugh as he continues to stare in awe.

"Okay, let's..."

"Wait," he says, stopping me, "I want to try it on."

He grabs the box and steps out of frame rushing to take his clothes off. I laugh looking at him as he almost trips out of his pants.

"You're really about to try that on now?"

"Absolutely!" He says with a firm nod.

"Well, while we wait for Santoro to try on his suit, let's talk. When I got in contact with Naviard, I asked him to make suits that would represent the both of us. Santoro loves the water so I made his background represent the water and this cute little cave we found on the island.

"Yeah, this might be the suit I wear all the time. Get me in fancy restaurants with no reservation."

"You have it on?" I ask before turning to the side seeing that he in fact does have it on.

He walks into frame posing in his suit. The jacket is unbuttoned against his bare skin, he opens the jacket to reveal the piece and his body.

"You can't tell me I don't look good." He says, posing again as if he is on the runway

"You look good, babe."He smiles satisfied before sitting down next to me, waiting for me to open my box.

"I think I know what yours is." He says as he stares intensely at the box.

"Hush! No guessing."

As I open the box, inside lay a lightly colored orange suit jacket. I hold up the piece to let the camera get a glimpse before opening the jacket to reveal a beautiful array of sunflowers.

"That's nice as hell." Santoro whistles slowly, "I thought it was going to be cupcakes though for sure."

I laugh as I show the inside of the suit jacket, revealing more details as I open up the jacket farther.

"Look at these details!" I gasp, stunned. "This is going to be my next Red Carpet outfit."

"Orange does look good on you, baby."

"I know it does."

He chuckles, "Don't get a big head now. Go try it on. I might change my mind."

I roll my eyes and smack his arm playfully as I walk out of view to change into the suit. The suit feels comfortable on my skin, the inside feeling like silk. I nod impressed, secretly needing more of these suits.

Once the outfit is on, I walk into frame posing in my suit as Santoro cheers me on.

"I'm starting to think you were meant to be on the runway."

I laugh, "I could never do that. Just being on camera is enough attention for me."

"Well, you certainly got my attention." Santoro says, staring at me the way I look at a sweet treat after a long day.

"Let me change out of this before you start something."

"You don't have to wear anything specific for me to start something." Santoro calls out to me as I change out of the suit.

I smile before putting the jacket back in the box. "I'm editing this conversation out.

He shakes his head, "No, leave it in." His smile is mischievous as he gives my body a once over. I turn to the camera ignoring his gaze before taking my seat next to him.

"Alright now, that's all we have left for this video. Make sure to like, comment and subscribe. And of course, I will see you in the next one."

I wave to the camera before turning it off. Santoro smiles before turning back to the corner to take off his suit.

"You have a lot to edit with that one." He says laughing as he pulls his shirt back over his head. I watch as he folds the suit jacket back properly.

"I know but I think the viewers will love it." I smile

"Of course, they will, because they love you."

I blush. "I wouldn't say all that."

Santoro steps forward, his hands touch my waist gently bringing me close to him. "I would." He smiles and places a gentle kiss on my lips.

"You're only saying that because I'm your girlfriend." I laugh, kissing his lips back ever so gently.

"You're not just my girlfriend. You're my love." He kisses my lips again and pulls me in the direction of the door.

"Where are we going?" I ask

"I think you deserve a sweet treat." He winks as he opens the door.

"You don't mean..." I gasp "The Cookie Monster Cupcake?"

He chuckles when he sees my face light up, "Oh, I mean it!"

"I love you." I say as I jump onto his back.

He squeezes my thighs as he walks us out the door. "I love you more, Cupcake."

The End

Acknowledgements

Growing up, I always loved to craft. My mom would always have us doing some type of activity, especially in the summer time. I remember building bird houses and jelwery boxes out of popsicle sticks, making things out of eraser caps and more. This book came to me while I was in the comfort of my room crocheting and knitting clothes, then two years later, Single & Crochet was born. Because crafters need love too. I wouldn't have been able to do this without God first and foremost but also my amazing readers and supporters from day 1. I'd like to thank my siblings who have supported my crochet addiction but also helped develop my story telling over the years. I'd like to thank my editor Sefora (you are amazing) and Treshell for this amazing cover. I hope you enjoy and I'll see you in book 2.

About the author

Ciana Smoak is an English teacher by day and an author by night. She loves to read and write black romance novels with all the feels. When Smoak is not reading or writing. She can be found baking, crocheting or spending time with her beloved niece and nephew.